"You test me sorely, Alice Kendall." His eyes met hers. "And you tempt me. That's the way it is with temptation. It's hard to resist."

As if he could do nothing else, he took the cup from her hands. He knew he should leave, shouldn't have returned. But he couldn't stand it any longer. He touched her then, as he had wanted to since the day he first saw her. He traced her cheek with the back of his finger, and without a word, he drew her into his arms.

Through the stiff folds of her gown, he could feel her tremble.

"What are you doing?" she asked on a shaky breath.

Lining her jaw with his palm, he said, "This." Then he bent his head and kissed her.

His body surged with desire, and he had been with enough women to know that she wanted him, too. . . .

By Linda Francis Lee
Published by Ivy Books:

DOVE'S WAY
SWAN'S GRACE
NIGHTINGALE'S GATE

NIGHTINGALE'S GATE

Linda Francis Lee

IVY BOOKS • NEW YORK

An Ivy Book
Published by The Ballantine Publishing Group
Copyright © 2001 by Linda Francis Lee

www.randomhouse.com/BB/

Library of Congress Catalog Card Number: 00-193502

ISBN 0-449-00207-1

Manufactured in the United States of America

First Edition: June 2001

10   9   8   7   6   5   4   3   2   1

Prologue

He could let them live. Or die. It was like playing God on Judgment Day.

The thought always made him sigh in pleasure.

Sitting back in the leather chair of his small but finely appointed study, he pulled out a pair of cigar scissors. They were small but sharp enough to make him smile. The brass reflected in the firelight as he snipped the end of the tightly rolled tobacco leaf. After a moment, he picked up a crystal snifter to savor his brandy, a fine, old cognac that went well with his cigar. Preparation for a woman. With white-blonde hair and milk-white skin. Painted. A courtesan, a prostitute like his mother, a woman with no morals.

He swirled the amber liquid around the glass, watched the legs run down the sides, then took a long slow sip. Murder was a precarious occupation, done only after much care and planning. He had done it before. Would do it again. But he was smart, smarter than those who would try to trip him up. He picked his prey carefully, and didn't succumb to the urge too often.

Tonight, however, it couldn't be put off any longer, he thought with a shrug of inevitability. He had made his decision earlier.

When all was quiet and the fire burned low, he set the snifter aside, no more than a sip or two gone. He placed the cigar at a perfect angle in the porcelain dish, next to the cutter. Then he carefully pulled a ring from the velvet-lined

1

box. He slipped it down the length of his finger and stared at it. A gold band with a hand-carved ebony nightingale embedded on top.

Now it was time.

A slow burn of excitement surged through him as he made his way through the darkened alley in the South End of town. The air hung still in the night, gauzy and leaden with humidity. But he hardly noticed. He relished the anticipation of a woman almost more than actually having her. Then he waited. Not long. She would be there soon; he knew her schedule intimately.

She appeared a few minutes late, which surprised him. But he wasn't surprised by her tears. A smile pulled on his lips at the thought that he was the cause of her distress.

Earlier in the week, she had told him she was pregnant, and that if he didn't take care of her, she'd reveal his identity. Such a pity. He hadn't been through with her yet, still enjoyed the way she purred beneath him, lifting her hips to take him fully. His body shuddered with intensity at the thought, swelling with hardness. But such was life. Frequently what one wanted didn't matter. She knew too much about him, so it couldn't be helped. Besides, he would have had "to take care of her," as she herself had put it, eventually anyway.

He waited until she was close before he stepped away from the pitted-brick wall. At the sight of him alarm blanched her face, until it was replaced with a knowing fear. She had made a terrible mistake by threatening him; he saw the realization in her startled green eyes.

She shivered in spite of the thick summer air. "What do you want?" she whispered.

He stepped toward her. "You, of course."

Her painted red mouth opened on a surprised breath. Relief curved her shoulders as she misunderstood his meaning. She looked around. "Here?"

He chuckled. "Yes, here. Though tonight, sweet Lucille,

I'm not interested in tasting the delights of your body." He pulled his gloves off slowly, revealing strong hands. "Or ever again."

Panic flared hot and bright in her eyes as he drew closer.

"Don't do this, please." Her words tangled with a choke of tears, before her eyes darted from side to side, as if at any second someone would step out of the darkness to her rescue.

Then she started to run. But her long, cheap skirts tangled in her legs. He caught her by the wrist, so tiny, so delicate, so easily broken, and pulled her close. She trembled with fear, intense and all-consuming, and he almost felt sorry for her. Almost.

Chapter One

The city sweltered.

Alice Kendall absently curled a loose tendril of white-blonde hair behind her ear. It was unbearably hot in her small law office in the South End of town, her long skirts and petticoats even more confining than usual. But she hardly noticed.

Pulling a folded rectangle of newsprint from a file, she reread the startling headline that she hadn't been able to get out of her mind.

PROMINENT SON CHARGED IN MURDER

Last week she had cut the article from the paper, though she couldn't say why. In the short nine months she had been a solicitor, she had made something of a name for herself by defending small but difficult cases. Even though a murder charge was well beyond what she could reasonably expect to take on at this point in her career, it was just the kind of case she dreamed of defending one day. Big and important.

Tapping the newsprint in thought, she started to read.

Lucas Hawthorne, son of prominent citizen Bradford Hawthorne, has been charged with the murder of Lucille Rouge, a well-known courtesan found dead in Beckman's alleyway in the early hours of Sunday morning. After his arrest Tuesday afternoon, Hawthorne was set free on a five-hundred-dollar bond.

Equally well known as the owner of the infamous gentlemen's club, Nightingale's Gate, Lucas Hawthorne was unavailable for comment. The elder Hawthorne son, Grayson, emphatically declared his brother's innocence. Matthew, the middle Hawthorne son, is reportedly returning to Boston from Africa. It is to be expected that the three Hawthorne brothers would show such solidarity. What is unexpected, however, is that Bradford Hawthorne, the venerable patriarch of the clan, has refused to make any comment at all.

The article went on, but Alice sat back and barely felt the bite of hard wood pressing her whalebone corset against her ribs. The Hawthorne brothers were well known throughout Boston. They were born of an autocratic, demanding father; and each, in turn, had grown up to be a breed apart. It was said they were exceedingly wealthy, impossibly handsome, and supremely arrogant.

Lucas Hawthorne, Alice had heard, was the wildest of the three, and so exceptionally handsome and charming that women had taken to lining the steps of the courthouse every time the man appeared before a judge for a pretrial hearing.

Alice had heard that the throng of females called out to him as he took the granite steps, straining to touch him, and cried after he disappeared through the thick, oak doors. She couldn't understand such a response to an accused murderer.

It was no secret Lucas was the youngest son of the very fine family, someone who seemed to relish his black-sheep image. Proper Boston didn't take kindly to a man who laughed in the face of propriety. Neither did her father, Boston's highly successful district attorney for the Commonwealth of Massachusetts.

No one within a hundred-mile radius dared cross Walker

Kendall. During his tenure as lead prosecutor for the Commonwealth, he had won far more cases than he had lost.

Alice cringed for the poor fool who would be faced with the task of defending Lucas Hawthorne. He didn't stand a chance against her father.

While she had never met any of the Hawthorne family, she felt sure given their name and money, not to mention the fact that Grayson Hawthorne was considered one of the finest lawyers in town, that there would be a fight.

Intrigued in spite of herself, she resolved to ask her father what he knew about the case when they met at noon for lunch at Locke-Ober's.

A sharp rap on the frosted window in the door shook her from her reverie. She blinked at the large, distorted form that stood behind the glass.

Instantly the article was forgotten. While she had successfully defended the few cases she had gotten, she had practically given her services away for free. As a new lawyer, not to mention as a *woman* lawyer, she didn't have clients banging down her door. Slowly she was developing a solid reputation. She knew that. But if Alice didn't start bringing in some sizable fees soon, she'd be hard pressed to stay in business. A solid reputation alone, she was fast learning, didn't pay the bills.

"Come in," she called out in her best professional voice, quickly dabbing the sweat from her brow before grabbing her pen and a file in hopes of looking busy just as the door swung open.

A man filled the doorway. A stranger. Her breath winged out of her at the sight.

Despite his expensively tailored suit, he looked dangerous. He was tall with broad shoulders, powerful, seemingly unfazed by the staggering heat. His hair was dark like a raven's wing. His jaw was hard and chiseled, just like the man. And his lips. Full and masterfully carved, sensuous.

The effect of such a mouth on a face so masculine was blatantly sexual.

Alice felt an odd tingle race through her, then settle low.

But it was his eyes that demanded her attention. A vivid shade of blue, they flickered over the interior of her office with quick efficiency, before settling on her—and when they did, his body went still and his eyes narrowed. His gaze was unnerving, intense, unreadable.

Locked in his stare, she couldn't move. Her world seemed to shift and change. Seconds ticked by in some distorted facsimile of time passing. An empty, hungry feeling flared unexpectedly inside her —a feeling she could hardly fathom, much less explain.

His gaze drifted over her like an insolent caress, judging, assessing. An embarrassing sense of inadequacy spun through her. She had a pretty enough face, she knew that. But not the porcelain features or curvaceous body to impress such a ruggedly handsome man.

Pulling up bravado like a shield, she gave him her coolest glare. "May I help you?" she asked, forcing her voice to be steady.

At the question he smiled, a slow quirk of lips making him look like a devilish schoolboy. "I think you can."

His tone made it clear that his words had nothing to do with the practice of law. He was making an inappropriate advance at her. Alice couldn't have been more surprised if he had fallen to his knees and begged her to marry him. Shaking the absurd thought away, she wrote her pounding heart off to outrage.

She pushed up from her seat in a stiff rustle of taffeta skirts and the scrape of chair against hardwood floor, certain he must be lost. Hoping he was lost. Or did she, she wondered when she felt a tiny flare of that odd, breathless feeling. Her gaze drifted to his lips, which just as quickly pulled into a wider smile.

Her head jerked up and she felt the instant burn in her face at his knowing look.

"Can I direct you somewhere?" she inquired crisply.

"I'm looking for Alice Kendall."

Her spine straightened in surprise. "For me?"

The man's indolent smile froze into a hard line. "*You* are Alice Kendall?" He glanced around the small office as if he expected to find someone else.

Her chin rose a notch, hating the fact that every time anyone met her they couldn't imagine she was old enough to practice law. This wasn't the first time someone had come into her office and assumed she was the receptionist. "Yes, I am."

His blue eyes narrowed dangerously. "What the hell?" he muttered, more to himself than her. "I need a lawyer, not a date for an ice-cream social."

She realized in that second that he was going to leave.

Instantly her brain raced, but not with thoughts of this massive man and what he made her feel, rather with thoughts of a client. A real, live, breathing client. And if his clothes were any indication, he could actually afford to pay her.

"You're looking for a lawyer?" she burst out.

He hesitated, his gaze no longer sensual. He regarded her with an inexplicable flare of anger.

But Alice wasn't about to be put off. She thrust out her hand like any good businessman, fighting off the very real desire she felt to dash out the door. "Alice Kendall, attorney at law, at your service."

He made no attempt to shake her hand, disdain shimmering around him like the waves of gauzy heat outside.

She tried to convince herself that he wasn't a hopelessly dangerous criminal. Truly, his clothes were nice. He shaved. His hair wasn't overly long. All right, so it was, she amended at the sight of dark hair brushing his collar. Even so, what did it matter. Didn't every man, woman, and thug deserve a lawyer?

Her heart did a little dance of excitement.

"Why do you need an attorney?" she asked, her mind spinning with thoughts of a breach of contract case, or a simple mistaken identity. Or given a criminal's frequently short life span, she'd even do a little estate planning if that was what he wanted. A client was a client.

But before he could answer, another man stepped in behind him.

This one was every bit as tall as the first, his hair as dark, though his eyes were black pools instead of blue. He looked familiar somehow, and she had the distinct impression that she should know him.

"Miss Kendall," he said, his voice smooth and polite, so different from the first man. "How nice finally to meet you."

She tilted her head in confusion as she tried to place him but couldn't. "Who are you?" she asked bluntly, forgetting all her hard-learned lessons in decorous behavior. "And why are you here?"

He didn't answer at first as he noticed the article lying forgotten on her desk. Before she knew what he was doing, he picked it up and glanced at the black print. With a sigh, he handed it to her, and said, "Everyone charged with murder needs representation."

Her mind jerked and spun, attempting to work, like gears trying to find purchase and take hold. "Murder?"

"Unfortunately, yes."

"You're Lucas Hawthorne?"

A brief flash of pure joy raced through her at the thought of such a client. But disappointment followed quickly on its heels. She needed a case she actually stood a chance of winning. The last thing she needed was for Lucas Hawthorne to walk into her office.

The man shook his head. "No, I'm not Lucas Hawthorne."

Relief, a resurgence of enthusiasm. Visions of solvency returned.

"He is."

Alice swung around to face the man who had taken her breath. Dark hair, vivid blue eyes. She stared at him in dumbfounded accusation. This was Lucas Hawthorne. In the flesh. Despite herself, she had a fleeting understanding of why women lined up outside the courthouse doors.

With a start, she shook the thought away, replacing it with another. So much for a nice little breach of contract case.

Damn.

"Why me?" she muttered.

"My question, exactly," Lucas Hawthorne stated, his eyes flickering over her frilly blue gown. "Aren't suffragettes supposed to be mannish and wear ties?"

"Lucas," the other man warned.

"For your information, I am not a suffragette. I'm a lawyer, and a good one, I might add," Alice snapped, her temper short as she swallowed the bitter pill that this wasn't a case she could reasonably take.

Lucas raised one black brow arrogantly and looked at her in a way that was meant to intimidate.

Alice was too disappointed to care, and she glared back. "Unless rumors are mistaken—"

"I've never been one to listen to rumors."

Her smile was thin and caustic. "I'm sure that makes your mother proud. I, on the other hand, enjoy a good rumor now and again. I'm always amazed at how much information they provide. And rumor has it that you have more money than God, and a brother who's a lawyer." She jerked around to the other man. "You're Grayson Hawthorne!"

The older brother nodded his regal head.

Stunned that two of the most well known men in New England were seeking her help, Alice sat down in her chair and refolded the article, then carefully straightened her already straight papers, giving herself time to think.

"So," Grayson said, "are you interested in the job?"

Her heart lurched. These weren't two run-of-the-mill thugs. They weren't lost, and they truly wanted her.

Okay, so only Grayson Hawthorne wanted her, but Grayson Hawthorne belonged to the pantheon of great lawyers as far as she was concerned.

Despite the fact that it was ludicrous to consider, blood drummed through her veins in exhilaration. This was what she had dreamed of for years. A big case. To be sought after and respected by the very lawyers who shaped the law.

But to defend a murder charge when she had only been practicing for less than a year? This was too big. Too soon. Any lawyer in town would know that. At least a good one would, and Grayson Hawthorne was a good one.

Disappointment flared once again, and her eyes narrowed suspiciously. "You never answered my question," she stated, looking at him directly. "Why me?"

Lucas Hawthorne leaned back against the wall and glanced wryly at Grayson. "Call me naïve, big brother, but shouldn't the lawyer be convincing us, rather than the other way around?"

"More than that, why aren't *you* defending him?" Alice challenged.

Grayson glanced back and forth between her and his brother.

"First of all, I deal in civil matters, not criminal. Beyond which, no jury in the land will believe that I can be objective about my own flesh and blood. We need someone from outside my firm."

"Then what about the slew of attorneys in this very building?" she asked, her tone acerbic.

"Not everyone here graduated number one in their class in law school, and not everyone aced the bar exam. You did."

A brush of pride washed over her at the words. Alice felt a slight softening in her stance, despite the fact that she knew she hadn't received a single compliment from anyone except her father since she'd decided to wear her hair up at eighteen. Undoubtedly she was desperate and susceptible to the most blatant forms of flattery, but still, it felt good.

"I've also heard you were the best strategist in your class," Grayson added. "We want someone new. Someone hungry." He eyed her carefully. "And if my guess is correct, you have something to prove. A winning combination, as far as I'm concerned."

She almost preened, would have, no doubt, if it hadn't become exceedingly clear that Lucas Hawthorne didn't agree. In fact, he looked downright antagonistic. She bit her lip and studied him. The man was angry. Dangerous. With large hands that easily could have ended a woman's life.

A shiver of something raced down her spine, but this time it had nothing to do with feeling drawn or intrigued.

"What is the charge?" she asked Grayson as if his brother weren't there. "Murder in the first degree? In the second? Manslaughter?"

"Murder in the first," Lucas answered for him, crossing his arms casually on his chest as if he didn't have a care in the world.

Her heart fluttered, and she tried to ignore him. "The Commonwealth must have some pretty solid evidence to go for such a charge."

Deep lines etched Grayson Hawthorne's face. "What they have is a very solid hatred for my brother and the way he has chosen to lead his life."

Unable to help herself, she turned to study Lucas, took in the half-angry, half-amused smile pulling at those lips that had made her heart flutter.

"Did you do it?" she asked without thinking.

The smile evaporated into the bleak office, and his arms dropped to his sides. His look of bored indifference disappeared until only the taut line of his jaw and the tense brace of his broad shoulders remained. The small office simmered with anger.

"I thought lawyers didn't ask questions like that," he said with harsh animosity.

"This lawyer does."

He pushed away from the wall and walked toward her desk with the smooth grace of a panther, as if all this time he had been holding back, containing the raw, furious power of his rage. "What do you think, Miss Kendall? Do you think I did it?"

She didn't lean back, though she wanted to, and she didn't answer his question. Instead she asked, "Where were you the night of the murder?"

The air in the room seemed sparse as he stared at her. She felt the barely contained power of him, the heat of his body overpowering the small space. It was all she could do to not look away.

"I was in my room at the club. In bed. Would you like to know what I was doing there?"

His voice was a deep, seductive brush of sound, and her breath hissed out of her.

"No, thank you," she managed. "But if indeed you were in . . . your room, how could anyone possibly think you did it?"

"They have an eyewitness."

Alice blinked. "An eyewitness?" she repeated, incredulous. "If someone saw you do it, you don't need a lawyer, Mr. Hawthorne, you need a miracle worker."

"That's why we came to you." Lucas drawled the last word with stinging contempt. "As Grayson said, you're smart, you're hungry." His smile returned, hard and dismissive. "And while you aren't at all what I expected, you *are* a woman."

"Lucas," Grayson snapped.

Her shoulders came back. "What is that supposed to mean?"

But Lucas wasn't put off. "What my dear brother has failed to mention is that he believes a woman lawyer will help my case."

"Most men would believe that a woman lawyer would do more harm than good."

Lucas shrugged, the gesture a lament. "I said as much myself. But Grayson feels that no woman would consider representing a guilty man. At least that's what he's counting on a jury believing."

She began to see where he was headed, and her stomach tightened with anger.

Grayson gave his brother a quelling look before he spoke. "The fact is, Miss Kendall, if you agree to represent Lucas I don't believe he will ever be indicted by the grand jury, much less convicted in a court of law. Yes, they have an eye-witness. But she is a woman of lesser virtue, and it will be her word against his."

"From what I hear, your brother is a *man* of lesser virtue." The words were out before Alice could stop them.

Grayson's countenance grew fierce. Lucas's eyes darkened to a deep shade of unfathomable blue, before he threw his head back and laughed.

"At least she's honest," he said. "Come on, big brother. We're wasting our time."

He headed for the door, looking pleased to be leaving. She stared at his retreating back, at the smooth grace of him. But Grayson didn't budge. He stood, staring at her, and at the last second Lucas cursed and turned back.

"*Are* we wasting our time?" Grayson asked.

Alice couldn't seem to look away from Lucas. Moments passed in silence as she thought about this man charged with murder, trying to understand what it was about him that drew her. He was arrogant, rude, and he had trouble written all over him. But something about him made her heart beat wildly and her knees feel weak.

It was foolish, idiotic, an insipidly female reaction. And

she had always prided herself on the fact that she had never been insipid.

"I'm sorry," she said finally, still looking at Lucas instead of his brother. "But I can't take the case."

A flash of something—hurt, fear—darkened in Lucas Hawthorne's blue eyes, but it was quickly covered by that wry indifference.

"Come on, let's go," he said.

Grayson pursed his lips and stared at her hard. "Just think about it, Miss Kendall," he said, his tone firm and exacting. "Lucas needs a lawyer who can counter the very reputation you mentioned." He glanced around the very sparse surroundings of her office with a knowing look. "And if my guess is correct, you need a client."

Then they were gone, the door closing with a rattle of glass in the wooden frame. Alice stared at the murky window, feeling shaken and angry. More than that, she felt a needling desire to take the case.

But to deal with a man whose disreputable lifestyle could very easily have led him to commit such a crime? And if he didn't do it, given his reputation, no court in the land would believe him.

No, she wasn't that foolish.

She pressed her hand against her heart. It raced inside her chest as Lucas Hawthorne's blue eyes flashed in her mind— the way he had looked at her, really looked for those few moments when he first entered the room, seeing her as no one else ever did.

What did he see, she wondered.

Shaking her head, she scoffed at her thoughts. She wasn't going to ask Lucas Hawthorne anything, not about what he saw . . . or about what he had done. Her decision was made. She wouldn't see him again. Case closed. End of story.

Chapter Two

Smoothing every loose strand of hair back into her chignon and carefully adjusting the folds of her voluminous skirt, Alice pulled the chair closer to the desk and got back to work.

Lucas Hawthorne might not be an option, but still she needed another client.

Every morning for the last three weeks, she had pored through the *Boston Herald* in search of crimes committed and any sort of roadway accident. If defendants weren't coming to her, she would just have to go to them.

There was a word for such practices, she knew it, and not a particularly nice one. But *solvency* was the only word these days that held any meaning for her. She had moved out of her family home—so it was only to the cottage behind the main house, but it was a move as far as she was concerned—and she was not about to move back. She cherished her uncle, adored her dear brother, and loved her father. But she wasn't interested in living the rest of her life with two bachelor relatives and her widowed parent.

Two hours later, with the paper read and a notepad filled with prospects, Alice noticed the clock. With a grimace, she barely took time to grab her hat, gloves, and parasol, before she dashed out of the office. Her father hated it when she was late.

She headed for Locke-Ober's, a bastion of fine dining since the early years, the spot where she and her father met every Thursday for lunch. It was also the place where important men about town congregated.

She wished she could tell her father about the Hawthorne brothers' visit. As her greatest supporter, he would be proud, she was sure, that such an important family had come to her for representation. But it was unethical to reveal the names of people whom an attorney chose not to represent.

And she wouldn't represent Lucas Hawthorne. Now that he was gone, she couldn't imagine why she had given even a glimmer of consideration to him or his case. Clearly he was trouble, and his case couldn't be won. And no doubt missing breakfast accounted for the odd hunger he made her feel.

Five minutes late, she arrived at the entrance of Locke-Ober's. With her chin decorously parallel to the floor, her breathing just barely even beneath the starched linen of her chemisette after having dashed the last handful of blocks, she entered.

"Mademoiselle Kendall, how good it is to see you," the maître d' greeted.

Alice smiled, genuinely happy to see the Frenchman. "Thank you, Jean George."

She peered into the restaurant. "Is my father here yet?"

"But of course," he answered, with a tsk. "Where else would he be on Thursday at noon?"

So much for her hope that he would be a few minutes late.

Jean George led her into the walnut-lined dining room. Her father sat at his usual table, with food already there, and he wasn't alone. Clark Kittridge, assistant district attorney for the Commonwealth beneath her father, or ADA as the lower-level attorneys were commonly called, was with him.

She could feel the rush of blood to her cheeks. There was no denying the fact that Clark was everything she wanted in a man. He was kind and caring. A man who shared her passion for the law. And everyone was certain that the two of them would marry. Alice included.

She wasn't sure if she was delighted at the sight of him or

annoyed that her father had allowed someone to breech their special time. But it was Clark, after all. And she really did want to see him, too.

"Hello," she said, approaching the table, her long gown rustling delicately with every step she took.

The men rose from their seats. Their dark suits, crisp shirts, and high collars were more respectable than fashionable. Her father was only a few inches taller than she, with a strong barrel chest, a thick, luxuriant mustache, and a crease between his brows that gave him the look of serious contemplation at all times.

Walker Kendall smiled at his daughter and opened his arms. "You're late," he stated as he kissed her fondly on the forehead.

"You look lovely," Clark offered.

"True, and thank you."

Her father chuckled. Clark offered her a wonderful smile. He really was a dream, and she sighed her pleasure at the ease he made her feel. Whatever ire she felt melted away as she sat down in the chair he held for her.

Without another word to her, Walker Kendall resumed his conversation with the younger man. She hardly noticed, however, as she took in Clark's sandy blond hair, the way he combed it back with just the right amount of pomade. Tall but not too tall, well built but not so massively chiseled.

So very different from Lucas Hawthorne.

The thought made her stiffen, and it was then that she realized her father had just said the man's name. Sitting back, she focused on the conversation just as the waiter set a peeled grapefruit and avocado salad in front of her, covered with poppy seed dressing. Her usual.

"We don't have much on him, sir," Clark was saying, "other than the statement given by the . . . um . . ." He glanced at Alice, then said, "the woman of the evening."

"We have enough," Walker countered in his all-knowing way, taking a bite of pork loin roast. "Trust me." He leaned forward and looked the younger man straight in the eyes, fork and knife still in his hands. "You know you are my handpicked choice to succeed me."

Alice's spine straightened. While it was assumed Clark would one day take over for her father, the words had never been stated out loud. For the last year Clark had said he needed to know where his life was going before he could make such a momentous decision as marriage.

Forget the fact that he was nearly thirty with a good income and an adequately respectable place in society. He hadn't been able to commit. Now, she was sure, he could. What a wonderful day she was having!

"However, you have to win a big case, Clark," Walker continued. "You've done well, but you need a significant conviction. This is your chance."

Clark beamed. "Well," he mused, "we do have that statement."

"Exactly," Walker said with a nod and another bite of his lunch.

"I just wish it were from a more model citizen."

"Doesn't matter. Prostitute or prude, she's an eyewitness, and anyone who saw the crime is enough—more than enough—to get an indictment."

After a person was charged with a crime, it was up to the prosecutors to convince a grand jury that there was enough evidence to indict the person. Only after an indictment was obtained did a defendant stand trial.

"And once you get the indictment," Walker added, "I have every confidence you will dazzle all of Boston with your prosecution. I'll let you have this case all to yourself, Clark. No reason for me to get involved directly."

The younger man's eyes went wide with delight. Alice's heart leaped and it was all she could do not to reach across the table and squeeze his hand.

"I'm telling you, Clark, this is your chance to make a

name for yourself. It also gets the likes of Lucas Hawthorne off the streets."

"Thank you, Mr. Kendall," Clark said excitedly, clearly pleased as he took a pad of paper from his suit coat pocket and hastily made a few notes. "I won't fail you."

"See that you don't."

At that, Walker turned his attention on his daughter and eyed her closely. "You certainly look pleased with yourself."

Her smile broadened. "I've had a good day."

"What have you done?" he asked with a raised brow and a chuckle, his suspicion born from years of experience with his only daughter.

"I haven't done anything, Father," she admonished fondly, and this time she did reach across and squeeze her father's hand. "I'm simply in a good mood. No crime in that."

Clark stopped writing and looked up. "Surely your high spirits have nothing to do with the fact that Lucas Hawthorne came to see you this morning."

Alice straightened in her chair, surprised that anyone knew about the meeting. "Where did you hear that?"

"Word gets around," Clark answered apologetically.

Walker studied his subordinate for a moment. "What else did you hear?"

"Nothing else, sir. Though my guess is that Hawthorne went to Alice to ask for representation."

Her heart hammered. She was half furious with Clark and half elated that her father heard that someone so important sought her out. She knew he'd be proud.

"That is ridiculous," Walker scoffed brusquely, then cut himself off and turned to Alice. "Is this true?"

Ridiculous? Alice sat very still, stunned at her father's reaction.

Her mother having died when Alice was only a year old, she had been raised by her father and her uncle. Her father had always been her greatest supporter—the one person who had always believed in her.

Doing her best to hold back her mounting confusion, she said, "You know I can't tell you that, it would be a violation of ethics."

"I am not the ethics board, Alice. I'm your father."

"Yes, but first and foremost, you are a lawyer. We both know that."

Walker's mouth pulled into a grim line. "Then let me put it to you this way. If he did come to you, and if he was insane enough to ask for representation, I hope you had the good sense to decline. If he is crazy enough to want you, he only wants you for one reason."

Her fingers curled around the arms of her chair. Her confusion mixed with a completely foreign and stinging sense of betrayal. "Why is that?" she asked very slowly.

"Because of me," he stated with the arrogance for which he was known.

Because of me. Crazy enough to want you.

The words were like a slap, for many reasons. She never would have believed her father could say something like this to her. But more than that, if the one person who had always believed in her didn't think her capable, what did that mean?

Ignoring the grapefruit salad, she forced herself to ease her grip on the chair, thinking of all the very credible reasons Grayson Hawthorne had given for wanting her—without a single mention of Walker Kendall. "That's absurd, Father. You said yourself that you won't be prosecuting him. This has nothing to do with you."

Or did it?

She hated this sudden sense of doubt.

"Don't be a child, Alice. This is an important case, and my office is prosecuting it. I'm sure he knows I will take an interest whether I prosecute it personally or not. Hawthorne also knows that I will take great pleasure in bringing him down. And I *am* going to bring him down," he added with a vehemence that sizzled through the room.

Clark's pencil halted in midstroke.

Walker calmed himself. "Rather, Clark is going to bring him down."

The younger man nodded and resumed writing.

"There is no need for you to be on the losing end of that stick, Alice. Whatever reason he wants you, do you really think you can win?"

Despite having thought that very same thing only hours ago, Alice was appalled. And hurt. Her father had always told her she could do anything if she put her mind to it. He had drummed in a soul-deep belief in herself and her abilities. He had never doubted her—at least he had never voiced any doubts. Now she wondered.

"You have always been a realist, Alice. And the reality is you're a woman."

His tone couldn't have been kinder or more solicitous if he had just told her she had a fatal disease.

"And," he continued, "can you deny that you have been coddled by me? I love you, and I don't want to see you make a fool of yourself. That's all."

Her thoughts spun like marzipan candy, messy and fragile, easily shattered as she searched for something to say. "But Father, I've won every case I've taken on. I graduated summa cum laude. I aced the bar."

Walker sat for a moment, his brow furrowed deeper than usual as he stared at his water glass. After a second, he gave a quick nod of decision, then said, "Woman or not, you are a lawyer, and you are my daughter. I'll see that you get some reasonable case." He glanced at Clark. "What can we funnel her way?"

"Funnel?" she sputtered.

Her father continued talking to Clark as if she hadn't uttered a word. "A case that we are prosecuting where the suspect needs a defense attorney?"

"Well, sir, off the top of my head I don't know."

Walker tapped the silver fork against the white linen tablecloth. "What has happened with that B&E Dickson is working on?"

B&E. Breaking and entering, Alice knew, though she could hardly believe her ears.

"You can't be serious, Father."

"Hmmm," Clark mused, considering. "That's not a bad idea."

Alice's mouth fell open as she listened to this ludicrous conversation going on around her as if she weren't there.

"Good," Walker stated with a decisive nod. "See to it that the suspect is given Alice's name and address for representation. The case shouldn't prove too difficult. Dickson needs a comeuppance. He's gotten too cocky of late."

"Yes, sir. I'll look into it as soon as I get back to the office. Dickson's case should do nicely."

Humiliated to the core, Alice searched for words. She felt adrift, her anchor cut loose, and she didn't know where to turn. "Are you saying that you don't think I'm good enough to be Lucas Hawthorne's lawyer?"

Her father focused on her, really focused, as if he understood that he had gone about things badly.

Reaching across, he smiled and patted her hand. "Of course you are good enough, princess."

She looked at him, wanting to believe that it had all been a misunderstanding, a mistake, that she had misheard what he had said.

"But do you honestly think a man like Lucas Hawthorne would risk his life in your hands? Would *you* risk your life in your hands?"

Fury hit like a thunderclap, burning fast and hot through her. But she welcomed the anger, preferred it over the very foreign despair. "Thank you, Father," she began, "for your vote of confidence."

"No need to thank me," he replied, clearly not listening.

"I know what is best," he added, seemingly unaware of the cauldron that began to boil before him.

"Father—"

"Go back to your office, and Clark will see what he can do about getting you some work." He glanced at his pocket watch. "I've got to get back to the courthouse. Your brother is meeting me there. We have an appointment with the governor this afternoon. I've recommended Max for the new committee on banking."

He wiped his mustache, tossed the napkin on the table, then stood. "Have whatever else you want. Jean George will put it on my tab. Ready, Clark?"

The assistant district attorney jumped up, leaving his food barely touched, then stuffed his pad of paper and pencil in his shirt pocket. "Yes, sir."

Walker retrieved his top hat and walking stick, nodded to the maitre d', and was gone. By then Alice was so stunned that she hardly noticed when Clark reached across and patted her shoulder kindly before he followed his boss. She was mad. Furious. Humiliated.

Pride surged, and she thought of how Lucas Hawthorne had sought her out. How Grayson Hawthorne had known of her achievements in law school, of her success with the Board of Examiners test.

She shouldn't take the case. Based on her father's reaction, she knew it would infuriate him. Beyond which, Lucas Hawthorne was probably guilty, and if not, at the very least, he was dangerous. And murder was too big to take on at this point in her career. She understood that.

But her father didn't believe in her. Didn't believe she could get her own cases, didn't believe she could succeed without his help. Funnel work to her, for mercy's sake.

Raised in a world of men, she knew Boston society thought her odd. But that had never bothered her, because she'd had the love and support of her family.

Sitting at the table in Locke-Ober's now, her world seemed

to have shifted and changed. Who was she if her father didn't believe in her?

She felt an all-too-familiar stubborn streak flare inside her, a streak that had gotten her into no end of trouble over the years. But it had also been that streak that had gotten her through law school, through years without a mother. She could do this, too. She was a good lawyer.

And before she realized what she was doing, she headed out of Locke-Ober's, hailed a hired hack, gathered her skirts, pulled herself into the cramped confines of cracked leather and grimy windows, and directed the driver to the infamous establishment known as Nightingale's Gate.

Lucas saw her the minute she walked in, felt the same unexpected heat flare through him at the sight, and he cursed.

Standing in the entrance of Nightingale's Gate in long sleeves and a high collar despite the sweltering heat, Alice Kendall looked out of place. Too prim against the backdrop of plush red velvets and smoky mirrors reflecting gilt-trimmed archways and dripping crystal chandeliers. Her eyes were wide with shock, making it clear she had never been in a place where women wore little in the way of clothing and men unabashedly enjoyed it.

Lucas would have smiled had he not been so damned angry at the sight of her as he sat in his loft office that overlooked the grand salon of his gentlemen's club. It was a space that allowed him to monitor what went on, but didn't force him to be a part of everything all the time. He had another private office upstairs in his suite of rooms. But much of his time was spent here, allowing him to see who came in and when. He couldn't have been more surprised when Alice Kendall showed up in his club.

He still couldn't believe Grayson wanted this prudishly dressed woman to represent him. Nor could he believe Grayson thought she could. God, she looked as if she should be teaching Sunday school, not going to court.

And how would she deal with his lifestyle? He knew it would be that, more than anything, which would be on trial if he was indicted. Even though Alice Kendall couldn't be that much younger than he was in age, Lucas was certain she was young and innocent in a way he hadn't been in years—if ever.

He muttered a virulent oath and raked his hair back with his hand.

At thirty, he had seen and done more than anyone he knew. He loved the women, the wildness.

He had the fleeting thought that he lived like he did, pushing to the edge, because he had lost sight of any other way to feel alive. But something about this woman made him feel . . . yearning? For what? Innocence?

He scoffed at the thought. He wouldn't deny that when he walked into her office something about her snared in his mind. The second he saw her his body responded. The reaction had been primal and intense. The way her amber eyes had first widened, then darkened with awareness—an awareness that seemed to catch her by surprise. Her full, red lips parting on a startled breath.

Instantly he had seen that she was beautiful in an understated way, if you looked beyond the prim gown and severely marshaled hair. There had also been a surprising provocative wildness that had flared in her eyes, which didn't match her very contained exterior. But then he had learned she was the lawyer.

The combination was a puzzle. That was what surprised him, he reasoned. He wanted to know what that wildness was. Nothing more, nothing less. Just as that was what snared his attention now.

A regular, who'd had more than his share of the club's fine whiskey, pawed at Alice's full, navy blue skirt. Lucas saw her wide eyes go even wider, and he stood from his chair.

"Howard."

One simple word, but spoken in such a way that everyone

in the room below stopped and turned toward him. Howard immediately dropped his hand away.

Lucas had his reservations about this man who frequented the club. It wasn't anything in particular that he did. He paid his bills and joked with the others. But Lucas didn't like the way he looked at the women when he thought he wasn't being observed.

"Got a new girl, did you?" Howard asked with a laugh.

Bright red flared in Miss Kendall's cheeks, though it looked to be a red of anger, not embarrassment. For half a second Lucas would have sworn she almost decked the man. The thought surprised him, and he discounted it just as quickly.

"A little prim," Howard added, "but pretty enough."

"She's not a new girl," Lucas stated with quiet command, "and if you don't step aside, I'll come down and personally see that you do." He glanced at his right-hand man. "Brutus, bring Miss Kendall upstairs."

Howard's eyes flashed heatedly, but then it was gone, and without a word of protest, he stepped aside with sharp precision. Lucas knew that while he had the most popular establishment around, patronized by many of the most important men in the city, there wasn't a person who frequented Nightingale's Gate who wasn't half afraid of him. Most of the time it served him well. But there were times . . .

He cut the thought off. He had spent years creating his life, honing it until it was just what he wanted, needed. And it was foolish that he felt tired of what he had created for even a second.

While both of his brothers were married, Lucas felt no pressing need to follow suit. He had never lacked for feminine companionship. His sexual appetites were strong. He enjoyed women immensely—their bodies, their faces—but he had no need of an heir. As a result, he didn't need a wife.

The thought of his sisters-in-law came to mind. He held

them both in high regard, and wished his brothers well. But Grayson and Matthew had been to hell and back to get them.

All Lucas had to say was, No, thank you.

Within minutes, Brutus escorted Alice Kendall into Lucas's office. He was still standing when she entered, but when he gestured to one of the two soft leather chairs that faced his desk, she didn't notice. She was too busy peering over the low half-wall like Alice peering into the rabbit's hole.

Lucas followed her gaze and noticed Janine, his newest dancing girl, sidling up to Howard. He felt a flare of temper. He had not been able to instill in the woman that the men could look but never touch. She encouraged them to do both. And just then Alice Kendall was getting an eyeful of the raven-haired beauty being felt up.

Lucas gave a subtle hand signal directing Brutus to the scene, then he returned his attention to the woman before him.

"Miss Kendall?"

She swung her head around. "Yes?"

"I'm flattered that Nightingale's Gate is so enthralling to you, but unless you've come to ask for a job as a dance girl"—there went those eyes again, wide, shocked . . . intrigued? Surely not—"then I suggest you get on with why you are here. I'm a busy man."

His words and tone were meant to intimidate. He wanted her gone, and fast. But Alice Kendall was anything but intimidated. She took a seat with the confidence of a queen and looked him straight in the eye.

"I've decided to represent you," she stated importantly, her hands clasped on top of her reticule, which lay in her lap.

Lucas felt his breath hiss out of him. "Hell."

"A simple thank-you would do."

The sounds from below became muted, distorted in his mind as he tried to make sense of this woman before him. She was an odd mix of prim, pious, and pushy. He didn't like her at all.

"Gratitude," he stated coolly, "generally comes from someone who is thankful."

She looked at him with a tight smile, her shoulders coming back, outlining the gentle but distinctive curve of her breasts, then said, "I'm beginning to see why you don't believe in listening to rumors."

Lucas's eyes narrowed dangerously. "And why is that?"

"Rumor has it that you are charming. As far as I can see, you are anything but."

Lucas sliced her a mocking smile. "I find myself short on charm when I am being accused of murder."

Unfazed, she shrugged. "Good point. Though I'd think by now you'd be accustomed to run-ins with the law."

Lucas raised a brow and was surprised by the sudden urge to laugh. She did that to him, just like this morning, saying something so straightforward and unblinkingly honest that he was amused. And the fact was it had been a long time since anyone had provoked him, gone up against him and not backed down. This tiny little thing didn't seem impressed or afraid. And suddenly he was intrigued.

"True, I've had my share," he conceded, goading her. "But judging from your demeanor, I'd guess you've had as many run-ins with polite society." He rocked back in his chair, his hands resting negligently on the armrests as he sliced her a devilish look. "Are you sure you're a proper lady, Miss Kendall?"

For half a second she seemed to blanch, but then her amber eyes sparked until they glowed nearly green in the flickering gaslight.

"What I'm sure of is that you wouldn't recognize a *lady* if she jumped up and bit you in the face."

He chuckled as his gaze drifted to her mouth, bow-shaped and red without the help of paint, and he had the unexpected urge to taste her. "I've never been much for biting, sweetheart," he said, his voice like gravel as heat sizzled low, "but if you insist, I'll let you jump up here and give it a try."

Her eyes went wide before she made a strange noise that he would have sworn was a snarl, and he would bet money she felt a desperate itch to wipe the smile right off his face. His smile grew broader.

Her mouth opened and closed, before sound finally took hold. "You, you—"

"I'm sure the courts are impressed with your articulate ability with words, Miss Kendall. I know I am. In fact, I can't think of anyone more suited to state my case."

"You arrogant, self-centered, insulting—"

"You forgot haughty, self-important, vainglorious—I rather like vainglorious—if you are trying to exhaust the thesaurus."

"Errrr—"

"Am I interrupting?"

Lucas watched as Alice snapped her lips shut and swiveled to Grayson, who stood in the doorway holding his top hat in his properly gloved hands.

Visibly, she worked to gather her calm.

"Miss Kendall," Grayson said in greeting, clearly pleased. "What brings you here?"

"I came to accept the case." She shot Lucas a scathing glare. "Or at least I was going to."

Grayson beamed as he glanced from one to the other. "Don't let Lucas put you off, Miss Kendall. He will be the perfect client." He glanced at Lucas pointedly. "I promise."

Every ounce of Lucas's good humor vanished in direct proportion to the satisfaction he saw returning to Alice Kendall.

"I'll have a desk ready for you at my office by first thing tomorrow morning," Grayson added.

"What are you talking about?" Alice demanded.

"An office. You don't think you can defend my brother properly from that hell—from your office."

"I happen to like my office," she said tightly. "And if you want me on this case, we do things my way. Understood?"

Grayson got that look about him, exacting and intimidating. As the oldest of the Hawthorne brothers, he had been the more responsible of the boys. Lucas knew Grayson had never been able to please their father. Matthew, the middle brother, had always been the favorite, at least he had been until the scandalous accident that had scarred his face. Lucas had tried to please their father once. Only once.

"No, I don't think *you* understand, Miss Kendall—"

"Enough," Lucas said, cutting him off. "I don't think either of you understand."

He came around the desk until he stood directly in front of Alice's chair. He leaned down and planted his hands on the wooden arms carved from the finest mahogany, trapping her. Alice had to crane her neck to meet his eyes. But she did meet his eyes, boldly.

"And what is that, Mr. Hawthorne?"

"That I run this show. Not you. Not Grayson."

They stared at each other, so close that he could easily touch her.

And he wanted to, badly. He wanted to feel the silkiness of her skin, the heat of her mouth.

He didn't understand the feeling, nor did he like it. But he couldn't seem to look away from the faint hint of freckles beneath her milk-white skin or the depths of her amber eyes. He felt drawn in by that certain wildness that hid beneath her very proper exterior—drawn in by the contradiction.

His reaction was swift and intense, and he became aware of the sudden tension that shimmered through her body.

In a flash of insight he realized that for all her bravado, she was afraid of him, but she was doing her best not to show it. He wasn't sure if that angered or disappointed him.

Despite her fear, she squared her shoulders. "Then you are a fool, Mr. Hawthorne."

Her words caught in his mind. He pulled a hard, sharp

breath, and straightened. "It has been a very long time since anyone called me a fool, Miss Kendall."

"Then they should have. You are accused of murder, Mr. Hawthorne. Not petty theft. Not picking flowers from the no-pick section of the Public Gardens. I'm the attorney, not you. If you want me as your lawyer, then we do it my way."

Her gall astounded him. But on the heels of that, the reality of the situation hit him square in the chest.

He wondered how he had gotten to this point. Suspected of murder. His name splashed across the newspapers connected to the most sensational case in Boston's history.

Years ago, his older brother Matthew had been involved in the biggest scandal to rock Boston. Then Grayson had married a woman who had nearly caused an uproar with the shock of her cello playing.

Now it looked as if it were his turn.

But none of what the others had done could compare with murder and the prospect of losing his freedom. Or his life. And the reality was, he was closer to indictment than not, with a woman barely out of law school for a defender. He couldn't imagine how Grayson thought this was a good idea.

But what were his choices? The truth was, Lucas had inquired into other lawyers, and there wasn't an attorney in Boston who wanted this case—not when the Commonwealth had an eyewitness and it was no secret that Walker Kendall had it in for him personally. What man wanted to go up against that?

"So, tell me," Alice stated crisply, her eyes flashing her ire, "do we have a deal?"

Unspoken words hung in the charged air between them. At length, Lucas was forced to concede that he didn't have much choice. Curtly, he nodded.

"Good."

Despite his nearness, she rose from her seat. He knew that she expected him to step back; ordinarily he would have. But not today. They stood so close that he could feel the brush of her gown against his thighs.

Desire snaked through him, hot and fast. His muscles contracted as awareness heightened when he caught the scent of her. Not harsh colognes that the dance girls wore. Not expensive perfumes that the more brazen wealthy women applied generously. Rather a soft, sweet scent. Like innocence.

He watched as the color of her eyes darkened as her gaze drifted to his lips. Satisfaction flared.

But then she blinked, as if coming back to herself. "I'll see you in my office tomorrow morning at nine o'clock," she stated tersely. "On the dot."

Lucas scowled. She faced him, half belligerent, half ready to flee. But still she stood there. Defiant, stronger than he would have guessed at first sight. And her eyes. Awareness melted into challenge, becoming fathomless in a way that drew him, made his body tighten with a palpable heat. He felt frustrated and angry, but underlying that he felt something else. Grudging admiration? Intense awareness that had nothing to do with the mess he was in?

The thought added to his anger.

"I'll be there," he replied, slicing her a narrow look.

She gave a decisive nod. "Fine. Don't be late."

With that Alice Kendall elbowed him out of the way and left the office, her head held self-assuredly high. And this time when she passed through the main room below, she didn't so much as glance at the women who wore such provocative clothes or the men who watched her much too intently.

Chapter Three

"What the hell was that all about?" Grayson demanded as soon as Alice was out the door.

Tossing his hat aside, the older Hawthorne brother yanked off his gloves, crushing them in a tight fist.

Lucas walked back to his seat with barely contained anger and lowered himself into the supple leather with a nonchalance he didn't feel. What *had* that been about, he wondered. The intensity. The need to make her see that he wasn't someone she could toy with.

The need to touch her. The desire to pull her close, press her body to his.

Heat flared low as he remembered, and he muttered a curse.

He could still see her delicately boned face, her pale, milk-white skin—without powder or, worse yet, small doses of strychnine that some of the dance girls foolishly took to whiten their skin.

He rubbed his temples. "I don't like her."

Grayson looked at him incredulously, and Lucas couldn't blame him. He knew he sounded like a fool. But he *didn't* like her, or rather, he didn't like the way she made him feel. Off balance in a way he had never felt before.

"She's a lightweight," he offered instead. "You're crazy if you think she will be anything but a hindrance to my case. Any lawyer in Boston will walk right over her."

"She didn't let either of us walk right over her. In fact, I'd say she held her own." Grayson looked him in the eye. "Furthermore, you are going to do what she says. You need every advantage you can get."

"What about the advantage of my innocence?" he asked with a snarl.

"All any judge and jury cares about is what can be proved. Last I heard, you didn't have a way to prove your innocence. As a result, we'll have to make you look like a model citizen. Mother living here now may be a godsend after all."

The discussion was interrupted when a woman walked into the main room below, dressed every inch as properly as Alice Kendall. The brothers turned in unison.

Grayson's tight grip eased and he shook his head, then chuckled. "Speaking of whom . . ."

But Grayson's chuckle trailed off when a second woman entered behind their mother. His hard, obsidian eyes flickered with intensity when he saw his wife, Sophie.

Lucas groaned. Women, too many women, at least of the proper sort. Alice Kendall, Sophie Hawthorne. But most especially his mother, Emmaline, dressed in a handsome walking gown, holding a matching lace parasol, her soft gray hair pulled up underneath a wide-brimmed flowered hat, looking ready to attend a woman's sewing social. Instead she walked into his crowded establishment, moving among faro tables, dancing couples, and scantily clad women who dispensed freely flowing liquor, talking to each as if she was among a group of old friends.

Emmaline, his sainted mother—the woman whom all of Boston knew as the epitome of everything proper—had suddenly announced that she needed to *find herself*.

Find herself?

Lucas shook his head, rolling his shirt cuffs down out of habit when his mother was near. After raising three sons, Emmaline Hawthorne had announced that she no longer felt purposeful. Now she intended to find a new way to live. Her first step had been to leave her husband, Bradford, the patriarch of the Hawthorne clan. A scandalous endeavor, to say the least. Not that Lucas could blame her. He and his father rarely spoke, and only when they had no other choice. They didn't get along, and Lucas doubted they ever would.

Bradford Hawthorne didn't approve of his youngest son's appreciation for the finer things in life. What the man didn't understand, however, was that Lucas wasn't guided by cigars or fine, aged brandies. And he especially wasn't guided by women. He had many, enjoyed them all. But he didn't love them. If Lucas had learned anything at all from his father worth remembering, it was that there was no such thing as love.

The older man had done nothing but cause heartache and grief for Lucas's brothers, Grayson and Matthew, not to mention for their mother. It was no wonder that Matthew had left Boston to live with his wonderful wife, Finnea.

A flash of anticipation sparked at the thought that Matthew was coming home. Lucas hated the circumstances under which their middle brother was returning, but still he was pleased. He had sent word that Matthew didn't need to make the trip. But he imagined the missive wouldn't arrive in time before Matthew and his young family had boarded a ship for America.

But just then it was Emmaline who was the concern. Not only had she left her husband, but she had taken to living in Nightingale's Gate like a duck takes to water, and not a word from either him or Grayson could persuade her to live elsewhere.

When Emmaline had sent a note informing him that she planned to move into his gentlemen's club, he had fired off his reply. Short, sweet, to the point.

Not on your life.

He wouldn't have his mother staying in an establishment known for gambling, drinking, and ... things done by women *not* like his mother. What was she thinking? Grayson had gotten a good laugh out of his sudden flash of righteous modesty. But hell, she was a mother—*his* mother.

Emmaline Hawthorne, however, had been adamant. If Lucas didn't put her up, she would find a place that would.

Lucas groaned again at the memory.

No amount of arguing or trying to convince her to stay with Grayson and Sophie at their respectable Back Bay town house called Swan's Grace had swayed her.

Hanging his head, Lucas had conceded to her wish, but only on the belief that both she and his father would regain their senses and Emmaline would return to her respectable life. But that hadn't happened. And now, afraid she would never move out, Lucas had purchased the dilapidated town house next door to his and was in the process of transforming the run-down place into a proper home. That way his mother would be away from the goings-on of a gentlemen's club, but close enough that he could keep his eye on her.

"We've been to Harvard College," Emmaline stated, as she and Sophie entered the office without knocking, setting a stack of books on his desk. "Haven't we, dear?"

Sophie wasn't paying attention as she smiled shyly at her husband. Not that his sister-in-law was shy. Lucas had learned that she was anything but. And his brother, a completely reserved, no-nonsense sort, looked at his wife as if he would take her in his arms right there. The couple had been married three months before—only days after his mother had announced her independence—and they still acted like newlyweds who couldn't seem to get enough of each other.

Lucas turned away sharply and picked up one of the books. *"Introduction to Jurisprudence?"* He raised a brow. "Are you enrolling in law school, Mother?" he asked dryly.

Emmaline raised a brow of her own. "No, son," she replied, her voice chastising, as if he were still in short pants.

"Though perhaps I should. A woman can do anything a man can do."

Lucas's wry expression melted into a fond smile as he tossed the book aside and crooked his arm around her delicate shoulders to kiss her forehead. "Remind me not to go up against you in a court of law if you decide to pursue a degree."

Emmaline remained in his embrace for a long second, and he could feel her gathering her strength. And suddenly he understood, and a slow dread began to fill him. She had gotten the books in order to help defend him.

"I am not about to sit idly by while my child is being wrongly accused of murder," she stated, pushing back.

He fought to maintain a lightness he didn't feel. "I'm no longer a child, Mother."

She scoffed as she pulled her white gloves from her hands, then folded them into her reticule. "You'll always be my child, dear."

Grayson laughed out loud, and when Lucas turned around, he found Sophie curled against his brother's side. Lucas could see the ease in his brother that happened only when his wife was nearby.

His brow furrowed, and he didn't understand the twist in his heart that he felt at the sight.

He wrote it off to the sudden tumult of his life. Who wouldn't be edgy with his mother living under his roof, not to mention being accused of murder? But somehow it seemed more than that.

If he were truthful with himself, he would admit that for months now his life hadn't been satisfactory. Walking the edge, pushing the limits wasn't enough anymore. Even the women no longer brought the same pleasure.

More and more, while it was still easy to bring both himself and the women he chose to sexual gratification, afterward he pushed up from the tangle of sheets to stand at the window alone, feeling hollow and distant—as if he wanted something more.

The flicker of thought swept through him that after so much decadence in his life it took more to gratify him. Next, he thought darkly, it would take some sort of physical perversions to make him feel alive.

A cold shudder raced down his spine at the idea. But as quickly as the notion came, it was gone. Perversion held no interest for him, never had. Oddly, it was Alice Kendall and her untainted innocence that kept circling through his mind.

Lucas pushed the thoughts of discontent away as he did every time it surfaced. He'd had more money and pleasure in the last few years than most men had in a lifetime.

"Your mother very easily could go to law school," Sophie explained, her hand resting on her husband's chest in a proprietary fashion. "Even the library clerk was amazed at how easily she grasped the concepts."

Lucas shoved his hands into his pockets. "I thought you went out looking for wallpaper."

Emmaline scoffed. "As far as I'm concerned, it's a foolish waste of time and money to redo that house next door when I am perfectly happy here."

Here. In his home. Filled with gamblers and dancing girls. Like she belonged in a den for the fallen.

He realized with a certainty that she was going to fight him every step of the way.

This day couldn't get any worse.

Hard, pounding footsteps hammered in the grand salon below. Grayson cursed just as Lucas glanced over the railing to find their father slamming into Nightingale's Gate, coming to a halt on the high-glossed hardwood floor.

On second thought, the day could get worse.

Bradford Hawthorne was a tall man, as tall as his sons, his hair just as black, his shoulders just as broad, with the same blue eyes as Lucas. No doubt when Bradford had been younger, he had looked just like his youngest son. Still looked a great deal like him, in fact.

His broadcloth coat was expensively, though severely cut. His waistcoat was trim and respectable, no hint of color that might suggest any kind of ease. The hat on his head could have belonged to a preacher.

Brutus hurried across the room to him, but Bradford ignored the massive man just as he ignored one of the girls who sidled up beside him. He shook her off and looked up to the loft.

"Mother, where are you?" he demanded, his low, deep voice carrying through the high-ceilinged room with authority.

The patrons of the club stopped what they were doing to watch.

"No need to shout, Bradford. I'm up here."

Emmaline said the words regally, like a dowager countess. Bradford glowered, took off his hat, clamped it in a tight grip, before he headed for the stairs.

Bradford pushed Brutus aside with little thought that the fierce man hired to guard the portals of Nightingale's Gate could pummel him to a pulp without so much as breaking a sweat. Bradford pounded up the steps and didn't bother to knock.

"I am not shouting," he bellowed. "I am here to discuss your failure to do your duty."

Emmaline pshawed. "If you want to talk about duty, let's start with your duty to your son."

His eyes flashed.

"In case you haven't heard," she continued, "your son has been charged with murder."

Bradford shifted his gaze to his youngest son. "I heard. Though I can't say I was surprised."

Lucas tensed.

"Some fellow from the *Boston Globe* has been camped out in front of Hawthorne House for days trying to get at me. But I'm smarter than that. I send Hastings out the front door, and I slip out the back. Works every time."

"Why don't you talk to the reporter?" Grayson asked, the ease of only moments before evaporating at the sight of his father. "Your silence isn't helping matters."

"I don't have anything to say. No one is going to accuse me of being a bad parent. I was not lax in my duties! I will not be put on trial in the newspapers when I did my best!"

Grayson's eyes narrowed, his expression surprised. Emmaline sucked in her breath. But Lucas only laughed harshly. "Yes, Father, you were a great role model."

"Enough, you two," Grayson interrupted. "Whatever you feel about Lucas, I'd think you'd care about the Hawthorne name. If Lucas goes down, you go down, too, Father."

"Like hell I will. I survived Matthew. And you. I'll survive this, too."

"Then why the hell are you here?" Grayson demanded.

"To get my wife." Bradford turned to Emmaline. "I gave you a chance to come to your senses. I should have known that wouldn't happen. But now with those damned newspapermen lurking everywhere, you need to be where you belong—by my side at Hawthorne House. Not in some . . . some house of ill repute."

Emmaline's delicate hands knotted at her sides. "I might as well live in a real house of ill repute since I was nothing but a kept woman in yours. And not a well-kept woman at that."

"Mother!" Bradford exclaimed, scandalized.

"And that's another thing," Emmaline said. "I am not your mother! I have a name, for mercy's sake. Though I can't remember the last time you used it."

Bradford glared at her and forcibly calmed himself. "Fine," he said through tightly clenched teeth. "Emmaline, it is time you give up this nonsense and return home."

"Nonsense?" Emmaline set her shoulders. "The only nonsense going on around here is your idiotic belief that I am ever going anywhere with you again," she stated, raising her chin. "It's time you understood that I'm serious about this, serious enough that I'm getting a divorcement."

"Divorcement?" Bradford, Grayson, and Lucas bellowed the word at the same time.

The patrons below had their heads tilted so far back to see that Lucas was sure they'd tip over.

"Why don't we take this to my private office upstairs," Lucas suggested.

"Go by yourself," Emmaline quipped, holding her ground. "I'm staying right here. I have started my new life. I've been taken advantage of for long enough."

Bradford glared, thoughts clearly careening through his head. Would he attempt to remove her forcibly, which was his right? Though any fool understood he would have to deal with two of his sons before he could get anywhere. But Bradford Hawthorne was not one to be intimidated, especially by his sons. Or maybe he would attempt to say something nice, something conciliatory.

At length he said, "Fine. Stay. See if I care."

Then he stormed out of the room, slamming the door, making it clear that there would be no reconciliation.

Lucas hung his head. His mother was there to stay.

Alice headed straight for the courthouse. It was all she could do to put one foot in front of the other as she hurried to Tremont Street where she could catch the trolley. Her legs felt like jelly, and her stomach quivered. She had to be mad to have taken this case.

How many times did she have to remind herself that Lucas Hawthorne was bad news. Anyone with half a brain could see that. He was a reprobate, a saloon owner. He cavorted with fallen women and no doubt led men toward a similar fate. But the truth was, she wanted the job.

She still couldn't get over her father's reaction at lunch. She half hoped that when she arrived at the courthouse he would hug her tight and apologize. But she knew all too well that Kendalls didn't offer apologies. They moved on. Hurt feelings were left alone to be gotten over.

And her feelings definitely were hurt. A lesser woman would have burst into tears. But a smarter woman wouldn't be in the position in the first place.

Could her father truly not believe in her?

On Tremont, with no trolley in sight, she hailed a hired hack and tried to let the jostle and sway of the tiny carriage lull her as they made their way through the Theatre District, then along Boston Common, finally stopping at the massive stone building where justice was dealt.

But it wasn't the ride that finally calmed her. It was the realization that despite everything, she had a big case. After her disappointing lunch with her father, and the heated interactions with Lucas, reality finally had a chance to sink in. She had a client. A real, live, breathing client who would pay her fees.

Her first job was to go to the district attorney's office and obtain all the evidence they had, which meant a trip to see her father.

Taking a deep breath, she turned the brass handle and pushed through the door to his office. How angry could he be?

"Alice, dear," Louise Lemmons greeted with surprised pleasure as she looked up from a neatly organized desk. "What brings you here? I thought you just saw your father at lunch."

Alice clutched her reticule. "I did, but I need to speak to him privately."

"I'll have to see, dear. He is terribly busy. Backed up after the governor meeting, and what with all the stir over the Hawthorne situation."

"What stir is that?"

"You know how your father gets whenever a high-profile case comes in. Though he's over the moon about this one.

It's going to be all the talk in the newspapers. What with Lucas Hawthorne being so famous, or should I say infamous." Louise gave a soft, girlish laugh. "And you couldn't ask for a more outrageous name than Cindy Pop for your star witness. People are going to be curious."

"Cindy Pop?" Alice asked with a wry face.

"Yes. Cindy Pop is the witness, and the victim was called Lucille Rouge. An entire cast of characters that the press is going to adore. And you know how your father loves the press."

"Yes, I do." He often used it to his advantage, and no doubt would use it again. "Could you tell him I'm here?"

Louise started to protest.

"It will just take a few minutes, I promise."

With a sigh and a shake of her head, Louise went to the door that led off from her office. Knocking once, she entered. Seconds later Alice was led inside.

Walker Kendall set his pen aside and smiled at the sight of his daughter. He sat behind his government-issued hard-oak desk. Two plain oak chairs faced the wide expanse, and a well-polished though scratched cabinet stood behind him. Other men who had gained such success would have replaced the furniture. But Walker Kendall took pride in being a man of the people, watching over their interests, prosecuting the men and women who had dared to do them wrong. For his efforts he had received awards and commendations, and every one of them was either hung on the walls or displayed in the cabinet. The office was a veritable shrine to his success.

Alice had the sudden thought that Lucas Hawthorne's office hadn't had a single award or photo, very little to tell her anything about the man. The office had been impressive but subdued. So different from her father's.

She tried to ignore the traitorous thought that she was more at ease in the Nightingale's Gate office than here. Not that she had been all that comfortable at the gentlemen's club with Lucas leaning so close, the heat of him wrapping around her senses. She'd experienced the same shiver of awareness she had that first time he walked into her office. The desire to be close, the curiosity about what it would feel like if he leaned down and pressed his lips to hers. She inhaled with a shiver of longing.

But then she shook the thoughts away. Good heavens, she was as bad as the women who flocked to the courthouse steps to catch a glimpse of him. And she didn't have to look any further than the morning newspaper to learn all she needed to know about the man. He was a murderer.

Suspected murderer, she corrected herself. One she intended to get acquitted.

"What is it, Alice?"

She blinked, then focused. With succinct formality, she said, "I'm here on behalf of my client."

Her father's kind smile evaporated. Slowly, he sat back and raised a brow. "Your client?"

"Yes. I need to get—"

"Tell me Clark worked faster than I realized and you've already received the case I referred to at lunch."

"—the police reports," she finished, before adding, "and no, this is not in reference to the case you mentioned at lunch."

He stared at her for a moment, his fingers drumming on the desk. "Don't tell me you've taken on Lucas Hawthorne."

"I have. I was officially retained by Mr. Hawthorne just minutes ago."

Silence surrounded them as his fingers stilled on the hard wood, the deep lines of his countenance shifting into stern lines, as if he were not certain how to deal with a wayward child.

"Alice," he said, his tone warning.

Years of growing up underneath his loving guidance surged in her memory. She had never had the ability to stand up to him before, though in truth, she had never really wanted or needed to. Until now.

The fact was she wanted this case, for more reasons than her sudden realization that her father doubted her abilities. She was tired of sitting on the sidelines while life passed her by. And she couldn't deny that since Lucas Hawthorne had walked into her life, she had felt more alive than she had in years.

"I am here to obtain all pertinent documentation you have regarding the *Commonwealth vs. Lucas Hawthorne*." She heard the slight shake of her voice, but laced with that shake was determination.

"Damn it, Alice." His fist slammed against his desk, making his ink pen clatter. "What do you think you're doing? I told you not to take this case."

Alice stepped back in surprise at the anger. She had never seen her father lash out like that. Equally surprised, Louise popped her head into the office as if she had been standing just outside the door.

"Is there a problem here?" she asked.

Both Walker and Alice said, "No."

Louise hesitated, then backed out reluctantly.

Alice summoned every ounce of her conviction. "Despite what you think, Father, I know what I'm doing."

"Do you, Alice? Do you understand what kind of man Lucas Hawthorne is? A derelict, a man who thinks he's above the law. A man who belongs behind bars." His eyes narrowed. "He's a murderer."

She felt something inside her click, the confidence she had built over a lifetime rearing up—too strong to be quelled by one lunch gone awry. "Alleged, Father. He is an *alleged* murderer. Don't forget that very important word when you're talking about my client."

Walker's face suffused in an angry red. "This is not a friendly debate at home, Alice. This is real. In a court. With a judge and a jury."

"Don't you think I know that?"

He pulled a deep, calming breath, his shirt tacks straining over his barrel chest for half a second. "He is going to get what he has deserved for years. I am going to get a conviction."

"First, the grand jury has to indict. From what Clark said at lunch, you don't have much of a case."

"We have enough."

"So you keep saying. I'm not so sure. Regardless, I am here for discovery. I want a complete listing of all the evidence you have obtained thus far."

He leaned back, the metal coil on the wooden chair creaking. "Clark won't go easy on you."

"I wouldn't have it any other way."

The silence returned as he studied her, but this time she was aware of voices muted by the walls, muffled footsteps pounding down the corridors. Someone strode across the floor in the office above them.

"*I* won't go easy on you," he added, his expression hard and closed.

A chill raced through her despite the oppressive heat of the day. "I wouldn't expect you to treat me any differently than you treat any other lawyer who has come up against this office. With a fair hand and respect. Isn't that what you always say?" she challenged.

While he had uttered those very words for every newspaperman who had interviewed him, they both knew they weren't true. Walker Kendall was ruthless. He would insist Clark prosecute in the same manner.

He studied her coldly. "I'll send the information over when we have it compiled."

"I find it hard to believe you don't have it together yet. The grand jury hearing is in three days."

"Believe what you want." With that he retrieved his pen, then turned his attention to the letter he had been writing when she entered. She was dismissed, just like that. The coldness stunned her.

How had things changed so abruptly? Just this morning before leaving for work, she had gone to the main house. Her small family had laughed and joked, her brother charming them all with stories of his escapades. Their love had been clear and unquestioned.

But suddenly that seemed to have altered. All because of Lucas Hawthorne.

Frustration washed over her. She started to speak, but stopped herself just in time. What else was there to say? Nothing. She had gone too far for regrets. And she wouldn't drop the case.

When she got to the door, he stopped her.

"Alice."

She turned back, hope against hope flaring in her breast that he would offer her some kind words.

"I want a statement of disclosure. I want in writing that Hawthorne knows you are my daughter. And that you are engaged to Clark."

Unaccustomed embarrassment flashed through her. "Father, we both know that Clark has never officially asked you for my hand."

Would he ever?

The question startled her.

He came to call, had dinner with her family, took her for carriage rides in the country. But he had never done anything that was even slightly romantic. Like kiss her. Or send her roses. Since she was young, she had always dreamed of a man sending her roses, any color would do. And marriage. Building a home together, with an elegant fence around gardens filled with flowers of every kind. Though especially roses.

"You're as good as engaged as far as I'm concerned. I'm not going to give Hawthorne any grounds to ask for a new trial after we win."

The words set her teeth on edge. In the few cases she had defended against the Commonwealth, her father had never asked for a statement of disclosure. "You'll get it. Rest assured, there will be no mistrial. And if I were you, I'd remind myself that this is Clark's case, not yours."

Then she walked out of the office with as much calm as she could muster, holding on with every step she took.

"Dear God," she whispered, leaning up against a lamppost once she got outside. "What have I gotten myself into?"

Chapter Four

The following morning Lucas Hawthorne was waiting for her in her office when she arrived. Some days it didn't pay to get out of bed, Alice thought glumly as she pushed open the door and found him.

He sat behind her desk, fine-leather-booted feet propped up as he looked out the small office window to the bustling city streets below. He sat without moving, as if he didn't realize she was there. Sun filtered through the grimy streaks, distorting the world beyond, highlighting his profile. Yet again she was surprised by the beauty of the man.

How could anyone so striking be a killer?

But how could a man from such a fine family own and run a gaming hell with half-naked women and licentious men as prevalent as liquor?

The world didn't always make sense, she conceded.

"Glad to see you've made yourself comfortable," she said in a cool, flat voice.

Lucas glanced over at her. The minute he saw her his gaze drifted to her lips, and she saw the heat that flared in his eyes. The look made her feel breathless, with tingles streaking down her spine, and that made her angry.

She pursed her lips. Though all that got her was a broad, irritating smile. He consistently seemed amused by her ire. Regardless, his dangerous mood from yesterday was gone.

Swinging his long legs down from the desk, he stood. He was larger than she remembered. His shoulders were wide, and he was a full head taller, making her tilt her head to look him in the eye.

"Comfortable?" He glanced at the hard chair and grimaced. "Let's just say I'm doing as instructed, ma'am," he offered, his voice as smooth and sweet as the bourbon and honey she allowed herself on the rare occasions she had the influenza.

"I believe you said you wanted me here at nine o'clock. On the dot," he added with mischievous good humor. He glanced at the clock that said as plain as day that it was nine-thirty, and raised a brow. "I was here as instructed."

And she was not. But she'd had errands to run.

While her family had a fine old name, they didn't have a great deal of money to go with it. And while she lived only a few steps from home, she tried to maintain some semblance of independence by taking care of her own laundry and cooking her own breakfast and luncheon, if not supper. She didn't like to admit how often her stomach was growling loudly by the time Uncle Harry set supper on the table.

This morning, after dragging herself out of bed, she had found she didn't have a single thing to eat in her small kitchenette. And when she dashed to the main house, her father had already left for court; her uncle, the chief of Boston's police force, had left for the station; Max had gone to his position at the bank; with all breakfast fare neatly stored in the cool box, the coffeepot washed and put away. Not even a crumb of bread was left out. She cursed that three unmarried men were better equipped at domesticity than she was.

To add insult to injury, all her work-appropriate chemisettes lay on the overstuffed chair in a pile she had mentally tagged, *To be washed*.

Focusing her thoughts, she found Lucas staring at her, or rather her attire.

"What?" she demanded, piqued.

His full lips quirked, and his blue eyes sparkled with mirth. "Nothing. Just couldn't help but admire the fact that not only do you push the boundaries of acceptable women's work, you push the boundaries with clothing, as well."

He laughed out loud when she growled at him, then marched over to her desk, nudged him out of the way without thinking, and banged her satchel down.

"I hardly call a white cotton shirt pushing boundaries, Mr. Hawthorne."

"No," he agreed, "unless it's a white cotton *man's* shirt."

He had her there. But it had been that or no shirt at all. She didn't think a frilly pink lace blouse from her seventeenth birthday would have been any better.

"Haven't you heard," she began, gesturing to her shirt and skirt. "This is all the rage. I'd think someone dealing with the masses as you do would be aware of the latest trends."

"If that's a trend, it's one I'd rather not promote in my establishment."

Ignoring her hunger pains and the desperate desire for a cup of steaming coffee, despite the already hazy, hot, and humid morning air, she gave him a dry smile, then started pulling files out of the leather satchel. She might not have had a clean chemisette to wear, or anything to eat that morning, but she had gotten a great deal of work done last night.

She had drawn up the documents needed to start working on the case. Afterward she had gone to the main house and her father's study. Utilizing the extensive array of law books he kept at home, she had gone over the Commonwealth's murder statute. Sitting in the old swivel chair that she so loved, sipping a cup of tea her uncle had sleepily brought her, she had made up a list of possible defenses. As soon as she got the file of evidence from the district attorney's office, she planned to go to the courthouse and start searching every case in the past five years that had similar facts.

This was all work that was generally done after a grand jury indicted. But Alice wasn't taking any chances. She wanted to be prepared. The grand jury hearing was only days away, and if Lucas Hawthorne was indicted, they'd have little more than four weeks to devise their defense.

"Here are the forms you'll need to sign before we can get started." She set them out on the desktop with the nonchalance she had practiced last night. "Read each carefully."

Lucas glanced from her to the papers, one brow raised in question, then picked them up and began to read. He held the sheets in his fingers, long and strong, seemingly carved like granite. He read quickly, but thoroughly, his concentration intense. She had a fleeting glimpse of how the man could be so successful. He might run a house of ill repute, but he obviously ran it paying close attention to details.

When he finished, he glanced at her. "A consent form stipulating that you are my attorney?"

"Yes."

"And another stating that I am aware you are the daughter of Walker Kendall, district attorney. Of course I know that. Everyone knows that."

She grimaced at the words. "No doubt," she said through gritted teeth. "But the law requires written disclosure of that fact. While technically my father isn't trying the case, they don't want any surprises. Your signature proves that I told you and that you consented. That way, if we lose, you can't tell an appellate court that you need a new trial because you didn't know I was related to the man in charge of your prosecution."

Instantly whatever good humor he had was gone, his features becoming coldly implacable. Turning back to the window, he braced his hands on the windowsill, and she could all but feel the tension that radiated through his body.

"I have no intention of losing, Miss Kendall."

The declaration was cold and ruthless, invincible.

"Neither do I. But that doesn't make the paperwork any less necessary. My father knows the law better than anyone in town, and I know my father. He will not let this case proceed until this paper is signed. And a delay can only hurt you as it will give the press more time to drag you through the mud."

Lucas raked his hand through his hair and started to pace. "This is crazy. The police don't have anything."

"You said yourself that they have an eyewitness."

"I also said that it wasn't me," he stated, enunciating each syllable.

"Do you have proof of that?"

He muttered something not altogether nice under his breath.

"I'll take that as no, in which case, a simple, 'I didn't do it,' isn't good enough. I don't think I need to remind you that your reputation is less than stellar."

"What I choose to do with my life is no one's business," he snapped.

But Alice wasn't swayed. She planted her hands on her desk and leaned forward. "Tell that to a jury of your peers— those men who work hard all day long and come home tired to a wife and children with problems and concerns that they feel obligated to solve. Those men are not likely to look kindly on a man who has turned his back on the very responsibilities they struggle to shoulder each day."

They stared at each other, his jaw tense. His anger was overwhelming, much like the man himself.

"It sounds as if I need to convince you," he said in a low, dangerous voice that was undermined by a flare of emotion behind his lethal facade.

Yes, convince me.

The demand nearly tumbled from her lips, drawn out by the grim emotion she knew was shadowed in his blue eyes. But she swallowed the words back. She was a professional, and despite what she had said at their first meeting, she knew that as a defense lawyer guilt or innocence was not the issue. Getting her client acquitted was.

Alice closed her eyes for a brief second, then pushed back. "No, you don't need to convince me. Our best hope is that you are not indicted at all, then we won't have to worry about trials or proving anything. You simply must convince the grand jury that they shouldn't indict you. And once you sign those papers, we'll start preparing you for just that."

The room was charged, his expression furious, cornered, before he snatched up the pen and signed with quick, decisive strokes.

"Good." She refused to feel anything for this man— neither compassion nor intrigue. They had become attorney-client. A professional relationship. Anything else wouldn't serve either one of them well. They why did her gaze drift to his mouth again and again?

With crisp decision she returned the forms to the folder. "Now, tell me what happened the night of the murder."

Lucas sighed angrily and looked out the window. "I told you, I was at the club. In bed."

"Did you know the victim?"

"Yes."

She waited for him to expand. He didn't.

"Did she work for you?"

"No."

"Did you sleep with her?"

He glanced at her with disdain. "No."

"Did you see her that night?"

"No."

"Were you in the alleyway at all around the time of the murder?"

"No."

She leaned forward. "I might find your one-word, mono-syllabic answers irritating, Mr. Hawthorne, but a jury will take them as indications that you are unfeeling and don't care that a woman was murdered in an alleyway behind your establishment. More than that, they can very easily go one step further and take your apparent indifference to mean that you killed her."

His jaw muscles ticked. "Did that little speech of yours make you feel better?"

Frustration flared, but she tamped it down. "What will make me feel better is an ounce of concern on your part. You are not making this easy."

"Life isn't easy, sweetheart." His dry tone suggested cynical amusement.

"I am not your sweetheart," she bit out, before she sighed, then struggled for a reasonable tone. "Mr. Hawthorne. If you want me to help you, you must help yourself. That means working with me."

The very air in the room seemed to grow charged, and his blue eyes sparked. "And by that you mean . . ."

The words were spoken softly, deep and low. His look turned unabashedly sexual as he gaze drifted to her lips. She had the odd and surprising thought that this man wanted to kiss her. A sizzle of tingling tension raced through her.

Giving herself a mental shake, she determinedly ignored his innuendo and her body's reaction.

"What I mean is for you to take your situation seriously. Now," she said primly, "this is what I have so far. You didn't see the victim, you weren't in the alley, and you were in your bed sleeping. . . ."

He leaned back against the wall and crossed his arms. He looked at her, his eyes taking her in, his gaze hot and sensual. "I didn't say I was sleeping."

It took a second, but when his meaning came clear, she nearly choked. "Fine, you were in your bed *not* sleeping, but the fact remains, you are now charged with murder."

His gaze drifted lower, like a caress, making her body shimmer.

"That about sums it up," he replied.

Drawing a deep, sobering breath, she forced her thoughts into some coherent order. She knew he was trying to make her uncomfortable—and succeeding. But she had bigger problems on her plate. Either Lucas wasn't telling her everything or her father had lost his mind. The charges against her client made no sense.

She worried her lip and considered. "All right. I need to prepare you for your grand jury testimony."

"Grayson said I wouldn't be testifying."

"He's wrong."

Lucas raised a brow.

"Your only advocate in a grand jury proceeding is yourself. I'm not allowed inside."

His attention shifted from her lips, and his gaze narrowed severely. "Because you're a woman?"

"No. Because the defense, be they men or women, is never allowed in the room."

"Why not?"

"Only the prosecution, the witnesses, and the prosecuting attorney trying the case are heard. The prosecution can ask whatever he wants. The men on the jury can ask whatever they want, same with the judge. But the defense doesn't get to ask anything. I can only prepare you as best as I can for what might come up."

"That hardly seems fair."

"Take it up with the legislature," she stated dryly. "The good news is that eyewitnesses are historically unreliable. Misidentification happens all the time." She glanced out the window as her thoughts grew troubled yet again. "Which makes me wonder why my father thinks they have a strong enough case to take to the grand jury." She shook her head. "But he does, and that's all that matters. The other thing we have going in our favor is that whether we want to admit it or not, juries are known to vote *not* to indict and even for acquittals because they find the defendant so infinitely believable and likable that they can't do anything else. The best chance we have is if you make them believe your story." This was the truth, and it was what she was counting on. "Talk *to* them. Look them in the eye. Tell them you were at home. Tell them you knew the girl, but you hadn't seen her.

You are sick about what happened to her. No one deserves to die like that. Show them sincerity. Do not be glib. Do not make jokes. In short, charm them, Mr. Hawthorne."

"I thought you doubted my abilities in that area."

"Doubt it? No. I simply think you turn it on when it suits you. Clearly, thus far in our dealings, it hasn't suited you."

He grinned appreciatively. "Far be it from you to mince words."

"I'm your lawyer, Mr. Hawthorne, not a paramour who must stroke a man's ego with hollow flattery to keep him interested."

His grin turned into a surprised burst of laughter.

Before he could respond, she went on. "But with any luck, we'll be celebrating the grand jury's decision next week."

That same devilishly sensual light flickered in his eyes. "How will we celebrate, counselor?"

Her heart leaped, and she had to clear her throat before she could ignore him and continue.

"Let's move on."

She sat down behind her desk. Only then did Lucas sit, though Alice wasn't sure he even realized he had waited. Such a contradiction in this man. Manners of a gentleman, but the lifestyle of a scoundrel. Who was he?

"Miss Kendall?"

Alice shook herself out of her thoughts.

"You were saying?" he prompted, amusement still pulling on his full, sensuous mouth.

She was saying? Her brain raced.

He had the audacity to smile. "I believe we were going to continue with the grand jury."

"Ah, yes," she managed. "As I said, you need to make them believe you. And to do that, you need to wear a suit."

He glanced down at his apparel. "Last I heard, that's what I was wearing."

Alice took in what she could see of his cutaway jacket,

and she didn't have to try hard to remember the tan wool pants that molded to his hard thighs like a glove. The black coat appeared molded to his broad shoulders, and she was certain that if he took it off, the broadness would have nothing to do with the padding on which so many men relied.

"A real suit, Mr. Hawthorne. Not a . . . a . . . gambler's getup more appropriate for a cathouse than a courtroom."

His lips quirked with heart-stopping amusement. "I'm not sure it's wise to take wardrobe advice from a woman who wears a man's shirt and calls it the latest fashion."

"Funny. But I'm not talking style; I'm talking about presenting yourself in the best possible manner. You need to go to a nice everyman's store like Jordan Marsh and find one of those ready-made, dark blue, conservative suits. Nothing fancy. Nothing handsomely sewed by an expensive tailor. Just something respectable, something any man on the jury could buy for himself. Perhaps one of those Prince Albert ensembles. The coat, vest, and pants would do nicely."

Lucas didn't look happy as he undoubtedly envisioned the long and boxy jacket and vest that showed only a hint of collar.

"Women wear ensembles, Miss Kendall," he stated stiffly, rising from his seat.

"Ensemble, outfit. Call it what you will, just make sure you wear one. And a top hat."

"Next you'll want me to carry a walking stick."

"Absolutely not. You'd look like a fraud."

"And I won't in a Prince Albert suit?"

She rose as well and pinned him in her gaze. "No. You'll look distinguished and respectable, and incapable of murdering some poor girl in an alleyway."

Silence sliced through the room.

"You can't leave that alone, can you?"

He drawled the words, but she could feel the coiled tension in him.

"No, I can't leave it alone, Mr. Hawthorne, because it's the only reason we are here. You better get used to it. Clark Kittridge is going to say it every chance he gets. As will my father. Now, might we proceed?"

"By all means," he replied dryly.

Alice glanced at him, before returning to her notes. "Wear an understated tie, conservative shoes, and get a haircut."

"I will not cut my hair."

Alice sighed, a lock of white-blonde hair falling free from her hastily pulled back chignon. Impatiently she curled it behind her ear. "Are you going to fight me at every turn?"

"I don't see what my hair has to do with anything."

"It's too long, and even if you dress up like the most conservative, hardworking fellow there, your hair screams the fact that you aren't working at a factory, or a publishing house, or a mill pushing paper from morning until night. And I have no intention of continuing with this case for a second longer if you can't see fit to do as I say. So, what will it be? Me or your hair?"

Tension crackled in the air as he stared at her for an eternity. In that second Alice was certain he was going to choose his hair. She couldn't decide if she wanted to rejoice or cry.

But he surprised her.

"Have you ever had sex, Miss Kendall?"

She felt as if she had swallowed a watermelon whole. "What?" she sputtered.

"I'm curious if you've ever engaged in—"

"I heard you."

He shrugged, his all-too-knowing smile having slipped back into place.

"That is none of your business."

"True," he agreed. "I just thought that a little sex might ease that pinched look you keep getting on your face."

"Pinched? I'll have you know that my pinched look is caused by you, sir, not by my lack of . . . of . . . relations!"

"Ah, so you have had sex."

"I have not!"

"I didn't think so." His voice lowered to a gruff brush of sound. "If you'd like, I'd be happy to introduce you to the pleasures."

She was fit to be tied. "We are lawyer and client, Mr. Hawthorne. Not moon-eyed sweethearts who steal kisses behind potted palms."

He chuckled softly. "I wasn't thinking along the lines of something so innocent. But," he glanced around the room, "while I don't see a potted palm handy," he looked back, the humor in his eyes vanishing, "I'd let you steal a kiss."

Her heart leaped, and her breathing grew shallow. "Kissing has no place in a professional relationship and would do nothing but cause endless problems."

He leaned down and planted his hands on her desk. "Only if you let it."

He was close, too close, and if she moved just so she would touch him. With her mind reeling, she felt the very real desire to disregard everything she knew to be right and sane and lean closer.

"But not to worry," he added, a slow, knowing grin pulling at his lips. "I won't do anything you don't want me to. I can wait."

Her brain jarred, and she sucked in her breath as he pushed away, then headed for the door, so large and powerfully arrogant.

She wished to God she could wipe the smart look from his face. But she was mature, she reminded herself, not a child, and she would not lower herself to his level.

"Your hair," she called out, barely able to get the measured syllables past her gritted teeth, "are you or are you not going to cut it?"

He stopped at the door and turned back, his cocky smile evaporating. "I'll get it trimmed," he conceded, his voice terse.

Foolish relief shot through her.

"But don't ever give me an ultimatum again, Miss Kendall, do you understand?"

"What I understand is that it is my job to tell you what I think is best."

Their gazes locked, the tension nearly tangible in the small room.

After a moment Alice cleared her throat. "If you'll return to your seat, we can move on to your demeanor."

"Let's not." He turned the brass knob.

"We aren't finished!"

"Yes we are. If I stay here a second longer, I'll—"

"You'll what?"

She felt off balance and upset, though she wasn't altogether certain why. Then her breath caught at the look on his face. Trapped, furious.

"What, Mr. Hawthorne, what will you do?" She couldn't seem to stop herself. "Ask me more inappropriate questions? Try to unnerve me by undressing me with your eyes? Strangle me? Is that the real you? Is that what really happened to the girl in the alley? Is this all a waste of time?"

She had crossed a line; she saw it in his expression. Fury leaped like flames. But he contained the fire, pulled it back as if he had done it a thousand times before.

"Are you a gambling woman, Miss Kendall?"

Her shoulders came back. "Of course not."

"I think you are. I think that's why you took this case. Because you want to see how far can you push the boundaries before you fall."

Offended, she swallowed back a curse. "That is ridiculous."

"Is it?"

She couldn't think of an answer, much less formulate it into words.

"I'll be in touch," he said when it was clear she wouldn't answer. Then he quit the office without another word.

Alice stared at the murky glass in the door for a long time, unable to move. Her breath rushed out of her as she sat back in her chair, hard.

There was no denying it, no glossing over the truth. She was in over her head. The only chance they had of succeeding was for him to convince a grand jury that he didn't deserve to be indicted. Because she didn't stand a chance in hell of bringing this man to heel.

Chapter Five

He was in her office again the next morning when she arrived. His high-polished boots were crossed on the desk, chair tilted back, hands up cradling his head. Though this time he wasn't staring out the window without seeing. He looked at her, his blue eyes filled with humor, his lips crooked devilishly.

The sight of him made her breath grow shallow, with a squishy feeling in her stomach that she tried to tell herself was due to lack of sleep. She wasn't quite convinced, however. And that made her mad.

She got even madder when she told herself that after yesterday's display, he should have the good grace to look apologetic. Heck, at the very least he should look chagrined.

"How do you keep getting in here?" she groused.

Not only had she worked late last night, but she'd had to stop at the market, then do laundry. Given the nighttime hour, she couldn't hang her things up to dry on the line in the yard. She'd had to hang them around her small cottage. Now, obviously not enough hours later, her chemisette was still damp. Ugh. She really did need to send her clothes out to be cleaned. But for that she needed money.

She focused on Lucas and had to force the vision of money-bags from her mind when she looked at him. He was a client, not a cast-iron, bell-ringing, drawer-opening cash register. Lying in bed at three in the morning, she had conceded that she really needed to find a way to make this case work.

"I found the key on the ledge of the doorjamb," he replied without the slightest hint of guilt, swinging his legs down before he stood. "You really should be more careful. Who knows what kind of riffraff could have found that key."

"The same kind that already did," she shot back unkindly.

His chuckle rumbled through the tiny office as he rocked back on his heels, his hands in his pockets. She all but growled when he ran his eyes over her in quiet assessment, taking her in, his gaze like a heated caress.

When he looked back, he grinned. "Has anyone ever told you you're alluring as hell when you're mad?"

Heat flashed so bright and hot in her face that she was sure that if dry kindling had been close she would have set it on fire. "No." She scowled. "Until I met you, I haven't been in the habit of keeping company with people who make me mad."

Lucas tipped his head back and laughed out loud. It was a wonderful laugh, deep and infectious, and in spite of herself, she felt an ease settle in her tense muscles.

"I brought some coffee," he said. "Yesterday I noticed you didn't have any."

She thought she had smelled something delicious. "Is this your way of apologizing?"

"No. I just figured it was in my best interest for my lawyer to be awake and alert." He poured out a cup. "You look like you could use some."

"First you break into my office, then you insult me." Someone else might have refused his offer. Alice weighed the options. Delicious-smelling coffee? Her pride? Alice reached out and took the cup.

Just the smell made her want to swoon. And the first sip? Heaven. She felt a pleasurable sigh trying to break across her lips.

"Had I known you were this easy," he quipped, "I would have brought coffee over sooner."

She eyed him over the rim. "Easy? Me?"

Lucas smiled. "No, I don't suspect anything is easy with you."

She started toward her chair. "That's right, and don't you forget it."

He stood in her way, and she couldn't get by.

"Enough of the verbal swordplay," she said. "I'm glad you've arrived. We have lots to do. After you stormed out yesterday I thought your feelings were hurt and I'd never see you again."

"Stormed out? Hurt feelings? I thought the verbal swordplay was to be set aside."

"Sorry, couldn't resist."

He sat on the corner of her desk, bringing them face-to-face. "Just as I can't seem to resist you," he whispered.

Reaching out, his strong fingers drifted down the sleeve of her summer jacket. The touch was a shock—unexpected and compelling.

They both watched the progress, as if neither could look away. He stopped when he came to a bow at the cuff, attached to her chemisette underneath. He toyed with the satin. One simple tug and the bow would come free. She couldn't seem to breathe, and it was all she could do to hold on to her coffee.

She knew she should slap his hand away, bite out some sharp reprimand. But the words stuck in her throat.

He looked up, looked at her. "I shouldn't have mentioned sex yesterday," he said so softly she barely heard. "As you said, it isn't any of my business. More than that, it was unkind." He shook his head in a visible lament. "But you test me sorely, Alice Kendall." His eyes met hers. "And you tempt me. That's the way it is with temptation. It's hard to resist."

As if he could do nothing else, he took the cup from her hands. He knew he should leave, shouldn't have returned. But he couldn't stand it any longer. He touched her then, as he had wanted to since the day he first saw her. He traced her cheek with the back of his finger, and without a word, he drew her into his arms.

Despite the fact that she was a lawyer, her hair properly managed, her spine so often straight, her words always direct, she was surprisingly delicate to touch. Through the stiff folds of her gown, he could feel her tremble, could feel her innocent shock at the simple contact.

He'd be willing to bet that she had never been held before, no other man having tasted her sweetness. Her innocence pleased him greatly, though it shouldn't.

"What are you doing?" she asked on a shaky breath.

Lining her jaw with his palm, he said, "This." Then he bent his head and kissed her.

She opened her mouth on a startled intake of breath, her fingers seeming to find his shirt front of their own accord—surprised when they got there, unable to move away. Innocent and provocative at the same time.

He felt the intense need to bury himself deep inside her even as he felt an unwelcome need to keep her safe. The contrasting emotions made his mind reel. He hardly knew her, but he wanted her—wanted her in a way that was primal as well as possessive.

His hands found the clips in her hair, working them free until the heavy mass tumbled down her back. Her fingers curled into his shirt, and he deepened the kiss. Then she leaned into him, and he could feel the tautness of her nipples beneath the fabric of her gown.

It was this that had haunted his dreams since he met her, this that his body had yearned for. His body surged with desire, wanting her. And he had been with enough women to know that she wanted him, too. Though she didn't like the wanting any more than he did.

Alice gave a soft cry when he pulled back, and he chuckled to cover the emotion that swelled at such a reaction. Women had wanted him for as long as he could remember. But somehow with this woman it was different. It had nothing to do with his name, or his money. Nothing to do with a wildness in him that women thought they could tame.

Alice Kendall wanted no part of him, but she was drawn to him regardless.

Slowly, he pulled her between his thighs and tasted her again. Her lips parted, and he touched her tongue. She gasped in surprise, but when he gentled her with his hand rubbing soothingly against her back, she moaned against him, then wrapped her arms around his shoulders.

"You have such passion," he whispered as he kissed the corner of her mouth.

Reality hit her like a splash of cold water. She also realized that she ached with a longing she could hardly fathom, with a heat that pooled low, made it hard to think. The truth was, in that second she didn't want to resist temptation. She had the outlandish thought that she wanted him to pull the tie, loosen her shirt. It was like those breathtaking visions of standing on a cliff, not knowing how to stop yourself from jumping. And allowing herself to be touched by Lucas Hawthorne would be like jumping off a cliff. Foolish and deadly. But the kiss was like heaven.

He wrapped her close. She could feel him through her skirts. His chest, his thighs, his strength. Perfect and wonderful.

Perfect? Wonderful? Her mind reeled.

Good God, what had come over her?

Using the one remaining intelligent ounce of brainpower she had left, she forced herself to pull free.

"Mr. Hawthorne, please!" she choked out, her legs weak as she made her way to her chair, her coffee forgotten. As best she could, she pulled up her hair and secured it with clumsy fingers. "We are professionals; let us remember that."

After a moment, he swiveled around to face her, then studied her, a sensual possessiveness swirling in his eyes. "You liked that, didn't you?"

"I'd like you to remember who I am and why we are here."

Her answer didn't bother him; in fact, he looked quite pleased with himself as his devilish smile returned.

"You told me that the only sure way to avoid indictment was to have an alibi," he said finally.

She felt a shiver of awareness, and she hardly heard what he said. "Yes."

"You might want to contact this person." He handed her a slip of paper. Their fingers touched as she took it, and she felt a jolt of feeling when he didn't instantly let go.

"Is something wrong?" he asked, goading her.

She sucked in her breath. "Not a thing," she stated crisply, forcing her murky senses to clear as she focused on the note.

The writing was bold and fast, but not messy. No doubt his writing. Just like the man.

"Who is this?" she asked, her eyes narrowing.

"My alibi."

"Suddenly you have an alibi?"

He shrugged his broad shoulders. "I hadn't wanted to involve anyone else. Alas, it doesn't seem possible."

This time she really looked at the name. Not Michael James as she had read quickly the first time, but Michaela James. A woman. And he had already said he was in his room at the club. In bed.

Foolishly, completely inappropriately, she felt betrayed. Had he kissed this woman like he had just kissed her?

"You were alone with her in your bedroom?"

He gave one, brief nod of his head, the look in his eyes clearly meant to look regretful.

"Do you practice that choirboy expression in the mirror?" she asked caustically.

But she didn't wait for an answer. She folded the note and turned away. She still couldn't believe that she had allowed Lucas to kiss her. Heavens, she couldn't believe she had kissed him back. And she didn't understand the feelings that swept through her. She didn't care that Lucas had been with this other woman, she told herself firmly. Beyond which, she wasn't surprised. It meant nothing to her other than it helped her cause. But something else bothered her.

The idea of spending time alone with a man, in the intimacy of his bedroom. Would she ever have that in her life? The taste she'd had of such a thing made her legs grow weak.

She thought of Clark, and she had to swallow back a guilty gasp that finally she remembered him. The fact was, he was perfect for her. He was smart, funny. And kind without having to try.

But did he think she was *alluring as hell*?

She shook the thought away. No respectable man thought of the woman meant to be his wife in such terms. But still she couldn't let it go. Was Clark at all romantic? He had never brought her flowers. Never held her hand. And he certainly had never kissed her.

"If you need anything else, let me know," Lucas said. "I've got to get back to the Gate."

She swung around. "Ah, yes, good. I'll contact Miss James."

"You do that."

He pulled open the door, but just before it closed she spoke.

"Do you ever buy your Miss James roses?"

Lucas stopped and looked at her like she had lost her mind. "Roses?"

"Yes."

"First, she is not *my* Miss James. Second, I'm not much for giving any woman flowers. I prefer to give jewels."

"Flowers would be cheaper and probably get better results."

Lucas laughed, his blue eyes glittering like the jewels that he preferred to give. "I don't give gifts for results, Miss

Kendall. Moreover," he added with grim amusement, "you clearly are not acquainted with the women I know."

"Yes, of course." She waved the discussion away, couldn't imagine why she had asked. "I'll send word when I have spoken to Miss James."

"Do that."

But still he couldn't get out of the office because just then Clark arrived.

"Clark!" Her surprise at the sight of him, mixed with the guilt she felt over having kissed Lucas Hawthorne, made her call out with exaggerated enthusiasm.

Lucas cocked his head and raised a brow.

Wishing she could ignore him, but knowing she had to make polite introductions, she said, "You know Mr. Hawthorne. Mr. Hawthorne, this is Mr. Clark Kittridge."

Clark, ever righteous, but also ever the gentleman, looked fit to be tied as he tried to determine what he should do. Shake the criminal's hand or snub the son of an important man? Alice felt the bite of irritation but quickly tamped it down. What did she expect? He was coming face-to-face with a man he was attempting to convict of murder. He was not meeting a peer at a social engagement.

Lucas, she noticed, looked grimly amused. He also looked as if he wasn't going anywhere when he leaned up against the doorjamb, crossing his arms on his chest.

Staring at Lucas, Clark said to Alice, "I came by to discuss—" He grew more uncomfortable. "—the Darnells' gala this evening. Are you going?"

"I am," she blurted.

She had hoped Clark would ask her to attend with him.

This got another eyebrow raise from Lucas.

"Weren't you just leaving?" she asked him pointedly.

"I didn't think you were finished."

"But *you* were." She uttered the words as politely as she could.

Lucas's eyes darkened for a long second as he took her in.

The look was intimate, knowing, and Alice was certain Clark would realize just what had transpired in this room before he arrived.

But the second passed, and Lucas simply shrugged his shoulders and said, "True. As much as I'd love to stay and watch this little tête-à-tête, I can't."

She would have cheerfully given him a left hook to the jaw, and her expression no doubt told him as much. But he only chuckled in his all-too-confident way, then departed.

Alice stared at the closed office door. "I'm sorry about that," she said absently. "Please sit down."

"I can't," Clark said. "I don't have much time."

She swung around to face him. "But you just got here."

"I really came because your father told me that you have agreed to represent Hawthorne." His tone was severe and troubled, like a parent reprimanding a child.

"I thought you were here about the gala."

"Oh that. No, the chances of me finding the time to attend aren't very good. But I didn't want to mention the case in front of Hawthorne."

Disappointment flared, but she masked it with irritation. "Of course not," she said tightly. "You wouldn't want the man to be present when you discuss his case."

Clark gave her an odd look, as if he wasn't sure what had come over her, then he cleared his throat and added, "That's hardly the point. I can't believe you agreed, Alice."

"Why?"

They eyed each other over her desk in the small and cramped confines. The window was open to let in a welcome draft of air. The sound of metal wheels over cobbles echoed as carriages rolled by in the streets.

"Because *Commonwealth vs. Lucas Hawthorne* is hugely important to our office," he explained.

"Based on lunch yesterday, I'd say this is more important to *you*."

"All right. It is important to me. It's my first opportunity to make a name for myself. Don't you want that, Alice? Don't you want me to become successful?"

"Of course I do."

"Then back out. When the press finds out you are representing Hawthorne, they'll go crazy. What a story that would make—you against your father's office in one of the biggest cases in decades. You against his handpicked successor. The facts of the case will be obscured. It will be a freak show, not a trial." The frustrated lines of his face softened. "You know how hard I have worked. Don't ruin it for me now."

For the first time since lunching with her father Alice began to waver. How could she go up against this man whom she cared for? How could she actually try to defeat a man who needed to win in order to marry her?

The realization brought her up short.

But then he added, "And how will I look when I embarrass you in court?"

Alice tensed. "Embarrass me?"

"Sorry, that was harsh. But face it, you're a novice."

"You seem to forget that I have tried several cases since I opened my practice, and I have defended them all successfully."

He rolled his eyes. "Come on, Alice. Three of them never got beyond indictments, and you plea-bargained two."

"Those three easily could have been indictments, and you know it. But my clients were prepared when they got on the stand while the prosecution wasn't. As to the plea bargains, I got them off with time served. And you forgot to mention *Harold vs. Channey*, where I won outright. Not bad for a novice, I'd say."

"Fine," he conceded. "You won one outright. But you forget the fact that, being a woman in the *Commonwealth vs. Lucas Hawthorne*, you are at a grave disadvantage."

Alice marveled that this man didn't seem to understand that he was digging himself in deeper and deeper with every word he spoke. "That is ridiculous."

"Is it? This is murder we are talking about. Murder of a woman who sold her body for money. This is not a subject fit for a lady to hear, much less defend! Doesn't that bother you, Alice? Do you truly think it's appropriate for you to be acquainted with such facts?"

"First and foremost, I am a lawyer." Her father's words ingrained in her over a lifetime. "And as a lawyer, I am going to do my job and defend my client to the best of my abilities—which some people think are considerable."

They faced off, frustration and disappointment scudding across Clark's normally kind features.

"I'm not going to talk you out of this, am I?"

"No, Clark."

He sighed heavily. "So be it. Here is the witness list."

After a second, she took the folder and scanned the contents. Her upset with Clark was instantly forgotten when she got to the end. "I can't believe this is all you have."

"We don't need much. We have the eyewitness."

She remembered Louise mentioning this. "Cindy Pop?"

Clark's brow furrowed. "Where did you hear that?"

"From Louise."

"Louise must be working too hard, because I don't know anyone by that name. Our witness is Tawny Green."

"Are you sure?"

"Mercy, Alice," he stated, dashing his hand through his hair with sudden impatience. "Do you think I wouldn't know the name of my own witness?"

She hesitated. "Of course not. Anyway, if you have nothing else for me, I have work to do," she said.

She didn't think her dismissal could have surprised him any more than if she had grown two heads.

"Yes, well, fine. I'll just be going."

When she didn't disagree, he turned abruptly and departed. She listened until his footsteps dissipated in the echoing hallway.

She had been so thrilled when he arrived, and now she

was relieved to see him gone. Guilt pricked at her. Since Clark had gone to work for her father, they had shared an affinity. For as long as she could remember, she and her father had discussed the law. She loved those special times they shared, just the two of them, and she had been surprised at how much she had enjoyed when Clark started joining in. Intelligent debates, good-natured teasing. Sitting out on the porch afterward just the two of them, comfortable in silence.

Alice couldn't imagine a better life.

But in truth, she had noticed that he had started treating her like a child.

Was this really the man she wanted to marry?

She pushed the thought away, tried to erase his anger with the memory of his gentle face. But it was the trial that commandeered her mind.

Giving in, she returned her attention to the folder and went over the list once again, this time slower. Included were the patrolman who had been the first on the crime scene, then the sergeant who had interviewed the witness, and the coroner. Truly, not much on which to charge a man. Especially if that man had an alibi.

The woman in his bedroom.

A shiver of something raced down her spine. Disapproval, she told herself firmly.

What would this Michaela James look like? Would she be too beautiful for words?

It certainly didn't matter, she quickly told herself. Her only concern was if the woman could provide a true and believable account of Lucas Hawthorne's whereabouts on the night of the crime.

Alice placed the folder in her satchel, snatched up her hat, and headed out the door.

After stepping down onto the granite walkway, Alice handed the hack driver fifty cents. The address Lucas had given her proved to be of a grander residence than Alice had anticipated.

The house was not far from her father's in Beacon Hill, though this one was much larger with a columned portico and a sprawling front garden. Boston's most prestigious neighborhood had sprung up along what had once been narrow cow paths that wound their way through the most elevated part of town. As a result, long ago when someone decided to make the paths into roads and cobble them, there wasn't much room. It was rare to find a home with enough space for a sprawling anything, much less a yard and a portico.

Clearly, Lucas's alibi had money.

Not quite as enthusiastic, Alice banged the brass knocker. A liveried footman answered the door.

"May I help you?"

"Yes, my name is Alice Kendall. And I am here to see Miss Michaela James."

The footman raised a brow, and belatedly she remembered her manners. Quickly, she rummaged through her bag and came up with a card that had seen better days. It was times like these when she wished she had paid better attention to the etiquette lessons her father and uncle had insisted she attend. She knew she was supposed to fold down a corner or something. But she couldn't remember which one.

She simply set it on his silver card tray and hoped for the best.

Waiting in the parlor to see if the lady of the house was receiving, Alice took in her surroundings. Plush and ornate, with gold-trimmed doorways and multitiered chandeliers. Not at all to her style. For years she had dreamed of a simple but elegant town house. Tall and stately, with red bricks and slate blue shutters, instead of the more traditional black. And flowers. Lots of flowers lining a small front yard. Not just one color, but lots of colors. Red and yellow, white and pink.

How many times had she dreamed of wearing a wide-brimmed straw hat and spending the morning in her garden with pruning sheers and a basket? Snip, snip. Gathering the buds to fill a crystal vase.

But her dream of being a lawyer had always interfered. How could she be both? She had told herself she could, but was it true? After Clark's reaction, for the first time she had to wonder.

"Mrs. James will see you now," the footman intoned.

Alice followed the man up a sweeping curve of stairs, then down a long, dark hallway. Gas sconces lined the way, though they didn't burn with light. She caught a glimpse of oil portraits, but it was too dark to make out any features. She liked the house less and less as she went.

But when the footman opened the doors at the end of the hall, bright summer sunlight made Alice squint. She had never seen such a room. Windows lined the walls, bringing in streams of light. The room was decorated with furniture covered in a welcoming floral print over two-inch yellow-and-white stripes, with hints of green. Alice felt as if she had stepped into a garden.

"Miss Kendall. I take it you are here because of my dear Lucas."

So much for small talk.

"Yes, ma'am."

It took a moment to find the woman. She lounged on a sofa, and, indeed, she was too beautiful for words. She was older than Alice, but not significantly so. Her hair was a rich auburn. Her eyes were a bright shade of green, like jade, while her skin was a creamy white without a single blemish. Lying on the sofa, she easily could be a model for a famous artist.

"I told him to send you. He wouldn't at first, insisting that I not say a word about being with him. Always the gentleman, you know. Or do you?" She considered her. "He told me that you think he's guilty. He's not."

"And you can provide him with an alibi?"

The woman's laugh was deep and throaty. "You're different than I thought you'd be."

Alice bristled.

"I've offended you. I'm sorry."

"I'm not here for apologies, I simply need to verify that you can provide Mr. Hawthorne with an alibi for the night of July the twenty-third."

"He said you were direct, and not easily distracted."

"Is that a yes or a no?"

The woman laughed out loud at this, then sighed, waving her hand as if waving the words away. "Of course I will provide my dear Lucas with an alibi."

Alice noticed the ring on the woman's left hand, and suddenly realized the footman had called her *Mrs.* James, not Miss. Alice was appalled.

"Ah, I see you have noticed my Alfred's ring. Alas, Alfred is deceased, and doesn't every widow need male companionship on occasion?"

Alice might not be an expert on etiquette, but she did know that women of good breeding never discussed such things.

"You really know nothing at all about Lucas, dear. And before you can defend him properly, you'd best learn."

Alice had to bite her tongue not to ask Mrs. James to tell her everything. How could she explain the need she felt to see his alibi in a way that had nothing to do with the trial, to see whom he had been with? How to explain the sharp stab of pain at seeing this beautiful woman?

Was it jealousy? Envy?

Mrs. Alfred James was everything Alice would never be. Alice knew her blonde hair should be combined with blue eyes in order to make her distinctive. Her pale skin shouldn't be freckled. Her breasts should have been full. But they weren't.

Michaela James was beautiful and at ease with that

beauty. She was unconcerned with what the world thought of her.

Alice longed for that same freedom. What got her into trouble was that often she did live her life the way she wanted to, but then she frequently hated the consequences of her actions.

Looking at this woman, Alice, who had always been considered strong and knowing, came face-to-face with a strength she realized she didn't have.

Could she gain it? Could she learn not to care?

"Whatever you think of me isn't at issue, Mrs. James. Are you willing to testify in court if necessary?"

"Yes, yes. I'll tell them he was right here every second."

"He was here?"

The woman froze, though only for a second, before she laughed easily. "He was here every second before we made our way to Nightingale's Gate. Have you seen his bedroom, Miss Kendall?"

But Alice wasn't distracted by this sudden change of subjects.

"Thank you for your time, Mrs. James. I won't be needing your testimony. I'll be going."

She didn't wait for a response or for the footman to lead her below. Her mind raced. How dare Lucas make a fool of her?

Twenty-five minutes later, Alice shoved past a startled Brutus. The minute she walked into the grand salon, she glanced up at the loft. As expected, Lucas sat in the leather chair, busy at work.

This time she wasn't taken in by his striking looks or the devilish smile she had learned was never far away. She marched up the stairs before Brutus could stop her.

"What is the meaning of getting someone to lie on your behalf?"

Brutus was out of breath when he finally flew into the room behind her.

Lucas leaned back, steepled his hands, looking completely unfazed by her outrage. And that outraged her even more.

"What do you take me for? A fool?" she demanded.

"No, though throwing yourself at a twit like Clark Kittridge seems foolish."

Especially on the heels of having been in Lucas's arms.

The words hung unspoken, but clear as day.

Her mind jerked. She disregarded the thought that she was embarrassed.

"I did not throw myself. At anyone."

"Then what do you call that little display I witnessed at your office?"

"Being polite."

"Like hell you were."

"Why do you care? And what does that have to do with you lying to me about your alibi?"

He eyed her, then shrugged. "You said I needed one. Micki offered."

Micki? She pressed her lips shut.

"On top of that," he continued, "I don't like my attorney sleeping with the man who is prosecuting me. Or should I say, hoping to sleep with the man who is prosecuting me."

"What?" she gasped.

"I saw the way you looked at Kittridge."

She could hardly speak over her indignation. "How dare you say such a thing! I would never . . . I wouldn't dream—"

"Save it, honey." His eyes were cold and lethal. "You fawn all over a milquetoast like Kittridge, but you call me a murderer."

"That's because you probably *are* a murderer!"

Silence hissed through the room like a spew of breath. Alice couldn't believe what she had said.

"I'm sorry, I didn't mean that."

His countenance took on that dark, dangerous look that sent a shiver down her spine. This was the man whom other men didn't cross.

"You meant it. You've said it too many times not to. I don't care what Grayson thinks, I want you off the case."

Alice sucked in her breath, her mind swirling.

"What?" she managed.

"You're fired, Miss Kendall. I don't care if I have to defend myself. I want you off my case and out of my life."

Her shoulders came back like a military man's, pride surging up and replacing mortification. "Fine. I'll draw up the papers and send them over first thing in the morning."

"Good."

Standing there for a moment, she tried to understand what she felt. Freedom and relief, she told herself firmly. "Good."

She whirled past a shocked Brutus, then marched out into the muggy air. But she hadn't gotten much farther than the town house next door, piles of sand and construction workers everywhere, when her blood began to settle and reality seeped in.

She had been fired.

A sick feeling swelled in the pit of her stomach. She could hardly believe it, but she had failed. She felt hot and cold all over.

She had never failed at anything before—at least not when it came to her studies and now her work, she amended with a sigh. Failing at relationships seemed to be her most proficient pastime, at least failing at relationships with anyone not related by blood. And her family *had* to like her.

She walked without knowing where she was going, not stopping until a little girl carrying a wild bouquet of daisies ran into her path. Suddenly, Alice felt six years old, standing in Winchester Poole's kitchen. He had given her a daisy, plucked from Boston Common. But when she started itemizing the nature of his crime against the city, which owned the gardens, he had snatched the stem away, ripping it from her chubby hands, tearing the delicate petals off, and told her to go home.

So much for her first love.

So much for her first big case.

Two very different matters, but somehow standing in the hot, sweltering sun, they both made her feel the same.

Empty and alone.

Chapter Six

MURDER SUSPECT CHOOSES WOMAN LAWYER

Lucas cursed at the headline that screamed across the top of the evening edition of the *Boston Herald*.

"What the hell is this?" he demanded, the afternoon sun slanting across his private office.

He wore a snowy white shirt, royal blue waistcoat with a golden paisley design, and smooth-fitting riding pants tucked into high boots. He had tossed his jacket over a chair back and forgotten it.

Brutus came forward, his massive form and ruthless looks, as always, incongruous with his formal attire. "What is it, boss?"

"This," he grumbled, sliding the newsprint across the desk, then leaning back in his chair.

"What's wrong with that, boss?"

"What's wrong? Everything's wrong."

Lucas stood, intent on heading to his brother's downtown law office. But he was saved the trouble when Grayson entered, his dark suit respectable and refined, his own copy of the newspaper folded neatly underneath one arm.

"Good afternoon," Grayson said with an uncharacteristic lightness to his voice.

"Like hell it is. Have you seen the paper?"

"Right here. Great tactic."

"Tactic?" Lucas stood dumbfounded.

"Yes. It's the perfect way to get word out that Alice Kendall is representing you, and those jurors will undoubtedly walk into that hearing with the idea that a woman, a respectable woman, stands behind you. Though I wish you had discussed it with me first." His features grew troubled. "In fact, Alice Kendall won't discuss anything with me. I've sent notes, but she won't see me. She informed me that she was the lawyer, not me. If I wanted to discuss the case, I'm to do it with you."

Grayson grumbled, and Lucas would have smiled that anyone would dream of treating the oldest Hawthorne brother in such a way. But he was too damn mad.

"I didn't put it there," he stated. "I assumed you had. Hell, I fired her this morning."

Grayson's countenance grew ominous. "You what?"

Lucas didn't give him a second glance. "She thinks I'm guilty," he growled. "The way I see it, she's not the perfect person to defend me."

Not to mention that he couldn't get her out of his head. Her eyes, her hair, which had shimmered like spun silk when he had freed it from that damned bun. And her body. She kept it well hidden, but prim, little Alice Kendall's fit his own all too well.

Frustration snaked through him.

"She's a nuisance."

"A nuisance?" Grayson slapped the newspaper onto the desk. "Don't you understand the gravity of this situation? Do you think I'm exaggerating, that this is just a bad dream and in the morning you are going to wake up? You're not, little brother. This might be a nightmare, but it's real. And while she might be trying my patience by refusing to speak to me about what she has planned, I am smart enough to know that she's your only chance to make headway with Walker Kendall. Proof of which is in the fact that no other lawyer wanted to touch this case. Everyone in town knows

Kendall has had it in for you since the day you opened Nightingale's Gate."

Lucas's eyes narrowed. He hated the truth. "He's not trying the case," he stated stubbornly.

"He's not that stupid. This is personal, Lucas. He has made a career prosecuting men who toy with the law. You've stayed just far enough over the line that he hasn't been able to touch you. Now he's got his chance to bring you down for a whole lot more than just this murder, and you're smart enough to know it. Why else would he put his lapdog on the case? Kittridge gives him the perfect cover to stay involved while not appearing to be prosecuting you himself." Grayson paused, his dark eyes shining like slits of cool obsidian. "Or is it that you want to go down?"

"Don't be absurd."

"Am I? Don't think I haven't noticed how you push the limits, ride the edge as if daring life to beat you."

Lucas stared out the window without seeing.

When Lucas didn't respond, Grayson sighed. "Why are you making this so difficult? All I'm trying to do is help."

Lucas knew Grayson was right. But how to explain when he didn't understand himself why he didn't want the woman on the case—or why he pushed to the edge at every turn? "It's just that Alice Kendall bothers me," he finally answered.

Lucas felt his brother's cool-eyed speculation on his back. "She gets to you, doesn't she?"

Pivoting around, Lucas felt the dangerous pounding of blood through his veins. His brother's words might be true, but he wasn't about to admit it—much less do anything about it. He might respond to her body, but he wanted nothing to do with the repressed little church mouse who had wildness flickering in her eyes. Kissing her had been a lapse in good judgment that still amazed him. "You're crazy."

"Do you think? Or are you crazy? Maybe being around someone who doesn't get paid for her affections for a change is interesting to you."

"I do not pay for my women," he stated coldly.

Grayson conceded the point. "No, I don't suppose you have to pay for them. But you're surrounded by them. I think you're drawn by Alice Kendall's innocence, but put off by it at the same time."

"When did you become a philosopher? And forget Kendall. She's off the case."

"Damn it," Grayson snapped, his patience suddenly at an end. "When are you going to get it through your thick skull that you are in trouble? I can't make this go away. And there's not a lawyer in town who has gone up against Walker Kendall and won. You need his daughter on your side, whether you like it or not. Now you better find a way to re-hire her."

He hung his head, knowing his brother was right.

"It's not that easy." An amused smile suddenly pulled at his lips. "She would have quit had I not fired her."

"Why is that?"

"She said I needed an alibi; I provided her with one."

"How the hell did you do that? You said you were alone."

Lucas glanced casually over the newspaper, then tossed it back on the desk. "Micki insisted. I've never been one to refuse a lady."

"Damn it, Lucas! How could you do such a thing?" Grayson shook his head. "God, I don't understand what is going on with you."

All traces of humor evaporated into the plush room. Suddenly the space seemed oppressively hot, despite the paddle fan that normally kept things cool.

"Regardless," Grayson continued, "you better use that charm of yours and win Miss Kendall back. This is a battle, Lucas. And you need whatever advantage you can get. How many times do I have to tell you, Alice Kendall is the only advantage you've got? If I were you, I'd go see her right now. I don't have to remind you the grand jury hearing is Friday morning."

"She is attending the Darnells' party this evening. My visit will have to wait."

"The way I see it, you have a party to attend."

Alice tiptoed across the stone steps that traversed the back gardens. She didn't knock as she stepped into the main house dressed in her best silk gown. All right, it was her only silk gown, but she didn't think about that. She certainly couldn't afford another, and her father had better things to spend his money on than party attire.

She loved the dress, loved the vibrant jade that made her amber eyes look green, and made her white skin creamy versus just pale. The style was a tad young for her, she knew that; but it was one of the gowns her father had purchased for her five years ago when he had assumed she would enroll in social clubs and sewing circles rather than law school.

As soon as she came into the front parlor, her uncle saw her.

"Alice, you look beautiful."

Harry Kendall was shorter than her father, his hair slightly thinning, though his middle was not. He had taken care of her and her brother since their mother died. And while Harry had been busy working his way up through the ranks of the police department, he had never been as busy as her father. Alice adored him.

Smiling up into his kind gray eyes, she said, "Thank you, Uncle Harry. You look quite dashing yourself."

Harry glanced down at his cutaway jacket and starched white shirt front, ebony tacks, and black silk waistcoat that stretched just a tad too tightly over his middle, and smiled. "I don't get to dress up all that often. I'm glad you decided to go tonight. You really have to socialize more, Alice. It's not right for a young woman to lock herself away with law books and court cases." His bushy gray eyebrows furrowed together. "And despite what your father thinks, as far as I'm concerned, it's time you gave Clark a run for his money. Let him know you aren't sitting around while he makes up his mind. There are plenty of young bucks who would be thrilled to have you."

She patted his arms. "Yes, and they are trampling over each other trying to get through the front door."

Harry grumbled, though what else could he say. He knew as well as anyone that she was right. She knew that while her looks were acceptable, she had never mastered the fine art of flirting, smiling shyly, or making a man feel that he was the end-all. A drawback, she knew, to the world of courting. And of course there was that pesky little detail that she was a lawyer—a very unfeminine occupation. The only man yet who hadn't been put off by her path was Clark.

And Lucas, she thought without warning.

Her lips tingled as she remembered his kiss. No, being a lawyer hadn't put a damper on that.

"Alice?"

With a start, she came out of her reverie, her fingers coming to her lips guiltily. Then she grumbled at the direction of her thoughts.

"I haven't locked myself away." She held out her arms to display her gown, and wrinkled her nose. "But do I look terribly out of fashion?"

Just then her brother, Maxwell, came down the stairs. "In Boston, dear sister, nothing ever goes out of fashion. Women have been pulling the same gowns out of mothballs for decades."

Instantly she felt better. Her brother always had the ability to make her laugh. "You look smashing," she said as she took in his fine formal attire.

He bowed low. "Thank you."

His hair was dark, his eyes more gray than blue. Tall with

broad shoulders. So different from Clark. So very much like Lucas Hawthorne.

She tensed at the thought of the man, and forcefully told herself her beloved brother was nothing like the criminal ingrate who had fired her that very morning.

"What is this?" Maxwell admonished. "Is my little Alice nervous? You've certainly not cared so much about your attire before. What is going on tonight that has you jumpy? Is it that newspaper article?"

Alice groaned. She still couldn't believe that she had been the subject of a front-page article, especially since she had already been fired. What would the headline read in the morning? WOMAN LAWYER FIRED.

How had this happened?

"No, the article isn't the problem," she answered. "I'm just excited about going to a party after so long. Is Father going with us?" She peered past her uncle and brother into her father's study. No one was there.

"I'm not sure, Alice." Harry shuffled his feet. "He was pretty upset when he saw the paper. It's not every day a man has to see his daughter splashed across the front page."

She didn't tell him that the headline was incorrect and would no doubt be retracted. After this week's events, she no longer knew what to expect from her father. More anger with her? Relief that she was finally off the case? Or would he be his old self, kind and caring, her greatest support?

Only days before she had been secure in the knowledge that he would have pulled her into his strong arms and told her that she could do anything. Other cases would come along. But that was a few days ago. And since then, things had changed.

Yet again she had that feeling of not recognizing her life. Her father. Clark. The way Lucas Hawthorne made her feel. He stirred up things inside her that were better left alone.

Besides, the fact was she felt a tremendous sense of relief that she no longer had his case. It was the easy way out, no doubt, and part of her was angry that she would accept such a defeat. But in truth, she was in over her head with Lucas Hawthorne. And tomorrow she'd sit down with her father and find a way to explain the situation and put things right.

They departed the house, but once outside, Maxwell headed for the walkway instead of the waiting carriage.

"Where are you going?" Alice asked.

"To the party." He laughed, his black patent-leather shoes so shiny they reflected the moonlight. "But not in that paddy wagon. I'd rather walk."

Uncle Harry muttered, then guided Alice to the subdued, black police carriage driven by Sergeant Mazon, whose job it was to see that the chief of police got where he needed to go. As employees of the Commonwealth neither Harry nor Walker made a great deal of money. In fact, none of them, including Alice, would have been invited to an event at the socially prominent Darnells' if it hadn't been for the fact that the Kendalls were descendants of Boston's first citizens. They might not have a great deal of wealth, but they had a fine old name. And that was what mattered most in the social circles of Boston. Money simply would have made it easier to move among their peers.

The small carriage rolled down Charles Street from their centuries-old home in Beacon Hill. After only a few turns and a short distance past the rich green confines of the Public Garden, they pulled up in front of the entrance to the redbricked and black-shuttered town house in the newer, but still important, part of town called the Back Bay.

Outdoor gas lamps glistened in the clear black night. The police conveyance looked solid and utilitarian when bookended by long lines of richly enameled broughams and landaus. The single horse that pulled the somber carriage whickered and kicked at the cobbled pavement, impatient to move on.

Every nerve in Alice's body felt edgy and raw, insecurity wrapping around her like a winter cloak. Clark had said he wouldn't be there, and neither would her father. And they were the two people she depended on to get her through the intricacies of society.

"You're going to do just fine," her uncle whispered as he held out his arm, then led her inside.

The house was stunning: the sweeping staircases, the dripping crystal chandeliers, the crush of beautifully clad men and women. A footman took her cape, and the next thing she knew she stood in the ornate welcoming hall.

More than ever she felt like a rose garden in winter. Old and out of season, the thorns gaudily dressed up with a silly bow. Self-consciously, she reached up and checked her hair.

"If you're this uncomfortable," her uncle whispered, "we don't have to stay."

How dear of him. But she had to face these people sometime.

"I'm fine, Uncle. Really," she said, squeezing his arm.

Gleaming hardwood floors stretched out before them, an orchestra playing on a stage done up like a framed painting, suspended, somehow, off the ground. A few couples danced, but most guests still talked and greeted new arrivals. Just beyond, Alice could see accordion doors folded back to reveal tables laden with food and a towering ice sculpture in the center.

Men in formal attire exchanged greetings. Mothers in demure gowns showed off their daughters, while the young debutantes twittered behind gloved hands holding beautifully laced fans.

Had she ever been that young, Alice wondered. She couldn't imagine that she had.

"Alice, is that you?"

Alice and Harry turned to find Jessica Mayfield approaching. She wore a sapphire blue gown of taffeta, with a long train trailing behind her. This was not a gown pulled out of mothballs.

"It is you!" the woman exclaimed.

Jessica extended her hands, then kissed the air on either side of Alice's cheeks. She allowed Harry to shake her hand as was proper. "How good it is to see you, Mr. Kendall." She glanced around them. "Is Maxwell here tonight?"

"Not yet. But he is on his way," Harry replied.

"Oh, good. I so want to see him." She batted her lashes. "Such the elusive bachelor that no girl seems to be able to catch." She waved her fan. "And my father was saying he looked forward to seeing you, Mr. Kendall. He insists you are doing an outstanding job with the police. It is a very good thing, I am told, that one of our own is commanding the very men we pay to keep us safe." She leaned close, her smile dimming like a gaslight turned down. "We are safe, aren't we?"

"Boston has never been safer," he assured her.

"But what about that murder business? Surely it can't be true that Lucas Hawthorne did it?"

As if the mention of his name made him appear, Lucas chose that moment to walk through the door.

Conversation cut off as if a conductor had halted his baton. Alice could see the crowd's surprise at his attendance.

"I can't believe it," Jessica gasped, her green eyes glittering with scandal and intrigue. "What is he doing here? Lucas hasn't accepted an invitation during the social season in ages."

Alice felt sudden tension coming from her uncle, and her already unsteady smile froze on her face.

Lucas stood in the doorway, his black evening attire relieved only by the crisp white of his tie and waistcoat. A half-smile pulled at his sensual lips, but his blue eyes flashed with a keen intelligence, his countenance alert.

Everyone stared at him, as if waiting, though who knew for what. Lucas scanned the room, quickly, efficiently, his perusal not stopping until he found her.

Alice's heart leaped and hammered when he ignored the

stares and awkward greetings, and started toward her. He moved with a combination of polished elegance and raw virility, predatory, powerful. A panther among peacocks.

She watched him approach and thought of sin. Dark, dangerous, and deeply disturbing.

She had thought a lot about sin growing up, couldn't help it when surrounded by the worlds of her father and uncle— tales of sordid crimes and hideous deeds laced through dinnertime conversation. It had always set her apart from the other girls, who knew little more about the world than the current fashions or cross-stitch patterns. For as long as she could remember, she hadn't had anything in common with her peers.

But it was her life, and Alice wouldn't give up the close relationship she'd had with her father for a thousand frothy gowns or a hundred prim beaux. She needed only one man in her life—one man who could accept her as she was. And for that, she had Clark.

He understood that knowing about sin and acting them out were two entirely different propositions. Just like her father and uncle. They were subjected to sin but didn't give in to it.

Lucas Hawthorne, however, did.

"Oh my," Jessica breathed, her hand fluttering at her breast. "He's coming this way."

Indeed, Lucas didn't veer off, nor did he stop until he stood before them. His blue eyes locked with Alice's for one long moment, a shiver of unbidden sexual pleasure racing down her spine as if he had touched her, before he turned to Jessica. "Miss Mayfield," he said with a formal bow.

Jessica sighed, though in delight, and nearly swooned, generally making a fool of herself over Lucas Hawthorne.

"How interesting that you have joined us, Mr. Hawthorne," Jessica said, finally finding her voice. "You must come with me. No doubt everyone will want to talk to you."

She started to take his arm, but he gave her a look that

was both sensual and charming at the same time. "First, I must speak with Miss Kendall."

"Oh." Jessica eyed Alice more carefully.

But Alice found she couldn't look away from Lucas. He didn't say another word. Instead, he took her hand. White glove to white glove, but still she felt the heat of him. Then he bowed and brought her fingers to his lips. He didn't simply make the gesture as was proper, he kissed her knuckles. The touch sent liquid fire through her body. Never had she been touched like that. So innocently, but with such sensation.

Then just as quickly, he dropped her hand and addressed Uncle Harry.

"Mr. Kendall," he said formally. "I haven't seen you in, what, three weeks since my arrest?"

There was no mistaking the sarcasm in his voice. He threw the words down as some sort of archaic gauntlet. Jessica gasped and several heads turned their way. Her uncle bristled.

Harry pulled himself up to his full five-foot-nine inches. He might not have Lucas's height, but what he lacked in inches he made up for in solid muscle mass. "Yes, three weeks. Though if I'd had my way, you'd be socializing in the not-so-comfortable confines of a jail cell rather than in this fine salon."

Lucas's lips pulled into a crooked smile. "Alas, we can't all have our way."

Alice couldn't believe what she was seeing. Her uncle never lost his temper, nor was he ever so blatantly rude. Just then she was seeing a man she had never seen before. Callous and angry. Though in her uncle's defense, she had to admit that Lucas had a way of bringing out the worst in a person.

Without another word, Harry took Alice's arm and started to leave. But Lucas stopped them.

"Miss Kendall, I would appreciate the pleasure of this dance."

Jessica gasped again, and Alice started to decline. But Harry did it for her. "Not on your life, Hawthorne."

"I'd like a word with my attorney," he stated, his tone brooking no argument, "and unless you'd like me to take your niece into the back study to have said discussion alone, I suggest we do it in a dance."

Harry fumed.

Jessica's eyes were as wide as saucers. "You're his attorney?"

By now, several people had circled around curiously. A short, plump man stepped forward, his balding head sparsely covered with long hairs plastered over the top, his florid cheeks even brighter with drink. "It was all over the papers this afternoon," he explained.

"I saw that," Jessica exclaimed excitedly. "But I only read the headline. I never dreamed that the woman was our very own Alice. Though I should have guessed." She tsked. "You always did like to stir the pot."

A sick feeling swept through Alice at the fuss everyone was making over her being Lucas's lawyer. Though she knew she shouldn't be surprised. She wasn't naïve. But still she didn't like it.

As the crowd thickened around her, Alice became separated from her uncle, who looked fit to be tied over the commotion involving his niece. And without realizing how it happened, Alice found herself on the dance floor, a strong, though surprisingly gentle hand guiding her.

"I don't remember saying yes," she said, when Lucas pulled her close, not sure if she was relieved to be away from the tumult or miffed that he had so high-handedly dragged her away.

"I don't remember your saying no, either."

His deep, rich chuckle rumbled seductively in her ear. Amazingly, the sound filled her with an ease she hadn't felt since she had decided to attend this gala affair. The thought leaped out at her that she was more relaxed in the arms of a man accused of murder than with a crowd of her peers.

"Would you have taken no for an answer?" she asked, an unaccustomed teasing lightness finding its way into her voice.

He set her back a bit and looked down at her with an amused grin, before his gaze lowered even further, and he took in her lips. "If a lady says no, I always respect her wishes."

Both of them knew he wasn't referring to dancing, and Alice felt blood sting her cheeks.

"You're blushing." His smile faded away, and for a moment Alice thought he was going to reach up and touch her face.

"I can't tell you the last time I saw a woman blush," he said, as if unaware that he spoke.

Suddenly whatever good humor he had was gone. His arm circled round, and he pulled her even closer. "An innocent blush, the gown of a maiden. How old are you, Miss Kendall?"

"A gentleman never asks a lady her age."

"I've never pretended to be a gentleman."

"True, but you came here, didn't you. Isn't one of society's unspoken rules that a man who attends a social function must adhere to society's dictates? An unspoken agreement, if you will."

"If you are so enamored of society's dictates, why have you become a lawyer?"

She would have tripped had he not steadied her, his strong hands practically picking her up and carrying her for the few steps she missed.

"I see you don't have an answer." His smile resurfaced. "Though 'touché' certainly would seem appropriate."

But this time she wasn't taken in by his charm; his statement was too incisive for that. "As I see it, my having a job and your being a gentleman are two entirely different matters."

"I disagree. Your having a job seems very much like your not being a lady—at least that is what I would wager society believes. Therefore, your not being a lady is very much like my not being a gentleman." His eyes sparkled. "I never would have guessed that you and I had so much in common."

Alice sputtered over his convoluted reasoning. Had he just insulted her?

"Don't worry, Miss Kendall. I was never partial to proper ladies anyway."

"I am . . . I never . . ." She couldn't get the words out over her vexation—and her fear that this, indeed, was what everyone in Boston felt. That she wasn't a lady.

Her heart fluttered, and her chest felt tight. She wanted out of this place, out into the air where she could breathe.

Fears long suppressed wouldn't be held back any longer. Did the person she had been raised to be make it impossible for her to be thought of as a lady—or to become a wife? Should she have forced herself to learn to flirt and cross-stitch in order to have a child? Should she have squashed her very real love for the law to have the family that other women took for granted?

She thought of the many months she and everyone else seemed sure that Clark would propose—and hadn't. She thought of his long string of excuses as to why they should wait. Suddenly she felt sick. Would she never hold a child of her own? Would she spend the rest of her life alone, surrounded by two old bachelors and her brother with his family after he married? Would she be little more than a spinster aunt?

"I'm sorry."

The simple words cut into her spiraling thoughts, and she glanced up. Indeed Lucas appeared contrite, his blue eyes boring into her, and she felt a strange twisting in her heart.

"You are a lady," he said, almost a whisper, the words intense. "I never should have implied otherwise. But you are also smart and lively, beautiful and informed. So different from any woman I have ever met."

The words soothed her heart like a balm.

"And you look lovely tonight," he added softly.

Surprise mixed with renewed embarrassment at the thought of her gown. "I look like a grown woman in schoolgirl's attire."

"No, you are a beautiful young lady."

"I am not beautiful, nor am I young."

"By whose standard?"

"By anyone's."

"Not by mine. I have never found any woman under the age of twenty-four interesting. My guess is that you have just barely become interesting."

He said it in a way that she couldn't help but laugh. "Are you trying to prove to me that you do indeed have charm?"

The dance floor had grown crowded, forcing her even closer to his broad chest. She could smell the heat of him, like sun-dried grasses, fresh and clean. He lowered his eyes to look at her, his dark lashes like crescent moons.

"Am I charming you, Miss Kendall?"

The words made her breath skitter. His words washed over her like a caress, so simple, but sensual. Intimate, though she hardly knew him. Didn't want to know him.

She concentrated on the diamond tacks that marched down his shirtfront. Music surrounded them, violins and the deep yearning sound of the cello.

"No, Mr. Hawthorne, you aren't charming me. You are annoying me." She could barely get the words past her lips.

Mirth glittered in his eyes as he pulled her even closer to the hard planes of his body. "Yes, I can tell."

Alice grumbled. "Why are you seeking me out now?" she asked. "Just this morning you never wanted to see me again."

She felt his body tense.

"True," he answered honestly. "In fact, the sole reason I am here tonight is to apologize for my outburst in your office."

"Outburst?"

"When I fired you."

"Is that what you call it? Either way, you were right. My manners were sorely lacking. And so were yours." She felt heat rush to her cheeks but forced herself to continue. "A client and his lawyer have no business . . ."

"Kissing?"

"Yes, kissing. It is completely and utterly unprofessional. I shouldn't have allowed it. But something . . . I don't know. All that matters is that I did. We have no business working together. I'm sure your brother can easily find another attorney."

"I don't want another attorney."

Her head tilted back. "What are you saying?"

"I want you to represent me, not someone else."

Her heart fluttered, her palms felt moist. She was sure he could feel the heat coming through her gloves. Instinctually, she stepped away, but the crush of guests plus the iron strength of his formally gloved hand kept her there.

Her fingers gripped his shoulder to keep from losing her balance. "Why?"

In one smooth motion, he twirled her around, his strong thigh coming between her own for the briefest of moments.

"Because I want you."

The words crystallized in the warm air that buffered the room. Mere inches separated them, his words rumbling and provocative. Their gazes locked, his so filled with sensual heat that she felt dizzy.

"I want your knowledge of the law, I want your ability to speak and the truth that is clear in your eyes."

Facts, reality. Not sexual. Alice hated the bite of disappointment.

"Are you feeling all right?" he asked.

His countenance lined with concern, and he held her even more firmly as if supporting her. Supporting her as if he really cared. She had the fleeting thought that in this man's arms she could afford a few blessed moments of weakness.

"It won't work," she barely managed.

"Why?" He studied her intently, guiding her about the dance floor with ease. "Are you afraid?"

Alice blinked. "I am not afraid, Mr. Hawthorne."

"Are you worried that you will give in and kiss me again?"

"I did not kiss you! You kissed me. And you can lay money on the fact that I will never kiss you again!"

He smiled with utter confidence. "See, you've solved your problem. No more kissing. No reason not to work together then."

His teasing banter set her teeth on edge. "This is not a joking matter, Mr. Hawthorne."

With those words, all traces of laughter evaporated, and he stopped their progress on the dance floor.

"I know. And as much as I hate to admit it, I also know that I need you, Alice."

The rawness of his quiet words surprised her. For the first time she saw a trace of vulnerability in this strong man. She felt the sudden urge to wrap him in her arms, hold him, comfort him, press her hand against his heart.

But the suspended moment jerked to a halt when she felt someone take hold of her arm.

Turning abruptly, she came face-to-face with Clark. They were on the edge of the hardwood floor, and he was looking at her in harsh accusation, before his gaze slowly shifted to Lucas. His brown eyes narrowed into angry slits.

"Clark?" she gasped. "What are you doing here?"

"I managed to get away from the office." He looked at Lucas, then back. "Is there a problem?"

Lucas didn't bother to look at the shorter man; he looked only at her. "Is there?"

Time hung suspended. Yes, there was a problem. Everything was wrong. Her thoughts spun out of control.

"No," she said finally, steadying her breath. "I'm simply tired."

She turned to go and allowed Clark to take her arm. Gratefully? Reluctantly?

"Miss Kendall," Lucas called out, stopping her.

As if she could do nothing else, she turned back.

"Will I see you tomorrow at the hearing?" Lucas asked.

His eyes implored her. It was as if there was no other answer but one.

"Yes. I'll be there."

She saw the ease that instantly washed over him. Then that full and wonderful smile. "Good," he said with an arrogant nod.

She couldn't help her answering grin. "See that you wear that blue suit we discussed."

Clark made a noise, and before she could hear Lucas's reply, her father's assistant district attorney pulled her away.

Chapter Seven

Friday morning, Alice arrived at the courthouse half an hour early. Just as the newspapers had reported, women lined the steps, all holding handmade signs proclaiming Lucas's innocence. A few proclaimed their love.

Having heard about the flock of adoring women and seeing them in person were two very different matters. There were young women and old women, prim women and outrageously dressed women. But they all had one thing in common. Their devotion to and support of Lucas. The actuality stunned Alice, made her feel foolishly insignificant and plain.

Hurrying inside, her footsteps rang in the marbled hallway outside the grand jury room. She had marshaled her blonde hair in a respectable, severely appropriate twist. Her gown was dark blue, tailored, with a white blouse. Not a frill to be found. She was as ready as she was going to be.

Generally it was the assistant district attorneys rather than the defense lawyers who arrived before time and paced up and down the corridor waiting for their turn to present their findings in the proceedings.

Several cases would be heard that day, and if an ADA could present the evidence and convince the grand jury to indict, the prosecution was one step closer to going to trial. An assistant district attorney's career was made on wins. Alice knew that Clark needed a win today. Would he fight fairly or like a back-street alley cat to get it done?

The *good* news for Alice was that as the defense attorney she wasn't allowed in the grand jury room. The *bad* news for Alice was that as the defense attorney she wasn't allowed in the courtroom. A double-edged sword, as it were.

She couldn't present a defense, or object to anything. As a result, she had no reason to pace nervously like an ADA.

Alice, however, was as nervous as any prosecutor. But combined with her nervousness was a growing calm. The more she thought about it, the more she believed that no jury in the land would indict Lucas Hawthorne based on the flimsy, and no doubt entirely unreliable, evidence of an eyewitness whose moral character was dubious. A prostitute with nervous testimony would not stand up in a court of law, Alice felt certain.

The Commonwealth didn't have enough evidence. Could her father have given the case to Clark because he knew they didn't stand a reasonable chance of winning? As it was, if they won an indictment, her father looked good. If they lost, only Clark looked bad. Alice hated the thought that her father might do that.

The long hallway outside the grand jury room grew cluttered with prosecutors, witnesses, policemen, defendants who weren't locked up, and their families as they arrived to take part in the proceedings or provide support and encouragement for loved ones. But there was no sight of Lucas.

Clark appeared ten minutes before the proceedings began. When he saw her, he frowned, then shook his head and gave her a lamenting smile.

Holding his bulging satchel by the handle, he headed her way. He said hello to most every other prosecutor, shook hands with many of the defense attorneys present, politely greeted the patrolmen. When he made it to her end of the corridor, he set the satchel down and pulled a kerchief out of his pocket to dab his brow as he spoke.

"I can't believe you're really going through with this," he

said as he refolded the white linen into a neat square and put it away.

"Believe it; I am."

He raised a brow at her tone.

Before he could respond, however, Lucas arrived at the top of the stairs, as powerful and arrogant as always. At the sight of her he nodded his head with supreme satisfaction, and walked forward. Her heart skipped a beat at his bold expression. But then he noticed Clark. Instantly, Lucas's countenance shifted, and she saw that dangerous man she had seen the first day she met him.

He greeted him succinctly.

Clark cut him direct, and would have walked off if just then Grayson hadn't arrived at their sides. Grayson Hawthorne might be Lucas's brother, but he was too powerful of a lawyer, not to mention man about town, to snub.

"Hello, Grayson," Clark said genially.

"Mr. Kittridge," Grayson replied with a stern formality.

Clark, younger than Grayson, and clearly less successful, blushed crimson at the subtle set down.

Just then Walker Kendall surprised them all by arriving. Every prosecutor there, and most every defender, vied for his attention as he walked down the hall. The echoing din of voices against the marble surroundings grew deafening. Walker worked his way through the crowd like a politician, shaking hands and smiling broadly, talking and joking with lawyers and policemen alike. Alice watched with a great deal of pride at how clearly respected he was.

Because of her intense gaze, it took a moment to realize that Boston's county coroner was behind him.

Confusion raced through her, and her heart began to pound when Grayson caught her in his steely-eyed gaze. Coroners were rarely called to testify before a grand jury unless there was a question as to how the victim died.

"What's he doing here?" Grayson demanded.

"I don't know," she answered, her mind whirling with

concern. "I saw that the coroner was on the witness list, but there isn't any question about cause of death in this case. I can't imagine why he is here."

Clark's embarrassment had fled, and now he smiled, but he didn't say a word. Alice was instantly suspicious. And worried.

Pushing past the men, Alice didn't wait for her father to make it down the corridor. The large brass clock embedded in the marble wall showed that only one minute remained until the grand jury proceedings would begin.

"What is the coroner doing here, Father?" she demanded without preamble.

Walker raised a brow, though he didn't stop walking. "Is that any way to greet your father?"

For half a second, she nearly cringed and apologized. But in the next second the urge was gone, replaced by the fact that something was terribly wrong. First the coroner, then Clark's certain smile, and now her father's haughty surety.

"There is no dispute as to how the girl died," she said, forced to walk beside him, her long skirt swishing as they worked their way back to the opposite end of the corridor.

"No," Walker replied while acknowledging a well-known solicitor in the distance. "There isn't. But you just never know what you might need in an important case like this. It was Clark's idea, actually. I was impressed that he would think of it," he finished, just as they stopped in front of Grayson, Clark, and Lucas.

"Why is the coroner here, Walker?" Grayson asked.

"No specific reason," he answered with the utmost respect.

Grayson's eyes narrowed. "You're trying to pull something."

"Careful what you say, Grayson," Walker said coldly, his smile gone.

Grayson looked Walker straight in the eye, as if trying to read his thoughts, then he turned to Alice. "Ask for a postponement."

If only she could. "We have no cause. The coroner was listed."

"Ask anyway."

"What am I going to say? 'I have a funny feeling about this'?"

Grayson growled. Her father raised a brow. She was almost certain that Lucas chuckled.

"Damn," Grayson cursed.

Slowly, Alice turned until her eyes met Lucas's. He stood where she had left him, though now he leaned casually against the marble and wooden-wainscoted wall with one shoulder, his expression a cipher.

What was he thinking? Why was it that he never seemed to care what was going on around him, that his life hung in the balance? But at the Darnells' ball he had cared, she was certain. She had not imagined that rawness in his voice.

There was no time for words when the wide double doors were pushed open by the guard. The grand jury was ready to convene. Unless Alice was wrong about the triumphant look on her father's face, the coroner had something to say. And Lucas Hawthorne was going to be indicted.

Alice felt hot and sick and caught in a terrible trap.

She started to move away but looked back at the last minute, just in time to see Walker hand a file to Clark. "Good work," she overheard her father say.

Then the older man headed inside the grand jury room.

"Where are you going?" Alice demanded. "You said you weren't dealing with this case."

"I'm not. But that doesn't mean I don't want to see how my most promising ADA is doing." He smiled, a flash of white teeth. Then he walked in.

Alice watched him sit down in the back row. When she turned to Lucas, he was studying her, seemingly more interested in what she was feeling than in what was about to happen to him.

"You'd best go in," she told him, forcing her voice to be strong.

He looked at her for a second longer, then nodded his head. "Yep, I'd best get in to the lions."

"It might not be so bad," she offered. "It's still your word against theirs."

"So we hope."

Turning away, he sauntered inside as if he didn't have a care in the world. It wasn't until the wide oak doors swung closed that she realized he was wearing a dark blue Prince Albert suit.

Grayson sat on a hardwood bench, as calm and contained as stone. Alice admired his cool, but that was as close to it as she got. She paced, as nervous as any rookie assistant district attorney had ever been.

There was no telling how long it would be before the *Commonwealth vs. Lucas Hawthorne* was through. As the minutes passed, Grayson didn't move. Now and again he glanced at the clock. Though that was the only sign he was at all impatient.

After an hour Alice felt as if she had run ten miles. Her legs ached from walking back and forth over the hard marble floor. Her back was sore from so much standing. And all the while questions raced through her mind relentlessly.

Could the coroner have something to say that was not in his report? Had her father known about it and she hadn't?

But no answers as Lucas's fate was being decided inside.

At forty-three minutes past ten o'clock in the morning, Clark Kittridge strolled out of the courtroom, his smile wide and brimming. Her father was right behind him.

Alice felt a sick lurch to her stomach at the sight. But what made her want to cry was the sight of the double doors swinging shut with no sign of Lucas behind them.

"Your client has been indicted and remanded into custody," Clark stated triumphantly.

Alice sucked in her breath. Grayson cursed.

"The court has no business remanding my client," she said, barely controlling the shake in her voice. "A bond hearing was already held when he was arrested, and he posted bail. What do you think you're doing?"

Clark shrugged. "Ask your uncle. He took Lucas away."

"Hell," Grayson ground out.

After seeing how her uncle reacted to Lucas at the Darnells' party, Alice had to agree.

"I'll take care of this," Grayson added, his face set dangerously.

"No," Alice stated. "I'll handle it."

She looked at her father. "Get him out here, or I will press charges of false imprisonment. You know the law, as do I. Don't think for a second that I will allow you to play games with me."

Alice wasn't sure if she had ever seen her father so angry at the way she spoke to him. But he realized she wasn't kidding. And he had stepped beyond his power. He knew it. Alice knew it.

"We certainly haven't imprisoned the man, Alice," he replied, a smooth veneer over his anger. "We simply wanted to make sure that all our files were in order. It shouldn't take long."

"Get him out here now."

They eyed each other, toe to toe as they had never been before.

At length, he shrugged. "Clark," he said. "Go tell Harry to let Hawthorne go—I mean, let him deal with any file questions we have later."

Even so, it was another hour of pacing and stomach churning before Lucas was led out of confinement.

For a second after Lucas appeared, Alice thought he looked vulnerable, as if that time behind bars had shaken something loose inside him. But in a flash it was gone, his smile broad and carefree.

"It's not the Hotel Vendome, but it's not bad once you get to know the staff. I'll have to send Sergeant Bellows one of my best bottles of champagne."

"What happened?" Grayson demanded.

Lucas shrugged. "With some well-constructed prodding, the coroner suddenly remembered a tiny, but apparently significant, piece of evidence he had conveniently forgotten to mention."

Alice glared at her father. "Forgot to mention?"

"Are you implying something, daughter?"

A palpable tension shimmered through her father. She felt the shift in him immediately, and she braced herself for what she was about to learn.

"During the hearing," Lucas continued, "the coroner mentioned that there was a mark on the body of the victim."

"A mark?" Her mind whirled. By now Grayson and Clark stood on either side of her.

"Yes, there was a mark on the body." Lucas hesitated, drawing the moment out. "Of a nightingale. Just above the left breast. Like a brand, I believe his exact words were."

Walker shrugged. "The most unexpected things can happen in a trial. You should know that, Alice. If you had gone to the coroner yourself and asked a few questions, you could have learned that information."

All eyes turned to her, and her stomach plummeted. Dear God, she hadn't gone to talk to the man at all. How could she have not done something so simple, so elemental? So what if coroners were rarely brought into a grand jury hearing. So what if there had been no question as to the cause of death.

"Did you interview him, Miss Kendall?" Grayson asked.

"No," she said, trying to make her voice firm.

Her head felt light with mortification as her father looked at her. His anger when he found out that she had taken the case had been hard enough to take, but this blazing disappointment was infinitely worse.

"And if you had found that out, Alice, you also would have known to question your client."

Walker said the last words softly.

"If you had," he continued, "you would have learned what everyone else already knows. Lucas Hawthorne has worn a ring with that very distinctive and very unique nightingale on it for years."

She jerked around to face Lucas. "Is that true?"

He gave one of his infamous shrugs.

Frustration and anger surged up like a tidal wave.

"Is that true?" she demanded, each word enunciated.

"I'm afraid it is. Though for what it's worth, I lost the ring months ago."

Clark sneered. "Yeah, and if you believe that, I've got another story for you."

Instantly Lucas's smile vanished, and he had Clark by the collar, pressed against the marble wall. Clark struggled and gasped. His satchel dropped to the floor.

"Hey there," Walker called out, as Grayson leaped in and pried his younger brother away.

"There is no call for fisticuffs, young man," Walker said, "unless you'd like me to recall one of my brother's men to lock you up on new charges."

"He's only showing his true colors," Clark said, rubbing his shoulder. "You should have seen how he manhandled Alice just last night at the Darnells' ball."

Walker raised a dark bushy eyebrow ominously.

"That is ridiculous," Alice stated. "And this is not about dances. This is about my client."

Walker studied his daughter, then glanced at Lucas. "Be careful, Hawthorne. Make sure you don't do anything that I will make you regret. Alice might be your lawyer, but she's my daughter."

Her shoulders came back. "Father!"

But Walker Kendall was done with this encounter. "Come along, Clark. We have work to do."

They strode down the hall.

"Hell," Grayson bit out with a look so angry that Alice fought back the need to grimace, before he turned on his heels and headed for the doors himself.

Lucas watched them go, and this time when he looked back at Alice, he was serious and looked decades older than his thirty years.

"Don't let it get you down, sweetheart." He reached across to her, his full lips smiling crookedly as he gently nudged her chin. "What you and Grayson didn't understand was that I was going to be indicted all along. There was nothing anyone could have done to prevent it."

Then he turned away without another word and disappeared down the hallway.

Chapter Eight

Alice sat in her office, the sun fading in the distance. A pad of paper lay on the desk in front of her. Growing up, most girls wrote out what their names would be when they married. Mrs. Charles Dewherst. Mrs. Randolph Hastings.

But Alice had always written something else.

ALICE KENDALL, ATTORNEY AT LAW
ALICE KENDALL, ESQUIRE

She had always known she wanted to be a lawyer. But after this morning's efforts, she wondered. What qualified solicitor would make such a blatant error?

For one tiny moment, she allowed herself to close her eyes and press back in the chair, welcoming the bite of hardwood spindle, to feel the devastation of it all. But only for a moment.

Her thoughts were interrupted by a knock on the door. She could make out the dark, looming shape of a man behind the murky glass. Was it Lucas?

Her heartbeat quickened, though yet again she didn't know what it was she was feeling. Did she want him to be there or not? Was she ready to face him after letting him down?

And what about the ring? He had lost it. She could believe him, couldn't she?

Too many questions, and not enough answers. Though

answers didn't matter when it was her father who pushed through the doorway, not Lucas.

Her heart plunged to her stomach as Walker glanced around the small office, his blunt fingers smoothing his mustache. She wasn't sure what to expect. But when he turned back to her and actually smiled, kindly, fatherly, then opened his arms, she walked into his embrace and held tight. Though only for a second. Her father didn't abide weakness of any sort, and holding on too long had always been considered weak.

"My little Alice," he said, holding her at arm's length. "I'm sorry the Hawthorne case turned out this way for you."

"Oh, Father. This has been such a mess."

"I know, I know."

"I should have spoken to the coroner."

She felt a sudden tension in him, and he stepped back. He looked a tad uncomfortable, but then it was gone.

"That is water under the bridge now, Alice." He patted her hand. "We all live and learn. Now it's time to cut your losses and move on."

She cocked her head, then carefully pulled her hand away. "Cut my losses?"

"You know it's for the best. Get out of this case now before you embarrass yourself further."

"Embarrass myself?" Did it always have to come back to this?

"All you have to do is say you aren't experienced enough for a big trial. Everyone will understand."

"Too big of a trial for me?"

"I'll send you some cases, I really will. I kick myself for not taking care of that the day we had lunch. But I've been busy. Though I'll make certain you have some jobs that pay better than the cases you started out with. Or better yet," he added, glancing one last time around her office, "why don't you give up the pretense of making it on your own and come to work for me."

She felt frustration and hurt mix together in a volatile combination. "Why do you and Clark keep trying to get me off this case?"

If he heard the growing stiffness in her voice, he didn't let on. "Because we both care about you. Don't fool yourself, Alice. You only got this case because of me. Worse yet, if you are stubborn enough to stay involved, you only guarantee yourself more heartache. This will ruin your career. You worked long and hard to become a lawyer. I can't believe you would willfully throw it away because you were foolish enough to think you could actually win this case." He sighed and held her shoulders. "I love you, my sweet Alice. And as your father it's my duty to try to keep you from harm. That's all I'm trying to do."

A heavy sigh rushed out of her. "Oh, Father."

"Just think about it, is all I ask." He held her for a second, then kissed her hairline. "I'll see you at dinner. Harry is making your favorite. Pot roast and mashed potatoes."

The door rattled behind him as he left.

"That's your favorite," she whispered in the quiet room, something that she knew was insignificant somehow making her world shift a little bit more. "I hate pot roast and mashed potatoes."

Returning to her chair, she reviewed what she knew. Whether she had interviewed the coroner or not, how could Lucas Hawthorne explain away a mark on the victim that was said to be made by a ring he was widely known to wear? An eyewitness was surmountable. But an eyewitness, the supposedly distinctive nightingale mark, and no alibi made it next to impossible to ignore. And as she had already told her client, most of the men who would be on the jury would like nothing better than to convict him simply on principle. He owned a highly successful house of ill repute. He had plenty of women and a great deal of money. Exactly what most men didn't have—but wanted.

Alice stood and started putting files in her satchel when another knock sounded on the door.

She tensed when Clark entered. But he smiled at her, his face warm and open, his brown eyes once again kind.

"I just saw your father," he said.

"Yes," she said, sliding her hand into her glove.

"I'm sure I know why he was here."

"Why is that?" she asked, casting him a quick glance as she tugged on the second glove.

"To talk some sense into you."

Alice raised a brow wryly. "Don't tell me you're here for the same reason."

"No. I know you well enough to understand that you will make your own decisions. I just wanted to come by and tell you that I'm sorry things worked out as they have." He walked up to her and took her hands in his. Running his thumbs over the gloved backs, he looked into her eyes. "You are very special to me, Alice, and I would hate to think our . . . relationship would be ruined over this."

Did he mean it? "I'd hate that, too."

"Good." He squeezed her hands, then he leaned over and kissed her cheek. "I just wanted to make sure."

She hardly heard what he said. She felt giddy. He had finally kissed her.

Of course, it wasn't much of a kiss, more a brotherly peck than anything else. And truth be told, she had experienced none of the heat and yearning she had felt when Lucas had kissed her. But still it felt good. More than that she needed to forget about Lucas and the feel of his lips on hers.

"Whatever your decision is regarding this case, I'm behind you."

His words made her feel bold, and suddenly she felt it was time to take matters into her own hands. Time to make things clearer between them.

Before she could change her mind, she asked, "Would you like to have dinner with me?"

"That would be nice. I hear your uncle is making pot roast and mashed potatoes."

"Actually, I was thinking we could go to Locke-Ober's."

He sliced her a reproving look. "Alice, if I didn't know better, I'd swear you were asking me to step out."

"I am asking you to step out," she blurted.

His spine straightened, and his eyes widened. He seemed at a loss for words.

If Alice could have melted into the suddenly stiflingly hot room, she would have. But in the next second, Clark contained himself and smiled at her, taking her hand.

"I'm flattered," he said, composing himself. "That would be lovely."

Her heart skipped, then burgeoned with joy as his fingers wrapped around hers. He did care for her.

"I'm so glad," she said. "I didn't think I could be wrong about your feelings."

His grasp stiffened, but she hardly noticed as she rushed on, suddenly no longer able to stop herself from plunging down this path.

"I was certain you cared for me. Oh, Clark, we are perfect together, and we are getting too old to play games anymore."

"Games?" He stepped back, pulling his hands away.

An alarm went off in her head, but something stronger carried her on. "I care for you, and you care for me. This is silly that we keep holding back. Clark, I—"

"Alice."

He cut her off, and with that one word, her spiraling thoughts and emotions careened to a halt. She stared at him.

"I do care about you," he said, his gentle face lined with regret.

It was the regret that brought the world to a stop.

"But I'm not . . . attracted to you," he finished. "Not in the way a husband needs to be attracted to a wife. I love debating cases with you. God, I don't know anyone besides your father who knows more about the law. You're smart and independent. You're a wonderful woman." He hesitated, his features twisting with regret. "But if I marry, I want a wife who will be happy to stay at home, darn my socks, and see that my laundry is done. Regular things. The kind of things that would bore you to tears." He looked at his hands. "I know I should have made my intentions clear sooner."

He could have said many things that would have hurt her, embarrassed her, made her want to cry. But this leveled her as nothing else could have. It hit at a core so deep and vulnerable that it sent her reeling. Because she realized in that second that Clark was no different from the rest of the men she had encountered. None of them wanted a wife who knew so much about things women normally knew nothing about. She knew too much of the world to make any man a good wife. She might have the requisite lack of sexual experience that a husband demanded of the woman he married, but she lacked a true innocence—an innocence of what the world was really like.

Beyond that, she was too strong of a woman to sit back and accept a world consisting solely of a man and his needs. But she didn't have enough strength to accept a life without love and a family to call her own. The realization left her spinning in despair.

"Alice, I'm sorry."

"I think you should leave."

"Alice—"

"Just go!"

He started to leave but hesitated at the door. "Please let our office know how to proceed once you decide."

He left her then, and she stared at the firmly shut door. With effort, she tried to work. But in the end, she had to get out of her office.

The hot August air had eased some as the sun descended, and the darkening sky beckoned her. She gave little thought to the lengthening shadows. For a second, she had an unexpected sensation that someone was watching her, and she stopped. She felt a shiver of fear. But when she looked around, she saw only the young boys whose job it was to light the gas lanterns that brightened the dark nights.

She walked without thinking, with no thought as to where she was going. But she wasn't surprised when she found herself at Lucas Hawthorne's club.

For one long second her fingers curled around the ornate twists of the wrought-iron gate. A blue-black slate walkway, lined with perfectly tended gardens, led up to the massive front door. Nightingale's Gate appeared to be nothing more tawdry than the beautiful and refined home of a wealthy family. But it was in the wrong neighborhood, not to mention that the statue of a man kissing the long, graceful neck of a scantily clad woman on a carved granite bench announced to all who cared to notice that this was not an ordinary residence.

She told herself to leave. Her life had shifted precariously after her encounter with Clark, and the grand jury had left her profoundly shaken. She was a professional. She had no business seeing anyone when she was in such an emotional state. But she couldn't seem to stop herself.

A strong fragrance hit her when the front door pulled open. Mildly sweet, but musky. Somehow foreign.

Brutus gestured her toward the grand salon, but they were stopped by a staggering man who came up the walkway and demanded entrance. Brutus didn't look happy, and Alice didn't wait around to see what happened.

Inside the main room, the aroma was even stronger, drawing her in. A piano player performed in the corner, nothing outrageous or flashy. Rather a beautiful piece that was cheerful and refined. When she had arrived before, she had barely noticed her surroundings. Today she took in the high-ceilinged room, the paneled walls, the gleaming hardwood floor, several closed double doors that led off to who knew where. Then there was the loft office she had been to before with its plush leather and fine-grained woods.

The thought that this completely inappropriate gentlemen's club seemed more a haven away from the bustling streets of downtown than a place of decadence surprised her. And for the first time Alice wondered just what went on in this house of ill repute.

But whatever surprise she felt melted away at the sight of Lucas standing at the long oak and brass bar, a beautiful woman draped over his arm, the mirror behind the counter reflecting their image. The women pressed her ample breasts against his arm, and Alice felt embarrassment surge to her cheeks.

Lucas Hawthorne was well known for escorting an assortment of beautiful women around the Puritan confines of proper Boston. Rarely, Alice had heard, was he seen with the same woman twice, though each of them were supposedly very much the same.

Women of elegant beauty, generous curves. And fast reputations.

They dined at the best restaurants in the area, attended the opera, graced the symphony, sitting in box seats next to the mayor and his wife, or the governor and his mother. It was said that Lucas appeared to relish the snubs, rather than being reprimanded by them. Perhaps because those very same men lined his pockets with generous amounts of coin when they attended his notorious gentlemen's club.

How often had she heard her father lament this very fact? Too many times to count. And based on the crowd there now, she couldn't say that the murder charge splashed across the newspapers had made a dent in his business.

But Lucas seemed aware of no one else besides the woman on his arm. He cupped her chin and kissed her on the forehead. Not a proper, sweet kiss, rather one filled with promise.

Alice felt her cheeks grow warmer with those strange feelings she had experienced at the Widow James's home. Jealousy? Or was it disgust? The man was two steps away from jail, his life hung in the balance, and he laughed and carried on as if he wanted to make sure he savored every last decadence before he lost.

Seconds later Lucas extricated himself from the woman's embrace. The drunken man in the foyer still had Brutus's attention, leaving Alice to stand alone, watching Lucas as he picked up a crystal glass slightly filled with an amber-colored liquid. He stood at the bar looking down into his glass for long minutes. Revelry swirled around him, the woman now cozying up to the other men in the room. But Lucas seemed oblivious to it all.

Alice stood there and watched, unable to look away or call out to him. In that moment, much like those few minutes when he had first been let out of jail, he looked vulnerable—as if there were more to him than the laughter and wild rebelliousness.

Yet again, she felt something stir deep inside her, something primitive. Something she did her best to keep well hidden.

"Hey, boss!"

Alice jumped at the sound of Brutus calling across the room.

"Your lawyer lady is here."

Lucas looked up, and their gazes caught in the murky mirror. For a second, his eyes were bleak. But the second passed, and the bleakness swept away until only bright blue remained.

Slowly he turned. "Hello, lawyer lady," he said in his best molasses-smooth drawl. He picked up the crystal. "Can I get you a drink?"

"No, thank you."

Lucas leaned back against the bar and studied Alice. Her tone was prim, and she clutched her satchel in front of her like a shield, making him smile. As frequently happened, the smile made her mood worsen.

"Are you sure?" he asked. "Just a sip. It might ease those stiff shoulders of yours. Or would you like me to rub them?"

He could all but see offense snake down her spine as she assimilated his words.

Everyone else in the room laughed.

"It looks like it would take more than a rub to loosen up that stiffness," one man called out with a cackle.

"Looks like she needs them both," cried another. "A brandy *and* a good rub."

"Enough," Lucas said, standing away from the bar, his voice decisive and commanding.

The men glanced at Lucas warily, then swiveled back around on their stools and resumed their drinking.

She started across the room toward him. "If you said sit or roll over, would they do that, too?" she asked with a scoff.

Lucas raised a brow. Her mood was decidedly bad. "Why, Miss Kendall, I never would have guessed you had a sense of humor."

"I don't."

"That's right. You are serious, professional, and nothing if not disapproving of such goings-on as you see here."

"Speaking of *here*, that reminds me. I have a question."

She closed the distance between them, and he didn't like how glad he was to see her. All traces of humor evaporated, and he swore softly. He could hardly fathom how little control he had whenever he was around her. Never before had he been at the mercy of his body. Had she not pulled back when she had that day in her office, no doubt he would have taken her right there—probably on the desk. Though truth be told, his only regret was that he hadn't.

Damn those innocent eyes.

Unaware of what he was thinking, Alice came closer. But when she stopped in front of him and spoke, all images of desks and legs entwined died a quick death.

"What is that smell?" she demanded, waving her hand in front of her nose.

Lucas stiffened, and he stepped back. "What smell?"

She gestured through the room. "It's everywhere."

"Ah, that. It's a Middle Eastern incense. It's meant to relax you. Combine that with a drink, and you have the perfect combination to wash a man's worries away. Are you sure you don't want a brandy?"

"Don't try to liquor me up, Mr. Hawthorne."

" 'Liquor you up,' " he repeated, his brow furrowed in disbelief. "God, I can't remember the last time I heard that phrase. Maybe from my mother." Instantly he groaned.

"What's wrong?"

"Nothing. I just remembered that my mother wants to show me some paint samples. No doubt they are red or bright green, or a flashy yellow."

"Paint for what?"

"I'm renovating the town house next door for her."

He glanced over to a stack of papers lying out on the bar, along with an artist's rendering of what the finished structure would look like. He felt Alice's sudden, very keen interest, saw the way she reached out slowly, as if holding her breath, and traced the gracefully sculpted fence around what would one day be gardens.

"Do you like it?" he asked.

"It's wonderful," she said with awe, though he noted a hint of sadness in her tone. "Doesn't your mother already have a home? Hawthorne House, isn't it?"

"Yes," he muttered. "But no, she is not living there at present. She has moved in with me."

"Here?" Her head snapped back and she stared at him in disbelief. "In a gentlemen's club?"

"It's temporary," he stated with a scowl. "Though temporary has added up to three very long months. But as soon as I get the place habitable, she'll be packed up and relocated," he added, rubbing his eyebrows with the fingers of one hand. "That is unless my father finally comes to his senses and cajoles my mother back home."

He heard the edge in his tone at the mention of his father. Alice must have heard it, too, because her expression changed, and she looked at him oddly.

"Don't you like your father?" she asked.

"Let's just say we don't see eye to eye on many things."

Her face creased with disapproval. "He's your father," she stated, as prim as a schoolteacher. "Someone you should love and respect."

"Just like you do?"

Her shoulders came back. "I do love and respect my father. I admire him a great deal."

"Save your speeches for the jury."

Alice harrumphed. "Speaking of juries, they are going to want to know the exact nature of the business you carry on here at Nightingale's Gate."

"What do you mean?"

"I had assumed this was a club where men of means could gamble and drink."

"It is."

"Then why all the barely dressed women? I've begun to wonder if this place isn't really a brothel."

He wasn't sure if he was amused or furious. Though he knew he shouldn't be. But it had been years since anyone had questioned how far the women of his establishment would go. Everyone knew. The men who tested the boundaries received a lesson they would not soon forget. No one toyed with the women of Nightingale's Gate.

With tight control, he uttered his response. "Do you really think I would have my mother living in a brothel?"

She didn't answer.

"I am many things, Miss Kendall," he said coolly, "but not a whoremonger. I offer drinking, gambling, and dancing girls, not prostitutes. Men can look, but not touch."

If anything, Alice looked relieved, as if she had been testing the waters and praying for the right answer.

"More than that," he couldn't help adding unkindly, "it is

a place where men can come to sit in peace and quiet and enjoy a fine brandy, a cigar, and good conversation without being interrupted or harped at by a wife or child."

This part of the answer didn't please her nearly as well.

"Not all wives would harp or nag," she snapped. "In fact, some wives could be boon companions. A partner or helpmeet."

"When it comes to marriage, Miss Kendall, a man isn't thinking about a *boon companion*. He wants a woman who can take care of his home and family. A woman who will give him children and love them."

"I would give him children, and I would love him!"

The words burst out of her so loudly that everyone in the bar turned to look. Instantly she grew mortified, and Lucas studied her. If he didn't know better, he would think she was on the verge of crying.

"Alice," he began.

But the caring in his tone dried her tears, and her chin rose a notch.

"I'm speaking hypothetically, of course."

He studied her. "Are you?"

"Yes. But what is not hypothetical is the nightingale mark on the victim's body," she added crisply. "Please tell me about your ring."

Talk of women and children was forgotten. With a bang, he set down the crystal tumbler, his tall form towering over her.

"I told you, I haven't seen it in months."

"Though I suppose you don't have proof of that."

He shrugged.

"Did you report it lost or stolen?"

He didn't answer.

Her eyes narrowed. "So, you have no proof, not even a police report of stolen property."

"Nope. Regardless, they can't prove that I still have it."

Her amber gaze ignited with ire. "If I'm not mistaken,

they can find enough witnesses to prove that you owned it. And unless you can prove that it was stolen, or that it was not in your possession the night of the murder, you might as well go to the gallows and hang yourself!"

He stepped closer, too close, his stance threatening. Most men, not to mention women, would have moved back. Not Alice.

"I can't prove that I lost the ring, which means you can't prove it either. So you'll just have to do what you have been hired to do. Find some other way to get me acquitted."

"That's easy for you to say."

"You seem the sort that likes a challenge."

"Maybe you're right," she came back at him, her face pulled into wry lines. "But what I really want to know is why you want me as your lawyer. What is the real reason?"

He debated the wisdom of his answer. "For many reasons," he offered.

He studied her, then stepped closer. He could feel how she set her stance, forcing herself not to move back. "As I already told you, there's the benefit of your being a respectable woman. And yes, you are smart and good at what you do. But most of all, you're not afraid of me. The jury will see that, too." He gave a little laugh. "You're also not impressed by me. I admire that. For the first time I need someone, and I don't like it one bit. But I'm not fool enough to risk my life because you make me crazy at every turn. I'm smart enough to see that you truly are my saving grace in all this muddle."

Her breath caught as if he had read her very thoughts. With his strong fingers, he gently took her chin and tilted her head until their eyes met. "You aren't thinking about quitting on me now, are you?" he asked softly.

Alice realized she had been considering just that. Too much in her life had turned upside down. Clark. Her father's disapproval. The ring.

The realization that she had been inches from giving up stunned her. Because regardless of her concerns about what society thought of her, she couldn't resist the way her blood rushed through her veins at the idea of getting in front of a judge and jury.

She wanted to win, for reasons that had nothing to do with the way Lucas Hawthorne made her feel. She wanted to be something more than Walker Kendall's daughter, or Harry Kendall's niece. She wanted to succeed.

She realized as well that she couldn't rely on what she had done in the past. She had to prove herself now—prove that she could do this. And she would.

A beautifully elegant woman came down the stairs, drawing everyone's attention. Her skin was creamy, her gray eyes soft. She had white hair pulled up from her face, demure, elegant.

Alice knew on sight that this wasn't one of Lucas's women. Though it wasn't her age or her attire that made Alice so certain. It was the way she carried herself. At ease with the world around her, and in charge of her destiny.

This could only be Emmaline Hawthorne.

The woman smiled at everyone in the room, said hello to the bartender, and even knew the name of the scantily clad girl who had been hanging on her son's arm.

"Hello, Mrs. Hawthorne," they called out in return.

"Emmaline, please," the older woman said kindly but sternly, as if somehow the Mrs. and the Hawthorne bothered her.

The others went back to their drinks. Emmaline found her son and started toward him. Her stride hesitated at the sight of Alice, but then a look of determination came across her features.

"You must be Alice Kendall," she said, taking her hand in both of hers. "I was hoping I would have an opportunity to meet you, though I had my doubts since both Lucas and

Grayson are doing everything in their power to keep me out of the main room and off the streets. I had more freedom when I lived at Hawthorne House, and I had none then!"

"She used to be demure," Lucas said with a wry grin. "Anyone who knew her would have called her ethereal. Now we call her our resident pit bull." He tsked in mock severity. "You've been spending too much time around Sophie."

"Don't blame this on dear Sophie. I am simply finding myself again, as well you know."

"Yes, but if I weren't such a respectful and devoted son, I might be inclined to ask what you have found in the three months you've been looking."

Alice's eyes went wide. Emmaline only chuckled.

"Moreover," he continued, "I hardly call free reign of Nightingale's Gate, a carriage at your disposal, and daily excursions to who knows where, restrictions on your movements."

"True enough. But I don't like the idea of being relegated to the town house next door to live. I like being here." She gave a grand sweeping gesture to the room that was rapidly filling with customers. "Where life is pulsating."

"*Pulsating?* Mother, please," Lucas said with a grimace.

Emmaline laughed again. Alice couldn't help herself, she laughed as well at the prudish look on the very *un*prudish Mr. Hawthorne's face.

Turning to Alice, Emmaline said, "Such a beautiful laugh you have."

Flustered, Alice didn't know what to say.

"And modest, too."

Emmaline hooked their arms together as if they had known each other a lifetime. "I like you. I can tell already."

"Well, thank you, Mrs. Hawthorne."

"Emmaline," she corrected, then pulled Alice back toward the bar. "Come see something. My son has been less than obliging to my choices of paints and wallpapers."

Lucas followed. "Your son can't see painting walls colors that will shock the system," he clarified.

Emmaline snorted, surprising Alice.

"Yes," Emmaline sighed dramatically. "He wants cream, I want red. He wants demure hardwood floors, I want red and black marble. I want exotic plants, he wants—"

"A beautiful fence surrounding flower gardens."

It was Alice who had finished the sentence, and Lucas looked at her in surprise. Emmaline eyed her speculatively. "I'd say our Alice here has a fondness for fences and flowers."

"For gardens filled with roses," Alice whispered on a self-conscious laugh. Then she shook herself. "Regardless of what goes in those gardens, the house will be beautiful."

"Then darling, you should live there. I have no doubt that it will be lovely when it's finished." Suddenly she grew serious; the joy was gone, and her eyes grew distant. "But I've lived a lifetime of lovely and demure, and I never felt very much alive. I am ready to live now, to the fullest. And I want to do it any way I choose." She blinked, then focused on her son. "Is that so wrong?"

They looked at each other, and Alice felt extremely uncomfortable witnessing this private moment.

"No, Mother," he said with sincere feeling in his voice. "That isn't so wrong." He hooked his arm around her shoulders. "And I will do whatever I can to see that you are happy."

Emmaline looked directly at Alice. "There are many reasons why I know my son didn't kill that woman, Miss Kendall."

Alice saw the tension flash through Lucas.

"But the biggest reason of all," Emmaline continued, "is that my dear son has always helped women who are in need."

The statement stunned Alice. Moreover, she found it hard to believe. He ran a men's club with dancing girls, after all.

As if understanding her thoughts, Lucas cut Emmaline off. "Mother, enough."

"But it's true."

He shook his head and smiled, that easy quirk of lips, as if he didn't have a care in the world. "My mother is a kind and poetic soul." He kissed her temple with a fond chuckle. "And I guess it's to be expected that she has romantic ideas about who her son really is."

Emmaline's face fell, though if it was from disappointment that she was wrong, or disappointment that he could be so glib, Alice didn't know.

Emmaline turned to Alice. "Don't let him fool you, Miss Kendall. For reasons I have never understood, he spends a great deal of time and energy making people think the worst of him. He is a better man than he makes out to be. Prove that to the courts, and get my son acquitted." She hesitated. "You can do that, can't you?"

The look on the woman's face was both pleading and determined. Alice had the sudden thought that a conviction might kill her.

But to prove that he was a better man than people thought?

"I will do everything I can to see that your son walks free."

Lucas met her gaze, and she knew he understood the underlying meaning. Whether he was a better man or not wasn't at issue. Only the crime mattered.

"But do you think you can do it?" Emmaline persisted.

Silence surrounded them as doubts and concerns swam through her mind for the first time in years. She cursed Clark for making her doubt herself. But deep down she knew it had as much to do with her stumble with the grand jury hearing as with Clark's rejection.

But even knowing that didn't help. Could she do this? Could she truly succeed as someone else besides her father's daughter or her uncle's niece?

The thought was terrifying—but amazingly exhilarating

at the same time. She *could* do this. She would show them all.

With that, she reached back and squeezed the woman's hands. "I believe I can."

Chapter Nine

"What was I thinking?"

Alice sat at a long wooden table in the courthouse basement, mountains of case files scattered across the expanse, a dim gaslight flickering on the wall.

With a thud, she dropped her head onto *Commonwealth vs. Rupert Hennesey*—yet another of her father's cases that he had won in the last five years. The prosecution was flawless. As usual.

Alice banged her head a few times on the table, before sitting back and groaning. Her father was brilliant. Not that she hadn't already known that.

But first thing that morning she had gone to the courthouse and requested every file prosecuted by her father during the last five years in hopes of finding a chink in his armor. Some strategy aspect in which he was consistently weak.

To make matters worse, she had run into Grayson in the courthouse stairwell the minute she arrived. He would be informed of her progress regarding the case, or else. And who could blame him after the grand jury debacle.

So she had told him what she was doing and why. Satisfaction flowed through her at his look. He had been impressed. She had made one terrible mistake, but she wouldn't make another. They had also made plans to meet regularly to discuss the case.

But her satisfaction had evaporated incrementally with

each year of her father's trials she went through. As soon as she finished 1892, she had requested '91, then '90, until she had read every file as far back as '88. The results shouldn't have surprised her, and in any other circumstances she simply would have been proud.

There were no chinks in her father's armor as far as she could see. The Commonwealth rarely lost cases, and they lost none of the trials her father personally prosecuted. He was a formidable opponent. Her only hope lay in the fact that Clark was not her father.

Clark. Alice gave a tiny shudder. After a night of sleepless reeling that he was not attracted to her, she had woken in the morning with one very clear thought. How dare he not be attracted to her! She was smart, kind, and, quite frankly, not half bad to look at. He'd be lucky to have her. At least that was what she had been telling herself for the last several hours.

Thirty minutes later, she left the courthouse, her mind swirling with ideas on how she could possibly win this case. The sun glowed orange in the distance as it sank in the west. She knew it was nearly five and that by six her uncle would have supper on the table. But she wasn't in the mood for company.

Wasting a nickel she didn't have, she bought a frankfurter from a street vendor and ate as she walked home, thinking. She wove her way through the narrow streets of Beacon Hill, barely noticing the violets and petunias that struggled to stay alive in the heat, or the smell of summer-scorched cobbles as she approached the Kendalls' traditional redbrick town house on Cedar Lane Way. Still she was thinking. After slipping around the side yard, she went straight to her cottage rather than greet her family in the main house.

And by the time she finally fell into bed, she was still thinking. Her father's cases were perfect. Could they be too perfect?

The thought surprised her and made her feel guilty in

turn. Her father was a wonderful man, good and honest, and he would do nothing against the law.

First thing the next morning, Alice was in a hurry to get to work. She had woken up, the thought of Clark bringing only a grimace of remembered pain, and knew she needed a plan of action.

After dashing through her ablutions, she would have been on her way had her father not stuck his head out the back door, his napkin clenched in his hand as if he had been in the middle of eating when he saw her, and called out.

With a groan, Alice pivoted on her booted heel and headed for the house.

"Where were you last night?" he demanded, his forehead twitching with anger.

"At home."

"I didn't see any lights on."

Just then her uncle entered the room.

"I came in early and fell asleep. Good morning, Uncle Harry."

"Good morning, love. It looks to be a fine day."

"Beautiful," she agreed.

Max arrived next, in a hurry, late for the bank as usual. "Morning, little sis." He leaned over and pecked her on the cheek. "How goes the big case?"

"Good. In fact—"

"Is anyone listening to me?" her father demanded.

Max laughed wryly. "I'd recognize that tone of voice anywhere. You're on your own, Alice." Then he grabbed a roll and dashed out the door.

Wistfully, Alice watched him go.

"If you came home early," Walker barked, "then why weren't you at supper?"

Dragging her attention back, she explained. "I was exhausted. Besides, I'm an adult. You can't keep tabs on my every move."

"I can as long as you live under my roof!"

She went very still.

Harry muttered a curse. "Now you've done it, Walker."

"Father, I don't live under your roof."

"In the backyard, same difference."

"I am a practicing attorney now. As are you. How many times have you worked on a case late into the night, or through the night? How many suppers have you missed?"

They eyed each other in the spacious breakfast room.

"I am not sure what has gotten into you lately," he said, his tone cool, "and while you might have a degree in the law, you are still my daughter. And you will do as I say."

"I *will do as you say*?" she asked incredulously.

"Yes! I am your father whose responsibility it is to see to your welfare—which is not well served by you gallivanting around town defending murderers."

Alice nearly choked.

"That's right," he stated ominously, "I heard that you are still on the Hawthorne case. I will not have it, Alice. Do you hear me?"

Her head came back. "Yes, I hear you." She set her satchel down on the table with an ominous clatter of brass tacks on wood. Her heart pounded, and something she couldn't name pushed her on. "Now you hear me. Yes, I have committed my services to the Hawthorne case. No, I am not backing down, and I will not be intimidated by you." Blood rushed through her ears, but she couldn't seem to stop. "And furthermore, I am going to win."

She couldn't have surprised her father more had she stripped naked and danced on the table. She could see it in his face. She could also see when the surprise shifted, melding into anger. But she was past caring.

"What evidence you have is shaky at best. On top of that, you know juries better than anyone, Father. They'll want to know why a man of means would risk all to kill a prostitute, then mark her with a ring that everyone in town knows he wears. You know no jury in the land will convict him unless you can provide them with a motive. A motive! And the last I heard, you don't have one."

"I see you've learned your lessons well," he replied tightly. "I never thought I'd see the day when my daughter lectured *me*."

Walker tossed down his napkin, then strode angrily from the room.

Her uncle sighed. "Well, that didn't go so badly."

Alice half groaned, half laughed. "It was horrible."

She picked up her satchel and headed for the door. Harry followed.

"Alice."

"Yes?"

He studied her, his gaze intense. "I hope you know what you're doing."

She smiled and walked back to him. As she had done a thousand times in her life, she wrapped her arms around his middle and pressed her head to his heart. "I love you, you know that, don't you?"

He stroked her hair and sighed. "I do."

She pushed away and looked him in the eye. "You trust me, right?"

He sighed and nodded. "Yes, that, too."

"Good. Because I do know what I'm doing."

"All right." He wrapped his arm around her shoulders and walked with her to the front door.

Minutes later, Alice arrived at her first stop for the day. The coroner's office. She didn't imagine she would learn anything new, but she wanted to question the man and make sure there were no more surprises.

The place had a pungent smell of chemicals and death. It was all she could do to hold back a reflexive gag.

"Can I help you?" a tall, thin man asked.

His brow was deeply and permanently furrowed, his thin lips held in a firm, disapproving line.

"Yes, I am Miss Alice Kendall, esquire," she added with emphasis on her lawyer's title, "and I am here on behalf of my client—"

"No ladies allowed."

"Ah, but lawyers are, and I am a lawyer."

"But you're a lady first."

"So kind of you to notice," she said dryly. "But every client's attorney is entitled to question commonwealth officials over their findings. You are an official, are you not?"

"Yes."

"And you do having findings, true?"

His furrowed brow furrowed even more. "Correct."

"Then I am entitled to ask you questions on my client's behalf."

He stood belligerently, not relenting.

"Of course, if I need to, I can go to the presiding judge and force you to speak to me."

"You do that," he said, and started away.

That's not what she had hoped for. Her mind raced.

"Fine, I'll head on over to the courthouse. Of course, I will feel compelled to mention that you have more than one corpse back there," she leaned sideways to get a better look into the back room, "in varied states of . . . decomposition. Not the best method, I imagine, to keep body parts and evidence separate."

That got his attention. He turned back with a fierce scowl.

"What do you want to know?" he bit out.

"I want to see the mark on the victim in the *Commonwealth vs. Lucas Hawthorne*."

"Good God, lady! The woman has been dead for weeks! What do you think I do, have a bunch of dead people lying around here?"

She looked in the back again and shrugged. "Hard to say."

"The victim is dead and buried."

"Hmmm. Then show me the drawings you made of the mark."

"Lady, I already put that in the police report."

Her shoulders stiffened. "The police report?" she asked. "There is a police report that contains a drawing of this ring mark?"

The man grew decidedly uncomfortable. "I don't remember. No, actually, I'm thinking of a different case."

"Are you sure? Failure to disclose that information would be a federal offense, sir."

"I didn't hold anything back, do you hear me!"

Alice looked at him closely. "Okay. Then please draw the design for me now."

He looked as if he wouldn't do it, but at the last minute he snapped up a piece of paper and a pencil and sketched out the design. A nightingale caught in flight.

Without warning, a chill ran down her spine.

"Are you sure you didn't give this information to my unc— Rather, to the police?"

"I told you, I didn't think of it until I was in the grand jury hearing. Now I have work to do, lady. If you have any more questions, petition the court. Good day."

He marched to the back room and slammed the door shut. Feeling uneasy, her thoughts in a jumble, she left the coroner's office. As much as she wanted to go to her office and make sense of her thoughts, she knew she had to make one more stop. The crime scene.

The alley was narrow, lined with doors leading from the backs of four-story buildings. A strangeness came over her. There were no signs of mayhem, no signs that a woman had died on the hard dirt.

Unlit lanterns on lampposts dotted the way. Not many, only a few, placed here and there, that would be lit by lantern boys when it grew dark.

Continuing down the rutted road, Alice studied the backs of the buildings. Countless doors had access to the alley, and if it wasn't a door, there were high walls with thick wooden gates leading into narrow gardens. She went all the way to the end, then glanced back. She wasn't sure what she was looking for, but nothing leaped out at her.

After a moment, she headed around to the front. First, she came to the brothel listed in the crime report as being the victim's place of employment. The Flamingo. Next she came to Nightingale's Gate. A circumstantial piece of evidence, but given enough pieces, a good lawyer could make a case. Then, of course, there was the issue of the nightingale ring.

Back at her office Alice put her hat and gloves aside without much thought, then got to work. She had to make sense of what went on that night.

She reread the crime-scene report, the arrest record, the notes from the district attorney's office, and compared them to what she had seen in the alley. Concentrating, Alice drew up a diagram of the alley and the surrounding streets. She marked the spot where the woman had been slain. She also noted the gentlemen's club only steps away.

Something seemed wrong. But what?

Alice used a dotted line to show the alleged path the victim took from the brothel at the end of the block to the murder location one building down the way.

Still something didn't make sense.

Thumbing through the police reports, she scanned the information she had read and reread until she knew it by heart.

Lucille Rouge left the Flamingo at midnight, then she made her way down the alley. The eyewitness put the murder at a quarter to one in the morning. Which meant forty-five minutes passed between the time Lucille left work and the time she was killed.

What had gone on for that amount of time?

Alice glanced at the short distance on the map and felt certain that either Lucille hadn't left the Flamingo as reported, or she had gone someplace else first. But if so, where?

Alice jotted the questions down on a separate piece of paper.

Next, she made a timeline. At the top she wrote out Lucas's statement of being in his room all evening. At the bottom, she put the estimated time of death. The blank space between the two told of all the work she had to do to fill in the details of what had taken place that night.

But she would fill them in. The only chance she had of winning was to anticipate the prosecution's every move.

The thought reminded her of that niggling feeling that she was missing something from the five years of her father's cases she had gone over. But still, it wouldn't come.

Shaking her head, she tacked each of the pieces of paper up on the smooth white wall that most lawyers would have used to display their awards.

It was while staring at the disconcerting facts before her that someone knocked on the door.

Lucas entered the office and watched as Alice sat back in her creaky chair and looked at him. She wore the same type of unimaginative woman's suit like a prickly shield, with a white blouse underneath. Had he not held her in his arms, he wouldn't suspect the generous curves that she hid so well. His senses jolted at the remembered feel of her in his arms. The bossy lawyer lady had become shy, holding on tight, wrapping her arms around his shoulders as if she didn't want to let go.

Though she had, abruptly, as if she had needed to let go fast. As if holding tight was more than improper—rather weak.

Her blonde hair twisted in a knot at the back of her head. Everything looked the same, except the shadows beneath her eyes, as if she hadn't slept.

Did he keep her awake, or his case?

He could see that same flash of darkness in her eyes that he saw every time he appeared. Was it awareness? When she saw him, did she feel the same heated desire he felt? Or was she trying to assess if he could have killed someone?

The thought made him feel raw inside. Arrogance and pride surged. He could no longer deny that he wanted her to desire him, not question him.

He scoffed silently. Wouldn't Grayson have a fine laugh over the fact that after years of putting walls between himself and the women who tried to capture him, now he cursed the walls that Alice had constructed around herself?

He had been forced to concede the point when she had been happy to stay off the case.

Now he wanted to be found innocent. He wanted this finished. But how to help his defense without giving too much away. He knew too much about what went on in the alleyway that night, and he felt a powerless rage that it had happened.

But he wouldn't tell anyone about that night, not even his lawyer. He couldn't. Was it that he really wanted to go down?

Lucas ignored the thought. All that mattered was that he hated seeing that look in this woman's eyes—her wish to believe in him, but not knowing how.

Was it the taste of innocence, as Grayson had suggested?

Having his mother living with him hadn't stirred the emotion. With his mother he felt protective—and put out, he thought with a wry grin. But with this woman lawyer he felt the need to absorb her innocence. Find its meaning.

But more than that, he wanted her to want him. He wanted her to want the man who had tasted the darker aspects of life and didn't know how to give them up.

Could he give it up for her?

For the first time since that day long ago when he started wearing the nightingale's ring, he wanted a taste of purity. And he knew that he would do anything in his power to tear down the wall that Alice had built around herself. He wanted to make love to her, introduce her to the passion that he was certain lay just beneath the surface of her proper veneer.

"Impressive," he stated, instead of saying all the things he was thinking—things that would no doubt send her running for cover. He knew he had to give her time. He had to win her over. Find a way to make her trust him.

The thought made him feel as if his hands were tied. He wasn't used to holding back when he wanted something. But for Alice he would be patient. Rather, as patient as he could.

She tilted her head in confusion.

"The charts and timelines." He motioned to the wall. "It looks like a war room in here."

Confusion disappeared and that obstinate determination he had come to recognize took its place. A general couldn't have looked any fiercer.

"A good analogy, actually," she replied. "This is going to be a war. And our first line of defense is for you to help me fill in all those blank spaces in a way that makes it appear that you couldn't possibly have committed the crime."

"I thought we were trying to prove I'm innocent."

"Unless there are some pieces you haven't bothered to share with me, proving you're innocent isn't likely."

His eyes narrowed.

"Though that hardly matters. All we have to do is make the jury have reasonable doubt. And that, I believe, is realistic."

He sat down in the chair in front of her desk. "How do we do that?"

"You've got to help me understand a few things. Like why this eyewitness would name you if you didn't do it?"

Because he felt certain the woman *had* seen someone in the alley. Someone who had left Nightingale's Gate.

But he didn't say that. He placed his hands on the arm-rests and forced a calm he didn't feel.

"Because she doesn't like my hair. She thought it was too long." He found a smile, swallowing back the bitter taste of such a foolish answer. "Little did she know that all she had to do to get me to cut it was boss me around, badger me nearly to death, then threaten to quit."

Impatient anger sizzled through her eyes. "This is no time for jokes, Mr. Hawthorne."

"Your cheeks are red, Miss Kendall. Why is that?"

She cleared her throat uncomfortably, and he was sure she was fighting off a scorching blush.

"Do you know how arousing you are when you get like this?"

He expected a sputter or a stammer. Instead, she rose from her seat.

"Quite frankly, I don't give a flying flip if you land in jail for the rest of your life."

He stood slowly, planted his hands on her desk, and leaned close. He watched the wariness flare in her eyes—he also saw the stubbornness that wouldn't let her back away. He would have smiled had he not wanted to curse at this horrible, tangled mess.

"But you got me into this," she continued through clenched teeth, "and I'm not going to let you sit back and ruin it because of your arrogance and your desire to dance with danger. One of these days you'll lose. And I'm not interested in being on the dance floor with you when your number is up."

"Tell me, Miss Kendall, since you're such an expert on personalities, if I dance with danger, why do you work so hard to avoid it?"

"I don't avoid it. If I did, would I be sitting here with you?"

He chuckled softly, and let his gaze roam deliberately over her body. He had felt enough of her for his imagination to have plenty to work with. She flushed angrily, and he could tell she itched to cross her arms on her chest. "Very true," he conceded.

It took a second for her to manage her thoughts. She felt much too hot and cornered. The smell of him was wildly rugged and clean. A tantalizing mixture of long grasses and soap.

"Stop looking at me like that," she said testily.

"What way is that?"

"The way that has nothing to do with the case," she snapped.

His smile grew crooked, and he stepped back.

"Good. Now," with effort, she dragged her gaze away and looked at the papers on the wall, "what I know so far is that Lucille Rouge, a woman who works only yards from your gentlemen's club, was strangled to death in the alleyway behind Nightingale's Gate."

She watched him as she made the statement, looking for some sign of emotion over the words, but his expression remained unreadable.

"That is what I've been led to believe," he agreed.

"You probably also heard that the tips of the woman's fingers were snipped away."

This time he grimaced, though barely.

She drummed her nails against the desk. "My theory is that the victim scratched her killer."

"What good would it do to cut off her fingers?"

"So that detectives wouldn't think to search out a man who was scratched. We could have proved you weren't scratched, had we known. You are unscratched, aren't you?"

He held his arms wide. "Smooth as a baby's bu—"

"Good enough," she interrupted.

"I'd be happy to show you." He reached for his shirt fastenings.

"Don't bother, Mr. Hawthorne."

His smile grew heated and devilish. "I'm only trying to do my part to prove my innocence, Miss Kendall."

"Thank you. I'll keep that in mind. In the meantime, the scratches are pure speculation on my part. But it is these small details that we have to unearth. The tiniest thing can set this case on a whole new path. So let's start with what we know. The victim: Miss Rouge."

Lucas returned to his seat, and yet again she saw a flicker in his expression.

Regret that he had killed her? Was she fooling herself when she thought he was incapable of killing someone? Or regret that she had been killed? She wanted to know. Because the thought that wouldn't leave her alone was that her father didn't go after innocent men.

"Did Lucille Rouge always walk down that alleyway?"

"Yes."

"How do you know that?"

Alice saw a flicker of surprise in Lucas's expression. But he covered it quickly.

"Everyone knew that Lucille lived one block over. She got to her place from the alley."

"Did you ever see her walking home?"

He shrugged. "On occasion." He seemed to consider his answer, then added, "Actually, I saw her that night."

"Good God! Why didn't you tell me?"

"I was sure it would be misconstrued."

"When did you see her?"

"In the back hallway. She was with Brutus, and she was upset."

Alice couldn't believe what she was hearing. "What was she upset about?"

"That is none of your concern."

Blood hammered in her temples. "Like hell it isn't." The curse didn't even faze her; in fact, she felt like cursing a lot. "Nothing is private for you anymore, mister. If you want me to have any chance of defending you successfully, then I need to know every detail of your life. Where you live, how you live, who you see, and what they say. So once again, why was Miss Rouge upset?"

He eyed her for a moment. "She was pregnant."

Alice dropped her ink pen with a clatter. "Please tell me it wasn't by you."

His jaw tightened. "I've told you I did not have relations with her."

"You also told me you hadn't seen her that night."

He shrugged unapologetically. "Again, I didn't want the information misconstrued. However, the fact remains, I did not have relations with Lucille Rouge."

She heaved a sigh of relief. "Then who got her pregnant?"

"I don't know," he said.

She couldn't tell if he was lying.

"She wouldn't say. I told her I would help her in any way I could." He lowered his head and stared at his boot. "I didn't get the chance."

Was it an act? Was he sincere?

So many questions. Too many questions.

Alice felt her head spin. Because whether he was sincere or not hardly mattered. If her father or Clark found out the victim had been pregnant, they would have the final piece they needed to make a circumstantial case successful. A motive.

Chapter Ten

Alice needed to find enough evidence to build a case for reasonable doubt. She didn't have to prove Lucas didn't do it or that anyone else did. She just had to prove that there was reason to believe that *maybe* he didn't do it.

A frustration for the prosecution. A godsend for the defense.

It was late in the day when Alice left her office and headed for the brothel where Lucille Rouge had been employed before she had been murdered. Yet one more step she had to take to ensure she didn't make any more mistakes. To start with, she needed to find out more about the victim. Then she'd start on the eyewitness.

Evening approached as Alice arrived at the Flamingo, the brothel that was only one door away from Nightingale's Gate. But when she stepped inside, the place might as well have been a world away, given how different it was from Lucas Hawthorne's establishment.

The building was tall and narrow, the entry hall dark and garish, with more red velvet and gold fleck than Alice had seen in a lifetime. Smoked mirrors lined the walls, and even at this early-evening hour, the smell of liquor stung her nose.

A short wiry man came forward. He was dressed in gray trousers, shirtsleeves, and a gold-flecked vest that matched the walls.

"What do ya want?" he demanded, looking her up and down. "We don't need no do-gooders around here trying to convert the girls. So get away with ya!"

"Rest assured, I'm not here to reform anyone. I simply want to talk to the . . . owner of the Flamingo."

"She ain't here." He pushed her toward the door.

"Then I'll wait," even though she didn't want to, at least not if she had to wait anywhere near this man. Not that she was afraid. She wasn't. But he smelled to high heaven of pungent aftershave. Or was it a woman's perfume? Alice shuddered.

"No waitin' allowed."

"Is that in a rule book somewhere?"

He glanced at her, his eyes narrowed. "Are you funnin' me, lady?"

"Far be it from me to *fun* you. But as Lucas Hawthorne's attorney, I must speak to the owner—"

"You're the lady lawyer?" His craggy countenance took a decided turn for the better as his lips cracked open in what she assumed was a smile. "Why didn't ya say so?" He dragged her back inside. "May!" he hollered out, nearly bursting Alice's eardrum. "Lucas's lady lawyer is here!"

A woman of ample girth and the puffiest hair Alice had ever seen appeared at the top of the stairs.

Alice forced a smile. "Yes, I'm Alice Kendall, esquire. I take it you run this place of business."

"Run and own," she stated proudly.

"Well, good. I need to ask you a few questions."

"About time you showed up," the woman barked.

Everyone's a critic.

The woman called May came down the steps. It wasn't until she stood inches away that Alice could see the woman's face. Given the heavy velvet draperies that covered the windows, and the light that barely flickered in the gas sconces, everything had a hazy, softened image—until one got close. No doubt an intentional effect.

But the effect was not needed for this woman who ran a whorehouse. May was beautiful, with flawless skin. She was a large woman, her curves full and luscious rather than fat. Alice couldn't have been more surprised.

"Miss . . ."

"May, just May."

"Yes, fine. May. I need to ask you and your . . . employees about Lucille Rouge and the night she was murdered."

May took a kerchief from her ample breast and pressed the fine linen cloth to her eye. Alice had the fleeting thought that this madam had better manners than she did.

"Poor, poor Lucille. Such a sweet girl. And she was just getting good after we changed her hair."

"Her hair?"

"Yes. She was a mousy brown, didn't get much business. But once we changed her hair to white, white blonde, like yours, in fact, the men loved her." May stepped closer and took a long strand of Alice's hair. "How do you get it to look so natural?"

Alice's mouth fell open before she pulled her hair away self-consciously. "It is natural."

The man from the doorway scoffed.

"It is!" She stopped herself and shook her head. "Though it hardly matters. Could you tell me about Lucille? Who were her friends? Do you have any idea who might have done this?"

"Not Lucas Hawthorne, I can assure you," May stated staunchly. "As to friends, Lucille kept to herself mostly."

"Why is that?"

"Partly because she was just that way. And partly because she was the only girl I have that didn't reside at the Flamingo."

"What do you mean?"

"My girls live here. I take care of them. But Lucille came to me about ten months ago wanting a job. Lived down the way and couldn't make a living anymore cleaning house."

May shrugged. "Call me a softy, but I felt sorry for her. Gave her a job. Let her stay in her own house. She didn't live but a block over."

"Who was the last man . . . she was with?"

May blinked out of her reverie. "Can't say that I remember."

"You don't remember, or you don't want to."

The little man chuckled.

May flashed him a heated glare. "Doesn't matter which, really. Both get you the same answer."

"I'd like an opportunity to question the man. That's all."

"If I told you who visited my establishment I wouldn't have a bit of business left. Sorry, honey, no names."

"I can have you summoned to court."

"Go ahead. But do you think for a minute I'm going to discuss what goes on at the Flamingo? And do you think anyone who has ever been here is going to admit it?"

She had her there.

Alice's mind raced, and in the silence she became aware of women peering down at them. "Then can I talk to your girls?"

Immediately, several gasps sounded through the building, then footsteps hurried away, followed by doors banging closed.

"I think that answers your question."

Alice left minutes later, grumbling. Next on her list, Tawny Green, the eyewitness.

The woman lived close by, but when Alice knocked on the door, she was told gruffly that Tawny lived in the small house at the rear of the property. And no, she couldn't go through the house.

Alice had to work her way around to the back to gain access. Once there, she realized that she was yet again in the same alley where Lucille Rouge had been killed. By now the late-summer sun was nearly gone, and Alice felt a chill race down her spine. She couldn't have been more relieved when the lantern boys appeared, dashing up their ladders to light the fixtures.

Catching her breath, she stood for a moment as the boys worked. Then they were gone. Despite the light, the alley was surprisingly dark, and she couldn't wait to get away. But first she had to talk to Tawny Green.

She knocked once, then again at the wooden door that opened directly into the alley. When finally the door pulled open, a woman answered. She looked young and scared, with bad teeth and hair strangely styled and lips painted a bright shade of red.

"What?" she demanded suspiciously.

"Are you Tawny Green?"

"Who wants to know?"

"I'm Alice Kendall, attorney for Lucas Hawthorne."

She still stood there, her face a blank.

"You know, the man accused of killing Lucille Rouge."

In a burst, the door flew back and a rough-looking man appeared. Heavy jowls lined his face, making his dark eyes look beady. Her nostrils were being put through their paces today, as the smell of sweat and stale liquor made the Flamingo seem appealing.

Alice felt a start of incisive fear, and her stomach roiled. For the first time Alice questioned the wisdom of having gone on this hunt alone.

"Who are you?" he demanded, wiping the back of his meaty hand across his mouth. Food specs dotted his grimy skin.

Yuck, eck, disgusting. A nice diversion from her bone-deep, teeth-chattering panic.

She forced her voice to be steady. "I am Alice Kendall, attorney for—"

"Yeah, yeah. For that Hawthorne fellow. You remember, Tawny."

He said the words harshly, and the girl's vacant gaze flickered with something, perhaps recognition.

"You are listed as the eyewitness," Alice added.

"Yeah, you know," the man said, clamping her on the shoulder. "The murder you saw."

"Yes," she said softly. "Yes, I saw it."

Her gaze flickered with something. Alice realized then that it was horror for what she had seen. Clean this witness up and get her to talk, she would be a good addition to the prosecution's case if she showed that same horror. Alice had to stifle a groan.

"I'd like to ask you a few questions."

It took quite a bit of prodding from the man, but eventually Alice got her answers.

Alice shuddered, leaving as quickly as she could after learning nothing new. The woman had seen Lucas Hawthorne strangle the woman, then flee the scene. She was sure it was him.

Feeling sick and ineffectual, Alice headed down the alley, wanting to get home and take a long, hot bath. She wanted to wash away the memory of such grimy places, of such wasted lives.

She started walking, resisting the urge to run. She stumbled, unable to see the unevenness of the dirt road. The end of the alley beckoned. But she still had several buildings to go when she heard the footsteps. Great. Just what she needed at the end of a very bad day.

She nearly jumped out of her skin when a fancily dressed painted girl stepped out of the darkness. The girl looked up and down, then said, "The last man Lucille was with was Oliver Aldrich. The rich man on Beacon Hill."

Alice had heard the name, knew he was from one of the finest families in Boston.

"Talk to him," the girl pleaded. "And then someone's gotta talk to Cindy Pop."

The name leaped out at her, the name that Clark had assured her had nothing to do with this case. Alice's thoughts hardened at yet more proof that she was being manipulated by her father and Clark.

"Who is Cindy Pop?" she asked.

In the shadows on the opposite side of the alley, a twig snapped. The girl's eyes went wide with fright. Her fingers dug into Alice's forearm.

"You got to talk to Cindy and Aldrich."

Then without another word, she disappeared into the darkness.

Alice stood alone, her heart seeming to have stopped when the distinct sound of footsteps crunched on the dirt and gravel ground and they were too heavy to be the girl returning. Alice couldn't seem to move much less think.

The footsteps grew closer. With a start, she cried out and started to run. The footsteps followed, quickly gaining on her. The square of cobbled street that could be seen at the end of the alley appeared remote. She knew she wouldn't make it.

But just as suddenly as she made the realization, she saw the back door to Nightingale's Gate. If only she could make it that far.

Her lungs screamed, her foot caught in her dress. When she came to the door, her fingers fumbled with the latch. Belatedly, she realized it was locked.

She nearly cried out her despair as she heard the footsteps right behind her. But in that moment the door pulled open.

She heard the footsteps slide to a halt. Drunken revelers staggered out into the alley, arms locked over shoulders, the men singing.

The song broke off at the sight of Alice.

"Lookie here, boys."

It took a second to realize that one of the men was the awful Howard she had met in Nightingale's Gate. His gaze cleared, then grew licentious.

"Excuse me," Alice managed, trying to squeeze through the doorway.

Two of the men cackled. Howard put his hand out to stop her.

"You go on," he said to his friends, eyeing her speculatively.

She didn't like the sound of that. With a speed that surprised even her, she ducked underneath his arm and bolted inside. Before he knew what hit him, she slammed the door shut and threw the bolt home. When she finally opened her eyes, the tall, harsh-looking man was standing there.

Her yelp echoed in the long, tiled hallway as she wondered where he had come from.

"Brutus," she gasped. "You scared me to death!"

He didn't answer her at first, only stared. "I heard some commotion," he finally said. "I'll get the boss."

She couldn't think of anyone just that second whom she wanted to see more than Lucas Hawthorne. And that was ridiculous. Moreover, she was a lawyer, a professional, and the last thing she needed was for her client to see her in such a foolish state. And for all her efforts, what had she achieved?

Naught. Nil. Nothing.

But then she remembered the girl in the alleyway. No, she hadn't come away empty-handed. She had two people to track down to find out what they could tell her. It was best that she get home, go to bed, and regroup in the morning.

"No need to get Mr. Hawthorne. If you'll just guide me to the front door and perhaps hail me a hired hack, I'll be fine."

Brutus debated.

"Really, based on the noises coming from inside, I'd say Nightingale's Gate is in full swing, and your employer doesn't need to be bothered by me."

Brutus grunted, apparently in agreement, then led her through a series of hallways, the sound of voices and laughter getting louder with each step they took, until they came out in a foyer just off the grand salon. Peering inside, she could see that patrons packed the place.

For half a second, Alice stood mesmerized. She watched the finely dressed men who easily could have been at a gala social event, and the beautifully clad women. Which reminded her of her own less-than-beautiful gown, not to mention the recently ripped hem.

Without warning she caught sight of her reflection. She would have yelped her fright if her breath hadn't already been startled out of her. Dear God, she looked a wreck.

Lowering her head in hopes of no one noticing her, she hurried after Brutus who made his way through the throng of guests like a snowplow in winter.

But they hadn't gotten halfway across the gleaming floor when an all too familiar voice called out.

"Brutus."

The tone was as much questioning as a command.

Drat it all.

She practically ran into the granite wall of the massive man's back when he stopped abruptly. "Keep going, keep going," she whispered frantically.

Brutus looked down at her as if she had lost her mind.

"Yes, boss?"

"Bring our guest upstairs."

Alice considered making a dash for the front door, but she wasn't quite ready to face the dark alone. Lucas seemed the lesser of two evils.

By the time she arrived at the office, she realized she was shaking and she had to force herself to be calm.

"What's wrong?" he asked.

She had a sneaking suspicion that it had something to do with the shuddering fear she had felt in the alley. "It's been a rough night," she quipped, though even she could hear the quiver in her voice.

He came forward and stopped just in front of her. His eyes filled with concern as he took in her appearance. His finger twined with one long strand of her tousled hair that had come loose. "Something happened. Tell me what," he demanded.

The kindness in his voice threatened her trumped up bravado. But she held on, fought against the sudden threat of tears that burned in her eyes. Only sissies cried. She had learned that lesson well growing up in a house full of men.

She fought off tears with a scowl. "Nothing happened."

Lucas only stepped closer. "Alice?"

His voice rumbled through her mind like a caress, making her want to give in, but she couldn't.

"All right, if you must know," she said, with a levity she didn't feel. "I had an awkward moment in the alleyway, is all."

He looked at her hair and his expression grew fierce. He clutched her arms. "Did someone attack you?"

Suddenly it was too much. The threat of tears resurfaced, and she cursed.

But she was saved from embarrassment when they heard the sound of two feminine voices growing nearer.

"Damn. It's my mother and Sophie."

In a flash, he took her hand and pulled her unceremoniously through a door that she hadn't noticed before that lay flush with the dark wood wainscoting. They hurried through, and just as the door closed, Alice heard his mother call out to him.

"Lucas, where are you?"

But they didn't stop. Lucas pulled her down a long hallway, up a flight of stairs, then into another office.

"Now tell me, were you attacked?"

The room was expansive, with leather-bound books and all the things a man seemed to need in the place where he conducts business. Lots of hard, dark wood. A humidor, a decanter, and crystal glasses. Not so different from the office downstairs. Only this one was private.

"Alice, tell me what happened."

Alice felt the surge of fear again, and she started to pace.

"I think someone was following me as I walked down the alley."

"What the hell were you doing back there?" His eyes blazed with anger, but with something else, as well. A protectiveness, she thought, then discounted.

"After I went to the Flamingo—"

"The Flamingo?"

"—I wanted to question the eyewitness. She lives off the alley. If I wanted to talk to her, I had no choice."

"At night? By yourself? Hell."

"It was afternoon when I started out." All right, so it was late, late afternoon, more like evening, but she wasn't going to share that with him. She knew now she shouldn't have been traipsing around in dark alleyways in a not-so-great part of town.

Lucas growled. "I don't want you in that alley alone at night."

Fine by her. "If you insist."

She said the words like a petulant child, and he studied her. With a start, she had the fleeting thought that he had already known she had been in the alleyway. But that was absurd.

"So that upset you?" he asked.

"No, it was afterward. I saw one of the girls from the Flamingo, and we both heard someone. She ran off, and after that I am sure I was followed. I could feel him there." She tried to suppress the shudder.

"Him?"

"The footfalls were too heavy to be a woman's."

There it was again, that look as if he already knew what had happened before she told him.

Suddenly her stomach growled. Loudly. Cringing, she slapped her hand over her abdomen as if she could cover the sound. The noise startled Lucas, then he absorbed her expression. She saw something flare in his blue eyes, something deep but not sexual. Like concern. The sight was foreign to her. Growing up, if she'd been anything it was self-reliant. She hadn't needed any coddling or sissifying. No sir.

Suddenly it all seemed too much.

"What are you looking at?" she demanded crossly.

"At you. Are you hungry, sweetheart?"

"How many times do I have to tell you I'm not your sweetheart." She sniffed. "And I might be a tad on the starving side."

"Let me send for something."

"No, no. I'll go home." To her dark cottage at the back of the house.

She blamed it on lack of food, but those damned tears surged once again, and her lip started to tremble.

"What is it?" he asked quietly. "I think it's more than simple hunger."

Sinking her teeth into the soft flesh of her lower lip, she willed herself to be strong.

But then Lucas touched her, a gentle touch, the pad of his thumb brushing over her lips, and the dam burst.

Tears spilled over as if they had been waiting for decades. Angrily she dashed them away. But Lucas caught her hand and pulled her close. He held her, kindly, as if his sole purpose in life were to give her comfort.

"Tell me why you are so upset," he stated, his voice a gentle command.

Suddenly it was too much. "Nothing is wrong." The words tangled with tears that were so foreign to her.

He pressed her cheek against his chest and rubbed her back, stroking, calming, as her tears soaked into the fine linen of his shirt.

"I'm perfectly fine," she whispered, relishing the feel of his strength despite herself. "Never been better if you don't count the fact that my father is furious with me and my uncle is questioning my judgment." She shrugged her shoulders in despair. "Though who can blame any of them. I'm

stubborn, opinionated. Mule-headed and inflexible. I lack
every feminine attribute to attract a man." She pushed back,
her palms flattened against the hard muscles of his chest,
and looked at him with a scowl. "Feel free to contradict me
at any time."

He wrapped her tighter and chuckled into her hair.
"That's one of the things I like about you, the very sensible
way you say just what is on your mind."

Something that had always been buried deep inside her
fought to the surface. Boldness, the desire to toss propriety
to the wind and truly speak freely. "I don't always say what
is on my mind," she whispered, her gaze drifting to his lips.

The words spilled out of her before she could stop them.
If she had surprised herself, then she had managed to surprise this owner of a licentious men's club even more. The
connoisseur of women blinked.

She cursed whatever wildness had come over her, making
her bold. "I'm sorry. You must think I'm horrible."

But if he did, it was gone just as quickly, and his eyes
darkened.

He didn't have to be asked twice.

His kindness turned to something else, something pas-
sionate and burning. Like a man giving in to a vice he
couldn't afford.

He kissed her hair, then her forehead, his lips trailing
lower until he kissed her cheek. And then, amazing him, she
turned her head ever so slightly until her lips met his.

He groaned at the touch, running his hands up her arms to
her neck. The touch was just as she remembered it, as foreign as it was provocative. She felt stiff and ineffectual, but
she wanted this—as if she had been waiting for him to kiss
her again.

"Open for me," he whispered against her.

And she did.

His tongue drifted over her lips, and she moaned. His
body seemed to ignite, the heat of him burning through their

layers of clothes. Her spine arched deep as he bent to kiss her, pulling her lower body tight against his, his free hand seeking the small buttons at the neck of her blouse. With quick efficiency, he eased the mother of pearl orbs from their moorings, until she felt his fingers against her skin.

Their kiss became heated. He nibbled at her lips, his tongue flicking, feeling, all the while his fingers undid the long line of buttons of her blouse. Finally they fell free, and she shivered with longing when she felt the softness of his shirt brush unbidden against her naked skin.

Her body melted into his when their tongues intertwined. She pressed closer, as if seeking the fire his fingers ignited as they danced over her body.

His mouth slanted over hers, almost desperately. "Oh, God," he murmured against her.

His hand trailed down her back, pressing their bodies together. She felt his hardness against her belly, didn't understand what it was at first. Then a certain dawning washed through her. He wanted her, desired her. Despite her pale hair and nondescript eyes. Despite her lack of curves.

After Clark's rejection, the realization was especially gratifying, though it terrified her in turn.

"Yes, I want you," he murmured, his voice ragged.

He leaned back to see her. "How is it that you make me lose control?"

Before she could speak, he pulled her back with a groan, his lips capturing hers in a savage embrace.

She felt his heart pounding against his ribs, though they were pressed together so tightly she was uncertain where his heartbeat ended and hers began. Unwanted thoughts of reality tried to intrude, but she pushed them away as her fingers found their way into the thick strands of his glossy dark hair. Her senses reeled when his tongue demanded entry to the hidden recesses of her mouth once again to explore and taste, leaving her shaken with longing.

"Alice," he murmured.

Her body flushed with desire, awash with waves of a new and overwhelming need. With trembling limbs she clung to him, lost in the swirl of mounting passion that centered at the core of her being. Her body throbbed with sensation, and despite everything she knew to be right, she wanted more.

As if sensing her need, he worked her chemisette and undergarments free until she felt the brush of summer air against her skin.

She reveled in the freedom, working the fastenings of his shirt. But her fingers weren't as nimble as his, and seconds later he ripped off the cotton fabric. The touch of his bare skin to hers was like heaven. He trailed his lips down her jaw to her throat, his palm drifting down her sides, grazing the fullness of her breasts. She felt his hunger, just as she felt her own.

He kissed lower, and she cried out when he took one turgid nipple into his mouth and sucked. Her hands tangled in his hair, as if she couldn't get close enough. She opened up to the exquisite feel of his seeking lips, the rasp of his tongue, one hand holding her securely at her back, the other cupping her hips, pulling her tightly against him.

Together they sank to the floor, Lucas pressing her back into the plush oriental carpet. Her long skirts fell around her knees as he came between them, his palm caressing the heat of her beneath the layer of pantaloons.

Her father, her work, Clark were gone from her mind. Just as when she had started down the alleyway in the dark, she didn't think about consequences. She went headlong into this man's arms and desperately wanted to know where it would take her. If nothing else, she would not die without ever having known passion.

Just as the thought fluttered through her head, his strong finger slipped between the secret folds of her womanhood. The act shattered her to the core. The shuddering desire. The intimacy. Her body's gasp of yearning.

This is what love was about, she realized with blinding insight. But in that same second she also knew that the most important part of this act was love.

True and pure love.

The thought startled her at just the moment Lucas kissed her again. Sensation battled with sense, with the fact that she knew she couldn't go through with such an intimacy without being loved, truly loved.

As quickly as it had begun, she couldn't believe what she had started. And she had started it, no better, no different than one of the girls from the Flamingo.

With a jerk, she tried to pull away.

"Alice?" Lucas murmured.

"Let me go," she demanded, mortification that she could act so wantonly making her tone harsh.

Surprise gained her release, and she rolled to her knees, grabbing at her blouse.

The look on Lucas's face nearly ruined her resolve. The hurt, the fear, those same vulnerable emotions she had thought she had seen the first day she met him in her office.

Tilting his head, he reached out to her, intent on pulling her back.

"No, Lucas. We have to remember we have a professional relationship. Neither one of us can afford anything more."

He took her hand anyway, stared at the backs of her fingers as if seeing something else. "What if I said I wanted more than that?"

Though the words were said softly, they washed over her in a tantalizing heat, then just as quickly they stung. She hated to admit it but whenever she was near him, something primal and not at all acceptable rose up inside her. But if nothing else, she had always been truthful with herself.

"We can't have more than that, Lucas. Yes, there is desire, the kind of desire that threatens to burn me up. But once that initial hunger is satisfied, there's nothing left."

"That's ridiculous."

"Is it? Are you ready to give up Nightingale's Gate? Will you become the deacon of the church? How about raising children? What will you teach them? How to pour drinks? How to seduce women?"

With that, whatever vulnerability may or may not have been there vanished. He dropped his hand away.

Loss surrounded her. She could feel where his fingers had touched her, caressed her. Alice felt confused by this strange mix of emotions—desire and guilt.

But it was for the best. She was a protector of the law. And simply by being the owner of a gentlemen's club, he was someone who pushed the law to the limit. There could be no future for the two of them. They were different, too different. She had to keep telling herself that.

"I'll see you home," Lucas said tightly.

"No!" She couldn't be with him another second, or she would give in and brazenly go further. "No," she said more softly.

He stared at her forever. But what else was there to say.

"Finish dressing," he said, his voice having grown cold and emotionless. And once she had dressed, he yanked open the door. "Brutus."

Instantly the man was there.

"See to it that Miss Kendall gets home safely."

"Yes, boss."

The massive man looked her up and down, and she would have sworn she saw contempt in his expression. Or was it satisfaction.

He extended his arm, guiding the way. Alice went to the door, then stopped. At the last minute she looked back. But she was too late. Lucas was gone.

A coach waited discreetly out front. Brutus whisked her inside the confines, leaving her alone. She felt the carriage rock when he stood on the back fender, then he gave the command for the driver to depart.

Alice sank back in the seat. Plush velvet curtains, buttery

soft leather seats, shiny brass and wood paneling adorned the small space. A small fine wood cabinet filled with crystal decanters of liquor. Extravagance, decadence. Much like Nightingale's Gate. Much like Lucas. So different from any life she wanted to be a part of.

She wasn't wild. Didn't want to be, she told herself with conviction that even to her didn't sound real.

Within minutes, they pulled up in front of her father's house. Only one dim light glimmered in the study. The rest of the house stood dark. The thought of making her way around the back of the house by herself left her uneasy. So she hurried inside, intent on making her way out the back door as quickly as she could.

But the sight of her uncle stopped her cold.

He sat in her father's study, in his chair, a snifter of brandy set out on the desk. A cigar lay next to a cutter in sharp precision.

A gun lay out next to that.

Chapter Eleven

"Uncle, what are you doing?"

Harry Kendall whirled around, nearly knocking the brandy with his elbow. "Alice!"

The room was eerie and dark, only one old-fashioned hurricane lamp flickering with light, shadows dancing on the walls when a draft hit the flame.

"Where are Father and Max?"

Harry quickly put the unlit cigar and cutter in his pocket, then pushed the brandy aside. "They're out," he said, a strained smile on his face.

The darkness made Alice feel disjointed, the sound of her uncle's voice reminding her how much he and her father sounded alike. If she closed her eyes, she could easily mistake one for the other.

"I was just relaxing," he added. He took the gun and locked it in a metal box that stood open on the desk. "Just finished cleaning my weapon."

For the first time Alice thought about how long her uncle had lived in his brother's shadow, playing second fiddle to a man who was actually two years younger than himself. Why hadn't he ever married? And as the oldest, why didn't it seem as if this was his house instead of her father's?

Was her uncle jealous of Walker Kendall?

Her brow furrowed as she thought about Max. How did Harry feel about his nephew, who seemed to relish making decisions about the family and the household whenever their father wasn't there? Was there more going on between these three men than she knew?

Her uncle turned up the gaslights, making the study look as welcoming as it usually did, and she shook off every remnant of concern. This was her uncle, her family. She was jumpy from her escapades in the alley, not to mention the still rampant sensations coursing through her body from Lucas's touch, which had made her feel alive in a way that she hardly understood.

Harry was devoted to his brother, devoted to their family.

"What is it, Alice?" he asked, his voice as sympathetic as it had always been. "You look upset."

She shrugged as she pulled off her simple hat, tossed it aside, then walked farther into the room and plopped down in a brocade chair. She wasn't ready to go out to her cottage. She wasn't ready to be alone to remember the alley—or think about Lucas.

"Is it the Hawthorne case?" Harry asked, settling back in the matching chair next to hers.

"I suppose." She wrinkled her nose and hooked her booted heel under her knee. "The more I look into things, the more confusing they become."

"Welcome to police work."

His smile was kind and gentle, and Alice felt the tight coil inside her start to unwind. This was just what she needed, a calming talk with a man who knew what it was like to untwist mysteries.

"Generally a case gets more confusing before the facts start making sense," he added.

"I hope that's all it is."

"What has you bothered?"

She wanted to confide in her uncle, have him help her make sense of what she had learned. But she thought better of telling him anything. Walker and Harry Kendall discussed all the cases that went through their legal systems. She couldn't take a chance that Harry would talk to her father about what she had learned. She didn't need her father to know her every move.

The realization made her feel separate from her family for the first time ever. The thought was scary, disconcerting, but oddly exhilarating. Like freedom.

She thought of Nightingale's Gate. Of Lucas, and his claim that she pushed to the edge, wanted to see how far she could go.

Was he right?

Had he glimpsed something in her she had never realized before—or never admitted to?

She hesitated. "Uncle Harry, what was my mother like?"

The change of subject caught him by surprise. "What?" he sputtered.

"My mother. What did she look like? Was she happy?"

He managed to contain his surprise, and once he did, he sighed then leaned back, raking his thick hands through his hair.

"Yes, she was happy. Always happy. And fun." For a moment he lost himself in thought. "She had the most beautiful hair," he said softly. "Blonde. Just like yours. Pale as milk in a bowl. Men loved her."

"Did my father love her?"

His expression hardened, and his lips flattened to a hard line. "It's late, Alice. You'd best get to bed."

"But—"

"No buts. If you want to know how your father felt about your mother, ask him."

"But Father never discusses her."

"I'm sorry."

For now, however, it was enough. She felt gratified and somehow lightened to know that she had something in common with her mother, a woman who had been full of joy and laughter.

He tapped his blunt fingers on the small table between them. "And since you are doing your best to change the subject, I'd best tell you that I know you went to the Flamingo this evening."

"What?" she gasped. "How do you know that?"

"I am the chief of police. It's my job to know what is going on around town. But as your uncle—not as the chief of police—I felt I had to send word to your father."

"Uncle Harry! You had no right! I am a lawyer. A lawyer who has to go up against my father's office. He can't know everything I'm doing. And how am I supposed to build a defense if I can't interview witnesses?"

"You can't be gallivanting around such places, Alice. If you want to find things out, ask me."

His voice was lined with a sharp edge that surprised her.

Abruptly he stood. "It's late. We'd best get some sleep."

Disconcerted, Alice followed him from the study. But she jumped with fright when they came face-to-face with Max, who stood in the darkened foyer.

"Maxwell! You scared me to death."

"How long have you been there?" Harry demanded, his body suddenly tense.

Max glanced back and forth between his sister and uncle before a smile pulled across his face. "Just got here," he said.

Only then did Alice notice that his grin was actually lopsided.

"Max, you've been drinking."

"Just a wee bit," he said with a slurred laugh, then made his way to the staircase. "I'll just head on up to bed. See you in the morning."

Chapter Twelve

He needed a woman.

He felt antsy and caged. Pushing up from the fine leather seat, he started to pace. He had to be careful. Who would have believed that Lucille's death would cause such a stir?

One wrong step and he could be found out all too easily. More than ever, he had to watch his every move.

But the need had grown greater.

The brandy sat out on the desk. His cigar was there, the cutter. He should put them all away.

It was too soon. And people were talking.

Frustration snaked through him, but he willed it back. He was in control of himself. He was too smart to do something foolish.

Though he couldn't deny the need to kill had grown stronger.

Clenching his hand at his side, he fought for control. Fought to contain the desire that he had lived with for so many years. Why was it growing more fierce now?

He thought of Alice. With white-blonde hair and amber eyes. She was good at this. Though he wouldn't have guessed that when she started the case. She wasn't afraid to go anywhere, and she was learning too much. Such a shame because she was different from most women. But in the end, he sighed, they all were whores, some better at deceiving than others. Like all the women he had loved, including his mother.

Yes, Alice was learning too much and asking too many questions.

He toyed with the ring, the golden nightingale catching the light. He felt the need snake through him. But patience was a virtue. He had to sit tight, bide his time. No more killings until things calmed down.

Only fools were careless, and he was no fool.

But still he felt the need.

Chapter Thirteen

Lucas watched as Alice entered her office and froze.

He stood in front of the window, his shoulder braced against the casing as her expression took a hard, jarring skip at the sight of him.

It was the next morning, and overnight everything between them had changed. She had made it clear to him there could be nothing between them—their worlds were too far apart. He could see that in her expression. And the truth was, he knew it was true, had known it all along. But she made him forget.

Now, more than ever, he could see that he unnerved her. But he couldn't say if the change was caused by the fact that they had shared such intimacy. Or if she was unnerved because she had let a man accused of murder touch her so intimately.

Either way, he told himself he didn't care. She had pushed him away, telling him she didn't want him to touch her. The truth of her words had blazed in her eyes.

Despite that, standing so close to her, he felt the urge to pull her into his arms.

Merciless control quelled the desire—quelled the weakness. And she had made him weak. Around her he had allowed himself to care. But caring, he had learned long ago, caused only heartache. He would not be weak again.

What a fool he had been to have allowed himself to care about Alice Kendall.

Had the circumstances been different, he would have ruthlessly put her out of his mind. He would have gone on with the life he had built for himself. Busy, power laden, with people needing him, though he needed no one. But as much as he hated the fact, he still needed Alice in his life, he needed an attorney. And until the trial was finished, he had to continue seeing her.

He also understood from her expression that she would no longer be put off with glib responses. She wanted answers, and she planned to get them.

"Good morning," she stated crisply.

"Is it? I hadn't noticed."

"Fine, no small talk. What do you want?"

"I'd think we were beyond *small talk* after last night—"

"I'll thank you not to remind me of that."

Something flashed in her face, harsh and angry.

"I take it you got up on the wrong side of the bed," he quipped.

"Whether I did or not is none of your business."

"If you had stayed with me, you might have slept better. Or maybe not."

"Once again, you are showing how *un*charming you can be."

This made him chuckle. "I've got to practice on someone. As to my being here, I take it an 'I just wanted to see you' isn't going to do it."

"No."

"How about, I couldn't stay away."

"If I thought that were true, I'd tell you that you should."

"But you don't believe that?"

"No. I think for some curious reason you desire me. Perhaps like adding an oddity to your curio cabinet of women."

"You underestimate your charm."

She scoffed and busied herself with a file.

"Then how about, I brought you a gift."

She whirled around. "You did?" She cursed. "I mean, no thank you."

"I almost got you with that one," he laughed.

She threw up her hands in exasperation. "Aren't you even fazed by the situation you are in?"

"I'm fazed, I'm fazed. But the fact is, sweetheart, what good does it do me to hang my head and weep?"

"So you laugh and tell stupid jokes, instead?"

"Sounds good to me."

"That's great. You act like a moron, but since it's voluntary that makes it okay? What kind of an inadequate excuse is that?"

He felt his features harden, the devil-may-care attitude strained. "It's the only excuse you are going to get," he said tightly.

At that, she raised a brow.

But whatever she would have said was lost when Brutus burst into the office.

"Boss!"

Brutus was out of breath as if he had run the whole way. His impeccable black suit was stained from sweat and the sweltering August heat.

"Another girl got knocked off in the alley."

The air in the tiny room seemed to dissipate until there was nothing left to breathe. Alice stood stunned. But Lucas wasn't. He had come here on purpose and had made sure Brutus knew where to find him. A cold, hard inevitability filled him.

"What?" Alice demanded.

"A girl was killed," Brutus explained. "Last night, in the alley behind the club. Strangled just like Lucille."

"Dear God," she breathed.

"Boss, there are coppers all over the place. You got to see."

"Don't you dare." With effort, Alice regained her wits.

She knew her client would not be well served if he showed up at a murder scene.

"This is my neighborhood," Lucas said, his voice intense. "These are my friends. I am going."

Brutus and Lucas headed out. They were nearly to the small elevator before they realized Alice was behind them.

"What are you doing?" Lucas demanded.

"I'm going with you."

"This is no place for a lady."

"Maybe not, but it is the place for your lawyer. I don't want you at a crime scene without me."

"Suit yourself."

The same carriage from last night waited out front. Lucas sat inside with Alice; Brutus assumed his spot on the fender. They took off at breakneck speed, careening block after block from the office to the alley behind Nightingale's Gate.

When they arrived, it was like nothing Alice had ever seen before. Blue-uniformed patrolmen filled the alleyway. Austere black carriages parked every which way, as if they had just stopped and the passengers had leaped out.

Confusion reigned.

But then she saw Uncle Harry and her father standing over what she realized now was the body of a woman.

Her stomach clenched, and dread filled her. She didn't want to go any farther. She wanted to turn and run as fast as she could in the opposite direction.

"Go home, Alice."

She turned with a start and found Lucas.

"You don't want to see this."

True. She didn't want to see it. But what she wanted wasn't relevant. As she tried to build her case, she needed access to all evidence. And another girl dead in the alleyway undoubtedly was another piece of evidence.

"I'm not going anywhere," she said obstinately.

She walked ahead. Uniformed patrolmen surrounded the body. The closer Alice got, the more reluctant she became.

But little more than ten paces away, the uniforms parted, and the sight stopped her in her tracks.

The girl lay on the ground, seemingly asleep, peaceful, except for the unnatural position of her head. Alice felt the fear and revulsion rise up.

Hardly aware that she moved, Alice took the remaining steps until she stood over the body. From a distance, the girl had looked serene, pretty. But up close, serenity was gone.

A silent scream pulled at the woman's mouth, distorted and frozen, teeth bared, uneven and chipped. Her eyes stared sightlessly, bulging and glassy. Her hair looked like straw, and her skin, unnaturally white, brushed with sand and grit from the ground.

The alley smelled of dust and death, flies buzzing the corpse, and the climbing sun made it only worse. Alice resisted the urge to cover her face as her stomach heaved.

She desperately wanted to flee. But there was one more thing she had to do. While the patrolmen searched the rest of the area, her father and uncle deep in conference, she quickly bent down and moved the victim's collar aside. And there it was. Just as Alice had feared. The imprint of a nightingale.

She jerked her hand back as if burned. There hadn't been a single mention of the ring mark in the newspapers. Clark, no doubt at her father's insistence, had kept the piece of evidence a well-guarded secret. Which meant that the killer had to be the same. This hadn't been a random act. The man was still out there, still killing.

When she staggered to her feet, Lucas studied her, his expression ominous, as if he already knew what she'd seen.

Her mind staggered with questions as she stumbled away from the body, bracing herself against the solidity of the brick-and-mortar wall. Resting her forehead on her arm, Alice wanted to weep.

Lucas came up beside her, and he placed his hand between her shoulder blades, as if he wanted to give her strength.

The touch felt strong and good, comforting, though confusing. Her mind rocked back and forth between the murdered girl and this man. Who was he really?

But just as quickly the contact was gone.

"Get your hands off my daughter."

Walker Kendall's voice sliced through the muggy August heat. Pushing away from the wall, Alice stood back. Lucas and her father faced off, with her uncle just to the side.

"Stop!" she cried.

"I will not stand by while scum like you ruins my daughter. I'll not let you strangle her like you strangled the life out of these girls."

"Father!" She fought for control. "Father," she repeated more reasonably, but with force. "I'll thank you to watch what you say. This is my client, and I'll not stand by while you convict him without the benefit of a judge and jury."

"Say what you will, Alice," her uncle interjected. "But I'm taking this man into custody."

"You can't do that!"

"Watch me."

"Do I have to threaten to slap you with a lawsuit for false imprisonment?"

Harry stopped.

"Don't think I won't, Uncle. You don't have one shred of evidence that my client did this."

"I know what my gut tells me."

"Your gut isn't proof, so don't you dare lay a hand on Mr. Hawthorne. Until you convince a judge that you have evidence that he could reasonably be charged with this crime, he is coming with me."

She took Lucas's arm and headed back down the alley, praying that her uncle wouldn't force the issue. But they made it to the end of the road, with little more notice than her uncle's and father's hard gazes burning into their backs.

As soon as they rounded the corner, Alice fell back against the carriage fender.

"What's wrong?" Lucas asked.

She looked at him, really looked. What could she tell him? What could she tell anyone, she realized. Whom could she trust? Because what she hadn't told anyone, and what made her stomach roil with sadness and guilt, was the fact that the girl who lay dead in the alleyway was the same girl who had followed her out of the Flamingo and told her about Oliver Aldrich and Cindy Pop.

The girl would not die in vain.

Alone in her office, Alice fired off a note to one Oliver Aldrich, whom she found listed in the Boston book as living in the Back Bay. A moneyed man, to be sure.

She worked through the day and waited. She thought back to everyone she had mentioned her encounter to. Her uncle had already known about her visit to the Flamingo, and he had told her father. She had told Lucas. And Brutus knew. Not to mention those horrid men who had stepped out into the alleyway.

Had the girl been killed because she had given Alice information? Or had she been in the wrong place at the wrong time and suffered for it?

Alice remembered the fear she had experienced in that alley. The sensation of being followed, the desperate fear.

And she knew with certainty that had those men not stepped out the back door of Nightingale's Gate last night, she would have been the one found dead in the alleyway this morning.

Alice hardly noticed the time passing. But when finally she received her reply from Oliver Aldrich, the sun had sunk on the horizon.

The man was busy, too busy to see her.

Not good enough.

Alice rummaged around her desk drawer for a calling card,

packed up her bag, and headed for Commonwealth Avenue. She took the trolley, which dropped her off on Arlington Street, then walked the two blocks to the man's home.

She knocked, banging the heavy brass ring with determination. A starch-suited butler answered.

"I am Miss Alice Kendall, here to see Mr. Aldrich."

The man raised a brow, no doubt thinking about the fact that it was highly improper for a maiden lady to call on a man. Little did he know that this call was the least of the unmaidenly things she had been doing of late.

She shuddered at the thought but pushed it away. As a working woman she had already taken the leap into the improper. A continued series of tiny steps to further her travel could hardly be a surprise.

With the dignity of the perfect lady, Alice extended her card, placing it on the man's silver tray. "Please inform your employer of my arrival."

He nodded his head, then turned. He held the tray extended as, with heels clicking on tile, he disappeared down a long hallway. The house was beautiful even if it was decorated with dark woods and heavy furniture. Alice surmised the man wasn't married.

She couldn't imagine what Oliver Aldrich could have to do with the murders, and when she found herself standing before him in his study, the servant bowing out, she was at even more of a loss.

Tall and well built, the man looked regal and prosperous, not at all like a murderer. Though Alice was rapidly beginning to wonder what a murderer actually looked like.

"Miss Kendall."

He sat behind his desk, the room dark and gloomy. A large Persian cat purred in his lap. She itched to throw the heavy velvet curtains wide. Without good light, it was hard to tell his age. Thirty? Fifty?

"I thought I sent word that I was unavailable."

"You did. But as I said in my note, this is important."

He stroked the cat's fur as he considered her. After a long moment, he gestured toward a seat. "I should have surmised you wouldn't give up so easily."

"How so?"

"I read the article about you in the *Herald*."

"Oh, that."

She had been described as hardworking, smart. And beautiful. God, who would have guessed she'd be such a sucker for a compliment. Again and again she allowed them to turn her head. Heavens, had Grayson Hawthorne not complimented her in the first place, no doubt she wouldn't be in this mess. But no, toss her a single kind word, and she lapped it up like sweet cream on pie.

Never one to dwell on the negative, she had put the rest of the adjectives, the ones that hadn't been nearly as nice, from her mind.

"I was impressed," he added.

"Thank you."

"Of course I'm a determined bachelor who has little use for the ways of proper society, so perhaps I'm not much of a judge."

If he was trying to put her in her place in some back-handed sort of way, he wasn't succeeding. Not completely, at least.

"I'd like to ask you a few questions."

"About?"

"Lucille Rouge."

His features remained calm and unperturbed. But Alice noticed that his hand tightened ever so slightly in the fur of his cat. As if he realized what he had done, he loosened his grip and shooed the pet away.

"The name doesn't ring a bell."

She didn't believe him.

"What about Lucas Hawthorne? Does his name ring a bell?"

"Ah, Lucas. Of course I know the man. I went to school with him."

"School?"

"Yes, of course. We went to Boston Classics together. We were both boys really." He chuckled. "Though Lucas was much more . . . shall we say, mature than the rest of us. I think it was about that time that he got enamored of the nightingale."

"He liked the bird even back then?"

Oliver chuckled and steepled his hands in front of him. "Oh yes, we all liked the nightingale, Miss Kendall."

That's when she noticed the woodcut impression of a nightingale that hung on the wall. "I couldn't help but notice the woodcut."

His malleable features turned cold. "Which belonged to my father. Now enough of this nonsense. What do you want?"

Without thinking about consequences, she asked, "Where were you the night of July thirteenth?"

"Are you interrogating me?"

"Just wondering."

"I suggest you stop bothering respectable citizens, and face the facts that you are defending a guilty man."

He called for the butler, who appeared as if he were standing just beyond the door. Short of making them throw her out, she didn't see how she could stay a second longer.

As regally as he, she nodded her head. "Good day, Mr. Aldrich. I'll be in touch."

"I want to know why you haven't investigated a single other person besides Lucas Hawthorne."

Alice stood in the kitchen with her uncle, an apron wrapped around his thick midsection, as he cooked the family's evening meal. He still wore his dark blue pants and starched white shirt, but his uniform jacket hung over the back of a kitchen chair.

Harry scraped chopped garlic into a skillet of heated oil. The instant aroma of garlic sizzled and popped into the air.

Italian night at the Kendalls'.

"Uncle Harry, you aren't listening to me."

"I'm listening, I'm just not answering."

After the garlic had cooked, next came the onions, slow stirred with the garlic, then chopped tomatoes, until the whole house smelled like a succulent Italian kitchen.

"You have to answer to someone; it might as well be me. Your investigation started and ended with my client."

"No reason to look further. He did it."

"You don't know that!"

"Give me one other possibility."

"Oliver Aldrich."

Harry nearly dropped the skillet. "What are you talking about?"

"I went to his house today."

"Alone?"

"Of course alone."

Harry banged the skillet down. "I've had a less-than-stellar day, with you at the top of my list of people who are making me angry. The last thing I want to hear is that you have gone to an unmarried man's home alone."

"How else was I supposed to interview him?"

"Damn it, Alice! It's my job to do the interviewing. Not yours."

"If you had done your job, then I wouldn't have to."

Harry's eyes narrowed, and his jaw ticked. "Where did you get his name?"

"That's not important. What matters is that I got it, and when I went over there, I found a woodcut of a nightingale." Then she remembered something else. "He had a ring mark on his finger."

"And you want me to arrest him because of that?" he asked incredulously.

"Why not? You arrested Lucas for little more."

"That little more happened to be an eyewitness."

"Yes, an eyewitness who lives with a mean son of—"

Harry's eyes went dangerous.

"Mean son of the woman next door. Really. I think they were related."

Was that fast thinking or what?

"I will not have you talking like a street thug, Alice. I didn't raise a heathen."

"No, you raised me to use my mind and common sense. That eyewitness is lying. She is being told what to say, and someone out there is telling her to say it. Moreover, have you heard the name Cindy Pop?"

Harry went still. Time seemed distorted. Despite the apron Uncle Harry wore, he looked murderous.

"No, I haven't heard the name. And I suggest you haven't heard it, either."

Chapter Fourteen

Brutus led Alice to the top floor of Nightingale's Gate. They seemed to go up and up, floor after floor. The building was only four stories high, but somehow taking four floors at once, not to mention the late summer heat, made it seem even higher.

Once there, Alice had to grab the banister and take a few seconds to gain her breath. Last night she had gone to her cottage without staying for dinner. Now, midmorning, hours later without a single morsel of food, she felt light-headed and weak with hunger. She really had to go to the market.

Brutus looked down on her as if she were the most pathetic of specimens. She itched to issue a few choice words, but it hadn't been easy to get the guard dog of a man to bring her this far. Even then, she'd had to tell him it was an emergency and remind him that she was Lucas Hawthorne's attorney. After that, she kept her mouth shut for fear he wouldn't take her the remaining distance.

As her breathing eased, she became aware of a noise—rhythmic and primal, groaning and intense. What in God's name was Lucas Hawthorne doing?

Alice's first inclination was to turn around and dash back down the stairs. But a perverse sense of dread and curiosity kept her feet moving, one in front of the other.

She entered a room at the top of the building that was filled with an assortment of . . . items. Metal, leather, mirrors.

Lucas stood at the center, bare to his waist, sweat gleaming on the hard smooth planes of his back, tight-fitting pants molded to his thighs like a second skin. He looked like sheer power, raw and uncontained, as he pounded a stuffed bag that hung from a rope. The sight of broad shoulders, hard flat stomach, and narrow hips was stunning.

He punched the bag with a series of brutal jabs, only a thin cover of white linen on his knuckles; all the while his feet never stopped moving. She felt her heart skip at the sight of him. No more devilish smiles or glib, seemingly uncaring answers as if he didn't care about the events that had disrupted his life. It was as if the polished, sophisticated façade he kept so carefully around him had been stripped away.

Now he stood wild and untamed, so different from the proper men she knew. She felt something wild inside herself flare, making her heart pound. But, as always, she held it back. She might have broken rules by becoming a lawyer, but she was still a lady.

His rawness had an outlet in this room, and she envied him that. While people thought him improper, Alice doubted that many men could imagine this side of the man. What he let them see of him in Nightingale's Gate was tame in comparison.

She sensed the minute Brutus thought better of her being there. Without a word to his employer he grabbed her arm and started toward the door. But she wasn't going anywhere.

"Mr. Hawthorne!"

The sound of flesh on leather ceased abruptly as Lucas whipped around to face them.

A brutal wildness consumed him, a rage, Alice thought fleetingly. Something that burned inside him that was close to crazy, every muscle so tense that they tremored. His sweat gleamed in the sunlight that slanted through the tall windows, his blue eyes nearly black with blinding wrath.

She realized that despite all her thoughts about this man, she didn't know him at all.

"What the hell are you doing here?"

His voice was harsh and furious.

Brutus stammered. "I didn't think you'd—"

"No, you didn't think."

"Now really, Mr. Hawthorne. It's not Brutus's fault that I am here. He was told—"

"I don't give a damn what he was told. Get out."

Fury washed through the room like a tidal wave. She didn't like the feeling, nor did she understand it. Though, in truth, she couldn't say that she was scared. Off balance, disconcerted in a way that she couldn't name. But not frightened. Though she knew she should be.

"Can't do it," she replied with an apologetic shrug, seemingly indifferent to his unleashed rage that shimmered before her. "Unfortunately, we need to talk."

"Get her out," he answered through clenched teeth, his eyes like coals of menace.

"It's important, Lucas."

At the use of his name, he seemed to flinch. Then he pulled a ragged breath, as if trying to contain the power that coursed unchecked inside him, and said, "Take her to my suite. I'll see her there."

"Your suite? Your bedroom suite?" Sensation sizzled through her much as fury had sizzled through the room seconds ago.

"Suddenly you're concerned about propriety?" he asked with a sneer.

He had her there.

"Well, this just seems more . . . appropriate."

"Appropriate?" He looked at her as if she had lost her mind. "In my suite or not at all."

He appeared to mean it. "All right. Have it your way." Her tone was a lament, but she was aware of the giddy excitement at the thought of seeing his private chambers.

This time she let Brutus lead her out, though she tugged her arm away and raised her chin when she became aware of the disapproval that seemed to tighten his grip on her arm.

The guard dog led Alice back down to the third floor. Pushing open a wide, heavy oak door, he motioned her inside.

"Wait here."

As always, a man of few words.

Turning back, she found he had led her to the private office she had been to before. But this time she noticed an interior door that stood ajar. Beyond that she could see a masculine setting of chairs, bureaus. And a bed.

Her heart skittered at the intimacy of such a sight. Never had she been in a man's private chambers. Not even her father's, at least not since she was a child and would sneak in, practicing her sleuthing techniques on the secret safe he kept in the back of his closet. He had never learned that she had become a master at picking the lock.

A smile surfaced at the memory, only to flutter away when she heard a slamming door somewhere nearby. Clearly there was another entrance to this suite of rooms. But no one appeared. She heard footsteps, then the gush of water flowing from a spigot. It took a second to realize that Lucas must be in there washing up.

The knowledge sent a bolt of heat rushing through her that he could be so cavalier about her presence.

And then there was more of that damnable curiosity.

What would he look like with water sluicing down his body? Despite the fact that she had grown up in a house full of men, never had she seen so much of a man as she had in the boxing room. Never had she seen sculpted planes of flesh that looked so much like Michelangelo's David.

Forcefully she focused on her surroundings and noticed a series of photographs. Brown-and-white images. Looking closely, she made out Emmaline Hawthorne; Grayson, when he was young, standing next to another boy whom she guessed was the middle son, Matthew.

After looking closely, she noticed that only one of the photos was of Lucas.

She picked up the heavy silver frame and studied his image. She was certain it was him. Tall, even as a boy, and amazingly handsome. Not gangly or awkward. He must have made the girls swoon even then.

The biggest difference she saw between then and now was his smile. Not that he didn't smile as an adult. He did, but it was devilish, provocative. When he was younger, the smile had been full and free, innocent.

Yet again she wondered what had changed this man?

After looking at each of the photographs, it occurred to her that while she had never seen Bradford Hawthorne, she was sure there wasn't a single picture of him here. She remembered the coldness that had come into Lucas's voice at the mention of his father.

What, she wondered, had happened between the two men?

The opening door gained her attention, and she turned to find Lucas standing there, that glimpse of bed just behind him. The harshness was gone, as if he had washed it away with soap and water. But the smile had yet to return.

"Have you found anything interesting?" he asked, leaning his shoulder against the doorjamb, crossing his arms on his strong chest.

He wore an elegant, though thoroughly masculine pair of trousers, and a white shirt, no tie, unbuttoned at the top, revealing a hint of golden skin. A man at leisure in his private chambers. The whole of the scene flustered her. Suddenly she became aware of her heavily starched suit, her breasts seeming to strain against the material.

Self-consciously she smoothed her hair.

That got a smile out of him. But the smile was impersonal, distant, as if he had erected a wall around himself—as if somehow he stood detached from her in ways he hadn't before. Up until now, she had made him angry, she had intrigued him, she had made him laugh. But never had he seemed indifferent.

"Damn you," he all but whispered.

"What have I done now?"

"You look beautiful."

She felt the burn of red in her cheeks. So much for indifference.

Feeling awkward and well beyond the sort of topics she was comfortable with, Alice waved his comment away. "You and your sugar-coated platitudes."

The harshness flared, but only for a moment before impatience settled. "You said you had something important. What is it?"

Oh yes, that. "You told me you lost the nightingale ring. But you didn't tell me why you started wearing it in the first place." She thought of Oliver Aldrich's comments, and she understood that there was more to the nightingale than simply the love of a bird. "What is so special about a nightingale that you wore a nightingale ring and you named your club after it?"

He stared at her hard.

For the first time in years, Lucas grew uncomfortable. He glanced at the photograph he had seen Alice holding, the one of him as a child, and felt the shiver of yearning for the past. Finally he glanced back at her.

"Was there ever a time when you fit in?" he asked.

The question startled her. "What does that have to do with the ring?"

"Did you ever fit in?" he persisted.

She hesitated, as if considering the wisdom of replying. "No," she answered honestly.

"Not ever? There wasn't even one time when you did?"

"No," she said.

He could hear the truth in her voice, and a sadness he was certain she didn't allow herself to feel. Not Alice Kendall.

She lifted her chin. "I was raised by two men, one a bachelor, another a widower, both of whom loved their work. My way of fitting in at home precluded me from fitting in with people my own age."

"What way was that?"

"Discussing law cases or the latest crime spree. If I wanted to be a part of dinner conversation, I had to be able to discuss what my father and uncle were discussing."

"And that was their work."

"Exactly."

"But why are you so certain that you never fit in?"

She looked as if she wouldn't answer.

"Please," he asked her softly. He wanted to know for reasons that had nothing to do with the trial.

She sighed, then at the last minute gave in and began a lawyerlike recounting. "When I was eleven, I actually made a friend," she said without emotion. "A new girl who moved in a few doors down. Her father was a merchant who had made good, and not many of the parents in the neighborhood allowed their children to play with her. My father and uncle weren't snobs. And as far as I was concerned, a friend was a friend."

It was then that he saw the first hint of feeling, as if she had been holding it back with effort.

"She invited me over for a tea party with the most beautiful bone china I had ever seen. Small little cups and saucers. A tiny little teapot. Made just for her."

A smile pulled wistfully at her full lips, and he wondered what she had been like as a child. Shy but smart, too smart for the other children, with a dry wit that was beyond her age.

"We sat around the small table, and she said we would pretend to be grown-ups. And we talked. Finally, something I could do. She regaled me with stories of her parents and siblings." Alice laughed, a wonderfully free sound. "She told me delightfully wicked stories about brothers slipping out of the house and sisters sneaking kisses beneath the sprawling leaves of potted palms."

"Ah, that's where you got the idea about the potted palms."

She flashed him a wicked smile, then went on. "When it was my turn, I wanted my stories to be just as enthralling. I had no stories about my brother, so I told her about the only things I knew. The latest crime that my father and uncle had been consumed with for weeks."

At this, she grimaced, and suddenly Lucas knew this was where her happy memory ended.

"I told her every detail I could remember." She scoffed. "I thought her wide-eyed look was one of pure fascination. The next day, when her father stormed into our dining room, I learned that my friend had been wide-eyed with shock." Alice shook her head. "I truly didn't know that other girls would be terrified by such a conversation."

"What did your father do?" he asked gently.

At this she shook her head and laughed. Foolishly he wanted the smile to stay.

"He enrolled me in every sort of class for any kind of female endeavor. Needlepoint and etiquette, singing and dancing." She looked at him with a teasing tilt of brow. "Did you realize that your lawyer can play the pianoforte?"

"No, I didn't. But I do know that you dance quite well."

Alice laughed at this. "I loved dancing." Then her laughter faded to a fond smile. "I loved those lessons. But lessons cost money. Money two civil servants didn't have. And soon I was back at my father's table, listening to his tales of the law."

"I'm sorry," Lucas said, meaning it.

She tilted her head and shrugged. "No need to be. In truth, I loved those discussions, still do. I loved debating my father, loved coming up with possible trial strategies." She looked at him. "As much as I loved dancing, I loved those discussions with my father more."

"So while other girls your age worked their way through music scales and stitching patterns, you debated the law."

"I suppose."

"What happened to your mother?"

Her smile evaporated completely. "I don't know exactly. She died when I was very young. I don't remember her at all. Though my uncle said she was beautiful."

"Now I know where you got your looks."

That took the words right out of her mouth. After a moment, she managed, "Those sweet words might work on the rest of the women you know, but they won't work on me. You can't distract me any longer. Tell me what that ring means to you."

His laughter faded away, and despite all that he told himself about playing his cards close and not giving in to feelings for this woman, he felt the need to offer her something in return. Or perhaps it was seeing her there, in his private suite, holding that damn picture of him as a child. "It was a gift, and it represented the one time in my life when I fit in."

"I can't imagine your not fitting in."

"Do I fit in now?" he asked with a raised brow.

He could tell she didn't want to answer.

"You know I don't," he said. "And you'd better understand that fact when you step into the courtroom."

"I'd say you intentionally set yourself apart."

"No doubt you're right. But there are plenty of people who know about me, about my wild past. I started smoking at ten."

She waved the comment away. "I'm sure lots of children sneak cigarettes. A jury isn't going to convict you because of that."

He looked away, out the window at the people hurrying by below. "I had my first drink a year later."

He turned back to see her head tilt. "Well," she began, "kids will be kids, and kids are curious."

Whether he was trying to remind her or himself of the chasm that lay between them, he didn't know. He raked his hand through his hair and felt an unrelenting restlessness pushing him on.

"Listen to me, Alice. I have been this person that your father wants to convict longer than I've been anything else. I don't know how to be anything else."

"Is that why you and your father don't speak?"

"We don't speak because he resents me."

"A father resenting his son?"

He stared at her hard, not wanting to go forward, but knowing he had to, for many reasons.

"He resents me because I love my way of life. I have loved it for years. And as an adult, I haven't changed. I drink, I smoke." He hesitated but knew he couldn't stop now. Alice had to understand. "I make love to women I have no intention of marrying. Hell, I had sex for the first time when I was twelve. With a whore."

Her eyes went wide with shock. "A twelve-year-old with a paid courtesan? Good heavens, that is horrible."

"Horrible?" And then he knew he had to make her see, make her understand. "It was wonderful."

She couldn't seem to move, and he pressed forward. "I was twelve and she was older, old enough to know what she was doing, but still beautiful enough to fuel my imagination. A near dream of gentle but knowing hands caressing parts of me I had only just become aware of."

Alice looked away, and he couldn't tell if she was saddened or disgusted.

He glanced down at his finger, where he used to wear the ring. "The nightingale reminds me of that time."

Her brow furrowed as she looked back. "What specifically does it remind you of, Lucas? Of who you were, or who you have become?"

The question caught him off guard. Which was it? Did he want to forget that naïve young boy he had been? Or did he want to forget who he had become—a man who hardly understood the word *innocent* anymore?

"In truth, I don't know," he answered.

Alice stared at him, trying to take in all that he told her. She thought of what Oliver Aldrich had said, and she was certain Lucas wasn't making this up. She could also see that while Lucas told the story with determination, he hated the words, he hated the truth.

Suddenly she remembered his mother's words—the day Emmaline said that Lucas wasn't as bad as he made people believe.

It hit Alice in a fit of surprise that he *was* better than he made people believe, that the look in his eyes was not about guilt or depravity—rather true and utter despair.

Then another realization came on the heels of the first. He might not believe the truth any longer himself. But how to prove he wasn't a horrible man?

He had no alibi. She had no counter for the eyewitness. And he had no way to prove that he didn't still own a nightingale ring.

She had to find another way. Something that would prove without a shadow of a doubt that he was not the killer.

It hit her in an instant, hard and clear. She would have to find the killer herself.

A shiver of fear ran down her spine when she remembered being followed in the alley. Then the next morning when they found the girl dead. The nightingale killer had struck a second time. And she felt certain he would strike again.

"I have a plan," she said before she could think better of it. "A plan to prove your innocence."

"Ah, you and your plans." He chuckled ruefully.

Suddenly, asking him no longer seemed like such a good

idea. He'd probably say no. But she was here. And she didn't have to ask. She could simply tell him.

Taking a deep breath, she forged ahead. "I'm going undercover. I'll leave you now."

She pivoted and headed for the door, a loose strand of hair flying out. But she hadn't gone more than a few steps when he stopped her.

"Undercover?"

She tilted her head, debating the wording of her plan. Nothing too detailed, something that might sound rather innocuous. "Yes, I'm going undercover in the alley. Who knows what might turn up?"

"You're trying to lure the killer."

"Find? Lure?" She shrugged.

"Like hell you are." His countenance went stormy.

"You said yourself that it was my job to come up with a way to get you acquitted."

"No," he repeated, unfazed by her reasoning. "I won't allow it."

"Mr. Hawthorne—"

But it wasn't Lucas who cut her off, rather her stomach, which chose that inopportune second to growl . . . yet again. An ill-timed reminder to her that she hadn't had dinner last night or breakfast this morning.

Lucas shook his head and smiled as if he couldn't help himself, though the detachment was still there. He extended his hand. "Now that you have stated your plan and have your answer—"

"I wasn't asking, Lucas."

"—come with me."

"Where are you taking me?"

He pulled her into his bedroom.

"What are we going to do in here?"

Stopping, he turned back. They stood close. "What would you like to do?"

She glanced at his bed.

"Are you trying to seduce me, Miss Kendall? That's not very businesslike of you."

Shock shimmered through her, along with the desire to say yes. "Absolutely not."

Lucas smiled. His broad hand cupped her cheek. "Are you sure?" His voice deepened. "I'd let you."

Her breath came short and fast. His fingers lingered on her skin. The smell of soap and shaving cream wrapped around her. But as if her stomach knew that nothing good could come of this completely and utterly inappropriate situation, it growled yet again.

His full sensuous lips curved wider. "Let's deal with that stomach of yours first. We'll talk about your having your way with me later." He grasped her hand again and continued on.

"Mr. Hawthorne. Despite what you think," she stated, eyeing the bed, "I am not that kind of woman."

"I think you are."

Alice sucked in her breath.

"A hungry woman, that is."

They walked right past the bed, and for the first time Alice noticed the small kitchen.

"I'll make you something to eat," he said. "You can talk while I cook. Though I'm not sure I'll be able to hear you over the racket your stomach is making."

Alice's smile was brittle. "Didn't your mother teach you it's not nice to mention such things?"

"Yes, but as I see it, you're hungry, and so am I. No sense in standing around starving when we can do something about it." He stepped closer once again, his gaze darkening with some fathomless emotion as he ran his fingers over her lips. "Unless you can convince me to do something else."

Sensation raced down her spine.

"Eating is probably best," she managed to say.

"Of course."

The emotion disappeared, and he chuckled, then completed the last few steps to the kitchen. Alice followed, trying to remember what she had come here to talk about.

"How about ham and eggs?"

"You really cook?"

He shrugged and pulled out a skillet. "If you call ham and eggs cooking, then yes, I cook. Most of the time I go downstairs. But there are times when I prefer to eat in private."

"I'm impressed." And she was.

Within minutes he had whipped up eggs mixed with melting cheese, ham cooked to perfection, and slices of thick bread smoothed with creamy butter. He set the plates out on a small table in a bay window at the back of the house. She nearly swooned from the combination of heavenly smelling food and hunger.

"Do you ever eat?" he asked.

"Do you ever not ask every single thing that comes into your head?"

He held her chair and grinned. "I frequently don't say all the things that pop into my head—especially where you are concerned."

"Like what?"

She took the first bite and had to hold back a moan of pleasure. Alice didn't think a simple meal could taste so good.

"Like no matter how many times I tell myself you are my lawyer, and nothing more, I keep thinking about your beautiful eyes—about how they turn nearly green when they reflect the sun."

He poured her a glass of orange juice, then sat back and started to eat as if he had mentioned nothing more striking than the weather. As always, a contradiction.

"Are you trying to seduce me with good food and flattery?" she asked, afraid that his tactics were working all too well.

Lucas smiled wryly. "I'm simply trying to sustain the health of my lawyer. Besides, I'd never be that subtle."

She savored a buttery slice of bread smothered with strawberry jam he had produced from one of the cabinets. "No, subtle doesn't suit you. You are more the clubbing-over-the-head and dragging-to-your-cave type."

"I think I can eek out a bit more finesse than that."

He smiled at her in a way that made her insides melt much like the butter on the bread.

"Do you practice that smile when you're alone at night?" she asked over a bit of melted cheese and eggs.

"Do you practice your sharp barbs when *you're* home alone?"

"A question instead of an answer."

"I'm learning from you."

"Touché."

He gave her a mock bow of his head, then downed his orange juice.

"I didn't realize you were a boxer," she said.

"I'm not."

"You should be. You looked wonderful."

Humor flickered in his eyes and he leaned forward, planting his elbows on the table with no thought for proper manners. "You think I'm wonderful?"

"You boxed wonderfully well," she clarified, flustered.

"Admit it, Alice, you like me."

He was laughing at her. "I do not! I mean, I do not like you as a . . ."

The words trailed off. What was she going to say? As a suitor, a friend, a lover?

"I mean," she said with the utmost formality, "I like you fine as a client, Mr. Hawthorne."

"That's all I meant, sweetheart."

You did not! But she kept that to herself. "I am not your sweetheart. I am your lawyer. Speaking of which—"

"You didn't finish your breakfast."

She eyed that last bite of bread and jam. Common sense

told her to set the plate aside and get to work so she wouldn't look like a ravenous pig. Instead, she snatched up the morsel.

Lucas made quick work of clearing the table. Alice went to the sink to wash her hands. When she turned back, Lucas was there, setting the plates on the counter. They were so close she could touch him. But she had better sense than that. She started to step away. But Lucas stopped her when he reached out, setting down a plate on either side of her, his hard muscled arms trapping her against the sink.

She stared at his shirt tacks, so dark against the white, one left undone at his neck, her heart pounding in her chest. Then her head tilted back until their eyes met.

"Did you enjoy the meal?" he asked, his voice heavy and rich with sensuality.

"Yes," she managed. "Thank you. I couldn't have done better myself."

"I'm beginning to believe that's all too true. Do you even know how to cook?"

"Of course," she answered with a scoff. Which wasn't exactly accurate. She had been raised to battle wits, not cook meals. "I've just been a little short on time recently, what with an uncooperative client, and all."

Appreciative laughter shone in his blue eyes as he ran his hands down her arms. "I'm happy to cooperate now."

His voice held a ragged edge that made it clear he wasn't immune to her. The realization surprised her and made her breath catch. This man she didn't understand wanted her. Still.

He looked at her, his eyes like dark ocean pools drawing her, his gaze so intense that she wanted to surrender, the lure was so strong. But how? How to give in to a man who was a client, a man of lesser virtue? She couldn't afford this man, couldn't afford to be used, then discarded.

"I am your lawyer, Mr. Hawthorne, not one of your paramours, and I'll thank you to remember the difference."

He studied her with a speculative gleam in his eyes, and she was sure he was remembering their last encounter.

Doing her best to suppress the heat that wanted to flare in her cheeks, she hurried ahead. "I realize you have no reason to remember that since I . . . I . . ."

She floundered.

"Since you kissed me? Like a paramour?"

This time embarrassment flared hot and bright. But Alice would not run from responsibility. "Yes, I was unforgivably forward, then foolishly ran out like a child. It was a display unworthy of your paid advocate, and I apologize."

"Apology accepted."

His palms ran down her arms, and she knew she was in for trouble the minute he leaned toward her.

His lips grazed hers, softly, just a hint, as he leaned into her, a barely perceptible groan slipping out of him, and he deepened the kiss.

"Let me be forward this time," he said softly, "then you won't have anything to apologize for."

Had he not been so close, she knew her brain would have made sense of his words, found the illogic. But he was close, too close. Yet not close enough.

Her mind screamed run, but her body yearned for him. And her heart—it trembled with fear and exhilaration. But she couldn't move away.

Wisps of her hair had come free, curling down her neck. He ran his fingers along the light strands.

"That wasn't what I meant," she replied with a deep shiver of feeling drifting low.

"I know." His fingers continued their path, grazing her collarbone beneath the thin cotton of her gown. His voice was hoarse, and when he turned his hand over, skimming the back ever so gently lower, stopping just above the swell of her breast, he seemed to shudder.

"God forgive me, but I liked that," she whispered.

He pulled her against him, his mouth coming down on hers.

Her fingers curled into his shirtfront—though she shouldn't. She did nothing more than sigh when he pulled her chemisette from her waistband, his callused fingers sliding beneath the material to stroke her back. Then he coaxed her lips apart, and she tasted orange on his tongue. And when she leaned into him, she felt his deep moan.

"This isn't wise," he said against her open mouth.

"I haven't done a wise thing since you walked through my office door."

She felt him tense, and she cursed her tongue.

He closed his eyes, his fingers seemingly frozen. And she was sure he would step away and make her feel like the most forward of fools. His eyes opened, troubled, fathomless. But he didn't step away. He kissed her hairline, his lips drifting lower until he nipped at her neck. Her head fell back, and he put his hand on her abdomen, slowly trailing up, his lips nipping at her ear, before he cupped her breast.

The sensations were exquisite, amazing, the intensity she craved—that she never wanted to end, regardless of what it said about her. In that moment, right and wrong fled from her mind; propriety was not a thought.

She wrapped her arms around his neck, and he lifted her up until her body lined his.

"You make me want you," he whispered. "Badly. You make me want to explore every inch of you. You make me want to watch your face as I fill you, slip my hard length inside you."

Alice felt her body's reaction simply at the words, the image of their bodies lying entwined. His hard shaft filling her, slowly, insistently.

Her breath caught on passion, but shock as well.

"You make me feel as if I've never been with a woman before," he whispered, his voice gravelly as his hands cupped her hips.

He looked into her eyes, and she saw a depth of feeling inside him. Desire, yes. But feelings of wonder and innocence as well, which she would never have dreamed were possible.

"You make me feel like someone I'm not," he said, his voice a desperate accusation.

The innocence in his eyes fled at his words, like a reminder.

Abruptly he stepped away. But before he turned, she saw a stark emptiness of soul that cried out to her. As if she could do nothing else, she reached out and stopped him. Looking down, he stared at her pale hand on his arm, watched as her fingers curled into his sleeve. But he didn't give in.

Very carefully, as if he were afraid that she would break—or that he would—he took her hand away. For long seconds he didn't let go, only stared at her fingers, before he kissed each one.

"Go home, Alice," he said raggedly. "Go home, go back to work, whatever. I am not the man you are trying to convince yourself I am."

Chapter Fifteen

Late that night, Alice slipped out of her cottage, staying in the shadows to make sure no one saw her. Avoiding her father, uncle, and brother proved easy. Evading the frequently lurking newspapermen had been doable. But it took fifty cents to a hack driver to cause a diversion for her to slip past the growing flock of women who clamored outside of Nightingale's Gate in hopes of catching a glimpse of the establishment's owner. The women were everywhere now. At the courthouse, on his front doorstep.

Last night, she had heard, one had managed to slip inside the club and wasn't found until Lucas had retired. Fortunately, when he had found her naked in his bed, he'd had the presence of mind to have Brutus escort her safely home, though not before she was given a hot meal.

All said, it took Alice nearly an hour to get from her cottage to the inside of Nightingale's Gate, arriving at eleven in the evening.

Earlier that day, after leaving Lucas, she had sought out Grayson at his law office downtown. He had been no more receptive to her undercover plan than his younger brother had been. He also had never heard of Cindy Pop when she asked him about the woman.

But Emmaline had arrived unexpectedly in the office, and when she heard about the undercover plan, she had convinced Grayson to go along. The older woman had also said she'd see to it that Lucas agreed as well.

Now, slipping inside Nightingale's Gate, Emmaline was waiting for Alice as promised.

"Hurry, hurry," the older woman said, taking her hand and dashing up the stairs like a guilty schoolgirl. "I have everything ready in my room."

"What's wrong?" Alice asked, keeping up as best as she could.

Once the bedroom door was firmly shut, Emmaline breathed a sigh of relief and looked at Alice sheepishly. "Lucas still hasn't quite come around to your plan yet."

The older woman turned quickly away. The room was simple but beautiful, with yellow-and-white-striped draperies with floral overprints. Windows overlooked the gardens in the back, lush and full despite the summer heat.

Emmaline went to several pieces of clothing that were laid out on the bed. "I borrowed these from the girls. We'll have to see what fits and what doesn't. We also need to work on your hair."

"What's wrong with it?"

"Nothing, dear. It's beautiful. But it looks a tad matronly," she added apologetically. "First, however, we need to start with the clothes. You can try on things behind the screen."

Alice did as she was told, changing into the outfits Emmaline provided. With each change, she stepped out from behind the screen, and each time she stepped out, she found another of Lucas's dancing girls had come into the room.

They studied Alice as if she were a specimen under a microscope, foreign and not altogether appealing.

What had started out as a means to an end, a professional situation, suddenly made her feel as if she were young again, awkward and not fitting in with the rest of the girls.

"What?" she demanded finally, when she could take their silent scrutiny no longer.

Emmaline seemed to shake herself out of someplace

in her mind and said, "It's just that none of these outfits look . . . seem . . . none of them are quite right."

"What's wrong?"

A large-boned, red-headed woman with a revealing robe stood up. "Your damn skinny ass is the problem. You don't have enough flesh on you to make it worth a man's while to take a second look."

Alice wasn't sure if she was mortified or incensed. Not that she was surprised.

"Nattie," Emmaline reprimanded gently. "Alice has a nice figure."

"Nice doesn't cut it in this world, I tell you."

Alice had the very real and very sudden thought that she would have liked to have had a sister. And a mother whom she remembered. But whatever fondness she felt fled when the girl called Nattie pointed out her biggest flaw.

"You don't have enough in the way of breasts to satisfy a man."

"Nattie," Emmaline admonished sternly.

"It's the God's own truth, it is. Which makes me wonder what she is doing with this dressing-up business. No lady like her is gonna go to work in a place like this. Look at her."

All the girls and Emmaline peered at Alice. Red flared so bright in her cheeks that she could feel it burn.

"Don't you worry about why she is dressing up," Emmaline interjected. "We just need to worry about making her look the part."

The girls sighed, hemmed and hawed, before Nattie raced out of the room, then returned triumphant.

"This should do it!"

Alice gawked. "What are those?"

"Bust enhancers. In a place like this, where men can look but not touch, they don't know the difference."

Sure enough, within the next hour, Alice was buffed, shined, painted, and enhanced. When the women were through with her and she stood in front of the chevaled mirror, Alice hardly recognized herself.

"Oh, my," she breathed.

"Oh, my, indeed," Nattie said with a snort of approval.

Alice turned sideways, all but gawking at the voluminous curves that had sprouted. Without thinking, she ran her hands over her body, her eyes going wide when the girls burst out in a gale of laughter.

"Now you need a bit of practice. Lucas is . . . busy in his private suite." Emmaline grimaced at this, and she couldn't meet Alice's eyes.

Alice felt she had been kicked in the stomach at the thought that Lucas was upstairs with another woman. But why shouldn't he be, she told herself firmly.

But somehow what she felt was a wildness, that emotion she had been working so hard of late to contain. She walked to the door, painted and polished. No, not walked. She strolled, strutted, sauntered. She parted her lips and ran her tongue along the edge of her teeth. "I'm ready."

"Oh, my," Emmaline mused.

"That's more like it," Nattie said with an approving nod.

"Time to see if my . . . new look works."

Alice made it down the stairs, feeling a giddy excitement she wasn't used to, and into the grand salon.

The second Alice hit the floor, every eye turned in her direction. She sauntered and smiled, came up next to men, close, too close, but that was the intent. Besides, Lucas was upstairs with a woman.

"Miss!"

"Over here!"

"Would you like to dance?"

They circled around, each vying for her attention. This was what pretty girls experienced, she realized, understanding for the first time the power of beauty and curves. It turned men into mush.

Just then, Grayson came in the front door, the room echoing with calls of lurid appreciation.

"What's going on?" he asked.

A footman pointed. "The new girl, sir."

Grayson took in the room, finally finding the "new girl," though it took a moment for him to register who she was.

When he did, he nodded in approval, or perhaps resignation, then went to a table in the corner where two men waited for him. If . . . No, she amended, *when* Lucas got wind of this, there would be hell to pay.

Regardless, Grayson went over the plan with the men, then nodded for Alice to join them. After one last summary, Alice found herself in Beekman's alleyway, the thick night air wrapping around her like gauze.

Millions of stars dotted the black sky, and the moon was full and bright. But still she felt the darkness to her bones. There was a huge difference between thinking about being in the alley, and actually being there.

Not for the first time in her life, Alice wondered how in the world she had gotten herself into a particular situation.

Taking a deep breath, she quashed second thoughts and looked up to the two places the lookouts were supposed to be hiding. Both were there. Thank goodness. Now to act.

Her dress was made of red satin with black trim, cut low, though not too low since the bust enhancers had to be covered. Black-netted stockings covered her legs, disappearing into a sensible shoe, with a practical shawl thrown over her shoulders—as if to say, I just finished work, and now I'm going home.

She hadn't covered her pale blonde hair, rather Emmaline had done it up in an elaborate design that curled on her head, then fell alluringly down her shoulders.

She walked along, trying to remember how the girls had shown her. Swish, swish. Stumble. Damn.

In the grand salon she had been perfect. Out here, however, her nerves skittered. Suddenly things had taken on a decidedly more real aspect, and for the first time she questioned this impulsive idea of hers. Just the thought of a murderer coming out of the shadows made her blood run cold. What if the men couldn't get to her in time?

A little late to think about that now, she thought glumly. Though wasn't that frequently the way with her? Act first, think later. A bad habit, to say the least, though a habit until now that had never gotten her into too big of trouble.

But a mere thirty minutes later, she went from questioning her impulsive plan to cursing it. She had swished and flounced and trotted up and down the alleyway, and not a single soul had appeared. Not a rustle or creak of footsteps.

By one in the morning, her legs ached, her hair had gone limp, and she desperately wanted to go to bed. At one-thirty she gave the signal that she was done for the night. Minutes later, a carriage swept up.

"It didn't work," she stated glumly when Emmaline pulled her inside the confines of Grayson's carriage.

"Not tonight, but we still have three nights before the trial begins."

"You think we should try again tomorrow?"

"Yes, but we have to be careful. Lucas will be furious if he finds out we went ahead. If anything happens to you, so much as a scratch, he'll see that I regret it."

"True, no one can afford to lose his attorney just before his trial. Though," she added with a grim laugh, "it would provide him with a foolproof excuse for a continuance. I could come in handy after all."

Emmaline gave her a considering look that Alice didn't like one bit.

"What?" she had to ask.

"Lucas would care for more reasons than that, dear."

"Pshaw," she scoffed. "Your son might be happy to get thrown in jail just to get rid of me. Good heavens, he was upstairs tonight forgetting me quite easily apparently."

She willed back the childish words as soon as they spilled over her lips.

"Is that what you think?"

Alice waved the words away. "It hardly matters."

"Dear, dear," Emmaline said, patting her hand. "Lucas spent the night upstairs in the boxing room. He only goes up there when he's very, very upset."

Despite herself, relief, joy, and satisfaction rushed through her veins. Had they had more room, she might have jumped up and down. Though just as quickly, she quashed the feelings.

"Change now," Emmaline said.

Given the late hour, the streets were deserted. Emmaline turned away to give Alice some measure of privacy while she changed into her gown. Just as she finished, the carriage pulled up a block away from her house. Jumping down, she started away.

"Tomorrow night, then?" Emmaline whispered after her.

"Yes, tomorrow night."

Alice went straight to her office the following morning. In addition to her nocturnal endeavors, she still had to finish up preparations for the trial. She hoped it wouldn't come to that, but in case they didn't nab the man, the trial would proceed.

Then there was still the issue of Cindy Pop. Alice had been trying to find her since her name had resurfaced days ago. Whether people were being truthful or not, no one had heard of her. So the search continued.

After several hours of intense concentration, she set her pen in its holder and stretched her back, then checked the clock. Still hours to go.

She checked the clock a hundred more times before, finally, it struck five and she dashed home.

She barely said a word, and as soon as was possible, she yawned dramatically and said good night, despite the fact that it was little more than eight-thirty.

Walker, Harry, and Max hardly seemed to note that she was gone.

It was still early when she couldn't take it a second longer. With the late-summer sun down but still making the sky a dark shade of purple, she slipped out and headed for Nightingale's Gate.

Emmaline was surprised to see her when she sneaked back to her room.

"Didn't you get my note?" the older woman asked, her eyes red and puffy as if she had been crying.

"No, what's wrong?"

"You've wasted a trip here. Lucas got wind of the plan and has forbidden anyone from helping you do this. So I'm afraid the trial will have to proceed." Emmaline looked despondent.

"That's ridiculous, we just got started—"

"No, Alice." Emmaline stopped her. "Lucas was adamant, and in hindsight, I realize he's right. We can't put you at risk, dear."

Perhaps at another time Alice would have seen the truth in Emmaline's words. But just then Alice felt frustrated and ineffectual, disappointed that she couldn't see this through and avoid going to court. Because, in truth, she didn't see how she could win. The Commonwealth might have only a circumstantial case, but it was shaping up into a damn good one.

Barely offering a word of good-bye, Alice left Emmaline's room. But instead of leaving out the front, she headed for the back door. She might not be able to go undercover, but she could find Cindy Pop. This mystery woman must have some answers. And somebody living off the alley had to know where she was.

Just as she got to the back hallway, Brutus caught sight of her.

"Where are you going?" he asked, his dark eyes glimmering oddly.

"I'm meeting someone out back. Don't worry, one of my uncle's patrolmen is there as well," she lied.

She didn't wait for his response. She hurried out the back door to the alley, never seeing the hard look of speculation in Brutus's eyes.

The warm night surrounded her the minute she stepped out onto the hard dirt. It was dark, but not too dark, and it was still early enough that one or two people scurried to and from their homes.

She started at the first rough-planked door and knocked. Determined, committed, or perhaps just mule-headed, Alice went door to door, gate to gate. But everyone said they had never heard of Cindy Pop, though only a handful of residents spoke to her at all. Several slammed her out without a word. And with every slam, her mind circled faster. But she only marched to the next building, growing more frantic with each step she took. Someone had to know Cindy. There had to be some piece of evidence that she could find to help her case.

Caught up in her whirling thoughts, it took a second before she became aware of footsteps behind her. Spinning around, she peered into darkness dotted only with the light of a few gas lanterns.

"Who's there?" she demanded.

Silence greeted her.

Listening intently, the only sound she heard was the pounding of her heart in her chest. Alice shook her head, telling herself she only imagined footsteps. Forcing a manic little laugh, she started walking. Suddenly reality forced its way into her mind and she wanted out of the alley. She wanted to be at home, safe in her little cottage—or perhaps in a warm kitchen sipping tea with her uncle.

Concentrating on each step she took, she cursed the fact that the cobbled street was a long way away. But soon she couldn't deny that the footsteps weren't a part of her imagination. There was no mistaking the sound. In a distorted circle of thoughts, she realized she had succeeded. Inadvertently she had lured the killer out. Mission accomplished, though this night there were no backups in the shadows to leap out and help her.

She nearly threw her head back and laughed, because mixed with the fear that sent tendrils up her spine, there was stubborn exhilaration. Her plan had worked. She had not failed.

But all of that fled when the footsteps grew closer and terror finally, truly took hold, swelling in her throat.

Alice started to run, the toe of her shoe catching in her hem, sending her flying forward, sprawling in the dust and grit. But before she could scramble to her feet, a hand grabbed her from behind, pulling her to her feet in one swift and effortless motion.

She screamed, the sound piercing the night. But when she came face-to-face with the man, her mind careened to find Lucas towering over her in the darkened night, his face a ferocious mask.

His hands gripped her shoulders. "Are you all right?" he demanded, his gaze quickly taking her in, his expression fiercely protective.

Sensation spun through her, emotions tangling like overgrown vines.

"It's you," she whispered in a desperate rasp. Tears threatened, burning, aching, closing her throat. "It's only you."

She felt him stiffen with offense. But she didn't care. Everything pressed in on her, the night, the looming trial. The very real, though foolishly inappropriate, thought that she would be a spinster lawyer for the rest of her life.

"I can't even lure a killer!"

The words surprised Lucas. "What are you talking about?"

She gave a strangled cry, trying to break free, but he held her there.

"What do you mean?" he asked, his voice harsh, his dark eyes boring into her.

"I'm plain and unattractive, and I can't even lure a killer! He's out there; he's killing girls in this very alley, but he doesn't even give me a second glance!"

"Have you lost your mind?" His face lined with stunned accusation. "A murderer doesn't care about looks. And while I shouldn't begin to indulge this absurd conversation, let me tell you this. You are attractive, very attractive, and I would think you'd be smart enough to know that."

Her breathing was labored, her chest so tight that she felt she would scream. She knew he was right, she was being absurd, but something had pushed her to the edge, beyond caring. "Tell that to Clark, or any other man in Boston!"

"Clark?" An edge came into his voice. "What does that twit have to do with this?"

"That *twit*, as you called him, rejected me! I can't lure a killer! I can't lure a twit—"

She cut herself off, because there was no explaining to this man or anyone else. It was ridiculous, she knew. But how to explain her despair about a lifetime of not fitting in, about being someone whom others liked well enough on a superficial level, but not on a deeper level. She realized now that she lived a life of intellectual achievement because, deep down, she knew that was the only life available to her.

And she wasn't even succeeding at that.

Lucas stared at her, and she braced herself for some biting remark, actually wished for it. Anything to set her mind back to normal, to pull her back from this precarious edge. But he didn't offer some glib response. Instead, a depth of caring filled his dark eyes, making her throat tighten even more.

"Clark doesn't know his head from his ass," he said softly.

A tiny laugh burst out of her, but with that burst came the tears that she had valiantly held back.

"Alice." The word was a brush of sound as he braced his hands on her shoulders. "You are alluring. I've told you that. And from what I heard, you had every man in the club lusting after you last night."

"Yeah, paint me up and slap on a fake chest, and I'm a real treat." She snorted disdainfully.

"But the true beauty of you," he persisted, "is your innocence and your honesty. Painted women are a dime a dozen. But you, with your gentle beauty and welcome intelligence, are a rare find."

It was the kindness in his voice as much as his words that made her breath catch. She also saw that he didn't like the feelings he had expressed. But he couldn't seem to stop himself.

"I hate that you would cover up who you really are. Perhaps that's what I like the most about you. Your conviction, your pureness. It scares the hell out of me. But don't think for a moment that it isn't beautiful." He looked at her, his gaze intense. "There are plenty of men out there who would be honored to marry you."

"What about you?" she asked before she could stop.

The sound of revelers drifted to them from the distance. Lucas stilled, then cursed.

In seconds he whisked them down the alley and up a narrow set of stairs at the back of Nightingale's Gate, which she had never noticed before, that led to a small balcony with multipaned French doors. Once inside, she realized they were in his private suite of rooms.

Alice had the fleeting thought that Lucas could come and go without anyone knowing.

As soon as the door closed behind them, Lucas continued on as if he were going to lead her out to the hallway. But she stopped in the middle of his suite of rooms.

"You didn't answer me." She said the words out loud.

He stilled, but didn't turn back.

"Are you so different from Clark? Would you want me as a wife?"

"You don't want to marry me," he replied.

He turned around to face her, his expression shadowed with a dark yearning. Then, seemingly unable to stop himself, he walked back to her and took her by the shoulders.

"I am not the man for you to marry. Not the man to give you the children you deserve. Not the man who can give you a house with gardens filled with roses. I would only hurt you."

He watched, seemingly unable to look away, as his fingers drifted down the sleeves of her gown.

She realized with a start through the myriad emotions she was feeling, that she had been waiting for this, waiting for him to touch her again. Forever waiting.

With Lucas close, everything else faded away. Clark. Her father. The realization filled her with fear because she could think of nothing less possible than a future between herself and this man.

But then he leaned down to her and pressed his lips to the tender spot beneath her ear, and that realization along with the fear dissipated into the golden-lit room.

"Alice," he murmured. "God, I can't stay away."

Gently, he pulled back and stared at her. The same desperation that had flashed through his eyes when he talked about innocence lost. And like a drowning man reaching out for a lifeline, he took her hand, the tips of his fingers pressed to her pulse. With breathtaking slowness he trailed his fingers up her arm until he grasped her shoulder. And then he captured her mouth with his, finally, desperately.

She inhaled deeply, and when she did, she felt his tongue, fleetingly, against her lips. The intimacy never ceased to amaze her, as did the strange feeling that coursed through her body, making her want to press closer.

The dark alley was gone from her mind. Right or wrong vanquished. Only Lucas remained.

He wrapped his arms around her, and she went to him. His heat drew her, as his hands slid down her spine to cup her bottom, drawing her full against the hard planes of his body. She groaned into his mouth as he kissed her again, coaxing, his need insistent against her. And when he lifted her up as if she weighed nothing more than a feather, his arm hooking under her knees, then carried her to his bed, she didn't resist. In that second she wanted nothing more than for this to never end.

Setting her down, Lucas moved over her. She could feel the steely ripple of muscle beneath the thin cotton of his shirt. She wanted to touch him, explore his body, but she held back. As if sensing her trepidation, he brought her hand up and placed it on his chest.

"Touch me," he whispered against her ear.

Boldly, she worked the fastenings of his shirt, and she gasped when he hurriedly finished the job. She reveled in the smooth tautness of his skin, warm, his heart beating against her hand—strong and steady.

But her heart leaped when he started working the fastenings of her blouse. One by one, so assuredly. She put from her mind that given his skill he must have done this a thousand times before. All she wanted to think about then was the fact that he desired her. Her. Not someone else. He had seen her, knew her, spent time with her, saw her for everything she was . . . or wasn't. And still he wanted her.

In that moment it was enough. Perhaps tomorrow it wouldn't be. Maybe in the morning she would be overcome with regret. But right that second, she would go as far as Lucas would take her. She was well beyond the age when most girls were married and had children. For once, she would experience passion.

The thought of love reared its head. But she pushed that away, too. She wanted this man, and he wanted her.

Drunk on sensation, Alice let Lucas pull her blouse free. She gasped when he cupped her breast, and he caught the sound in his mouth, sucking it in, then stroking her tongue with his own, as if he couldn't get enough.

"Alice," he groaned into her mouth, before lowering his head to nuzzle the taut bud of her breast.

The touch sent her senses reeling, and she cried out, her back arching. "Lucas," she whispered again, awed.

His kisses turned to nips as he worked his way down her body, moving her clothes away. His teeth grazed her skin and the fine cotton of her underclothes. Impatient, he pulled off the chemise, then reached beneath the petticoat and tugged her pantaloons down her legs.

She had to bite back her gasp of shock. But she wouldn't stop now. She wanted to know.

He dipped his head and laved one nipple with his tongue. Her breath caught, and she felt his groan of satisfaction as the rose-colored tip pulled into a tight bud.

"You like that, don't you?" he murmured.

"You know I do."

He chuckled, then he ran his tongue around first one nipple, then the other, his teeth gently grazing the tender flesh. Her breath grew shallow as he trailed down her body, from the sensitive swell of her breasts to the waistband of her fine linen petticoat. He didn't take off her petticoat, he only slipped his hands under the hem. His hands skimmed slowly up to her belly, the gauzy material of her undergarment bunching against his wrists as he watched her eyes flutter closed.

Her mouth opened on a silent breath when the heel of his palm grazed the curls between her legs. Both of them were breathing rapidly as, gently, he brushed his hand back and forth.

"Alice," he whispered, then brushed his lips across her burning skin, his hand sliding lower.

She trembled, wanting, needing, desire beating in her veins.

He felt her need, felt her seeking something she didn't understand. But when he bent his head and tasted the bare silky flesh of her womanhood, her eyes flew open, and she cried out.

"Lucas!" she gasped, her fingers tangling in his dark hair.

Hard, consuming sensation shivered through him. His body pulsed with need, deep, powerful need that threatened to overwhelm them both.

With ironclad willpower, he pulled back. Reality reared, and he realized his demons had taken control, pushed him to this point, passion and desire for this woman winning over everything he knew to be true.

Since meeting her, he had tried to purge himself of thoughts of her. He had lain in bed, his body hard with desire. But the only woman he wanted was Alice. He wanted to part her thighs, press at her opening until she pulled him to her, then slide in, slowly. He wanted to feel every inch of her satiny warmth wrap around him. He had nearly done just that seconds ago.

And that couldn't happen. He wanted her, yes. And he could see in her eyes that she wanted him. However, it was the heat she wanted, the experience of passion that she sought. Not him.

But when he started to rock back on his heels and cover her, she grabbed his arms.

"Don't pull away from me."

"This has gone too far."

They were mere inches apart, both barely dressed.

"Please."

Her plea sank into his soul, and his body shimmered with barely controlled wanting. He had brought her to this point, his own driving need for this woman taking over.

"Don't make me beg," she whispered.

Unable to do anything else, he gave in, his groan rumbling through the room as his mouth slanted over hers. Their embrace turned to fire. Each giving in. Their legs tangling in the sheets.

"I'll give you what you want," he whispered against her skin.

Gently he pressed her back against the thick bedcoverings. Kissing her, he caressed her body. She met his passion, clinging to him, thrilling him with her naïve desire. The passion that would not be held back by inexperience.

His hand drifting low, his lips grazed the pulse at her neck as he pulled one of her knees up, her skirts floating down around her hips. And when he took one nipple deep in his mouth, he slipped his finger deep inside her.

She cried out, her back arching to his touch. His body leaped and made demands of its own. But he kept a fierce rein on himself. He stroked her sweet warmth, long strokes, deep and slow until her body began to move with him, low purring moans emanating from her.

Experience told him she was close, and experience told him to bring her close, but not there. Her mewling cries wound around him with the sharp bite of talons. Her mouth opened on a soundless cry when he stroked deep.

"Please," she managed.

With that, he gave her what she wanted. He saw the minute her body exploded. Sensation crystallized inside her, and she arched in silent, nearly torturous pleasure.

Release. The kind that went so deep that tension and the world around washed away. As potent as a drug. Lucas knew.

For one fleeting second, he wrapped her in his arms and held her tighter than he'd held anything in his life. Then, with the control he had mastered over nearly two decades, he pulled away from her.

Long minutes passed before her breathing grew even. At length she pulled up on one elbow. His hands stilled as he worked the fastenings of his shirt. She looked tousled and well satisfied, her blonde hair cascading about her shoulders, her lips full and red from passion. Her eyes had a stunned joy to them.

Concentrating on his tie, he steeled himself against the

desire to sink his flesh in hers, and love her as he wanted to. But he wouldn't do that.

"What about you?"

Her words surprised him, and his fingers stilled in their task. He saw her reflection in the mirror, her eyes wide at her words. Her innocent caring of him and his needs nearly brought him to his knees.

"There's more," she stated, a hint of the lawyer in her surfacing. "I know there is. I've read about . . ."

Her words trailed off, and his heart swelled. With a gentleness he had never felt before, he came back to her. But when she came up on her knees and would have wound her arms around his neck, he held them and kissed her forehead.

"That is all there will be, Alice. It's best this way."

She blinked.

"Now get dressed. It's time to get you home."

He stepped away and opened the door, calling out to Brutus. But Alice leaped off the bed and followed him, banging the door shut and flattening her back against it.

"Who are you to tell me what is best for me?" she demanded.

His expression grew fierce as he started to set her aside. But she grabbed his arm.

"I don't care about my virginity, Lucas."

He stared at her for an eternity. "But I do."

"Damn you! That's just an excuse."

His blazing gaze pinned her. She had no idea what their little interlude had cost him, giving her what she asked for, without taking for himself—when she was something he had wanted with an intensity he had never experienced. But he would not let her dissuade him.

"Call it what you will. The fact is, you got what you wanted. Pleasure. Mind-exploding pleasure that makes a person willing to dance with the devil. That's me, Alice. I dance with the devil. I seek that passion. The dark loss of control that makes a man lose his soul."

She stared at him, and he was certain she was seeing him as she never had before. But then she spoke.

"I don't think you're afraid to lose your soul to the devil—or even afraid that you already have. You're afraid to lose yourself to love, true love that you believe makes a man weak." Her eyes blazed, boldly meeting his. "It doesn't make you weak, Lucas. A man has to be strong to love. Are you that strong?"

Chapter Sixteen

Brutus came to the door and knocked.

Alice and Lucas stared at each other, their eyes locked, warring. But neither said a word.

"Boss?" Brutus called out. "Did you call for me?"

After a moment, Alice stepped away from the door, and angrily began to fix her clothes. "Go ahead, answer. Let him come in and take me away. Send me off. But just because I'm gone doesn't change the truth. You are a strong man, Lucas. A man who is more than you make out to be. I know it."

Lucas stood as still as stone, furious, upset in a way that he didn't understand—or didn't want to understand. It was easier to get angry than to try to make sense of what this woman made him feel—about her, about his life.

"You are naïve, and you haven't the first idea about the world I'm from. I won't taint you." He headed for the door.

"You aren't tainting me! And when are going to realize you aren't tainted yourself?"

Stopping midstride, he whirled to face her. "You have no idea what you're talking about," he stated. "You don't know the first thing about me. You ask questions and draw up diagrams, and you think you know who I am. But you don't."

"You told me about your childhood, Lucas."

He scoffed bitterly. "But I didn't tell you about the man I have become. About the hundreds of times I have lost myself in drink. The gambling—on anything from a horse race

220

to how quickly a man can lure a woman into his bed. The women into whom I have sunk my flesh—all to lose myself, all so I don't have to think."

His fingers curled around her arms. "That's just it, Alice, I don't want to think. Not about life, not about what I have done. Not about you." He let go harshly.

Unexpectedly, the image of himself as a boy came into his mind. Of smiles and laughter, or innocent games played with other boys in the street. Regular games, not games of chance. Stick ball and pirate escapades.

He turned away from the image. Alice was doing this to him, making him remember things that did him no good— made him wish for a life that he had lost.

His mind stilled at the thought and he cursed, then he quashed it with the ironclad willpower that had gotten him this far. Alice Kendall had nothing to do with the kind of life he *wanted* to lead, he told himself firmly. Nightingale's Gate was his lifeblood, for reasons that had nothing to do with money.

The club had given him purpose. Polite society had set his teeth on edge. The flirting, the vapid conversation. The inability to speak openly, truthfully, the real world hidden beneath yards of ruffled damasks much like the table legs proper women spent great stores of energy hiding.

Nightingale's Gate had provided him with a world that didn't make him feel restless. It made him feel alive. The danger, the darkness.

When he had agreed to hire Alice, he hadn't expected to come to care about her. Because of that caring, he didn't want her to get hurt. And if he wasn't careful, she would be.

Brutus waited in the hallway to do his bidding—and that bidding should be to take Alice home. But there he stood, the command left unspoken.

"God, Alice, don't you see, you want me to be a better man—the kind you don't have to feel guilty about wanting. You need a life of respectability and a husband who leads a regular life. I respect you too much to lead you down a path that you will only regret when your curiosity is quenched."

Her breath caught at his words, and he saw the truth flash through her eyes. Or was it fear? Was it possible that she herself didn't know?

But then her gaze filled with steely resolve. "Don't try to confuse me. Your brother would give his right arm for you. And your parents love you."

He had started to soften at the mention of Grayson, and the thought of Matthew arriving any day. They did care. But the mention of his parents made his blood run cold. "My father can go to hell."

She blushed as if she had forgotten that fact, but then said, "I can't imagine what has come between you and your father, but I happen to know that your mother loves you a great deal."

"A mother's love is blind. She accepts me despite who I am."

"Who you've become!" She sighed, frustrated. "Why do you go to such lengths to make people think the worst of you?"

"I'm not like you, Alice. No matter what you want to see, I am not innocent. I told you about the life I lead—and all of that barely makes me feel alive."

"Maybe that's because it has never been the life you wanted?"

"That's ridiculous," he bit out. "I set out to gain this world."

"For whatever reason, I believe you set out to thwart your father," she said with a quiet certainty.

Lucas felt as if a jolt of electricity had hit him square in the chest.

"Stop running, Lucas."

He hardened his heart. "Whatever my reason for becoming who I am, you can't put the layers of an onion back on once it's peeled."

"I don't doubt you've seen and experienced more than

most men, but that makes it all the purer when you get down to the core and find a man worth saving."

They stared at each other, each breathing hard.

"And for reasons I don't understand," she added, "that man, the promise of who you could be, scares you."

He didn't say a word, couldn't really.

At length, Alice shook her head and walked to the door. "Brutus," she said. "Could you be so kind as to see me home?"

His heart screamed to stop her, but his mind knew that he'd be a fool if he did. The door shut behind her, and as their footsteps grew distant, all he could wonder was what if she was right.

A sound woke Alice in the wee hours of the morning. Startled out of disturbing dreams of dark alleys and hands grabbing her out of nowhere, she sat up with a cry.

Sitting very still, her nightgown sticking to her from the heat, all she could hear was the pounding of her heart. Several seconds passed before she heard the noise again. A quiet knock on her cottage door.

Wishing desperately that she hadn't moved out of her father's home, Alice crept to the window. Peering into the brightening darkness, she saw a woman standing on the front step, looking furtively from side to side.

Better sense told Alice to remain quiet and do nothing. But Alice had never had a very good relationship with better sense. She answered the door.

"Miss Kendall?" the woman asked.

Standing eye to eye with Alice, even though she stood a step lower, the woman asked the question confidently.

"Yes, I'm Alice Kendall."

"I'm Cindy Pop, and I hear you've been looking for me."

Alice wasn't sure who she had thought this woman would turn out to be, but Cindy Pop wasn't it.

"Miss Pop?" Could that be a real name? "Please come in."

Cindy glanced around the yard one last time, then entered. Alice turned up a gaslight and found the woman looked tired and well older than she had at first sight. Her clothes were worn but clean, her stockings neatly mended.

"I assume you were looking for me because of Lucille."

"Well, yes. I was. Though no one I spoke to said they knew you."

Cindy shook her head as if Alice had no sense. "In my world, the less you know the better."

"But you do know, or rather, knew Lucille Rouge."

The woman's hard eyes softened, though only for a brief moment. "Yeah, I knew her. And I saw her get killed."

Alice's mind reeled. "Do the police know this?"

"Of course they do. I told them everything. But I haven't heard a word from them since I talked. Next thing I heard, they were saying that Tawny Green, a silly girl who's afraid of her own shadow, saw the murder."

Alice tried to assimilate the implications. Her uncle knew about this but had denied it. In fact, her father knew about this as well, she was certain, since it was from his secretary whom she first heard the name.

But did Clark know? Or had her father kept it from him?

Her mind spun with questions.

"All right," she said, giving herself a little shake, "tell me everything."

Cindy shifted her weight on her high heels.

"Please, sit down," Alice immediately offered.

"Thanks," the woman said, sitting with a grateful sigh of relief. "These shoes take a toll, I tell ya."

"I'm sure. Now, as to Lucille Rouge."

Cindy Pop's strong face seemed to fall. "She told me she was in love."

Alice remembered Lucas telling her that Lucille had been pregnant. "Who was she in love with?"

"Some important man. She never told me his name, said she had to keep it a secret for a while longer, but that he loved her as much as she loved him." Cindy sneered, the hard knowingness coming back into her lined features. "Lucille always was naïve. Important men don't love women like us; they use us." She turned away sharply. "That's the deal."

"Don't you have any clue at all who the man is?"

"No. The only other thing she told me was that she was pregnant by him."

"Did you tell that to the police?"

"Yes."

Alice stared, trying to fit this together with what she knew. But it made no sense. This woman had provided the Commonwealth with the one thing they lacked. A motive.

Then why wouldn't they have used Cindy? Why would they have suppressed her name?

"What else did you tell them?"

Cindy shrugged and reached down and rubbed her ankles. "I told them the killer disappeared inside one of the buildings off the alley. They wanted to know if I would say it was Lucas Hawthorne."

"They asked you that?"

"Yep. And I said I couldn't tell. It was dark."

The only reason Alice could imagine that the Commonwealth wouldn't want to use Cindy Pop was that they didn't *want* to risk the pregnancy coming out at trial.

But why wouldn't they want the jury to know that? *Who* wouldn't want the jury to know that?

It made no sense. "Miss Pop, perhaps the police have looked for you. I know I haven't been able to find you."

"They can find me, rest assured," she answered with a hint of dismay in her voice. "But that chief of police told me to my face I wasn't needed. Wasn't wanted. He told me that Tawny had come forward and had seen the crime from a better angle."

Was this true?

Then Alice thought of something else. "Miss Pop, did you see the killer bend over the dead body?"

Cindy squeezed her eyes closed. "Yes. And I hear on the street that the murderer marked Lucille with a nightingale."

Alice didn't agree or disagree. "Does the nightingale mark mean anything to you?"

She drew a deep breath. "There's a tale that used to circle around about a lady who had all the men enthralled. The Nightingale, they called her. She was more a legend, it always seemed to me. But now I'm not so sure. In fact, now that you mention it, Lucille asked about the Nightingale the night she told me about the fellow she was in love with."

"What did she ask?"

"If she was real. If she still existed."

"What did you tell her?"

Cindy shrugged. "I told her I didn't know. She seemed worried about it, though I can't imagine why."

A Nightingale lady? And suddenly she remembered Oliver Aldrich saying that many of them had loved the nightingale. At the time it hadn't made sense. Could he have been referring to this woman?

"Miss Pop, would you be willing to testify about this in court?"

"Sure, I already told the police that."

"Good. How can I find you when I need to get in touch?"

"Well," Cindy hesitated. "I'm staying at my ma's right now. I guess you can get me there."

Cindy gave her the address, a run-down neighborhood south of town, then started to leave. At the door she hesitated. "There's one other thing. I don't know if this is important or not, but one of the reasons I didn't realize what was about to happen was because he was acting so kind toward her."

Alice realized then that Cindy Pop felt guilty about the events, guilty that she hadn't done anything to stop the murder.

"Then the killer said something," she added.

"What?"

"It was like, 'You shouldn't have done it, Mother.' No one else was around that I could see. Then, lightning fast, Lucille was dead. It happened so quick like that there was no time to scream or do anything. In the next second the alley was empty except for me and Lucille's body."

Tears threatened in the woman's eyes, so at odds with her not-terribly-feminine features. Alice came forward and rested her hand on the woman's wrist. "You had no way of knowing what was going to happen. It wasn't your fault."

Cindy's shoulders came back, and she dashed at her eyes. "I know, I know," she said, though it was clear she was trying to make herself believe the words. "Send word to my ma if you need anything else. It's the least I can do."

She left then, slipping out just as the morning sun began to brighten the horizon.

Alice sat down at her small kitchen table, wondering how she could possibly win against the tactics that her father and uncle were clearly using. But to bring the charges to light would mean betraying her own flesh and blood.

Was this why her father had so adamantly not wanted her to take the case—because of what he was afraid she would find out?

How many times had her father said she was like a pit bull with a bone between its teeth when she tried to figure something out? He knew she would hunt and search until she learned everything. Had he wondered what she would do when she found out that he had withheld information? Because she didn't believe for a second that her uncle and father hadn't discussed everything they knew. The brothers, close since birth, so much the same that sometimes they were mistaken for twins, didn't keep secrets from each other.

But she had to know for certain.

Hurriedly, she sent word to Grayson and Lucas regarding the progress she had made. Then before she realized what she was doing, she was out the door and banging into the main house. It was Saturday, and her father, brother, and uncle sat around the parlor reading the morning papers.

"I want to know what in blazes is going on."

Uncle Harry all but leaped out of his seat; Maxwell pushed up casually and strode over to kiss her cheek. Walker Kendall, however, only lowered his newspaper and looked at her with a raised brow.

"Something wrong, daughter?"

"Yes, something is wrong," she stated, hands on hips.

"You are lovely when you're fierce, little sister. What have the poor hapless Kendall men done to gain the wrath of their only Kendall woman?"

"This has nothing to do with you, Maxwell," she stated. "And I'd appreciate a moment alone with our father and uncle."

For a second, a flash of wariness swept across Max's face, but then it was gone and he bowed. "Your wish is my command."

He left the room, but Alice didn't wait to hear his footsteps recede before she started to speak.

"Why did you suppress Cindy Pop's name?" she demanded.

Harry grimaced. Walker snapped the paper out to fold it neatly.

"What makes you think we have suppressed anything?" he asked with the controlled calm he was known for.

"I spoke to the woman myself."

That wiped the calm right off her father's face. She would have sworn Harry groaned.

Alice's stomach lurched. Up until that second she had hoped against hope that her father and uncle would truly be stunned by her accusation and have no idea who Cindy Pop was. But their reaction dashed what hope she had.

For as long as she remembered, her father had been beyond reproach in her mind. The perfect man, living a good and noble life, impossible to live up to. Now, watching as the gears in his quick-thinking mind churned, Alice felt betrayed. And disappointed. Walker Kendall was no better than most, doing what he had to do to get what he wanted.

"It's not what you think," Harry said when his brother remained silent.

"Isn't it?" she asked.

"No," Harry continued, "we had no way of knowing who she really was, no way of verifying anything she said. And when Tawny Green came forward, we didn't need her. Plus, more recently, we've not been able to find her."

She cast them a disbelieving glance as her father studied her. "She is living with her mother. How hard could someone's mother be to track down?"

"That's fine," Walker said, rising from his seat. "Now that you've found her, we'll talk to Miss Pop again."

Harry stared at his brother.

"We'll talk to her first thing in the morning," Walker added. "Won't we, Harry?"

Chapter Seventeen

Cindy Pop had to die.

It was a shame that it had come to this, killing and killing. But Cindy shouldn't have talked.

He took his cigar cutter from the drawer, snipping off the end of a fine cigar. Striking a match, he pulled a deep breath, lighting the tobacco. The rich, pungent smell filled the room, and he sighed as he leaned back and sipped his cognac. Life could be so complicated. But somehow it was the complications that made things seem interesting, made him feel alive.

Pity. Wouldn't it have been nice had his life been different, he wondered, not for the first time. But at the thought, his features hardened. His life would have been different if Mother hadn't made decisions that affected them all. Mostly, him.

Fury riddled his mind. With effort, he reigned in his careening thoughts. But in a matter of seconds, he marveled at his own power to control emotion. It was one of his greatest strengths.

He smiled into the dimly lit room and relaxed for one long second. Then he set down the cigar and cognac and retrieved his suit coat.

If Alice had to find Cindy, at least he learned about it before it was too late. Wouldn't Cindy be surprised when he reappeared at her side?

He chuckled into the warm air as he left through the back door.

Once on the street, he hailed a hired hack and rode quietly through the now-quiet city. It hadn't taken long to find out where Cindy Pop's mother lived. A few discreet inquiries.

Given the late hour, traffic was nearly nonexistent. The hack dropped him off a few blocks away; then he walked. He didn't bother to knock on the front door. Several tenement apartments divided the old house, filled with tired people trying to scrape by.

Cindy's mother lived on the bottom floor, the back apartment. He listened for a moment and found it quiet inside. Glancing around, he saw no one. So he tried the knob. It was unlocked.

Tsk, tsk, he thought with a chuckle.

Soundlessly he made his way down the long hall. Either no one was home, or everyone was in bed. His heart pounded as he moved through the darkness, pounded with excitement and anticipation.

Carefully he pushed open a door and found Cindy, sound asleep, harsh-looking even in repose.

He shuddered at the thought of touching her, so unlike the other girls. But a man had to do what a man had to do.

She didn't stir, making it all the easier. His grin broadened as he sank down beside her on his knees. Another time he would have stroked her cheek. But tonight was strictly business.

In a flash, his hand snaked out and he flattened it across her mouth. She came awake with a panicked flurry. But he was too strong for her.

As he held her, he felt the lightness drift from his mind, leaving only the burning ache that rarely left him. In that moment, as with every moment just before he killed, he wished that things had been different.

"You shouldn't have done it, Mother," he whispered, his throat growing tight.

For a moment, Cindy stilled and looked at him. And in that weak space of time, his hand slipped. As soon as it did, she fought, getting out half a scream. Rage surged through him, taking over, and in the next second the girl was dead, her throat snapped with a satisfying pop.

His head fell back, his eyes closed, his mouth opening on a silent exhale of pleasure. He pulled out his cigar cutters. He had been scratched before. He no longer took chances.

But his enjoyment was cut short when he heard movements in the house.

He would not panic. Voices grew louder as his mind raced with what to do. With a steady hand he shoved the cutters in his pocket.

A grimy window stood shut on the back wall. He leaped for it, struggling with the pane that clearly hadn't been opened in years. He fought and groaned as a voice called out to Cindy. Then footsteps.

Just as the door opened, the window yanked free and he was out into the night, landing on his feet on the dirt ground outside. He wasn't certain what stopped him, couldn't have said why he turned around. But he did. And for one quiet second, he looked up to a top floor where a woman stared down at him—not afraid, not disturbed. Only curious.

Could she see him?

Was there enough light?

His mind lurched. But it was too late to do anything about it. Wails floated out to him from the bedroom. Wails and cries of sorrow. How well he understood such sentiments. How well he knew the grief that followed when someone you loved was taken.

Then he was gone, walking out into the street and hailing a hired hack before anyone else noticed.

Chapter Eighteen

Sunday morning, only twenty-four hours before the trial, Alice woke with determination spurring her on. She had some very pointed questions to ask Lucas Hawthorne. Not about him, or the crazy desire he made her feel. Rather about the night of the murder and Cindy Pop.

But as soon as she finished rushing through her ablutions, hardly aware of what she threw on, then made her way into the dining room of the main house, her world turned upside down.

"Cindy Pop was murdered last night."

This from Maxwell who sat at the table, his chair pushed back, his legs crossed with leisurely indifference as he sipped a cup of steaming black coffee, despite the early-September heat.

Alice felt the color drain from her face. Standing there, she could do little more than stare at her brother in disbelief as a sickening dread started to come over her.

"No," she breathed.

Max shrugged, turning the morning newspaper toward her so she could read it herself. "Sorry, little sis."

But Alice didn't need to read to believe. She should have known something like this would happen. Closing her eyes, she realized she should have known not to tell anyone that Cindy had visited her.

Uncle Harry entered then, his craggy face haggard, his

casual shirtsleeves and pants looking grandfatherly and at odds with his thick, muscular form.

"How was she killed?" she asked her uncle immediately.

Harry shot Max a look of impatience. "You couldn't wait to tell Alice until after she'd had breakfast?"

Max shoveled eggs onto his plate. "I saw no reason to wait."

"Uncle!"

Harry turned to Alice. "The killer broke into the tenement where the victim was staying."

"Then surely someone saw who did it."

"Apparently so. However, we have nothing more than the fact that he had dark hair. He disappeared down the back alley."

The sickening dread swelled. Guilt and despair, a paralyzing fear deep down that she had been the cause of the murder. Not because she had sought Cindy out, but because she had told people that she had found her, had talked to her. The woman had been willing to testify.

She had told her father, her uncle, had even sent word to Grayson. Could they have told others?

And Lucas. She had sent him a note telling him that they needed to talk about Cindy and what she had said.

He set his coffee cup aside and pushed up from the table. For the first time, he felt frantic. Things were spiraling out of control. How could he have made such a foolish mistake as to allow himself to be seen?

But he knew why. Alice. She pushed him, made things difficult. Who would have believed she would be any good as a lawyer? Certainly not him.

And that was unacceptable.

Alice arrived at Nightingale's Gate like storm clouds on the horizon. Lucas watched her from his loft office, felt the unwanted easing in his soul at the sight of her familiar face.

He saw her in his dreams, when he was awake, the curious mixture of vulnerability and bravado, wildness and innocence. Every day he became more aware of how she had intertwined herself into his life; like threads in a tapestry, every strand needed to be complete.

He knew right away that she had heard about Cindy Pop.

Oddly, he had hoped the inevitable could be put off. One more moment standing close to her, a shared smile. The comfort that he liked more than he cared to admit. But that was not to be.

Events were unfolding in a way that was sure to drive her away. And with one look at her face he knew that things were about to take a nasty turn. She was upset and devastated. He would have to make a choice. This woman, or the truth.

As soon as she walked into the grand salon, she looked up. Their eyes met. God, such a shame, he thought. For the first time ever, he saw what he could have had if his life had been different.

But he was not a man for regrets.

"Good morning, Miss Kendall," he called down to her. "Can I take it that you've come to join me for breakfast?"

She didn't bother to answer, or wait to be invited, she came up the stairs and stood before his desk, he standing on the other side. Despite his determination to be indifferent, the sight of her so near brought a smile to his face.

"You move me," he couldn't help saying.

The words disconcerted her, throwing her off balance, he could see that, and it was all he could do not to reach out and trace her jaw.

"Don't," she stated, visibly regaining her composure. "Please. This isn't easy for me."

He sighed. "I know nothing good is brewing when you get that tone."

"My guess is that you knew nothing good was brewing before I ever walked through the door."

"You'll have to be a tad clearer."

"The latest murder. I don't think you did it, but I believe you know who did."

He stood very still. "I can't imagine why you think that."

"Because the murders have something to do with the Nightingale lady. And you know it."

Lucas had to fight the urge to lash out, not at her but at the situation. The frustration, the futile spiraling that he couldn't control. He stood there, fighting for nonchalance. The words hung suspended, the air charged around them.

"Ah, I see. You believe in the alphabet method of crime detection."

She narrowed her eyes.

"You know the type," he continued. "Clue A leads to clue F, and F to C, and forget B or D, just head on over to Z. Case solved."

"If you are trying to say my reasoning is convoluted—"

"Not *trying* to say, sweetheart—"

"Then tell me why else a nightingale would be tied up in the murders. And why else would Lucille Rouge be asking about the Nightingale lady, then end up dead?"

She asked the question in a way that made Lucas think she actually wanted him to say something that would absolve himself. But the truth was if he was brought before the witness from last night, he'd bet his club they'd point to him so fast his head would spin.

Lucas bit back a curse, then he pushed his coffee cup out of the way as he leaned back against the desk. He had to remain calm, had to think clearly.

The tense silence erupted when the front door crashed open and banging footsteps marched into Nightingale's Gate.

"Damn it!"

Lucas recognized his father's voice immediately, and his thoughts went still. Not now, he pleaded silently.

But Alice ignored the commotion downstairs, not even

bothering to turn around. She pressed him for an answer. "Tell me, Lucas. Who do you think killed those girls?"

"Damn it," his father shouted again, shaking some kind of paper in his hand. "I will not put up with this!"

It was early, so no one was at the bar. No girls, no bartender, no music man playing the piano in the corner. Emmaline strode into the main room, hastily pulling on her dressing gown.

"What are you going on about, Bradford?" she demanded, pulling the tie tight around her waist.

Despite the drama downstairs, Alice wouldn't relent. "Lucas, tell me! For once and for all, tell me why you won't help me prove your innocence?"

"This!" Bradford shouted, gesturing to the papers. He looked as if he had been up all night, his proper suit sagging and rumpled, his dark hair disheveled. "A divorcement, for mercy's sake!"

His heavy footfalls pounded across the floor, then he stopped directly in front of Emmaline. "You shouldn't have done it, Mother!"

At the words, Alice went still as stone. Her eyes widened, and her lips parted. Then she turned around and walked to the low half-wall that overlooked the main room. When she appeared, his father glanced up.

"Who the hell are you?" he demanded, his Hawthorne blue eyes blazing, the gray in his hair obscured by the light. Only dark remained.

Alice couldn't seem to move, much less speak, and Lucas felt his heart lurch. Then without ever uttering a word to the older man, she turned back to Lucas.

"He's the one," she whispered, her voice hoarse with shock. "All this time they thought it was you. But it was your father."

Reaching out, Alice grabbed a chair back. Her mind staggered and reeled as understanding rushed over her.

Bradford Hawthorne, who looked just like his youngest

son. From a distance, at night, it would be nearly impossible to tell the difference between the two men. And Bradford was a man who called his wife "Mother." Suddenly it all made sense.

"You are covering for your father," she managed.

Lucas looked from Alice to his father, and his expression turned dangerous. "You don't know what you're talking about."

"But I do. Cindy told me that the killer called his victim 'Mother.' In fact, he said those very words: 'You shouldn't have done it, Mother'!"

"You have no proof. Cindy is dead." His gaze was hard and obstinate.

She couldn't believe what she was hearing. "No proof? My guess is that a little digging will yield a great deal of proof. I'll get a postponement. We'll find—"

"No." His tone was adamant. "There will be no post-ponement. We go to trial tomorrow."

"Good God! You are one step away from hanging. You want me to defend you, but you constantly tie my hands behind my back. All for a man whom you don't even love!"

Lucas turned away, but not before she saw a flicker of emotion pass across his features. And suddenly she understood even more—understood in a way that she couldn't have only a few days ago. She thought of her father, thought of how he had suppressed evidence, and how she knew she would protect him.

The love for a parent regardless of what he had done. And the unconditional need to protect.

Lucas Hawthorne pretended to hate his father, when in truth, deep down, he loved him.

"Lucas, we need to talk about this. You can't hang simply because of some misplaced need to protect your father."

"I will not hang," he said, enunciating each syllable.

Frustrated, Alice turned to go. She needed to think, needed

to assimilate this new information. But Lucas stopped her at the door.

"And remember, Miss Kendall, your job is to get me acquitted, not to solve the crime."

Chapter Nineteen

The *Commonwealth vs. Lucas Hawthorne* began on a cloudy morning during the last week of September.

When Alice and Lucas arrived at the courthouse, women lined the steps, their plaques waving in the air. Protests of innocence. Demands that Lucas be set free. Proposals of marriage.

Alice thought she was used to the flock by now, but as she walked up the wide granite steps to the entrance, carefully holding her skirt with her properly gloved hand, one of the women threw herself at Lucas. Alice leaped back as Lucas caught the woman to keep her from falling. Tears streaked her face, and her eyes were swollen.

"They'll hang you," she cried, clutching his crisp lapels.

Alice searched for a patrolman. But Lucas only smiled down into the woman's eyes with an utter kindness that made Alice's heart go still. He set the woman gently upright, then cupped her cheek. "They won't hang me, darling. I'm going to be all right."

This calmed the woman, and when he nudged her chin, she offered him a watery smile. Then Lucas turned back toward the courthouse and proceeded forward. Alice couldn't seem to move, not understanding what she felt. This man was an enigma. So hard on the outside, so gentle and caring when caught off guard. And like this woman, Alice couldn't stand the thought of seeing him hang.

The halls were filled with men who worked for every

newspaper up and down the East Coast—be it rag sheet or respectable entity. The prosecution of Lucas Hawthorne had captured America's attention, as could be seen on the front steps of the courthouse. There wasn't a reporter around who wasn't going to take advantage of that fact. Any tidbit they could report about Lucas Hawthorne sold newspapers. He was handsome, rich, and unmarried. The public didn't seem terribly concerned about the tiny little detail that he supposedly had murdered a woman of the evening.

"Mr. Hawthorne!" they called out, waving their tablets in the air to gain his attention.

"How does it feel to finally go to trial?"

"Is your lawyer really qualified to defend such a big case?"

"Miss Kendall, who made your gown?"

The questions came all at once, half of them relevant to the day's proceedings, half not, all echoing against the pristine floors and high ceilings.

Lucas and Alice ignored them and made their way through the crowd, Lucas's broad hand securely at Alice's back, propelling her along.

"Hey, Lucas," one called out, "is your lady lawyer sweet on you?"

Alice saw Lucas's barely perceptible smile flicker on his lips, then it was gone.

Mixed in with the haggard-faced reporters with their tablets of paper and stubby pencil leads were a handful of photographers. They stood with their boxy equipment, perched high on three-legged pedestals, with drapes hanging off the back like locks of long black hair.

Just before Alice made it through the courtroom door, her father appeared at the top of the stairs. In a rush of booted heels on marble, the reporters swarmed Walker Kendall, firing off questions. Walker raised his hand to silence them, his politician's smile making him seem their ally.

"Fellows, fellows, I appreciate your interest, but my only

concern this day is justice. And it is justice that we will see done."

Alice had to stop herself from rolling her eyes.

Walker started away.

"But how will it feel to go up against your own daughter in the courtroom?"

He stopped at that, and looked the reporter in the eye, his smile still in place. "Clark Kittridge is trying this case. Not me. You boys know that," he said in a way that was friendly, but also put them in their places. "And while I have the highest confidence in my daughter's abilities as a lawyer, unfortunately, in this instance, the facts will show that Lucas Hawthorne murdered Lucille Rouge."

A roar of questions and comments erupted, but Walker didn't stop again.

Lucas guided Alice toward the defense table. He watched as she greeted opposing counsel, the bailiff, and even his family with polite formality. She was furious, Lucas knew that. But being the professional she was, he was the only one present who did.

Grayson wasn't any happier with him. Alice had seen to that.

Last night she had stormed over to Swan's Grace and demanded to see Grayson. Within minutes, the two of them were back at Nightingale's Gate. Grayson had been so angry he hadn't bothered with his coat or tie. He stood in the private office, his shirtsleeves rolled on his forearms, and tore into his younger brother with a verbal lashing, the likes of which Lucas had not experienced in decades—if ever.

All the while, Alice had stood cross-armed next to Grayson, nodding in agreement at everything the older Hawthorne said. But after he had spoken his piece, Alice ready to head for her uncle to tell him what she suspected, with Grayson going along to provide confirmation, Lucas had stopped them.

"No," he had said with cold finality. "Not a word. And as

my paid advocate, if you reveal so much as a hint about what we have discussed here, I'll have you disbarred for unethical behavior. The fact is, all you have is a vague suspicion, and don't you forget that."

Alice had fumed, not liking it one bit. But she had little choice. Though if he had learned nothing else about Alice Kendall, it was that she would not let this rest. She might proceed with the trial now, but he knew she would do her best to find a way to circumvent his mandate.

She'd be damned before she allowed one man to be convicted for what she believed was another man's crimes.

Lucas's mind hardened at the thought of what Alice might learn if she continued to dig. And the most damning piece of evidence of all wasn't about his father, rather about him. Despite what he had said, he still had the nightingale ring.

Clark sat at the prosecution's table, bent in heavy concentration over a file. Walker sat down in the first row behind Clark. Instantly, the younger man turned around and huddled with his boss.

Seconds later, Grayson entered, striding up the aisle with hard, determined steps. He didn't bother with hellos.

"Where is Mother?" he asked.

"I thought she was with you," Lucas stated, his expression focused. "She left Nightingale before I did. Could she be with Sophie?"

"Yes, they are together, but I don't know where. Something is going on, and I want to know what it is."

Their questions were answered when Emmaline hurried into the courtroom, her expression unreadable. Her dark blue gown was the perfect blend of a mourning gown and one that demanded respect. Pleased, Alice gave her a nod. Every juror there would look at Emmaline and see either their own mother or wife.

"Mother, what is it?" her sons asked in unison.

Emmaline stood for a moment, her face a frozen mask,

before tears spilled over onto her cheeks—though oddly, they might have been tears of joy.

Alice forgot about the ensemble they had picked out together, and felt a spurt of concern, but concern turned to confusion when a tall, blond-headed man with a distinctive scar marking his extraordinary good looks entered. She had the instant thought that the man would have been beautiful, too beautiful, if not for the scar.

He walked in behind Emmaline and wrapped a strong arm around her shoulders, his smile wide and good humored.

"Matthew!" Lucas and Grayson called out.

Alice stood at the table and watched, along with most everyone in the courtroom, as the men embraced. This man had to be the middle Hawthorne son, who had moved to Africa with his wife, Finnea.

For a moment, the charges, the trial, life and death were forgotten. The brothers reunited with an uninhibited love, suddenly looking like the three young boys they must have been growing up. Happy and carefree. Committed to one another no matter what.

Their focus didn't waver until the door pushed open again and in walked a woman Alice knew to be Sophie Hawthorne, and another woman she had never seen before. The second had red hair and green eyes, and the word *wild* popped up in Alice's mind.

Though a closer look at Sophie made it clear that neither of these two women appeared to care too terribly much about what others thought of them. Their clothes were beautiful, but not demure and proper. Their coiffures were neatly done, but nothing like Alice had ever seen.

The women had arms hooked together and looked like sisters of the heart if not sisters of blood. And Alice assumed that this must be Matthew's wife, Finnea. Even Alice had heard of her. And she remembered that she had come from Africa to Boston, and had shocked New Englanders with her odd and foreign ways.

But despite any oddness, the Hawthornes clearly loved this very different woman.

Alice felt a stab of yearning to have such friends and family, the sister whom she had never had. And then her yearning grew even more keen the moment that these women's husbands saw them. These powerful men, turning and seeing their wives, their love springing to life in their eyes.

But her heart started to pound at the look that came over Lucas. This man of power and money, who was dangerous and intense one minute, then devilishly playful the next, looked wistful.

He felt the same as she did.

Alice couldn't have been more surprised. Yet again she wondered about the contradictions of this man.

"Alice, dear," Emmaline called out to her. "Come meet the rest of my family."

For the first time when meeting a new woman, Alice didn't even think about what she had on or how her hair looked. It didn't matter that she wore rather mannish attire. She understood instantly that neither of these women cared, nor competed.

Alice loved Sophie and Finnea on the spot. They shook her hand and seemed genuinely pleased to meet her. Their concern for their brother-in-law was apparent, as was their faith that he wasn't guilty. Family first. Solidarity. The sentiment was clear. And this was further proven by the fact that Matthew Hawthorne had taken his family and traveled all the way from Africa to be at his brother's side during the trial.

Matthew and his wife hadn't arrived a second too soon. Having them there made a statement that could only help the perception the jurors would gain about Lucas.

"You'll meet our little Mary this evening," Emmaline added.

"She's waiting for us at Nightingale's Gate."

"You left her at the club?" Grayson demanded.

Matthew clapped him on the back. "We did, big brother. And knowing sweet Mary, she will have every woman and man there wrapped around her little finger by the time luncheon rolls around."

"The girls were definitely hovering around her like mother hens," Emmaline confirmed.

And then, finally, Alice was introduced to Matthew.

"Miss Kendall," he said with a gallant politeness that somehow went so well with the scar that slashed down his face. "Lucas and Grayson have told me what a skilled lawyer you are." The smile didn't leave his face, but his Hawthorne blue eyes became exacting. "We are counting on you to see that justice is done."

"Of course," she found herself saying.

Looking around her at this family, ending up with eyes locked on Lucas, she had never wanted something so badly. To do something for this wonderful group of people. And for Lucas. But what would happen if that meant bringing their father down?

"Rest assured," she continued, returning her attention to Matthew, "I will do everything in my power to exonerate your brother."

Matthew nodded, then led his wife, mother, and Sophie to the front row behind the defense table. Grayson nodded his head at Alice, then followed the others.

Only seconds after everyone had taken their seats, the bailiff called the court into order. When the judge entered and everyone stood, Alice felt her heart pound with nerves, but excitement as well.

Everything was in place. She had her notes, her opening, her line of defense. She had a list of witnesses who would attest to Lucas's character. And, most important of all, she had his highly respected family circling around him.

She couldn't imagine what could go wrong.

* * *

Judge Raymond Parks brought his gavel down at exactly nine o'clock. His hair was dark, and his sharp brown eyes stared out at the crowd. After making his opening comments, he got the trial under way.

Clark stood importantly, clearing his throat, then walked forward to address the court. He presented his opening statements with flare and conviction. He wore a somber, respectable suit, though he had a shiny gold watch fob dangling on his vest. Every time he pulled his coat back to rest his knuckles on his hips, the gold caught the light, drawing the jurors' attention. Alice even caught the judge looking at it once.

She smiled at this tiny error on Clark's part, and took it as a good sign. So it was only a watch fob, but she'd take what she could get. Things were going well.

Clark listed the reasons the Commonwealth believed Lucas to be guilty. And listening to him, Alice knew that the jury had to be thinking this was an open-and-shut case. But she knew otherwise. She almost rubbed her hands together in anticipation. While she wanted Bradford Hawthorne brought to justice, more and more she felt she could get Lucas off without that.

The Hawthornes sat with stern, unforgiving expressions narrowed on Clark. Emmaline dabbed a handkerchief to her eyes as if she couldn't stand one more hateful lie about her precious child. And Alice knew it was not an act. But Alice also knew that it wasn't as bad as it could have been. At least not until Clark paused and met each member of the jury's eyes, no longer unconsciously flashing his too-fancy chain, his tone suddenly, finally, more genuine.

"Lucas Hawthorne is guilty, gentlemen. Of course, we all know that the defense will attempt to prove otherwise. But when they try to contradict the evidence and bring on a string of men to attest to the murderer's good character, just remember one thing." He gestured to the defense's side of

the room, to Emmaline and Matthew, Grayson and the Hawthorne women. "For all the family that has come to show
their support of their kin, one very distinct person is not
here."

Alice felt her heart stop at the same time she noticed
Lucas's long fingers clench on the pen he was using to take
notes.

"Where is Bradford Hawthorne, good gentlemen? The
defendant's very own father is not present to show his undi-
vided support. I won't say what that means. But I think
every one in this room understands the implications."

And, of course, they did.

"But, you say," he continued, "perhaps the man is ill, or
something came up that prevented him from being here.
And I would say, good thought. I would never try to make a
point on such flimsy evidence—not with this, or any other
point. But in this case, I must tell you, on Miss Kendall's list
of witnesses, she has listed every adult member of the Hawthorne family. Every member, that is, except for the defendant's father. That, gentlemen of the jury, *is* telling."

Alice wanted to groan her dismay. If she had been alone,
she would have dropped her head to the table and cursed.

Alice paused for a half-second once the judge had invited
her to begin. A space of time, just long enough, to force the
jury to focus their attention as they waited for her to speak.

She had seen her father do it a thousand times. And as
soon as she stood, she felt the attention of each of the twelve
men settle and lock.

She nodded to the jury before she began her opening
statement. She had practiced what she would say in front of
her mirror in her cottage, would have liked to have practiced
in front of her father. But that wasn't going to happen. Not
with this case. And afterward, perhaps not with any other.

Her heart felt as if it would burst out of her chest it beat so
hard. She held a pen. She had found previously that it made

her look more professional. More than that, it gave her something to hold on to. But today her hands were so wet she felt as if it would slip through her grasp.

"Gentlemen of the jury, I must commend the prosecution for such a magnificent opening." She actually gave a nodding bow to Clark. The smile he returned to her was tight, and she could just make out a look of suspicion on her father's face as he sat one row back, his arms crossed on his barrel chest.

"A magnificent opening, I say, because the actors in Boston's very own gold-flocked, velvet-seated Theatre District could not have preformed such a fiction any better."

She would have sworn someone in the gallery snickered. With that her heart began to settle.

"But I've never been overly enamored of fiction. I prefer to deal with the facts. Hard facts. And the facts are these." She paused again, clasping her hands together at her waist. "The only evidence Clark Kittridge has against my client is the dubious testimony of a woman who claims to have been in the alley the night of the murder. He also has the mark of a nightingale on the victim. I will prove that his witness is less than reliable and that Mr. Hawthorne no longer owns the very ring that he is accused of using, and hasn't had it for some time."

Her thoughts raced with something she could add about the absence of Bradford. But what was there to say?

She started back toward the defense table, then stopped as inspiration came to her in a startling flash. Bradford's bragging about eluding reporters.

"And one more thing," she said, leaning back against the edge of the table. "Lucas Hawthorne's father. Mr. Kittridge stands before this court and leaves us with the impression that he doesn't support his son."

Alice would leave the jury with a different impression.

"Another fiction, gentlemen. Dramatic, yes. But truthful?

Absolutely not." She pushed away from the table for emphasis. "The truth is, Bradford Hawthorne is an old man."

She heard Emmaline's surprised gasp, but thankfully Alice didn't think anyone else heard.

She hurried on. "He is a man whom, I'm sure the vast number of reporters here would be willing to attest, has not been seen coming or going from his home in weeks." Thank God for small favors.

A low murmur of agreement shimmered through the back where the reporters clustered. She saw the jurors take this in, concede the point.

The implied point, she knew. That Bradford Hawthorne was not well enough to testify. Right or wrong, her father had taught her how to play this game.

She turned back and looked at Lucas, walked over to him, stood next to him, stood close, implying her support of this man. Then she returned her attention to the twelve men who had been selected the week before and would decide this case. "Lucas Hawthorne did not murder anyone, gentlemen. This man's only crime is that he has chosen a way of life that the prosecution deems unworthy. And because of that, he is being persecuted. That is what I will prove. Then it will be up to you to decide. Which will you believe? Fact or fiction? Thank you."

When she returned to her seat, every ounce of stress seeped away at the look of approval that flickered across Lucas Hawthorne's face.

After that, the day proceeded slowly. With the exception of a luncheon break, the prosecution brought on witness after witness going over every inch of the alleyway, not to mention every minute detail of the crime. It seemed to Alice that anyone within a half-mile of that alley on the night in question was paraded before the jury. Though she guessed she might have done the same had she had such flimsy evidence.

As a result, Alice declined to cross-examine the witnesses. No need to further hammer their points home.

Despite the sheer number of witnesses for the prosecution, each one's testimony was so short that Clark came to Tawny Green toward the end of the day.

The girl shook as she took the stand, holding up first her left then right hand to take the oath. Her skin looked unnaturally white against the black of the Bible.

"Miss Green," Clark began, his hand perched importantly just under the edge of his vest pocket, "could you tell the jury what exactly you saw the night of July thirteenth?"

When she started to speak, her voice was so soft the judge had to lean forward. "Speak up, woman."

His tone was gruff, and Tawny's eyes went wide; she looked as if she would cry.

Clark scowled at the judge. A mistake, Alice knew. So did Clark. He attempted to soothe his witness.

"You are doing just fine, Miss Green. You were saying . . ."

She wrung her hands, then began again. "I was walking down the alley."

"Going home?"

"Objection." Alice stood as she said the word.

Every juror turned to scrutinize her, and for a second she had the distinct thought that the men were put off by a woman interrupting a man. But she couldn't let that get in her way.

"The prosecution is leading the witness."

"Sustained," the judge said. "Rephrase, Mr. Kittridge."

Clark smiled thinly at Alice. "Fine." He returned his attention to Tawny. "Tell us, Miss Green, what were you doing in the alley?"

"I . . . I was going home."

Clark shot Alice a sour look that the jury couldn't see. "Thank you," he said dramatically. "Now, you were returning home, then what happened?"

"I heard footsteps and voices. So I stepped into the shadows."

"Why did you do that?"

"You never know what kind of man you might run into at night. A hooligan or a decently paying man."

Clark's eyes went wide, as did the jurors'. The judge cleared his throat. Alice felt an internal smile. The prosecution's witness had herself all but told the jury that she was a prostitute.

"I always stand in the shadows," Tawny continued, oblivious to Clark's concern, "until I can see if he might be worth my while—"

"Yes, thank you," Clark said, cutting her off. "On the night in question, what did you see from your place in the shadows?"

She seemed confused for a moment.

"The murder, Miss Green," Clark coaxed.

"Objection! He's prompting her, Your Honor."

"Careful, Mr. Kittridge," the judge warned. "We've barely started these proceedings, and I'd hate to think this is the way we are going to go."

"No, sir. Of course not." Clark composed himself. "Miss Green. You told the police that you saw something. Please tell the court what that something was."

"Yes, I know now. The murder. I saw Lucille Rouge get killed."

"And who, pray tell us, murdered that poor woman?"

For a second her eyes dimmed.

"Miss Green?"

"Lucas Hawthorne," she finally said.

Despite the fact that the details had been all over the newspapers for the last two months, a gasp shuddered through the courtroom like a wave undulating at sea, followed by hissing whispers.

"Quiet, quiet!" the judge demanded, banging his gavel.

Once the gallery had settled down, Clark continued.

"Miss Green, how did you know it was Lucas Hawthorne?"

"Well, the dark hair, mostly. Beautiful dark hair. It glistens in the light." This made her blush.

"Yes, and . . ."

"Uh . . . I've seen him a hundred times."

"Good, Miss Green. Now, could you please point out the man you saw kill Lucille Rouge?"

Dropping her head, she stared at her hands. After a moment, she cast a furtive glance in Lucas's direction, then averted her gaze and pointed at the defense table.

Another gasp, then the banging gavel. And Alice felt surrounded by Lucas's sizzle of anger. But she also knew with certainty that the girl was lying.

Glancing back at her father, Alice saw his pleased expression, before it settled into a calm mask. But something more than that bothered her, though she couldn't put her finger on it.

The courtroom was restless, and only thirty minutes remained before the judge would adjourn the proceedings for the day. But he wasn't about to stop yet. He was too strict for that. He asked Alice if she planned to cross-examine this witness.

"Yes, Your Honor."

With her head bowed in thought, Alice approached the witness stand. Clasping her hands in front of her, she looked up, looked straight at Tawny Green, and began.

"Miss Green, you said you were in the alleyway, going home. True?"

Her eyes flickered away, then back. "Yes, ma'am."

"Where were you coming home from?"

"From work."

"Work? What kind of work do you do, Miss Green?"

"Objection!"

When Clark didn't elaborate, the judge raised a brow and asked, "On what grounds?"

"Miss Green's employment has nothing to do with this case."

"Judge," Alice countered, "in order to determine how reliable the witness is, we must know something about her."

The judge nodded. "Objection overruled."

Clark all but grumbled, and Alice couldn't believe he had actually thought they could keep her occupation from the jury. Heavens, Tawny had all but told them herself.

"Miss Green, please continue."

"With . . . with what?" Her gazed darted around.

"Your occupation, Miss Green. What do you do to make a living?"

She stared at her lap again.

"Miss Green?"

"I'm a prostitute," she mumbled.

Alice leaned closer. "Please speak up."

She repeated her words, though barely.

"Miss Gre—"

"Miss Kendall," the judge barked, "we heard!"

Damn. She had pushed too hard. The episode shook her, disrupting her rhythm.

"Of course, Your Honor." She nodded demurely, then returned her attention to the witness. But Alice's performance went downhill from there. She couldn't get Tawny to budge on her story. The girl might mumble, but she mumbled consistently: she had been in the alley, the alley had gaslights, and she had seen Lucas with his dark hair.

When five o'clock rolled around, Alice breathed a sigh of relief.

"Your Honor, I have several more questions for the witness," she said, regardless of the fact that she had exhausted everything she had thought to ask. "But, given the time, might I suggest we break now, then I can continue in the morning?"

Time to regroup.

The judge eyed her, then leaned down to her. "I can't imagine what else you have to ask, but I'll give you some leeway. Go home and pull yourself together, Miss Kendall." He leaned back and stated to the court, "We will reconvene at nine in the morning." He hammered his gavel home. "Court adjourned."

Everyone stood as the judge disappeared into his chambers. The gallery filed out, then the prosecution. Alice made busy with her files, her head down as if concentrating. She didn't know if she could face the Hawthornes after such a dismal showing. And she especially didn't know how to face Lucas.

"That didn't go so badly," he said.

Her head shot up, and she wanted to melt at the look in his eyes, so kind and supportive.

Grayson and the rest of the Hawthornes were just as kind.

"The first day is always the hardest," Grayson offered. "Get some rest tonight. Then, tomorrow, try again to shake Miss Green. If you see it's not happening, move on."

The support of these two men nearly undid her. She knew what neither of them would say. She had to do better. And she would. She just needed to find a way to shake Tawny Green's testimony.

Lucas watched Alice go, her spine ramrod straight as she walked down the center aisle, her bulging satchel at her side.

As soon as she was gone, Lucas had the opportunity to talk to Matthew and Finnea. The men hugged again, that kind of fists-pounding-backs kind of hug.

"God, you look great," Lucas said.

Then he looked at Finnea. "Beautiful as ever," he said sincerely. "Africa is certainly treating you both well."

Matthew wrapped his arm around his wife, and Lucas could almost feel the love that flowed between them.

They made their way back to Nightingale's Gate, and Lucas felt a surge of love and poignancy when Mary raced forward and threw herself into his arms.

"You're not going to jail, are you, Uncle Lucas?"

Lucas pressed his forehead to hers.

"No, he is not," Grayson stated firmly.

She smiled then, and danced back to her father and Finnea. "Good," she stated, entwining her fingers with Finnea's. "Because Mama said that if people around here weren't careful, she'd have to deal a little African justice herself."

At first the family flinched, then they laughed. Lucas stood and gave his brother's wife a hug. "Thank you, Finnea."

"I don't think you are going to need my help, Lucas," she responded. "I think Alice Kendall is all you need. She has much strength. I sensed it in the courtroom."

"And we all know that our Finnea has the ability to understand things in a way that the rest of us don't," Emmaline commented.

Alice paced the small confines of her cottage.

She had missed something, she was sure of it. Racking her brain, she ran through every detail of the case, everything she had learned along the way. But the answer didn't come.

"I can't do this," she growled, throwing her head back and closing her eyes. "I'm terrible. I should have been a housekeeper!"

"Based on the state of this room, I'd have to say you're a better lawyer."

Alice whirled around and gasped at the sight of Lucas standing in her kitchen. "How did you get in here?"

"You left the door open."

Sure enough, the door gaped. But she had been hot, and opening the windows hadn't been enough. "Well, you should have knocked," she groused unkindly.

"I did, but you were too busy berating yourself."

"Someone's got to do it."

Lucas chuckled before his expression grew serious and he pushed the door shut with the toe of his gleaming black boot.

Chapter Twenty

Alice felt a tremor of awareness run down her spine. She wore little more than a light wrapper with her long hair hanging loose down her back.

"What brings you here?" she asked, her ire evaporating at the look in his eyes. "A social call at one in the morning?"

"I couldn't sleep."

"A trial can have that effect on people."

He made a sound deep in his throat, then started moving around her home. She had an unobserved moment during which she could just look at him. Tall, more handsome than any one man had a right to be, caressed by the flickering gaslight.

She felt a tightening in her chest. The world seemed to close in around her, her thoughts echoing in her head. He was beautiful.

He moved with that predator's grace, smoothly, no wasted energy. His steps were long and unhurried. But tonight he wasn't at ease.

The black pants he wore were creased, his shirt crisp and white despite the late hour, though he wasn't wearing a coat or tie. He'd had his hair cut for the trial, but still it looked rakish.

Her body tingled at the sight of him. He was the embodiment of maleness, dark and sexual, virile and dangerous. He was everything she shouldn't want but did.

He picked up a book, then set it down. He studied a

photograph of her and her family, though he didn't say a word. She felt a nearly overwhelming desire to cross the room to him. But she had been around him long enough to know that something was bothering him.

"You've come to fire me again."

She braced herself as he came closer, expecting him to agree. Instead he looked at her with the eyes of a conqueror.

"I don't blame you, if you do," she added, her voice barely a whisper.

"That's not why I'm here, Alice."

Her heart began to pound, her pulse racing. "Then why?"

He stared at her for what seemed like an eternity. "I couldn't stay away."

Her heart burgeoned and soared, and unable to do anything else, she flew into his arms. He caught her in a fierce embrace. His muscles tremored when she clung to him. And his breath sighed out of him when she brushed her lips against his.

With a ravenous groan, his mouth slanted over hers, his strong hands molding her to him. The contact was like fire, searing her. He had shown her what passion was, the intense all-consuming, ravaging part of life that she wanted more of.

"Lucas," she breathed.

His lips trailed back along her jaw.

"Lucas—"

"Love me, Alice," he said on a faint breath of air as he nipped her ear, half plea, half demand.

A shiver of yearning coursed down her spine. Her hands clutched him to steady herself. His hard chest brushed against the folds of her nightgown, the sensation like liquid fire.

"Let me hold you."

It was this that she had been waiting for. More than anything, she wanted to be held by this man. She wanted to feel his arms around her, their bodies pressed together. She wanted to feel the pounding of his heart.

Her desire overwhelming whatever fragments of sense she had left, she ran her hands up his arms to his shoulders. She relished the feel of hard sinew beneath her fingers. She relished as well his jagged intake of breath.

"Alice," he groaned against her ear. "I want you as I have never wanted anything in my life."

She knew he did. She could feel his yearning in the pounding of his heart. The understanding filled her with a deep abiding joy, and confidence.

He coaxed her lips apart. He tasted of brandy and cigars, but of sunshine and long grasses as well. When she groaned her pleasure, he pulled her even closer, his hand loosening the tie of her wrapper until it fell open. Pushing the material aside, he cupped the fullness of her breast beneath her thin nightgown, then brushed his palms across the peaks, his tongue tasting her.

"Yes, love," he said, pulling her full lower lip gently between his teeth.

He pushed the wrapper from her shoulders, and it dropped to the floor in a puddle around her feet. She knew her soft gown was all but see-through from long years of wear.

She started to cover herself.

"No," he whispered. "You are beautiful."

She looked down at the faded blue flowers. When she looked back up, he was smiling.

"You look cute," he clarified.

Alice rolled her eyes. "I'm not particularly interested in looking *cute* right this second."

His smile turned devilish. "That problem is easily solved. You can get rid of the gown."

Her breath caught, then with a boldness she never would have believed possible, she gathered the hem and pulled the worn cotton over her head.

She would have laughed at the stunned look that came over Lucas's face. Who would have believed that such a man could be surprised? But in the next second his surprise was replaced by awe.

She saw it, recognized it for what it was, and felt a shimmering power that nearly took her breath.

Then, with the palm of his hands, he traced her shoulders down to her arms, until his fingertips touched hers. But when he would have twined them together, she reached for the fastenings of his shirt.

He seemed to hold his breath as she worked her way down. But when she tugged at his belt, he caught her hand with a startled oath.

She stared up at him in challenge. For a moment, the darkness in his eyes flared with a surprised humor, after which he made short order of his clothes, then caught her up against his body with a growl.

He pressed her hips into his arousal, and she relished the power she felt when she moved against him.

"Hell," he groaned, his lips against her hair.

But she was not about to be put off. "I've been a virgin far too long."

"It takes two willing people for virginity to be lost, sweetheart."

"I'm doing my part." She kissed his chest.

He expelled a rush of breath. "No doubt about that," he managed. "But I'm not here to corrupt an innocent."

"You're not corrupting anyone. I know a whole lot more about this than you realize."

With an inventive curse, he pushed back and stared at her in disbelief. She only smiled.

"You taught me about pleasure the other night. And I read about the rest," she answered.

His brow raised.

"Not every book in the library pertains to etiquette or the law. Some are of an explanatory type."

Leaning forward, she caught one nipple in her mouth. She wasn't sure what happened to his brow after that, but she heard him groan, his hands capturing her head. She knew he wanted to pull her away, but with one flick of her tongue, his hands melted down her body.

"The author of that book should be shot," he barely managed to say. "You shouldn't know these things."

And then he gave in. He swept her up and carried her to the narrow bed that stood just out of sight. Bracing himself with one knee, he set her down, following in her wake.

With exquisite slowness, he leaned over her and brushed his lips against her skin, making her body quiver with sensation. And everything was forgotten.

"Lucas," she whispered, unable to get anything else beyond her throat.

Her body trembled as he rolled onto his back, pulling her between his legs.

His erection pressed against her as his hands ran down her arms to her hands, making her tremble. With incredible gentleness, he kissed her. "I have never met anyone like you," he whispered against her skin. "So pure and good, but bold and wild, as well. You humble me every time I'm near you."

Her eyes burned. She could see the reverence in his gaze, the sincerity. And when his hands drifted up her belly, over her ribs to her breasts, she did nothing more than sigh.

Winding her fingers through his hair, she gasped when he pulled one nipple deep into his mouth. His tongue laved the bud into a taut peak before taking the other, sucking and laving, a slow lava beginning to churn low in her body.

She felt demanding and greedy. She wanted to explore. It was madness, surely, but a madness she could no more stop than she could halt the progress of the moon.

She came up on her knees and straddled him. Instantly he started to push up. But she flattened him back with her hand.

"Alice," he said, his tone warning, "you're playing with fire."

The words caught in his throat when in that second she wrapped her hand around his arousal.

She could all but feel the shock that shot through him, the fire that burned through his limbs.

Her hand stilled as she looked at his face, eyes closed, lips set, his expression one of tight control. She couldn't believe how bold she was being, but she couldn't deny the thrill that raced through her at the silken feel of him. Biting her lips, she stroked his hard length. He shuddered, then fell back against the sheets.

She stroked again. When he reached out and caught her hand, her mouth opened to protest. But he only covered her hand with his, tightening the pressure against him.

Electricity shimmered through her. Emboldened, she caressed him. His body lay out before her, massive, dwarfing her tiny bed, his muscles carved like granite, his skin golden. Such a powerful man.

His body was tense, his hands fisted in the sheets, until finally he pulled her hand away, rolling her over in such a quick motion that she hardly knew what happened.

He leaned over her, his hands capturing her wrists above her head. "I am a mere mortal, and I can only take so much."

"So much until what?" she teased, her lips quirking devilishly.

"Until I embarrass myself like a schoolboy."

His hair fell forward on his brow, and, indeed, he did look a bit boyish. And terribly endearing. Pulling her hands free, she cupped his face, her heart swelling with all she felt.

She was forced to think about the fact that if she didn't win the trial, this man would be put to death. His vibrancy gone, his smile lost. And just as suddenly she couldn't imagine a life without either one of those things. She wanted him. She wanted him in a deep, primal way, as if she sensed her mate.

It hit her then, with their bodies entwined, that she wanted to be with this man for reasons that had nothing to do with the desire to taste passion. She wanted to be with this man because she loved him.

The thought took her breath. Lucas Hawthorne, who ran a gentlemen's club. A man who did his best to make people think the worst of him. She loved him.

Her eyes widened in wonder. She had never loved Clark. She had never felt like this, as if at any moment she could fly. For the first time in her life she felt truly alive.

She loved him. She loved Lucas Hawthorne. For who he was. In his entirety.

The shock of it stole her breath, and she rolled away, surprising him. But she couldn't hold back any longer. Not her joy, not her feelings. "I love you, Lucas."

She felt him suck in his breath with a hiss, and it took a second for her to realize that his fine, bold features had darkened.

"You don't love me," he stated forcefully, pushing up from the tangle of sheets.

He started to pace, without regard to his nakedness. For a second she could only stare at the beauty of him, the hard, muscled planes that rippled with each step he took; his manhood, thick and heavy, still half swollen with passion.

"But I do love you. It surprises me as much as it surprises you. And I'm going to save you."

His head came back and his eyes glittered dangerously. "What are you talking about?"

It took a second for her to realize what she had said. "I mean, I'm going to get you acquitted."

"You might get me acquitted, Alice, but you will never save me. I have been beyond redemption since I was ten years old. And you know that."

Not about to be put off, she smiled at him with all the love she felt. "All I know is that whatever you have done is out of goodness."

"Goodness? I learned about life in the arms of a paid courtesan." His gaze grew intense, fire burning. He seemed determined to make her see the man he saw. "As long as I live, I'll never forget her. I'll never forget her—a woman who so many others had already had."

Alice turned her face away.

But Lucas continued on, ruthlessly. "She was a whore, Alice. A beautiful, wonderful whore who had lost her innocence when she was too young. Just like me. That's what I'm like. A whore."

Her heart pounded, and she looked back, unable to stop herself from asking, "Did you love her?"

She saw him tense.

"Love her?" After a moment, he sighed. "No. But I cared. She used men, powerful men. But she truly seemed to care about me."

"What happened to her?" Alice didn't think she wanted to know. What if she were still in his life, working at Nightingale's Gate? What if she was wrong about everything?

"She killed herself not long after I met her. But she haunts my dreams. Still." His brow furrowed in memory. "She was highly desired for her talents."

Alice felt a stab of grief for the woman, but she was encouraged. "You feel guilty about her death, but you didn't love her. Just as you are not like her."

With that, she grew fierce. "You don't sell your body. You're not trying to please people."

And that's when understanding blazed like sun hitting ice, and she marched up to face him. "You're like me."

The expression on his face was so stunned it would have been comical had the situation not been so utterly awful.

"We are two of a kind, Lucas Hawthorne. So different yet the same. Surrounded by people who care, families with their concerns. But ultimately, each of us is alone, not fitting into the worlds of those who love us, having been someone so different for so long that it is hard to imagine how to be anything else."

Lucas stood as still as stone, but she could see he was shaken.

Her voice gentled, and she reached up and pressed her hand to his heart. "I do love you, Lucas. I love you because you are different. I love you because in some elemental way, we are so much the same."

And then her mind stilled as something else occurred to her. "What was her name? The woman." She grabbed his arms. "Tell me her name."

She felt his tense shrug. "I don't know. I never knew it."

Her fingers dug into his flesh. "A woman with no name. She's the nightingale lady. She's the Nightingale!"

Lucas looked at her sharply but didn't answer.

"She is! I know it. And you said yourself that she had been with other men. I am willing to bet that she gave you that ring." Alice suddenly remembered the ring mark on Oliver Aldrich's finger. "And I bet she gave other men the ring as well."

Chapter Twenty-one

There had to be more than one ring.

Lucas hadn't denied it, and Alice realized he must know that his father had one also. But if Lucas had told her about it, he would have felt he was implicating family. She, however, saw it as a way to muddy the waters. She felt certain that a case against Bradford Hawthorne would prove as circumstantial as the case against his son. How could any jury convict, knowing that someone else out there had one of those rings? Heavens, how could the Commonwealth continue the case knowing such a thing? She just needed proof that her instincts were correct and more than one of those rings existed.

Alice hurried through the streets the following morning. The sun was just a hint on the horizon. Lucas had left her cottage without another word, and she had paced madly, concentrating on the ring.

She wouldn't let herself think about how bold she had been. The intimacy. The feel of his skin beneath her touch. The shuddering desire and passion.

No, she'd save that for later. For now, she had to get some information. And Emmaline Hawthorne could help her find it.

There was something else the woman could do as an added bonus. She could speak to her husband and convince him to testify on his son's behalf.

Then maybe, just maybe, Alice could pull out information

that would make her father and the judge sit up and take notice without going against her client's expressed wishes.

Judge Parks entered the courtroom at one minute after nine o'clock in the morning. The gavel slammed down moments later.

Court was in session.

Lucas sat quietly next to Alice, heat radiating from his strong body, and she could feel his intense awareness. Alice had to force herself to focus instead of staring at the chiseled hands he had used to touch her.

When they had arrived at the courthouse, the crowds of women were still there, mixed with the throng of reporters on the front steps. Lucas had put his hand at Alice's back and guided her protectively through the crowd. But he hadn't said a word to her other than hello when his carriage picked her up.

Tawny Green returned to the stand, clearly reluctant. Alice knew she had to pick up where she left off, but she also had to stall until Emmaline arrived. And Alice prayed Emmaline could find what she needed.

"Miss Green, could you please repeat to the court where exactly you were in the alley when you saw Miss Rouge murdered?"

"Objection, Your Honor," Clark called out. "We've been over this endlessly."

Alice faced the judge. "It is imperative that the jury have a very clear understanding of the logistics, sir." She also wanted to see if the witness could remember what she had said the day before.

"I'll allow the question," Judge Parks ruled.

"Miss Green?" Alice prompted.

Tawny looked uncertain, and she furtively met Clark's gaze. Alice caught the barely perceptible nod he gave her.

Hardly listening to the answer, understanding locked Alice's thoughts into place. Feeling certain she was right, she fired off another question just as Tawny finished answering the last.

"You said you were on the north side of the alley?"

But Alice casually strode to the opposite side of the room, making it impossible for Tawny to see Clark unless she turned explicitly toward him. Which she did.

"Miss Green?" Alice demanded. "I'm over here."

"Um . . . yes. The north side," she agreed, though not until Clark had given her the barest hint of a nod. Had Alice not been watching him instead of the witness, she never would have seen it.

Alice fired off questions rapidly then, making it awkward for Tawny to keep looking at the prosecutor's table. The witness grew flustered, stammering her answers.

Yesterday when Tawny had stuck so determinedly to her responses, she seemed infinitely believable. Today, having to look back and forth across the room from Clark to Alice, a crack began to show in her plausible façade.

Tension built in the confined space. Alice could feel the growing excitement in the gallery. She saw the tight line of her father's lips. The best sign yet that she was making progress.

In the middle of one of Tawny's stammering answers, the courtroom door swung open and Emmaline hurried up the aisle. The judge flashed her an annoyed look for disrupting the proceedings. Emmaline grimaced apologetically and sat down in the front row next to Grayson.

When Alice turned to her, Emmaline gave her a smile and an emphatic nod.

Not wasting any time, Alice addressed the judge.

"Your Honor, I would like to request a ten-minute recess."

The judge raised a questioning brow, glanced between Alice and Emmaline, but finally agreed. The gallery seemed to sigh their disappointment that the proceedings were put on hold just when the defense was on a roll. But Alice paid them no mind.

Once the judge had left the bench, Alice and Emmaline huddled together.

"What is going on here?" Grayson demanded, his ire evident on his face. "You had her on the ropes, but now she'll have time to regroup."

Lucas sat back and crossed his ankle on his knee, looking at her with a speculative gleam in his eyes.

Alice met his gaze, felt the way he looked at her with approval. And that was all that mattered.

She looked back at Grayson. "Let her regroup. But I needed this recess."

"Why?"

"I don't have time to go over that now. Your mother and I have to talk."

And they did. Emmaline excitedly told Alice everything she had learned. Then she handed her a thin file.

"This should be everything you need," the older woman added. But just before she resumed her seat next to Grayson, she added, "I spoke to Bradford. I'm sorry, dear, but he won't testify."

Alice couldn't let that bother her. Not now. When the judge returned to the bench and court was called to order, Alice walked up to the witness stand, the file lying closed on the defense table.

"Miss Green," she began once again, excitement coursing through her veins, "you stated that the perpetrator had dark hair, correct?"

She looked at Clark.

"Miss Green, I asked the question, not Mr. Kittridge."

Tawny flushed red.

"Yes, yes, he had dark hair."

"How could you tell?"

"Objection!" Clark said. "She has eyes in her head, for mercy's sake. We have been over this time and time again,

Your Honor. I see no reason to badger the witness with re-
petitive testimony."

Grayson grumbled, as if agreeing. But Alice held on to
her temper. She knew what she was doing. The knowledge
felt good, intoxicating. And with the prospect of success
drumming through her mind, she addressed the judge.

"Your Honor, while we have been over this testimony, I
believe if you will allow me to continue, we will unearth
new information."

"That is ridiculous!" Clark burst out.

The judge eyed her, his dark brows furrowed. "I'll allow
it, Miss Kendall. But there better be something new out of
this."

"Yes, sir."

Clark sat down, but the sigh she expected didn't come.
Instead he looked worried. Her father did, too.

As well they should.

"Miss Green," she continued, "you were just about to tell
the court how it was you could tell the murderer had dark
hair."

"Well, um, it was the light that made me see him."

"What kind of light, Miss Green? Moonlight?"

"Ah, no." She frantically looked over at the prosecution.
"I already told you. There's a gas lantern right over the spot.
I remember it."

The witness seemed relieved by her answer. And Alice
had no doubt that she was relieved to have remembered the
fact. But there was something more that Tawny didn't appear to know.

Every time Alice had been in that alley she had been unnerved by the darkness. At those moments, however, she
had been too consumed with the eerie night and the sense of
being followed. When she had been there during the day,
she had seen the gas lanterns, so damning since one indeed
stood directly over the murder spot. But this morning it had
hit her.

"Miss Green, are you saying that due to a gas lamp above the murder location, you were able to see the perpetrator's hair color?"

"Well, um, yes."

"What if I told you that the gas lantern above that very spot is not working, in fact, hasn't been working since early April."

A gasp raced through the gallery. She felt Clark's stunned surprise.

Alice hurried to hammer home her point. "Aside from the fact that our fine city needs to repair the lantern, Miss Green, what else does this mean?"

Clark leaped to his feet. "Your Honor," he stated, "I have no idea what the defense is talking about. And if she is going to say such a thing, she had best be prepared to prove it."

The judge got a look on his face as if he had just eaten sour grapes. "Thank you, Mr. Kittridge, for explaining my job."

Clark didn't even cringe. He was too upset.

"Your Honor," Alice said, "this morning I obtained verification from the gas utilities that the lantern in question is not working. I only just got the file, which was the reason for the recess I requested." She walked to her desk, met Lucas's eyes, which showed a faint glimmer of pride—not relief for himself—simply utter pride at her success. The knowledge filled her heart.

Taking the file, she returned to the judge and placed the information before him.

The man quickly scanned the document, then looked at Clark. "It would appear the lantern is not functioning, just as Miss Kendall has suggested."

Clark sputtered.

"Miss Kendall," the judge said, "you may continue."

"Thank you, Your Honor. And if the court would indulge the defense a second longer, might I ask that the light fixture near the bailiff be turned out briefly?"

Clark leaped up, but the judge cut him off. "Don't bother, Mr. Kittridge. I will allow the defense her request."

At this point Judge Parks looked as if he was enjoying himself. "Bernie," he said, signaling to the bailiff who stood next to the knob. "Go ahead."

Everyone watched as the man turned down the light until it was gone. Despite the other fixtures, the man stood in shadows.

"Miss Green," Alice said in the dimmed light. "Could you please tell the court what color hair the bailiff has?"

Tawny stammered.

"Miss Green?" Alice prompted.

"I don't know," she finally whispered. "He just looks dark."

"Lights, please," Alice called out.

In seconds, the courtroom sprang into full life. And everyone there could see that the bailiff had hair that was not dark at all, rather blond.

"Miss Green," Alice pressed relentlessly, "are you still certain that the man who murdered Miss Rouge had dark hair?"

Frantically Tawny turned to Clark. Alice turned to Clark as well, daring him to make a single move.

"Miss Green, please answer the question," she said. "On your own."

"Yes, um, no. I mean yes. Oh, I don't know!"

Alice pressed her advantage. "Miss Green, did you ever know the color of the assailant's hair, or did the prosecution tell you it was dark?"

"This is ridiculous!" Clark bellowed, flying out of his seat.

"Is that an objection, Mr. Kittridge?" the judge asked, his brow raised.

"Yes, sir," he stated, fuming.

"Overruled. I'd like to hear the answer to this question. It hasn't escaped my notice that the witness has appeared overly interested in looking at you. Perhaps she has designs on you personally, Mr. Kittridge . . ."

Clark's eyes went wide.

". . . or perhaps she is looking at you for other reasons," he finished, his tone shifting into a dire warning.

Alice walked right up to the witness stand and leaned close, showing all the sympathy that she felt for this woman who suddenly found herself at the whim of men and a court system she didn't understand.

"Miss Green, did you really see Lucas Hawthorne in the alleyway the night that Lucille Rouge was murdered?"

"No, I mean yes, I mean they said it was him! Why would they lie?"

The courtroom erupted. Tawny began to cry. Judge Parks slammed his gavel down to no avail. And in the midst of the chaos, Alice saw her father stand up from his seat and walk down the center aisle, his broad back disappearing through the wide oak doors.

Was he impressed with her display? Or furious?

But Alice couldn't worry about that. She had a trial to finish. A trial that had just turned in her favor.

Chapter Twenty-two

Alice declined Emmaline's invitation to dine at Nightingale's Gate. She had work to do. She wanted to capitalize on the progress she had made.

Lucas stood beside his mother in the hallway outside the courtroom, and for a moment it looked as if he would insist. But in the end, he simply brushed Alice's cheek with the backs of his fingers and said he'd see her in the morning.

Would it be morning, or would he come to her again in the night?

For the rest of the evening, Alice sat in her small office and forced herself to forget about the sensual thrill that had raced through her at Lucas's touch. Intently, she went over all the facts of the case for the hundredth time. And she would go over them a hundred more times, if necessary, to be sure she remembered every element of what had transpired before, during, and after the murder.

But well after sunset, when the streets had grown quiet, nothing new had come to her. So she packed up her satchel and headed home. When she alighted from a hired hack, the main house was dark. As usual, she didn't have anything to eat in her cottage.

With the thought, or hope, of finding some leftover dinner in the main house, she entered through the front door. Not three steps inside she made out the silhouette in her father's study. The only light came from the muted moonlight that drifted through the windows.

Her pulse drummed at the thought of what her father would say to her about the trial. Right that second, she wasn't sure she wanted to know.

All of the sudden finding something to eat didn't sound like such a good idea. Perhaps if she turned around carefully, she could make it back out the front door without gaining Walker Kendall's attention.

But she didn't get very far.

"Alice?"

The voice was slurred, sounding odd. So unlike her father. He sounded drunk, surprising her. Walker Kendall never showed weakness of any kind, especially not the kind of weakness brought on by drink. She hated that she might have played a hand in bringing him to this point.

"You are going to win," he said, his voice unclear when she came to the doorway of the study. "I've been watching you."

"Of course you've been watching," she said with an uncomfortable chuckle, peering into the darkened room. "And I know I'm winning," she added truthfully.

He gave a distorted, muffled laugh. "You always were very sure of yourself."

A shudder ran down her spine. This encounter seemed off and disjointed somehow.

His arm moved, she could see the dark silhouette, could see that he took a long sip from one of the crystal glasses kept next to the decanter of brandy.

"Are you all right?" she asked, coming forward. But her footsteps stilled at the words he spoke next.

"Hawthorne never should have opened up the Nightingale. He's made too many people angry."

Every nerve on edge, she headed for the hurricane lamp that sat on the desk. "What are you talking about?"

Just as her fingers reached the lamp knob, the wall sconce flared.

"What's going on here?"

Alice whirled around to find Max in the doorway.

"Max," she began, wanting him to leave them in private, "Father and I—"

But the words cut off when she turned back and found that it was her uncle who sat in her father's chair.

"Uncle Harry!"

Her thoughts collided. Had Harry been pretending to be her father? Had she just assumed?

Her mind went back to the night she found him in this very chair, a gun laid out before him. The gun would be there now, sitting in its box to the side. What was wrong with her uncle? For the last few months he had seemed different.

At the sound of footsteps, she dragged her attention away. Walker Kendall entered the house, his face a mask of irritated distraction. He didn't seem to notice any of them.

"Father?"

Walker looked up and noticed his family. "Maxwell. Harry. What are you doing up this late, Alice? You should be in bed. You've got a long day ahead of you tomorrow. If you aren't asleep, at least you should be preparing."

Always the taskmaster. Never before had it bothered her.

"I am prepared, Father." She looked at her uncle and wondered what his cryptic remark meant.

She turned away. "Who is upset that Lucas Hawthorne opened Nightingale's Gate?"

Her father blinked, then shifted his gaze to his brother. His lips settled into a firm line before he said, "No one gives a damn about Nightingale's Gate. All respectable Boston cares about is that someone like Lucas Hawthorne isn't allowed to get away with murder."

"He did not murder anyone, Father. And you can't win this case."

His shoulders straightened.

"That's right," she continued. "Lucas Hawthorne isn't

guilty. And I think you know it." She hesitated, then made her decision. "I am certain a jury won't convict him."

"Ah, he's not guilty. There's a new thought." Walker Kendall scoffed into the high-ceilinged foyer. With a shake of his head, he set his satchel down on the aged marble floor, and came to stand before his daughter. "He's not guilty just like the rest of the men Harry holds in his jail cells who swear they are wrongly accused."

"Lucas Hawthorne isn't guilty," she repeated with all the passion and conviction that she felt. "He is a wonderful man who is misunderstood."

"You sound more like a woman in love than a lawyer," Max commented with a laugh.

"That's because I do love him!"

The laughter trailed off, replaced by three questioning gazes from three very strong Kendall men. Max groaned; Harry shook his head. And her father, Walker Kendall, attorney at law first and foremost, looked at her with a speculative gleam that made her wish with all her heart she hadn't said such careless words.

Every day that passed brought larger crowds to watch the trial. Anyone who couldn't get in waited outside for news of the proceedings. What could be bigger news than the infamous rake, Lucas Hawthorne, being defended by a woman attorney—the daughter of Boston's most powerful lawyer?

Lucas hated the spectacle. The fact that he was being written about in the newspapers every day didn't thrill him, but he felt the slow burn of frustration that he couldn't protect Alice from the same scrutiny.

A familiar tension took hold of him, and he cursed. But close on the heels of that tension was an emotion he didn't recognize. An odd feeling that went beyond his need to protect Alice, beyond his need to surround himself with her untutored but wildly provocative passion. He had thought a taste would quench his thirst for her. But each encounter had only left him wanting more.

And wanting and taking from her only put her in jeopardy that someone would find out. If the newspapers got ahold of that, she would be ruined.

Fortunately, so far they had said very little that could truly embarrass her. She was a fine lawyer, and that was acknowledged more often than not.

He hoped the whole blasted debacle would be behind them soon. Lucas had to believe Alice would get him acquitted.

In a meeting with Grayson and himself, Alice had said that after Tawny Green had been discredited, she felt all the prosecution had left was the ring—she had shot him a sharp look—and his less-than-stellar reputation. Lucas knew she intended to deal with his character starting today.

Lucas entered the courtroom with Grayson, the family behind them. Alice had stopped outside, then entered by herself. Watching her walk up the aisle, thoughts of the trial fled from Lucas's mind. He felt the same sensual heat he always felt when he saw her.

Today, like every other day in court, she looked every inch the professional, cool and composed. No more men's shirts or old-fashioned dresses. She wore tailored gowns with matching jackets. Only he knew what lay underneath the proper layers of her clothes.

He thought of her declaration that she loved him. He hated to think how much those simple words meant to him. The thought of a lifetime with her. Children and family. Raising a son of his own. But the truth was, they weren't simple words—nothing was simple about a woman like Alice Kendall loving a man like him. He didn't know the first thing about leading a respectable life. And Alice needed to understand that.

"Good morning," she said, with a shy smile that only he could see.

"It is a good morning now that I've seen you."

Red flared in her cheeks.

Without any thought for the world around them, Lucas reached out and touched her skin, barely, softly, but enough that it took her breath away.

"You are so beautiful when you blush," he added softly.

Somehow even such a small thing bolstered Alice's spirits. She was okay just as she was. Her looks. Her abilities.

The day's proceedings began with Alice's presentation of character witnesses. Her confidence grew exponentially with each person who attested to the quality of Lucas Hawthorne's reputation. His family, his banker, his friends, respected members of the community. And all the while the prosecution didn't attempt to cross-examine a single one of them.

Pride surged through her as she called Brutus to the stand. He attested to his loyalty to his employer. His knowledge of the inner workings of the club. Of Lucas's life. And, he added, the man was beyond reproach and couldn't have murdered that girl.

With a nod to Clark, Alice took her seat. When the judge asked halfheartedly if the Commonwealth wanted to cross-examine the witness, this time the ADA said yes, her father seated in the first row all but preening.

And that's when the tides turned, the slow ebb of water returning to sea taking what progress Alice had made with it.

Clark Kendall stood from his seat, tugged at his ultra-respectable cuffs, then proceeded to address the jury. Suddenly the young prosecutor moved with a confidence he hadn't exhibited thus far. Alice saw her father sit back and stroke his mustache, a sure sign that he was confident. Alice's palms grew moist.

"Mr. Hall," Clark began with the utmost formality, addressing the massive man by his proper name, "it sounds as if you are an exemplary employee."

Brutus got a little taller in his seat. "I try, sir."

"Then you know where Mr. Hawthorne is at most times."

"At *all* times," he corrected proudly.

"When he comes and when he goes? When he is with someone and when he's not?" Clark elaborated.

"Yes, sir."

"Do you know when he sees people in his private apartments?"

"Of course. As I said, I am within a voice's reach at all times."

Clark's lips flickered, as if in distaste, before he stepped closer and leaned his elbow on the witness stand as if the two of them were friends. Alice's mind raced, trying to come up with some reason to object. But she had no idea where he was going with his questions. Then she watched, dread filling her, as Clark glanced at her father. After a moment's hesitation, Walker Kendall gave Clark a barely perceptible nod.

"Can you tell me how well you know the defense attorney?" Clark then asked.

The question surprised everyone there. Including Alice. She could feel the tension in Lucas.

"Objection!"

"On what grounds, Miss Kendall?"

"There's no relevance."

"And no harm done, as I see it," the judge finished off. "You may answer the question, Mr. Hall."

Alice felt her heart begin to pound.

"I don't know what you mean," Brutus managed, suddenly wary.

"Have you seen Miss Kendall often?"

"Well, yes. She comes to Nightingale's Gate a lot."

Alice staggered back to her feet. "Objection! I have been at Nightingale's Gate to meet with my client."

The judge looked between Alice and Clark.

Clark shrugged his shoulders with great innocence. "If that is true, I don't see why you should object to my line of questioning, counselor."

What could she say?

"Objection overruled," the judge said.

Alice sank in her seat much as her stomach had.

"Mr. Hall," Clark continued, "is it not so that Mr. Hawthorne conducts his business from an office that overlooks the main room? The grand salon, I believe it is called."

"Uhm, yes."

"And isn't it true that Mr. Hawthorne has a more private office . . . just off his bed chamber?"

"Well, yes, sir."

Alice felt a deep, painful throbbing start in her temples.

"Does Mr. Hawthorne see business associates in this private office?"

"Not usually," Brutus stammered.

"But he does see Miss Kendall in this bedroom office."

"Objection!"

Clark ignored her. "Mr. Hall, have you seen *Miss* Kendall in this private office?"

The courtroom erupted with shocked gasps. Alice had to place her hand on Lucas's thigh when he started to leap out of his seat. Lucas's being protective of her at this juncture would only hurt him—confirming to the jury that she had indeed been in his bedroom.

She looked at her father. Everyone else was looking at him, too. He wore a mask of outrage at what had been implied about his daughter. But she knew her father well enough to know that his anger was feigned. This was the kind of tactic he used all the time, implying facts that may or may not be true. But she never would have believed he would use such tactics against his own daughter. The realization left her cold and spinning with devastation, the sound of voices and gasps echoing in her mind.

"Order in the court!" the judge called out, bringing his gavel down.

After a moment, a tense silence settled. Judge Parks glowered. "What I want to know, Mr. Kittridge, is what your line of questioning has to do with this case?"

Clark shot her father a furtive glance before he turned back to the judge. Alice felt light-headed. The lights seemed too bright and the room cramped, the walls closing in on her.

"Your Honor," Clark stated carefully, "the prosecution believes that Miss Kendall has become intimate with the defendant."

The courtroom erupted once again, just as Lucas leaped to his feet and launched at Clark. Thankfully Grayson and Matthew caught him and held him back. But this time no amount of hammering of the gavel brought them to order. Newspapermen ran one another down in their haste to exit, no doubt heading for their respective papers to report the developments.

Alice could do little more than sit in her chair, her ears buzzing with humiliation. Stunned, she turned slowly and looked at her father. "Why?" she mouthed.

He stared at her for one long second, before he looked away.

"I said order in the court!" the judge bellowed.

When finally order returned, the man called Alice and Clark to the bench.

"I will not put up with your shenanigans, Mr. Kittridge," he hissed. "Not in my courtroom!"

"This is no game, Your Honor," he replied, staying formal. "I have reason to believe that Miss Kendall has formed a relationship with her client that exceeds the bounds of her professional duties. The jury has a right to know that she is consorting with her client, manipulated by the impossible hope of affection from a notorious ladies' man like Hawthorne."

Alice was too stunned to speak. She was mortified and wounded to the core.

"Is that what you think of me?" she could barely ask. "That I'm an ineffectual spinster who is so desperate to be loved that she would be blinded to truth?"

Judge Parks turned to Alice and surveyed her. "Are you smitten, Miss Kendall?"

"Or course not!"

They suddenly became aware that the room had grown quiet and everyone there had heard.

Alice pressed her eyes closed. "Spinster or not, I am perfectly capable of doing my job, Your Honor."

Clark raised a doubtful eyebrow.

"And I think we both know that the prosecution is grasping at straws," she said, forcing steel into her voice to cover her devastation. "The Commonwealth is losing this case, and they know it. As far as I'm concerned, this case should be dismissed. Their eyewitness is completely and utterly unreliable, if not out and out coerced."

"That's a lie!" Clark blurted.

"Quiet, young man. I happen to agree with the defense— about the witness, and about the fact that whatever Miss Kendall feels for the defendant is none of our business." The judge sighed and focused on Alice. "But as much as I agree with you on that, I can't discount the fact that there is still the issue of the ring. I have no grounds on which to dismiss the case."

Alice held back a frustrated curse as Clark raised his chin and barely held back his satisfied smile.

"But you'd best be careful, Mr. Kittridge," the judge added. "I will not allow for any more theatrics."

Alice sought Lucas out at Nightingale's Gate. She needed to see him.

Despite what had been stated in court, and in spite of the fact that reporters could be watching for any sort of proof, she couldn't stay away.

She closed her eyes against the weakness. As his paid advocate, it was up to her to be objective, not become personally involved. She had known that all along. But he filled her dreams.

When she entered the club, the atmosphere was somber. The regulars were there, but they sat quietly sipping their drinks. As she passed through the grand salon, the awful regular named Howard glared at her.

Since the first time she came here, this man had made her uncomfortable. And those few short minutes in the alley had seared her with a fear she had never known before.

Alice didn't waste any time heading for the stairs where Brutus waited.

"Sorry about my testimony, Miss Kendall," the massive man said.

It was the first time he had been nice to her.

Pressing her hand to his forearm, she smiled kindly. "You told the truth, and that's all you can do."

He didn't lead her to the loft office. Instead, they made their way to Lucas's private chambers.

When they entered, Lucas stood at the bank of windows, staring out at the world below. Turning around, he leaned back against the sill, his gaze troubled as their eyes met. "That will be all, Brutus," he said.

As soon as they were alone, Alice bit her lip. As always, the beauty of him took her breath. His dark hair was wet, as if he had just left the shower. His clothes were perfectly pressed, but casual. His gaze somber but sensual. Seeing the man in private was both thrilling and intimate.

"I don't know why I'm here," she whispered.

"I didn't ask."

Then she was in his arms, holding on.

"Shhh. It's going to be all right," he murmured against her hair.

"But those things Clark said in the courtroom!"

"Hey," he replied, his tone teasing, "don't worry. I know how much you really hate me."

Pushing away, she looked at him through teary eyes. "That's the problem. You know I don't."

He stared at her, the momentary flicker of lightness in his eyes disappearing. "I know," he said softly.

But nothing came after that. No "I don't hate you either." No "I'm glad." Tonight his lack of response made her angry.

"Doesn't that mean anything to you?" she demanded.

Lucas stepped back and ran his hand through his dark hair.

"Doesn't it?"

A guttural noise sounded deep in his chest, but he didn't answer. Instead, he turned back to her fiercely, then leaned down and pressed his lips against hers. Like giving in to a greater power, his fingers trailed back to her ear, sweeping a long tendril of white-blonde hair back. Her breath came to her in a rasping shudder.

"No," she breathed again, pushing at his chest. "Answer me!"

He felt as much as saw her intake of breath. He noticed as well the flutter of her pulse in her neck that betrayed her. She was here now, with him, and he couldn't imagine letting her go. But no matter how she felt about him, it didn't change the fact that he could only ruin her—as was proved today in court with the prosecution's accusations.

"Of course it means something to me," he said. "It means a lot."

"But not enough for you to return the sentiment?"

He ran his palms down her arms. "I don't hate you either," he whispered.

"Oh, great! Just great! You don't hate me."

He had hurt her; he could see it in her eyes. He swore an oath, knowing he should tell her to leave. He should show her to the door, because to answer her would be like giving in to fire. Both of them would be burned.

Frustration assailed him. But he knew that he wouldn't, no, couldn't make her leave. "Everything you said means a great deal to me. *You* mean a great deal to me. When you are near I can't think straight. When you're gone, I want you back at my side. I think about you, I dream about you." He grasped her arms. "I want you every second of the day."

He didn't wait for a response, didn't want one. He pulled her close, crushing her to him.

"I need you, Alice," he whispered raggedly. And he understood in that moment that he needed her in a way that had nothing to do with his trial. This wasn't about acquittals or convictions.

Without another word, he lowered his head to hers, capturing her lips in a kiss. One strong hand traced a path down her back, pressing them close as the kiss became a demand— long and slow, deep, unyielding.

With a moan, she encircled his shoulders, clinging to him with a fierceness that startled him, left him breathless. He kissed her temple before his mouth slanted over hers hungrily. She opened to him, then nipped at his lower lip, clearly wanting him as much as he wanted her.

That was one of the many things he cherished about her. The boldness that mixed with a startling innocence.

He groaned into her mouth, his tongue tangling with hers. His lips trailed down her neck until he kissed the ripe swell of one breast beneath the fabric of her gown.

She shuddered when he ran his tongue along the pulse in her neck. Very slowly he kissed her, a sensual dance of lips and tongue tangling with hers, tantalizing, tempting.

Then she took his breath away when she stepped back.

Intense need seared him, his hard arousal throbbing insistently. But he wouldn't stop her. If she wanted to leave, he'd let her.

He was certain she would head for the door, but she surprised him when she started working the fastenings of her gown. One by one they gave way until her clothes lay in a puddle around her ankles.

Humbled beyond imagining, Lucas felt young and exposed. He almost hated the emotion. Hardly recognized it. But this woman had a way of making him act and think in manners that were foreign to him.

"Love me, Lucas," she said boldly. "Completely."

The words nearly brought him to his knees, that such a woman would give herself to him unselfishly. For no gain. Simply because she loved him.

Dear God, he felt it. Understood it down to his soul. Never would he have believed that such a pure person could feel such an emotion for him.

But he could see the vulnerability in her expression—the vulnerability that he would reject her. And with his throat tight with emotion, he went to her, taking her in his arms with fierce abandon.

She clung to him, reveling in the feel of his hard body pressed to hers.

Her fingers found purchase in his hair, his mouth nipping and sucking, making her yearn impatiently. She tore at his shirt, wanting to feel his skin next to hers. Willingly he obliged. In seconds, he shed his clothes and tossed them aside. He stood in all his startling glory.

"God, you are beautiful," she whispered in awe.

His sex was hard and heavy with arousal, the muscles along his chest and abdomen quivering with his barely maintained control. He kissed her again, urgently, his palms caressing her back, trailing down until he cupped her bottom. She couldn't help but respond to his coaxing, melting against him—seeking what she knew he could provide.

"Yes, Alice." He nudged her knees apart with his own, his muscular leg brushing against the juncture between her thighs.

The sensation was exquisite, and she couldn't hold back the moan that started deep in her throat.

With fervent desire, she ran her palms over his chest, feeling the contours, reveling in the sheer sculpted planes of him.

His body quivered as he sucked in his breath. Then he groaned when her fingers slipped lower, as she had done before, and she wrapped her hand around his length.

Lucas opened his mouth, silently drawing breath, his

eyes closed. The power she had over this invincible man amazed her and awed her in turn.

But he surprised her when he took steps back toward the bed, tugging her along. When the backs of his knees hit the mattress, he sat. Pulling her with him.

Before she knew it, her thighs straddled his, her knees pressing into the thick coverlet. His male flesh hard and insistent between her legs.

"Oh, my," she squeaked.

Lucas half chuckled, half groaned. "Move over me," he managed.

"Move over you?"

"I thought you had read a bunch of books."

"Well, not a bunch . . ."

His grimace held humor, and her heart raced with excitement, but also with the full realization of where this was headed. She felt nervous and insistent at the same time. She was both desperate to leap forward and fearful of where it would lead.

But the desire for this man won out when his strong hands brushed up her sides, nudging her closer, then gently guided her down to his shaft.

When the secret folds of her flesh touched his slick hardness, her body quivered with longing. But his sheer size made her tremble with trepidation.

With his hands instructing her, he moved her on him, slowly circling her hips, tantalizing her until her head fell back and all thought evaporated. She sought the pleasure he had given her before—though this time she sought something greater, something that pulled at her, something primal and innate. Instinctually, she understood that she yearned to feel him deep inside her. His flesh impaling her.

Seeking, her body heated, she began to move without his guidance. She felt him suck in his breath when she tried to slide lower, taking more of him.

"God," he whispered on a strangled breath.

She moved again, but despite her body's insistent desire, she couldn't go further.

Expelling his breath, he grabbed her hips and guided her back until they were nearly parted. But then he pulled her to him. Over and over again, slowly, deliciously, until she started moving again on her own. Moving and sliding, up and down, still seeking.

She looked at this man, his jaw locked, his body hard and tense like stone.

Unable to help herself, she leaned over him, her hair falling free to drape about them. And she pressed her lips to his. For one long, breathless moment, he wrapped her in his arms. Then without warning, he lifted her up and had her on her back, sinking into the bed beneath long rays of moonlight.

He came over her, pinning her into the downy sheets. His eyes met hers, his elbows planted on either side of her, his hands framing her face.

"I'm going to make love to you, Alice."

She didn't reply. Couldn't.

"Tell me you want me to," he demanded.

She did, so badly. "Yes, I want you to," she whispered.

His gaze locked with hers, he came between her knees, almost reverently, lowering himself slowly until the swollen tip of his manhood brushed against her. This time there was no thought that he was too large. She only wanted him.

Their bodies pressed together until there was nothing between them, joining in a centuries-old caress. Their eyes met and held. "It will hurt the first time," he said, his muscles leaping beneath his skin with barely held control. "But then there will be nothing but pleasure."

Her only answer was to move against him, her breath ragged, her body stirring, yearning, no longer able to wait. Then he called her name as he plunged into her with a single hard thrust.

She felt her virginity give way, as did he. He stilled, allowing her body time to adjust to the length of him. Then, slowly, he began to move inside her, carefully, gently—too gently, she understood at some primal level.

With a frustrated cry she moved against him. Almost reverently he laughed, then matched her thrusts, until they were both seeking. He cupped her hips, pulling her body up to meet his bold, fevered thrusts.

She clutched his shoulders, panting, needing. And then it happened. She felt her body convulse with spiraling intensity, every sense reeling and alive. Only then did she feel an explosive shudder rack the hard length of his body. He cried out her name, grasping her tightly to his heart as he buried his face in her hair.

For long minutes they laid that way, the heaviness of him comforting. After a moment, he rolled to his side, bringing her with him. She could feel the beat of his heart, strong and rapid. They lay wrapped together, silence all around them.

And just as she started drifting off to sleep, moved beyond comprehension, Alice knew she couldn't lose this man. She would fight for him— for his love, for his freedom. She would do whatever she had to do to see that Lucas walked out of the courtroom acquitted of the crime.

She could only pray he'd still want her once he was free.

Chapter Twenty-three

At six o'clock the following morning, with the sun threatening on the horizon, Alice furtively attempted to make it around her father's house to her cottage without being noticed. She had done her best to put herself together before she left Nightingale's Gate, but she never had been much of a morning person. Just remembering waking up in Lucas's room made her groan.

She had stretched, startled to find plenty of room on the mattress and incredibly soft sheets. Her tiny bed had rough muslin coverings, and her mind tried to process the information.

Then she had remembered. She wasn't in *her* bed.

Whipping her eyes open, she had taken in her surroundings. Lots of windows, gleaming hardwood, luxurious carpets, thick high-poster bed. And Lucas. Standing in the doorway in dark trousers, no shirt, with a cup of coffee in his hand.

"I just finished making breakfast. Are you hungry?" he asked, his smile rich and sensual.

A part of Alice wanted to yank the covers back over her head. How many times had Max told her she could scare the warts off of a toad with the way she looked when she woke in the morning?

Tangled hair. Sheet-marked face. And she couldn't imagine she came out looking any better *this* morning.

"Ah, no," she managed, glancing toward the window in hopes of lessening the amount of her that he could actually see. "Amazingly enough, I don't think I could eat a thing."

Lucas set the cup aside, and crossed the room to her.

With a wolfish smile, he reached out and pulled her close. "You, not hungry?"

"Believe it or not, I do more than think about eating."

"I'd like to think about something besides eating right now."

He stroked her cheek, and heat rose inside her. Heat and a deliciously silky feeling.

"I like seeing you in my bed," he said gruffly.

And somehow she believed him. It might not mean love, but it was a step in the right direction.

Alice nearly twirled in response.

"I woke up last night," she said, "and you weren't here."

Her words startled him, or so she thought. But when he looked back at her he only chuckled. "I was here all the time. You must have been dreaming."

He kissed her then, deeply. Her body yearned for what it now knew it could have. His absence from last night was forgotten. He made love to her in the early-morning hours, and only when a clock tolled the hour in the distance did she remember that they had a trial to attend.

She dressed as quickly as she could, praying she could get home without her father realizing she had been gone all night. He already suspected that she was intimate with Lucas. No sense providing proof. No telling what he would do with that.

Now, as she tiptoed along the brick side path, she had nearly made it around the house when her uncle appeared out the back door.

Damn, she was caught.

"Uncle Harry," she said, quickly reversing directions in the vain attempt to pretend she was just leaving the cottage rather than trying to sneak in.

But her efforts were for naught. Distraction marred her uncle's face.

"What's wrong?" she asked, forgetting her predicament.

He seemed to shake himself out of his thoughts. "Alice," he said, startled. "I didn't see you." His eyes focused. "Off to work so early?"

"Yes, yes." Whew. "Is something wrong? You seem upset."

Harry's face contorted. "Another girl was killed last night."

Shock stole through her. "Another girl?" she whispered, as startled as her uncle had looked moments before. "Dead?"

"Yes, they found her a few hours ago." He looked off at the lightening sky. "In Beekman's alley. We believe it was by the same man."

Her mind reeled, her chest seeming to squeeze. "What makes you think that?"

He hesitated, eyeing her. "I can't discuss the details as the matter is still under investigation. But I'll let you know this, I am on my way to Nightingale's Gate."

Alice gasped. "What for?"

"To take Hawthorne into custody for questioning."

"You can't do that!"

"But I can."

Her brain spun as she tried to sort through her thoughts and make a decision. But the decision had been made last night when she went to sleep in Lucas Hawthorne's bed.

"Not if he has an alibi."

"He can tell me all about that when I'm questioning him."

"No." Her tone of voice stopped him. "As my uncle, you need to know now."

He must have realized that something hitched in her voice because his head tilted dangerously.

"*I* am Lucas Hawthorne's alibi," she said rapidly before she could lose her nerve.

His craggy face went still. "What are you saying, Alice?"

She held out her arms to display her rumpled gown, then motioned to her less than perfectly marshaled hair. "I didn't come home last night, Uncle Harry. I was with Lucas Hawthorne at Nightingale's Gate."

His lips compressed into a hard line. "Doing what?" he finally asked.

"That hardly matters. We were together."

"Like hell it doesn't! You have been at a notorious scoundrel's place of business all night, and you say it doesn't matter? What were you doing until all hours? Gambling? Drinking?"

She cringed, hating to disappoint this man she loved. "Let's just say Clark was right about what he said in the courtroom yesterday. I have visited Lucas's bed chamber."

Harry's shoulders came back and his eyes widened. "Are you telling me you . . . you . . . had relations with that lowlife bastard?"

The words were a hiss of barely contained fury.

She had gotten herself into it now. Though there was nothing to do but forge ahead. "Yes, that is what I'm telling you," she responded, lifting her chin.

"How could you be such a fool? I didn't raise an idiot! I didn't raise a loose woman, either!" His face went red, a telltale vein bulging on his forehead.

"Say what you will, Uncle, but I love Lucas. And I know he couldn't have killed any of those women, and he certainly couldn't have murdered anyone last night since he was with me."

Then it hit her. Had he been? she thought suddenly. The hours seemed like a dream now. A blur of hours and minutes of being held by Lucas. Had she really woken up and found him gone, or had her mind played tricks on her—dreaming of what she feared would happen, dreaming that Lucas had left her.

"Love?" he bellowed. "Half the women in Boston swear they are in love with him, too. He's a predator, Alice! He lures women in with a fake demeanor that naïve females take as charm, then he tosses them aside like so much dirty laundry when he's finished. That, or he kills them!" He shook his head. "Good God, Alice, can't you see how he's using you? First, to go up against your father, and now, by blinding you by coaxing you into his bed. God, he's clever. The one thing he didn't have was an alibi! He's gotten that from you! At your expense!"

The words bothered her more than she let on. She didn't believe he could have killed anyone. But had he used her?

For now, she had to concentrate on Lucas as her client.

"I'm sorry that I've distressed you, Uncle Harry. But there is little you can do about this. I am an independent woman, an adult. I can do as I please. Beyond that, you now understand that you have no reason to question my client."

Harry grumbled. "Like hell I don't."

"The man has an alibi," she stated forcefully. "And if you so much as set foot in Nightingale's Gate, I will tell anyone who will listen that you clearly have a personal agenda against Lucas Hawthorne since there is no reason for you to be questioning him."

"You're going to tell everyone that you stayed there?" he asked, as if he didn't believe her for a second.

"If you force me to, I will."

Harry didn't look happy, but what could he do? He knew her all too well.

After several seconds had passed, and it appeared she had won this battle, she shrugged her shoulders apologetically, then added, "I'd like to see the file on the girl who was killed last night."

"You'll have it as soon as it's ready. But if you're so convinced your client had nothing to do with it, why read it?"

"Because it might give us clues as to who really *did* kill the girl," she said pointedly. "Clues that lead to someone who is still out there, whom you are too stubborn to look for." She started away, then stopped. "And I'd prefer that you let me be the one to tell Father about where I was last night."

One minute tough and professional, the next a trembling schoolgirl afraid to get in trouble with her father. She shook her head in disgust.

He studied her long and hard. "Fine."

"I'll do it right now."

Harry turned away. "He isn't here. You weren't the only one who stayed out all night."

Having narrowly escaped dealing with her father at this juncture, Alice cleaned up and got ready for court. First, however, she was going to see Bradford Hawthorne.

She arrived at the splendid town house called Hawthorne House at eight in the morning. She hoped that Bradford was home and awake. She didn't have time to be sent away.

An aged butler answered the door. His dour expression didn't give her hope, but she had barely uttered her name when he gasped then all but dragged her into the house.

"How is the trial going?" the man asked, his eyes pleading.

She must have looked doubtful that she should answer him, because he hurried on.

"I'm Hastings. I've been with the Hawthornes since before the boys were born. Young master Lucas is like a son."

His aged eyes actually teared up. "Everything I read in the newspapers doesn't sound favorable."

He was right, of course. The papers had become brutal recently, to her and to Lucas. And it had not gone unnoticed by the press that Bradford had yet to appear in court on his son's behalf. She had tried to do it Lucas's way. But she wasn't willing to take the risk any longer. Especially when another girl had been killed.

Alice's blood boiled at the thought of a father allowing his son to go to prison for a crime he may have committed. Today she planned to confront that man.

"I'm hoping to speak with Mr. Hawthorne today to see if he might help us," she explained.

Hastings groaned. "Mr. Hawthorne won't see anyone. He's sequestered himself in the back room."

Alice tapped her chin. "But if a bossy woman lawyer barged in, what is a nice man like you to do?"

She shrugged innocently. Hastings looked half appalled, half convinced it could work.

"Just point the way, Mr. Hastings, then start making noise like you're going to summon the police."

The butler gathered his courage then pointed.

No sooner had she started down a wide hallway than he started protesting—so convincingly that she almost stopped.

"What is going on?" a voice demanded.

She came face-to-face with Bradford Hawthorne. Standing so close, he was larger than she had realized. Tall like Lucas, his shoulders broad. How could a man who looked so much like his son be so different?

"You're that lawyer lady," he accused.

"I'd like to speak to you, sir."

"I have nothing to say." He turned to go.

"But I do," she stated crisply.

That stopped him. He eyed her with menace and a shiver ran down her spine.

"I don't like pushy women."

"I don't like fathers who turn their backs on their children."

If he was the murderer, that probably hadn't been the best thing to say, given the sheer rage that came over his face. But Hastings was there, she reasoned, hardly able to hear herself think over the blood pounding in her ears.

"Get out!"

"Not until we talk," she said with a calm she didn't feel. "Your son is on the verge of going to jail for a crime he didn't commit."

Bradford didn't say anything, and she knew this was the moment when she had to state what she suspected.

"A crime," she added, "he believes you committed."

A half-beat passed as her meaning settled in.

"What?" His outraged bellow exploded in the hallway.

Not even Alice could deny the sheer and genuine surprise that contorted the man's face. Or was he a consummate actor? Her head began to throb.

"Lucas isn't talking about his suspicions," she added, "and he's doing nothing to help himself because he believes he is protecting you."

"That is the most ridiculous thing I have ever heard."

"Is it?" she asked pointedly.

"What is going on in here?"

They turned to find Emmaline standing in the doorway.

Alice caught sight of the look that came over Bradford's face. Wistful, moved. Then hardening into stubborn anger.

"Mind your own business, Mother."

"My business is my son's welfare." She looked at Alice. "I have no doubt you are here to convince this bull-headed man to testify on Lucas's behalf, and I thank you for that. I can also guess that you aren't getting anywhere. It's eight-thirty, and you need to be in court by nine. Why don't you go now? I'd like to have a word alone with Mr. Hawthorne."

Alice didn't know what else to do besides leave.

Hastings showed her to the door, shaking his head in misery. "She isn't going to get anywhere with that stubborn, bull-headed excuse for a man."

"But she'll try."

Emmaline felt her throat tighten with emotion. Returning to the house that she and her husband had built for their growing family brought back a surge of memories. How she had loved this house, loved her life. Her boys, her activities. But she had hated how she and Bradford had grown apart.

Poignancy filled her as she took in the graceful columns and beautiful marble floors. Just the kind of house Lucas wanted to build for her now.

Would he ever understand that she had loved her early life? And every time she saw this house or another like it, it simply reminded her of what she had lost? The only way she would live like this again would be if she and her husband could recapture what they had had in the beginning.

And that wouldn't happen.

Bradford Hawthorne was set in his ways, wouldn't change for anyone, especially not a woman.

"I knew you would return."

"But I haven't, Bradford."

His expression soured, and it was then that Emmaline noticed that he didn't look well. He appeared tired, and old, just like Alice had said in court. For the first time, Emmaline realized that he wasn't a vital young man any longer.

The thought surprised her. Bradford Hawthorne had always been a force to be reckoned with, a powerful male full of vitality. This man standing there in shirtsleeves and a sweater, his trousers baggy and not perfectly pressed, looked like the grandfather that she realized he was.

Clearly, his son's trial was taking more of a toll on him than he was willing to admit.

"I've come to talk to you," she added.

"There's nothing to talk about," he grumbled, turning away, heading to the back of the house.

Emmaline followed him, arriving in the sunroom. Just in the short time she had been away, the house seemed different. It was still impeccably clean and ordered, but it was tiny things that she noticed. The lack of fresh flowers and music.

The sunroom was different as well. Instead of her basket of crocheting, piles of newspapers lay about in disarray.

Hastings appeared at her side. "I've tried to clean this room, but he won't allow any of the staff near it, including me." He shifted his weight. "If I might be so presumptuous as to say, I believe Mr. Hawthorne misses you."

At this, Emmaline scoffed kindly.

"I mean it," Hastings insisted. "I believe this is the one room that reminds him of you."

She didn't believe it for a second. "That is nice of you to

say, Hastings, and I appreciate your concern. But right now, our only concern is Lucas."

Hastings's face etched with sadness.

Bradford snorted over his shoulder. "I might be old, but my ears still work. And if the two of you want to go off and chat, do so. But quit yapping in here."

Hastings blushed, then he hurriedly departed.

"That was uncalled for," she reprimanded.

"Fine, fine, why are you here?"

"I want you to testify on behalf of Lucas."

"Like hell I will."

He walked to an oversized flowered chair and sat without helping her to a seat, putting his carpet slippers up on the matching ottoman as if he didn't know the first thing about good manners. Emmaline knew the move was intentionally insulting.

Insults, however, were the least of her concerns.

She walked further inside, having to step over stacks of newspapers, nearly slipping on an open section of the Monday morning *Globe*.

"I didn't extend an invitation," he spat.

"Whether either of us likes it or not, this is still my house."

"This is my house!"

"If you will recall, it was my money that paid for it."

His face suffused in red.

"I didn't come here to argue. I came to talk about our son. He needs you."

"He doesn't need me! He never has!"

Emmaline sighed, then sat down on a plump ottoman across from him and leaned forward. "There was a time when he did—a time when he ran to you with open arms, followed you everywhere you went. He even imitated the way you dressed." The memories leaped out at her, taking her back. She felt her heart go soft in a way it hadn't since her boys were young. "I remember when Lucas insisted on having a dressing robe exactly like yours with matching dressing trousers. Gray paisley silk." She looked at her husband, noticed that some of the harshness had faded. "Do you remember that?"

She saw that he did, saw that his mind had tumbled back. "And slippers. He wanted matching slippers."

"So he could stand next to me in the lavatory while I shaved," he said, with gruff softness.

"You made him a blunt razor."

Bradford sighed. "He loved that silly scrap of wood."

Emmaline hesitated, waiting, wondering how to proceed. "What happened, Bradford? What happened that changed things between you?"

His mood altered as quickly as lightning striking. He slammed his newspaper down on the table and leaped up from his chair. "I didn't do anything! Nothing! And I will not have you saying I didn't raise my son right."

Emmaline fell back against the chair. Her husband was many things, but he had never been violent. It occurred to her that something was very wrong.

"Bradford, what is it?"

"Nothing! Why does everyone keep asking me what is wrong? First Grayson. Now you?"

"Grayson was here?"

His expression closed up, and he waved the question away. "So you want me to testify. I say no. What else do you want?"

Her lips pursed, and her mind raced. "You said not long ago that you wanted me back."

A flicker of hope flared in his eyes, before he tamped it back. "And?"

"I can't come back, Bradford, not when you act like this. Do you even remember the man you used to be? The man I fell in love with? The man whose son idolized him?"

He stared at her for an eternity, and she began to feel hope build. How could a father not love his son? Bradford would do what was best for their child. Surely.

And when he did, what would that mean? How would she feel about him and their future? Was it possible for the man to change?

"If you love me at all, Bradford, if you ever felt anything for me, come to the courthouse today. Please testify for our son."

Chapter Twenty-four

Alice arrived at the courthouse with little more than seconds to spare. Lucas was already seated at the long oak table. Grayson and the Hawthornes were seated as usual in the row behind him. Lucas, Matthew, and Grayson conferred while Finnea and Sophie talked quietly and somberly.

The minute Alice entered, Lucas turned as if sensing she was there. His eyes shimmered with passion, and something more. Standing up from his seat, he looked as if he would touch her. Her breath caught.

Her thoughts broke off, however, when her father entered the courtroom. Without a word to anyone, he pushed through the low swinging gates that separated the gallery from the counsel tables and seated himself in the first chair for the prosecution.

Anyone who was watching understood in that second that he had taken over the case. Confirmation came when Clark didn't arrive.

Alice felt her stomach drop when Walker Kendall ran his fingers over his luxurious mustache. An age-old sign that he was preparing for battle.

"Damn," she heard Grayson mutter behind her.

Lucas only reached under the table and squeezed her hand. "You are a great attorney. Don't let your father throw you."

Sitting down hard, it took a moment for Alice to notice

the file marked to her attention that lay on the table in front of her. Just when she opened it and noticed that it was the crime report for last night's murder, the bailiff announced the judge, and she was forced to close the file and rise.

The judge sat and cleared his throat, then looked out at them. "I received word this morning that Clark Kittridge has been removed from the case and the Commonwealth's lead attorney will be taking over. While I can imagine why Kittridge was removed after yesterday's display, unfortunately in this case I don't mind telling you I don't like this at all. It puts us in the position of a father combating his daughter in a court of law."

"Your Honor," Walker interrupted, standing from his seat.

Not many men could get away with such a thing.

"Walker," the judge said, cutting him off. "I understand why you wouldn't want that man to continue after what he said about your daughter in court—"

"My relationship to the defense has no bearing on this case, Your Honor. I'm sure the court has noticed that months ago the prosecution presented documents to the defendant disclosing my relationship to his chosen counsel."

The judge grumbled. "Yes, I'm aware of the documents. I'm also aware of the fact that the documents make it impossible for me to do anything other than proceed, with you as lead counsel."

Alice sat with hands curled tightly around her pen. She could see her father's orchestrations all over this. Had he planned this all along?

Regardless of the answer, there was no denying that it was utterly and truly her against her father now. She prayed Emmaline would succeed in getting Bradford into court. While she had discredited Tawny Green, then paraded a series of character witnesses before the jury, there was still the issue of a father unwilling to testify on behalf of his son. And then there was the ring.

Today she would go out on a limb and tell the jury that there was more than one. Bradford Hawthorne, guilty himself or not, had one of those rings. She felt certain. If she could just get him on the stand to prove it.

Seconds later she got her wish when the doors banged open and in stormed Bradford Hawthorne. Relief and joy made Alice want to weep.

But when she glanced at Lucas, his eyes were dark and desperate, though oddly wistful.

What had happened between father and son, Alice wondered yet again? It had to be more than Lucas's way of life.

But the fact was, her only interest was in the ring. Though she'd have to lead the man to it. Her heart began to surge with the excitement of a warrior going to battle.

"Bradford!" Judge Parks bellowed, slamming his gavel down. "That is no way to enter my courtroom."

"I've come to testify! I'm sick and tired of everyone and their brother speculating about me. I am here to set the record straight once and for all."

Walker sat at attention, processing the scene with a professional's eye.

"You aren't on the witness list, Bradford," the judge said, a longtime friend of the Hawthornes.

"I don't care if I'm not; it is my right to testify."

"Someone has to call you, and as far as I can see, no one has." The judge turned to Alice. "Do you want him to testify?"

She composed herself as well as a stage actress. If her father knew she wanted the testimony, he would do everything in his power to thwart her.

Alice thought back to long years of Walker's tutelage, working a situation to her advantage—though not letting the opposition know what she really wanted. She wanted Bradford to testify about the ring.

She made a nervous but polite smile. An act. And a gamble. Would her father fall for it? "I can't imagine the prosecution will agree at this late date," she said nervously, then hurried on. "So why don't we simply move on to closing arguments."

Slowly Walker stood, eyeing his daughter. "Actually, I have no objections, Your Honor. If the man's father wants to testify, far be it from me to keep that from happening."

Success.

Alice's smile grew genuine, making Walker's eyes narrow. Though in truth, both she and her father were taking a risk. Who knew what Bradford Hawthorne had to say?

"Fine," the judge said. "Bailiff, swear Mr. Hawthorne in."

"No."

One word, slicing through the courtroom. All eyes turned on Lucas, who stood from his seat.

"No?" the judge inquired. Then he leaned over so the jury couldn't hear him. "You better have a damned good reason for this, son. As I see it, you need all the help you can get."

Alice willed him to sit. But it was Grayson who put his hand on his brother's shoulder and gently pushed him down. Like an animal caught in a trap, Lucas's eyes darkened with emotion—hatred, fury. Fear?

Bradford and Lucas stared at each other, but when Lucas made no further attempts to object, Alice could hear Emmaline's sigh of relief.

Within minutes Bradford was seated on the witness stand and ready. The gallery sat on the edge of their seats.

"Mr. Hawthorne," Alice began formally, "will you please state your relationship to the defendant."

"Good God," he chided. "Everyone here knows who I am. You come barging into my house at an ungodly hour to badger me to testify. Well, I'm here. So get on with it."

Walker Kendall's furrowed brows furrowed even more at this, realizing in that second that he had been manipulated by his daughter. Alice had the fleeting thought that they might not ever be able to move beyond this trial.

"Then my wife shows up and does the same thing," Bradford continued. "Well, let me tell you, missy, I'm not about to be pushed around by a bunch of women!"

He said that to the men in the room, which was just about everyone. Alice felt the knot in her stomach tighten. Had she made a grave tactical mistake in putting him on the stand?

"But let me tell you another thing," he spat, "I also won't put up with a bunch of misinformed newspaper sorts saying things about me not testifying and how that must mean Lucas is guilty. Well, to hell with that!"

Judge Parks hammered his gavel and groaned. "Bradford, please."

"Do you blame me, Raymond? Since the day Walker Kendall took office, that upstart has been angling for Lucas."

"Objection!" Walker bellowed.

"That's right, object all you want!" Bradford bellowed back. "I object, too, to the way you are dealing with this situation. Using me. Feeding information to the newspapers. And don't I know that those blasted stories are coming out of the prosecution's office!"

Walker fumed, and Alice felt as if she were falling down a long tunnel.

"Hell," he continued. "Do you think I like it that Lucas owns a saloon?"

"Mr. Hawthorne," Alice interjected, gathering her wits, needing to take control of the situation. "Lucas Hawthorne owns a gentlemen's club, not a saloon. An establishment that is frequented by many respectable men."

The gallery, not to mention the jury, shifted uncomfortably in their seats.

"Call it what you will," Bradford scoffed. "But it's not the kind of place any father wants his son to be involved with."

The man was unruly, and Alice grew nervous that she couldn't control him. She feared next that Bradford would launch into a diatribe about Lucas's misbegotten ways. And her nervousness grew when her father started to calm down. She saw as much as sensed the ease that came into his shoulders, the way he sat back just a tad. Confirmation that she had lost control.

At that moment, Alice realized she had nothing to lose.

"Mr. Hawthorne, you say you're not pleased with your son's chosen vocation—"

"You're damned right, I'm not."

"But the fact is, even though he owns Nightingale's Gate, you still call him 'son.' Clearly he means something to you."

With those words, all the bluster and bellowing seemed to fizzle out of Bradford, leaving him spent. Sitting there with all eyes trained on him, he couldn't hide how her words had startled him.

For the first time he appeared to take in his surroundings, the court, the bailiff with his uniform and gun. The jury of twelve men sitting in judgment of his youngest child.

"Son," he whispered. "My son."

"Yes, Mr. Hawthorne, he is your son."

He looked up at her, seemingly lost. She almost felt sorry for him. Almost.

"How can a father sit back and let the prosecution, not to mention those *blasted* newspapers, as you call them, rip your flesh and blood to shreds?"

She could hardly breathe for fear of the answer. Never ask a question you don't already know the answer to. Number one rule for lawyers. But something else pushed her on, something less pragmatic. Something primal. Like her love for Lucas.

"You ask me how I can sit back," he said, the words barely audible. "A better question, Miss Kendall, is to ask why my son took the road he has in the first place."

"Don't, Father."

Lucas's voice sizzled through the room. The two men

stared at each other, one barely controlling his fury, the other suddenly old, regretful.

Without breaking his gaze from his son's, Bradford said, "He took that road because I showed him how."

A surprised gasp washed through the courtroom like a wave as they tried to assimilate that this respectable man could know anything about the licentious life they knew his son lived, much less have led him there.

But it was Emmaline's intake of breath that stood out in Alice's mind. It must have been the same for Lucas, because he leaned forward. The anger was gone, only desperation remained. "Don't, Father. Don't do this."

Bradford looked as if he were wavering, as if suddenly he realized where he was and what he was about to say. But Alice managed to contain her shock over this revelation, and she knew in her heart that this was what she needed. Lucas was tarnished, yes, but dear God, if he had been pushed there by his father . . .

"Mr. Hawthorne, please tell us what you mean."

She felt Lucas's resurgence of fury, this time directed at her.

Bradford seemed to understand how important this was.

"I haven't been a good father," he told the courtroom.

"Objection!" Walker fired off.

Alice ignored the objection. She plunged ahead. Let the judge stop her if he wanted.

"Mr. Hawthorne, what do you mean when you say you haven't been a good father?"

"Your Honor?"

"Be quiet, Walker," the judge said.

Walker was so shocked he sat back in his seat with a thud.

Bradford shook his head, then seemed to look every juror in the eye. "No man wants to admit that he hasn't been a good father." He turned to where his sons sat close together in this court of law. "But I haven't been. Not to Grayson, not to Matthew. And certainly not to Lucas. I can't undo the past. But I can try to do the right thing now. I've tried to deny my part in Lucas's path to wine and women and gambling. But I can't any longer, because the truth is, I gave Lucas his first cigar."

Her mind staggered as she remembered the rest of Lucas's story. She turned slowly and looked at this man she loved. Sitting in the courtroom with his father facing him now, Lucas looked taut and dangerous in a way that Alice couldn't have imagined. But vulnerable as well.

Suddenly she didn't want to dredge up the past, not after the pain that she could see in Lucas's eyes. But that came from the woman who loved him.

The woman who was his lawyer had to put that from her mind.

"Mr. Hawthorne," she continued, her heart pounding for fear that she already knew the answer. "How old was Lucas when you gave him that cigar?"

"Eleven, twelve? I'm not quite sure."

"I think he was ten."

A disapproving murmur raced through the courtroom.

But Alice forged on, understanding coming so clear in her head that it felt like fragile crystal reflecting harshly over too-bright sunlight—painful, making one want to look away. "And what about his first drink?" she continued. "Did you give him that, too?"

"Alice." One word, a warning, Lucas's voice a strange mixture of fury and desperation.

"Please answer the question, Mr. Hawthorne," she prodded relentlessly.

Bradford caught sight of Emmaline, and he grew uncomfortable.

"Mr. Bradford," Alice said, her tone warning, "you have sworn to tell the truth. Please answer the question."

"Yes, I gave it to him. He was eleven. Whiskey straight up. Just like a man."

"Enough, Father!" Lucas stood up from his chair, his strong hands planted on the table.

"Your Honor," Alice responded, "please instruct the defendant to be silent."

"Please sit down and be quiet," the judge said, "or I'll be forced to hold you in contempt."

Lucas looked at her as if she had betrayed him, stunned that she would take what he had shared with her in private and air it here in a public forum.

The expression made Alice sick, but let him hate her. She wouldn't allow him to go to jail. She'd do whatever was necessary to see that didn't happen.

With anger blazing in his eyes, Lucas sat down. And Alice forced herself to turn back to his father.

"Mr. Hawthorne, it sounds to me as if you once had a close relationship with your youngest son."

Bradford seemed to forget where he was, and he looked at Lucas. His blue eyes blurred with unexpected tears. "You were so much like me. More than the other boys. And God, how you loved me," he stated intensely. "You loved me, you looked up to me, and I took you everywhere, had you at my side all the time. It just seemed natural to introduce you to the things that I knew you would eventually learn about yourself. I turned you into a little man, my little man." He shook his head, and turned back to the court. "I also introduced my son to his first woman."

"Don't do this, Father."

"But I have to, I see that now."

Lucas closed up, his face a sharp blank.

Bradford looked at his hands. "I took him to her bed."

A shudder of disbelief passed over the gallery.

"And do you know what that girl did afterward?"

Alice had difficulty keeping the lawyer separate from the woman in love. She felt weak, and her head spun. Every person in that courtroom leaned forward in their seats, clearly wanting to know.

"She killed herself," he said.

Shock reverberated against the walls, and Alice felt Lucas's soul-deep sadness.

The Nightingale. She was one step away from proving Bradford Hawthorne had introduced his son to that elusive lady, and that he had no doubt been with her himself first. Leading Alice to the nightingale ring.

Walker leaped to his feet. "I don't know what the hell is going on here, but I want a recess. Good God, Lucas Hawthorne must have killed that girl, too."

"My son didn't kill her," Bradford bellowed, "or the one he's being tried for right now." Then he dropped his head into his hands. "He didn't kill her; he tried to save her."

"This is ridiculous!"

"Sit down, Walker," the judge barked.

"Mr. Hawthorne," Alice prompted. "Please continue."

"They found her diary. She had written how kind and caring Lucas had been. My son cared about a whore. He had tried to find her a respectable job after that. Imagine. A thirteen-year-old. You might also imagine that no one would hire her, no one would give her a respectable job. Not even me, who understood how much this meant to my son." Bradford looked away. "Lucas has been caring for whores and the misbegotten ever since. The only person he has never tried to save is himself." He shook his head. "I heard today that Lucas hasn't helped his own defense because he believed I was the killer. And no wonder. I was in the alley that night."

The gallery reeled, and Walker slammed his fist down. "This whole testimony is ridiculous and should be stricken from the record."

Alice faced her father. "You were the one who said we should let him testify."

The prosecutor stared at his only daughter. What could he say? With menace in his eyes, he returned to his seat.

But Alice hardly noticed. She couldn't believe her good fortune. Success was so close she could taste it.

"Mr. Hawthorne," she continued, breaking into the stunned silence that had descended over the courtroom. "What were you doing in the alley?"

Bradford sighed. "I saw the girl who was killed—though she wasn't dead yet. I just saw her walking along. I was stunned when I heard that a girl had been killed that night."

"But you didn't kill her?"

"Good God, no! I was on my way *into* Nightingale's Gate when I saw her."

"Do you have proof of that, sir?"

"Brutus knows. I went most every night."

Alice felt Lucas's surprised tension. "What did you do there?"

Bradford looked at his hands. "I went to see Emmaline."

His wife gasped, and Alice felt a whirling sense of confusion.

"I saw her many nights, though she didn't see me. Hell, she wouldn't see me. But I couldn't seem to stay away. I just needed to see her to make sure she was all right before I could go to sleep at night." He looked out at Emmaline. "I didn't realize how used to having you near me I was." Then he looked at Lucas. "My son was bound to see me at some point."

"Why would Brutus help you?" she asked incredulously.

He grew uncomfortable. "I hired Brutus to watch after Lucas when he was still in short pants."

Out of the corner of her eye, she saw Lucas sit back in shock, his fingers curling around the table's edge. But she couldn't stop.

"You seem to have an odd relationship with your youngest son, Mr. Hawthorne. Earlier, you mentioned that you brought Lucas to his first woman. Correct?"

"Stop this," Lucas hissed under his breath.

Alice ignored him as brittle silence flared, along with a

few undeniable blushes from several of the men in the room. Women, Alice knew, didn't talk about such things. But she didn't care.

"Yes, that is true," he responded.

"Did you sleep with that woman as well?"

Now every man in the room was unhappy. Alice had definitely trod into an area she was not welcome in.

"Mr. Hawthorne, please answer the question," Alice demanded.

"I've had enough!" Lucas roared.

The judge looked at the defendant. "I can't say I blame you, son, but you hired her, not me. She's your lawyer, and she asked the question."

"Then she's fired."

"Fire me! You can't fire me!" She whirled around to the judge knowing it was time to gamble. "The fact is, I am sure that the woman Bradford Hawthorne took his son to gave the defendant the nightingale's ring. And it is that one remaining piece of evidence that ties my client to the crime. I believe that Mr. Bradford Hawthorne has a similar ring."

An audible gasp shuddered through the room.

The judge's brows rose. "And why, pray tell, do you believe that, Miss Kendall?"

Lucas sat very still, murderous.

"Because Lucas Hawthorne's first woman was called the Nightingale. And I have reason to believe she gave every man she—"

For the first time Alice realized just what it was she was talking about in a public forum. Dear God, she'd be ostracized.

But she was too far into this to turn back now. She was also stubborn. In her heart she knew she was right—she had to be right.

"—every man she had relations with got a ring." She turned to Bradford. "She gave you one of those rings, didn't she, sir?"

"Yes," he stated with menace. "But that doesn't make me guilty any more than it makes my son guilty!"

"I agree," she offered, euphoric that her hunch had proved correct. "All it proves is that Lucas Hawthorne isn't the only man in Boston who has one. The woman had relations with more men besides you and your son."

"Objection!" Walker called out, leaping out of his seat.

But Alice ignored him as her uncle's strange comments leaped into her head, clarity coming with them.

"In fact, I'd hazard a guess that there are other men in this very room who once received a nightingale ring. Too many powerful men had that ring, and none of them was about to go down for a murder involving the ring. When Lucille Rouge died in the alley behind Nightingale's Gate, who better to take the fall? The very man who rubbed their faces in their pasts by naming his club after the woman."

"Judge, this is ridiculous!"

"Miss Kendall, I'm warning you. You are treading on very thin ice here. This is a respectable courtroom."

"Judge Parks, I believe there are men who don't dare admit having one of these rings because that is to admit that he's had relations with a fallen woman. Men from all walks of life. Heavens," she added, throwing her hands up in the air dramatically, "my own father, a picture of what all Boston finds respectable, could have one of those rings."

"That is enough, young lady!" Walker bellowed.

But she didn't have to be told again as her mind froze. Her heart seemed to stop in her chest as she turned in slow motion to stare at her father. His gaze met hers with a moment of such intense hatred that she sucked in her breath. But then he gathered himself, so quickly that no one else could have noticed the fury.

"Your Honor," Walker said, "this has gotten out of hand."

Alice didn't listen to another word, couldn't listen as her mind shifted and rocked. Had he known all along that Lucas Hawthorne wasn't the only man in Boston who had the ring? Had he gone after Lucas with virtually no proof, no case—other than the one he had fabricated?

Then another thought hit her square in the chest. *Did* her father have one of those rings?

She found it hard to breathe as she thought of the pieces of this case that hadn't made sense. The manipulation of the facts by the prosecution.

Did her father have something to do with the crime?

Alice wanted to slap her hands over her ears to still the circling thoughts. But she couldn't run away from this.

She looked back at her father, then said, "I think we should approach the bench." She had to clear her throat and say it again before she was heard.

Lucas stood and reached for her hand. Their eyes met, and she knew he understood. Had he understood all along?

In truth, she had understood that he was protecting someone. She had believed it was his own father. But had she been wrong? Had he come to a place where he had tried to protect her? Had he hired her originally because he and Grayson had believed that with her on the case, Walker Kendall wouldn't have moved forward?

Like moving in muddy water, Alice walked to the judge's bench.

"Drop the charges," she said to her father, her voice monotone.

"Absolutely not."

"Drop them, Father." She leaned close so only Walker could hear. "Or I'll be forced to ask questions."

"Like what?" he scoffed.

She expelled her breath in short, staccato bursts, and she tried to get enough air to breathe. But her mind refused to wrap around the possibility of her father's involvement on any other level than as an overzealous prosecuting attorney.

"I will see to it that you are prosecuted for tampering with evidence, lying in a federal courthouse, and coercing testimony."

"I did no such thing."

"Then how do you explain the coroner's evidence that was withheld? Or the coerced witness? And what about the leaks to the newspapers as Bradford pointed out, that could have come only from someone who has access to the Commonwealth's case?"

Walker eyed his daughter. "Playing hardball, I see."

"I learned it from a consummate hardball player."

"I don't believe you'll bring that up to the judge," he said. "I'm your father."

She stared at him forever. "I've learned something about fathers during this trial. More important, I've learned a lot about you. If you don't drop the charges against Lucas right now, I'll turn around and tell Judge Parks exactly what I suspect."

The judge leaned forward. "What are you two going on about?"

Father and daughter stared at each other, their gazes locked in heated battle.

"I'll do it, I swear. Long ago you taught me that winning matters above all else. You proved that when you had Clark use my feelings for Lucas against me. Don't underestimate me, Father."

"You disappoint me, Alice."

"Really?" she said caustically. "I would think you'd be proud. I followed in your footsteps."

With eyes narrowed, Walker straightened his shoulders and turned to the bench. He hesitated for what seemed like an eternity, before he cursed beneath his breath.

"Your Honor, given the evidence we have just learned, the Commonwealth has decided to drop all charges against Mr. Hawthorne at this time."

Raymond Parks leaned back against his chair with a start. "I have never seen such a display in all my years. Are you sure about this, Walker?"

He glanced furiously at Alice. "Yes, I'm sure."

"Good God." Without another second passing, the judge said, "This case is dismissed," then he slammed his gavel down. He looked at Lucas. "You are free to go."

The gallery broke out in a chorus of shocked murmurs and joyous cheers. Women who had crowded into the back of the room tried to race forward, the guards barely able to hold them back.

Walker returned to the prosecution's table with jerking strides, not offering Alice another word.

Alice started back to the defense table, stunned, not knowing what she felt. And she hardly noticed when the Hawthorne family circled round and hugged her tight.

Chapter Twenty-five

When Alice arrived at Nightingale's Gate several hours later, she arrived to a celebration.

Emmaline was there, along with Grayson and Matthew and their families. But Lucas was nowhere to be found. They had won, though Alice felt little more than confused devastation about her father. Soon, she knew, she'd have to examine her thoughts—and have to decide what to do.

For now, she only wanted to see Lucas. She needed to witness for herself what she would see in his eyes. Dismissal? Would he be done with her?

Pride surged and damned her for such insecurity. And if he were so shallow as to have used her so callously, she was better off without him, she told herself forcefully. Too bad her heart was having trouble getting in line with her brain.

Would he be polite? Would he slowly move away from her over time? Would he ever forgive her for airing private matters in a court of law?

Or would he pull her close?

Her heart surged with hope just as her body tingled with sensation at the thought of being held.

After exchanging brief words with the family, Alice searched out Lucas. She found him in his suite, staring out the window, his strong shoulder braced against the window casing.

Emotion swelled in her throat at the sight of him, always so beautiful in a hard, chiseled way.

He stood there, so much like that day she found him in her office looking out. Vulnerable. A look so at odds with the fact he had just won his freedom.

"I know you're there," he said.

He turned around and leaned back against the casing. No smiles, no devilish quirk of brow.

"Why did you do it?" he asked.

"What? Get you acquitted? I thought that's what you hired me for."

"I didn't hire you to air family secrets."

She understood that he was angry. He was an intensely private man. "I didn't have a choice."

"We all have choices, Alice."

"No, not this time. Hate me if you want. But I love you too much to lose you to a noose, even if that means I lose you myself." She pulled herself up to her full height. "I would do it again in a heartbeat."

He stared at her, and she had no idea what he was thinking. His expression was dark and stormy.

"Come here," he said, his voice a rasp of sound.

She wanted to go to him, needed to, but she had to know. "Can you forgive me?"

"Forgive you?" He laughed, though the sound held no mirth. "How can I not? Now come here. Please," he added. Vulnerable again.

She took the steps that separated them, stopping so close that if she reached out they would touch.

When she couldn't reach out, he twined his fingers with hers and pulled her to him. Her heart pounded with a burgeoning love that was nearly painful.

He wrapped her in his arms, her head coming just beneath his chin, and he held her tight, his lips pressed to her hair.

She felt the ease that came over him once she was there, felt his heart beating strongly against hers.

"Why aren't you downstairs celebrating with your family?" she asked.

He hesitated. "I don't want to see the look in their eyes. I have always been the man who pushed the limits, a man who was wild because he relished it. Now they don't know what to think about me."

She knew they would feel guilty. She knew how her heart had broken for this man at his father's words, the pieces of the puzzle finally falling into place.

"I know what to think of you," she whispered.

He chuckled into her hair, then held her at arm's length. His blue eyes filled with something she wanted to say was love. But still he didn't utter the word.

"That's because you understand me. You didn't have a childhood either."

Her shoulders tensed. "Of course I did."

"No," he said. "You discussed murders when you should have been discussing the latest gowns. You discussed trial strategies when other girls were flirting with boys. You've lived with the realities of crime when you should have known about nothing more than crocheting and tea."

"I don't regret my childhood."

"I don't either. It's mine. It's all I have, and regret isn't going to change anything. But as you told me yourself before, we aren't the same as others. We've seen too much in a world that spends great stores of energy covering up the realities of life. At the time, I didn't believe you. I couldn't see how two people could be more different. But now I know you were right. We are different from those around us—our families who love and care about us. We stand apart, not intentionally, but because of circumstances beyond our control. I realize now that's why you drew me from the first moment I saw you. For all your innocence and proper clothes, you know more about life than someone like you should."

As much as she didn't want to admit it, she knew he was right. Why had their fathers done what they had?

Alice realized she might never know. She also realized she would have to make some kind of a decision about her father and the nightingale's ring.

Her stomach churned, and she felt ill.

And when Lucas swept her up into his arms and carried her to his bed, she didn't resist. She wanted to forget, not to think. At least not yet. She also couldn't bear the thought of going home.

But when he laid her down, he didn't work the fastenings of her gown or kiss her. He wrapped her in his arms, her back pressed against his chest. And within minutes, she realized this strong wonderful man, whom she loved so much, had fallen asleep holding her close to his heart.

She woke in the dark, disoriented. It took a few seconds for her to realize that she had fallen asleep in Lucas's arms. He still slept, though she could tell that soon the sun would begin to brighten the sky.

As the new day began, she understood she couldn't put off dealing with her father any longer.

She had to know if Walker Kendall had a ring. And if she wasn't mistaken, if he had one, she would find that ring in his safe.

Her stomach churned, and her mind spun as she remembered the nights her father had come home late. Or not at all. Where had he been?

But before those questions would be answered, she knew she had to go to that safe she had mastered as a child.

With a trembling sigh, she got out of bed, then padded over to her satchel. Before she headed home, she wanted to read the crime file her uncle had set on the defense table, which contained the information on the latest murder. She wanted to know every detail before she faced her father.

Could he have been the murderer all along?

Sick, she started to read. The crime was much the same.

The victim found in the alleyway, with her fingers snipped off. Though this time not all fingers were gone—as if the murderer had been caught in the act. And from that slip, the police were able to determine the girl had scratched her assailant.

Alice sat back. It was just as she had assumed. Why else would a murderer take the time to snip the fingers if he hadn't been scratched?

Knowing she had to go to her father's house, she moved quietly back to Lucas.

He had rolled over, one arm flung back over his head, the other across his chest. Unable to help herself, she relished the moments of being able to look at him, study him. Touch him.

She traced his jaw, his lips. Just barely.

The shirt he had not taken off last night had come loose around his neck, and she traced her finger down his chin, his neck, feeling the slow but steady beat of his heart.

But she felt something else as well.

As if burned, she jerked her hand back, her breath hissing in through her nose. She stared at him, her mind trying to work.

The woman had scratched her assailant.

Alice felt her stomach roil as she remembered the night she had found Lucas gone from bed. And the next morning another girl had been killed. She had told her uncle that Lucas had been with her all night—when he hadn't been.

Sweat beaded on her brow, and she stared at Lucas's sleeping form. Please let it be a mistake, she pleaded silently.

As if she had no will of her own, she reached back, her fingers trembling as she moved his shirt collar away. And saw three long scratches on his neck.

A silent scream froze on her lips, as her mind denied what she saw.

But she couldn't leave it alone. She had to know.

Quietly, she got off the unmade bed and crept out of the

room into Lucas's private office. She prayed she wouldn't find anything damning, and after going through each drawer, she closed her eyes in relief when all she found were ledgers and pens, work files and documents.

But just when she pushed up from the chair she caught sight of a small cabinet across the room beneath a low table. Her heart stopped when she pulled it open and found a cigar cutter and a nightingale ring.

The ring he had sworn he'd lost.

Her mind screamed in denial. Had he played her? Used her innocence? Used the charm she had known about all along, pulling her in with blind infatuation, just as her uncle had said.

Dear God. She thought of the way he hadn't helped her case, had thwarted her at every turn. Left her with cryptic information that led her to believe things that weren't true. Like his supposed belief that his father had been the guilty one. The way he reeled her in, kissing her when he hardly knew her, making her believe that someone so sought after and virile would truly desire a plain woman like her.

Fury flared, hot and burning.

With fumbling hands she gathered the things from the cabinet and shoved them in her pocket. But the cutters caught and fell to the carpet with a muffled thud.

She froze, realizing that at any second Lucas could wake up. But there wasn't any sound, no noise, no rustling of the bed.

Frantically, she shoved the cutter into her pocket, then stood. And just when she would have reached for the small cabinet to shut the door, she sensed someone behind her.

When she turned, she found Lucas, his hair rumpled from sleep, his hands on his hips.

"I wondered where you had gotten to," he said.

From the tone of his voice, she couldn't tell if he realized what she was doing. Thankfully, since the cabinet was beneath the table, he couldn't see it from where he stood. But one more step inside, and he would.

"I was just . . . looking out the window," she managed, hoping he couldn't see the trembling of her hands.

He smiled at her and started forward.

"No!"

His smile went hard.

"I mean, *no* need to look out this window. I love the one in the bedroom better."

He looked at her oddly, but when she walked toward him, hating every step, he didn't say a word. He didn't look into his office. But he didn't follow her either.

The sun had started to rise, brightening the room. And the brighter it got, the more she could see of the cabinet. She had to get out of there before he noticed.

She was sick and angry. She felt used and betrayed and wanted nothing more than to scream her fury at him.

She had to get to her father's house, had to find her father and uncle.

"What's wrong, Alice?" he asked, stepping closer.

"Nothing, nothing's wrong. I just have to get home. Father is going to be furious if he finds out I was here all night."

"I'd like to speak to your father about our future."

Her nostrils flared when he touched her cheeks, gently, so gently, as if nothing were amiss. Her head jerked back.

His hand froze, and his eyes narrowed. Tilting his head ever so slightly, he asked, "Are you sure there's nothing you want to tell me?"

A knock sounded at the door, and seconds later Brutus pushed through with a tray of coffee items. At the sight of Alice, she could tell he didn't know what to do.

"I'd think you would learn to wait until you were called," Lucas said dangerously.

Brutus stammered and started to back out of the room. But Alice took the distraction as an opportunity.

"I've really got to go," she said. Then, with a quick wave,

she dashed around Brutus, putting the massive man between her and Lucas.

She was down the stairs and out the door before Lucas could respond. He stared at Brutus's quickly disappearing back and wondered what had just happened.

Lucas pulled a deep breath and thought about the fear that had been in Alice's eyes. He thought as well about the fact that he had found her in his office.

What had she found?

What had put that fear in her eyes?

As soon as he reentered his office he saw the small cabinet, its door ajar, and he knew. The ring. She had found the nightingale ring.

Another knock sounded, and he whirled around. But it was Grayson who stood at the door, not Alice.

Grayson entered, his dark eyes blazing with fury.

But then Grayson spoke, and Lucas's hand clenched at his side.

"I just learned who killed those girls."

Lucas worked to steady his breathing as he took the file that Grayson held out to him. What would be inside? What would it show? And how would he respond?

Carefully, he opened the file and stared down at what turned out to be a photograph. At the sight his mind spun. But he knew he didn't have time to think things through. Time was of the essence. And with sickness in his heart, knowing what he had to do, he caught Grayson by surprise as he charged forward.

Chapter Twenty-six

He hated that it had come to this. His perfectly constructed plan going so awry.

The scratches. Someone coming upon the scene before he could snip all the fingers away.

And now there was the matter of Alice.

She knew too much.

Eventually she would put it all together, if she hadn't already.

Damn her!

With effort he tamped his anger down. He would not let emotion take hold as he had earlier. He would not let all his hard work come undone.

Everything had been going so well, working out. But at the end it had all unraveled on him. First because of his mother. Now because of Alice. Whores, all of them.

Now it was time to fix things. Finally, completely.

He entered the house on Beacon Hill, knowing that the only person there was Alice. He had watched for her, made sure she was alone.

He almost smiled at the thought that God was in the details.

But his smile evaporated at the thought of Alice ruining it all.

His footsteps were nearly silent as he made his way through the foyer to the back of the house. He flinched when he hit a loose board and a creak bit into the silence.

He heard her footsteps stop at the sound. Then nothing. But he didn't worry. He had secured the back door before he came through the front. She couldn't get out unless she came back toward him.

And, of course, she still couldn't get out.

A chuckle wafted into the high-ceilinged room as he no longer cared what she heard.

"Alice," he whispered, his voice taunting. "Oh, Alice."

Chapter Twenty-seven

She had fallen in love with a murderer.

As Alice had rushed through the streets, her mind tried to settle. She closed her eyes and willed herself to be wrong. Surely there was some explanation, some reason that Lucas had lied about the ring. Arriving at home, she prayed she had jumped to conclusions. But what if she hadn't?

Could she live with the fact that her gullibility had helped set a man free? That her naïveté had led her to forget everything she knew about the law?

Her eyes flew open at the sound of the quiet click of the front door.

"Father? Max?" She waited. "Uncle Harry?" But everyone had already left for work. "Hello?" she called out.

No answer.

A chill raced down her spine. Her heart leaped in her chest when she heard careful footsteps coming down the foyer steps to the entry hall.

Panic flared when she tried the back door and found it jammed. Telling herself to be calm, she made her way to the hallway. She glanced around frantically, but there was no place to hide. As carefully as she could, she slipped into the nook beneath the stairs, her blood thundering through her veins. She was afraid to move, afraid to breathe in the all-too-quiet house.

Fear crashed through her at the sound of someone moving through the house. She cursed herself for having called out. With her mind spinning, she realized her only hope now was to run for it.

As the footsteps came closer, she fought to stay in control.

And just when the intruder rounded the corner Alice leaped out. But at the sight that met her eyes, she stopped dead in her tracks.

"Clark!"

Clark Kittridge jumped in surprise. "Good God, Alice, you scared me to death!"

"Oh, my heavens! Clark!"

She staggered back, one hand steadying herself against the mahogany wainscoting, the other pressed against her racing heart. "Why didn't you say something when I called out?"

Clark eyed her, then cast a quick glance at the door behind her. "Did you call out? I didn't hear you," he offered with an apologetic smile.

"That's all right," she said, relief settling her racing heart. She sighed and smiled at the same time. "In fact, I'm glad it's you." She started to go around him. "No doubt you've come to see my father. But he isn't here."

"Yes, I know that. He's at the courthouse already." He shoved his hands in his pockets. "No one's here but us. Though, actually, it's you I want to see. I thought I might catch you before you left for the office."

She tilted her head. "What do you need?"

"I haven't been able to put you out of my mind. I feel terrible that this trial came between us. Everything was fine until then."

Reaching out, she touched his arm. "Oh, Clark, that is nice of you. But it was more than the trial. We were never meant for each other."

"That's not true!"

She took a step back, and he calmed himself. He placed

his hand over hers. "Come for a ride with me. Out to the country. We can stop and pick up a basket lunch. We'll talk."

"I can't." The thought of Lucas loomed in her mind, and fear and tears swelled once again. "I have to find my father."

She started to pull her hand away, but his fingers tightened over hers. Surprised, she looked up at him. "Clark?"

His kind smile seemed to grow brittle, and his grip grew painful on her hand.

"Clark?" she repeated, trying to understand.

Still he didn't answer. He glanced at the door, his breathing growing agitated. "We have a little problem, Alice." He shrugged. "You see, you have caused me a great deal of dismay."

He sighed dramatically, in a way that made him seem very different from the kind man she had come to know.

"You got Lucas off. He's free now. And everyone is wondering, If Hawthorne isn't the killer, then who is? I know your father. He'll start wondering about a few things that happened during the trial. Things that he knows you blame him for. The coroner's information that suddenly came out at the grand jury hearing. Tawny's seemingly coerced testimony." He gave one brief, nervous chuckle before he tsked. "If Walker doesn't start questioning, I know it's only a matter of time before someone else does. And then people will demand answers. They will want to know who was responsible for the . . ." He shrugged. "The less than ethical, but extremely necessary, behavior." He sighed dramatically. "You really should have let that lowlife Hawthorne hang."

A sharp light of understanding pierced through her mind, making her feel faint.

Alice thought back to her demonstration in the courtroom. The lights turned out, the witness asked to identify the bailiff's hair color. "It's dark," Tawny had mumbled. When in truth, the man's hair had been blond, looking dark only because of the extinguished light.

Her nostrils flared with alarm when she took in Clark's blond hair.

"Clark," she whispered, her head spinning. "Did you kill those girls?"

"Aren't you a regular Sherlock Holmes."

"Dear God, why?" she breathed.

"Because they deserved it!" he blurted out. "Just as every whore deserves to die!"

Visibly he calmed himself, then reached out and traced her cheek.

She flinched at the contact, and his expression went hard, but he didn't drop his hand away.

"Just a matter of weeks ago," he hissed, "you were panting for my touch."

Revulsion surged up, and she hated the truth of his words. She had wanted him to touch her. Wanted him to marry her. All because she had been afraid of her feelings for Lucas Hawthorne. The man she had wrongly accused not once, when she first met him, but again now, dashing out of his room and into the real killer's path.

He backed her up, until they stood in her father's study, her hips pressed against the table along the wall.

"I'll make you pant for my touch now, my sweet. I will, because you are no different than the rest. You are a whore, Alice Kendall. Proof of that is the fact that you slept with Lucas Hawthorne."

Lucas leaped past Grayson, knocking the file to the ground. An aged photograph spilled across the carpet. Aged and worn. A photograph that Bradford and Emmaline had come across as they sat together going over their past, trying to find a way to rebuild a future.

It was a photograph from Lucas's days at Boston Classics, a photo of his entire class. Him. Oliver Aldrich. And a little boy who had attended the private school on a charity scholarship arranged by rich men for a special woman.

But Lucas had barely taken that information in. He had to find Alice. In one blinding moment it all came clear.

Lucas cursed himself for not having understood earlier. But he hadn't. And now, based on the cutter and the ring Alice had found in the cabinet, Lucas knew she thought it was him. He also understood that Alice was in danger.

Flying out of Nightingale's Gate at a dead run, Lucas headed for Beacon Hill. Drivers jerked their reins to keep from running him down, but Lucas refused to stop. He had to get to Alice. To save her. To beg her forgiveness for not telling her that he still had the ring.

Would she understand that he hadn't known what to believe had happened the night in the alley? And whatever it was, it would lead to his past. That he hadn't wanted anyone to know that his world had been carefully constructed? He had told the truth when he said that he could live with people thinking him wild for wildness's sake. But he had lived nearly two decades determined that he would never be weak again. He had wanted to be acquitted, and he believed he would be—their case had always been circumstantial. He had done his best to ensure that he was set free without pointing to his father, or using his past. But Alice had found out anyway.

Would she forgive him? Would she believe him? Especially when he told her that he loved her.

Dear God, he had never told her. He had been afraid to tell her. But would it be too late?

Knowing he would make better time if he cut across the Public Garden, he grabbed the wrought-iron fence and leaped over in one easy motion.

Lucas ran, praying with an intensity that he had never felt before. He took a chance Alice had gone home, intent on finding her father. When finally he saw the Kendalls' house, all looked quiet. He wished as he had wished for little else that Alice had fled. If she had not fled, then he prayed that no one else had gotten inside.

Please God, don't let me be too late.

The door was locked. With wildness consuming him, he kicked in the glass side window, and turned the lock. Lucas hurtled through the entrance, wild and dangerous. But the scream that suddenly filled the house stopped him cold in his tracks.

"Alice," Lucas breathed, the hairs on his arms standing up.

With a warrior's cry, he lunged into the study.

"Don't come any closer!"

Lucas halted, panting, his eyes wild. With an ironclad control, he found Alice, and quickly glanced over her to see if she were harmed. Only then did he turn his gaze on Boston's assistant district attorney.

"Claus," Lucas said to Clark with a casualness he didn't feel. "Funny how things turn out, isn't it."

"I am not Claus!" he shouted, shrill and demented, the words careening against the walls. He jerked Alice in front of him, pulling out a knife and holding it to her neck. "Don't call me that! My name is Clark."

"Perhaps now, but you and I both know at Boston Classics you were Claus Kitowsky."

"I am no longer that boy!"

"No, I can see that. You've changed a great deal since you were twelve years old. I didn't recognize you. Though I suspect that was the point."

"That's right," he sneered, "I'm no longer the poor kid whose mother slept with rich men so her son could rub elbows with their sons. But I was never good enough. Each and every one of you snubbed me."

"We didn't know you, Clark."

"You didn't want to know me! Then I work hard and return to this town, and people still snub me. But someone as cheap and corrupt as a saloon owner is still welcomed with open arms. Those women who flocked to the courthouse every day of your trial were sickening. Sickening!"

Lucas tensed, his hard chiseled body growing taut with fear and regret. Carefully he eased a step closer. Clark's movements became more agitated, and the knife jerked, nicking Alice's skin.

"Ahhhg," Alice cried out at the pain, bringing Lucas to a halt.

Clark smiled with growing menace. "Though who would have believed it would be so easy for all those fancy Boston types to go against you at the mere mention of murder. Walker Kendall all but wet in his pants at the thought of bringing you down. If you only knew how easy it was for him to believe it was you." He laughed harshly. "God, it was easy to manipulate the case. A bribe here and a threat there. You'd be amazed at what people will do." His eyes narrowed. "But this little bitch here had to come into the picture and ruin everything. Everything!" he shouted, the knife jostling once again.

Lucas could sense her fear. But he also saw a light burning deep in her eyes. She would survive. She was a fighter, just as she had fought for him.

"But people know me now," Clark continued. "I've worked hard to get where I am!"

"You've worked hard to become a lawyer with a fondness for killing women."

"Killing whores!" he raged, the knife pricking her skin again. "Whores like my mother!"

"But she was a good woman, a caring woman," Lucas stated with a deadly calm.

Lucas could feel Alice's questioning gaze.

"Your mother loved you," Lucas added, his tone meant to soothe.

"She loved *you*!"

The words careened and staggered through the room, and Clark's rage mixed with furious despair.

Clark's bravado seeped away. "She loved you," he bit out despondently. "I saw the diary, just like everyone else! My mother, the whore. My mother, the Nightingale! I saw how she went on about you and your kindness, you and your caring, you and your desire to help her!"

"She needed someone, Clark."

"You were a boy! A stupid kid!"

He had been. As his father had explained in court, he had been young and naïve, not understanding the world his father had thrust him into without the benefit of age or explanation. He had tried to make sense of it all at a time when his body had been brought to life by the knowledgeable hands of a woman who was paid for her talents.

What boy wouldn't have done what he could to help the woman who stirred that newfound emotion?

What boy would have known that those sentiments couldn't have saved her?

Old, familiar anger and guilt surged inside him, threatening to strangle him. She had committed suicide because he couldn't find a way to help her.

"Well," Clark continued, "she wasn't going to embarrass me anymore. I took care of that."

Lucas's mind reeled.

Clark smiled triumphantly. "Yes, I killed her. Then I took her last nightingale ring. My, how it has come in handy all these years later. Marking the girls with the ring." He chuckled. "Inspired, I thought."

Lucas could hardly wrap his mind around the implication.

Clark sneered. "It could have stopped there. But no. You had to open a gentleman's club and name it after that whore, making too many important men remember. And that's what you wanted. I know it. I know you didn't want all those men to forget her. Threw it in their faces. Threw it in my face! And I won't have it!"

Lucas lunged then, catching Clark off guard. Alice broke free, staggering away, Lucas and Clark locked in combat, the blade flashing angrily. Both men were strong, but long years of pent-up anger and rage caught Lucas by surprise.

"You bastard!" Clark screamed.

Alice stood stunned for a heartbeat, her mind filled with desperation as the knife connected with flesh. Fear and panic made her blood pound, deafening her as it rushed through her veins. Terror pushing her on, she lurched to the box where her uncle kept his guns.

With hands clumsy and wooden, she fumbled with the key until finally the box snapped open. When she turned back, she screamed at the sight of Lucas lying wounded and bloody on the floor, unaware that Clark stood above him ready to attack again.

Crying out a savage oath, Alice squeezed the trigger just as Clark arched back to strike.

Clark's face pulled into a startled mask. Alice staggered back, her mouth opened in a silent cry as she dropped the gun.

Just then, Grayson and her father raced through the front door.

"Are you all right—" But Grayson cut himself off at the sight of Clark lying dead on the floor.

And his brother.

"Lucas." The word jerked out of Grayson's throat at the sight. Blood marked the wall.

Alice raced forward, dropping down next to Lucas.

"Sweet Jesus," Grayson whispered, stricken.

But as soon as Alice touched Lucas's cheek, he opened his eyes. Unfocused and disoriented. Until he saw her.

Instantly, the warrior's gaze resurfaced, and he struggled to rise.

"He's dead," she whispered, pressing her hands to his chest. "I'm safe."

She saw the relief that swept through him.

"Alice," he began, struggling to get up.

"Shhh, be still. We'll get a doctor."

"No." He struggled to gather strength, then took her hand in a firm but gentle grip. "I don't need a doctor."

Despite the pain, a smile pulled on his lips, devilish and

disarming, a lock of hair falling forward on his forehead as he pulled her closer.

"I only need you, Alice Kendall," he whispered. "I only need you for the rest of my life."

Epilogue

Nightingale's Gate was packed, though not with customers. The Kendalls and Hawthornes filled most of the room.

Only Lucas wasn't there.

Alice paced, her long taffeta skirts rustling, her hat long gone, her white-blonde hair soft around her face. She barely listened to her father as he offered his apologies that he had been so blind to Clark's deceit.

Uncle Harry wrung his hands and explained that they simply hadn't known what the assistant district attorney had been doing.

"But I asked you about the discrepancies," she pointed out.

"Sometimes," Harry said with an apologetic shrug, "certain things have to be overlooked when we know a man is guilty."

She whipped around at that, her amber eyes flashing green. "But Lucas wasn't guilty."

That shut him up.

And Max. He pulled her into a tight hug, regardless of her ire, and kissed her on the forehead. "You might be upset with them now, but you love us all anyway. You'll forgive them."

Alice grumbled. "You're right."

It was then that Lucas finally entered. Alice had never been so glad to see anyone in her life. So tall and handsome. So strong despite the knife wound to his shoulder. The doctor announced that he would recover fully. He'd have to be careful with his arm for a while, and he'd have a scar, though it wouldn't show.

"Too bad it's not more visible," Matthew called out, displaying the scar he had gotten not so long ago, much lessened now since Finnea had come into his life. "It's amazing how a little scar can enthrall the women." He pulled his wife close and kissed her forehead. "Though I only care about enthralling one woman in my life."

At that, Bradford stepped forward; he looked at his three sons, and the room grew quiet. He looked from Grayson to Matthew, who stood suddenly tense. To Lucas.

Bradford's countenance was filled with remorse. But he didn't say a word until he turned to Alice.

"I have much to regret," he stated clearly. "A lifetime of not doing what is best for anyone besides myself. Having relationships with people I shouldn't have, relationships that led my son to believe that I was capable of killing someone. It took a little slip of a lawyer lady to make me see straight. I can never repay you. You've given me back my family." He turned to Emmaline. "And you've given me back my wife."

Emmaline walked to his side, and he wrapped his arm around her. "I'm sorry," he said raggedly.

"As well you should be," she responded with tears in her eyes. But they were tears of joy, and they smiled at each other like newlyweds.

The families drifted away, Matthew once again whole despite his scar, Grayson at peace in the world with Sophie at his side. And Emmaline and Bradford, having moved beyond the past to find a new life together.

Walker, Harry, and Max stood shoulder to shoulder at the bar, having come to the understanding that there is more to life than work. Winning was not worth the cost if that price was honesty or family.

They toasted one another, shook hands with the Hawthornes, then left. But not before each of them kissed Alice.

They loved her. They were proud of her. She had proved herself beyond a reasonable doubt.

But in the end, it was another man who mattered most.

Alice turned to Lucas. His white bandage was stark against his bronzed skin.

"No doubt by tomorrow morning, once word gets out about your success," Lucas said with his devilish smile, "you'll have clients lined up around the block begging for your services. You won't need a single troublesome Hawthorne or Kendall."

"But I need you," she whispered.

His smile vanished, and emotion darkened his eyes. "And I need you. I have needed you from the first, but was too damn stubborn to admit it."

"Stubborn, mule-headed, obstinate—"

He chuckled, though there was a hint of sadness. "I should bronze that thesaurus of yours." He took a step closer. "But call it what you will, there is no denying that you saved me." Slowly he reached out and ran his finger down her cheek. "You saved me from hanging, you saved me from being killed by Claus, and you saved me from myself."

"But you wouldn't have almost been killed if I hadn't doubted you."

Lucas shook his head. "How could you not? After all you had been through with me, it's no wonder you doubted when you saw that ring. I just didn't know how to tell you that I still had it. I wanted you to believe in me. I cherished the look in your eyes when you were certain I couldn't be guilty—and hated the one that told me you were unsure. The ring was the one piece of evidence that I knew would be next to impossible to get around—not without explaining how I got it. So there is no denying that you saved me."

"I just did what I could, as a lawyer, then as someone who loves you very much."

"And I love you. More than you can know."

She went into his arms and held him tight. It had nothing

to do with being forward or experimenting. It had to do with love and the sense of acceptance he made her feel.

After a moment, he held her at arm's length, wincing just a bit when he moved his shoulder too quickly. "I have something to show you."

She tilted her head in question.

He simply took her hand and led her out the front door, out to the street, then down the walkway for a few steps until they came to the town house next door.

"Lucas," she said on a breath.

"When I started this project, I thought I was redoing it for my mother. But even she knew all along that *you* belonged here. She said as much that first day she met you. Once I realized that, I did what I knew would truly make it your home."

"The rose bushes," she whispered.

"With an elegant fence all around."

"Oh Lucas, you remembered."

"I remember everything. I remember when I first walked into your office, the way you stood up to me. The way your amber eyes brightened to green when you wanted me to kiss you." He hesitated. "The way you stood up against a courtroom full of men to defend me."

He looked over the garden filled with color. "There are roses here of every type, of every color—for everything you've done for me."

"How did you get them here without anyone knowing?"

"What do you think I was doing in the middle of the night that time you found me gone?"

"The scratches! They were from the thorns!"

"What did you think?"

Alice cringed. "It wasn't just the ring that made me believe you had murdered the girls. Last night, I also saw the scratches. Oh Lucas, how could I have done that? How will you ever forgive me?"

His eyes glittered with mischief. "I can think of a few things that might put you in my good graces."

But Alice no longer felt the need to flee as she had that first day. She smiled right back. "What did you have in mind?"

He grew more serious than she had ever seen him, and he took her hands in his. "First, you have to marry me."

Her mouth opened on a startled breath.

"And second, you must never stop loving me. I need you, Alice Kendall. In my life, on my side. Next to me as my wife."

Emotion made her speechless, and when she didn't utter a word, Lucas grew determined. "Alice, please—"

But just like weeks ago when she had startled him because she asked him to kiss her, she didn't have to be asked twice.

"Yes, I'll marry you."

He took her into his arms and twirled her around with an innocent fun he hadn't known in years. "Mrs. Lucas Hawthorne," he said, setting her down. "I like the sound of that."

This time a devilish grin pulled on her lips. "Hmmm, actually I kind of like the sound of *Mr.* Lucas *Kendall*."

He threw his head back and laughed, then cupped her cheek. "I'll take that under advisement, counselor. Otherwise, do we have a deal?"

"Yes. Oh yes!"

Then he pressed his lips to hers, long and slow, sealing the deal with a kiss.

If you enjoyed *NIGHTINGALE'S GATE*, don't miss the first two books in the Hawthorne trilogy, and the stories of Grayson and Matthew.

Please turn the page for more details about the Hawthorne brothers...

DOVE'S WAY

by Linda Francis Lee

Matthew Hawthorne saved Finnea Winslet's life one day on a train in Africa. But Finnea didn't know that on that day she saved his soul. Destroyed by scandal, Matthew would have been ostracized completely by the unyielding society of his birth had he not been such a powerful man. Matthew doesn't let himself care about anyone or anything—until Finnea arrives unexpectedly in Boston.

Raised in Africa, Finnea is as foreign to Bostonians as they are to her. Yet she is determined to make a life for herself there, so she turns to Matthew to learn the ways of that rigid town. But can Matthew help Finnea without losing what is left of his heart?

Published by Ivy Books.
Available in bookstores everywhere.

A LIGHT ON THE VERANDA

by Ciji Ware

When Daphne Duvallon left New Orleans in the middle of her own wedding and ran away to New York, she vowed never to return to the land of her ancestors. Now she has come back to the South, to Natchez, Mississippi, a city as mysterious and compelling as the ghostly voices that haunt Daphne's dreams. A hasty visit to play the harp at her brother's wedding becomes an unexpected rendezvous with destiny when she meets Simon Hopkins, a nationally renowned nature photographer with dark secrets of his own. For the first time in years Daphne knows what she wants—until shadows from another life that cannot forget or forgive threaten to silence the music in her life and destroy her only real chance for happiness.

Published by Ivy Books.
Available in bookstores everywhere.

SWAN'S GRACE

by Linda Francis Lee

Grayson Hawthorne is everything blue-blooded
Boston society admires—rich, ruthless, untainted by
scandal. While always keeping a tight rein on his
emotions, he has never forgotten Sophie Wentworth,
the spirited but awkward child who captivated his
youth with music and a young girl's adoration. But
one night long ago, she left the city unexpectedly.
Now the toast of Europe, Boston's ugly duckling is
returning home with the grace of a swan.

Through provocative performances, Sophie has
found great fame as a concert cellist. She hopes to
keep her past and her new life a secret—until she
discovers that her family has bargained her away to
Grayson, the lonely boy she once loved—now a
cold, forbidding man with the power to break her
tattered heart. At that moment, she vows to bring
Boston. . .and Grayson. . .to their knees.

Published by Ivy Books.
Available in bookstores everywhere.